RETURN OF THE GUNHAWK

Brad Dennison

Author of
THE LONG TRAIL and *TENNESSEE*

Published by Pine Bookshelf
Buford, Georgia

Return of the Gunhawk is a work of fiction. Names, characters, places, and incidents are either the product of the author's imagination or are used fictitiously. Any resemblance to actual persons, living or dead, events or locales is entirely coincidental.

Copyright 2014 by Bradley A. Dennison
All Rights Reserved

Editor: Kay Jordan

Copy Editor: Loretta Yike

Cover Design: Donna Dennison

Cover Art: The Free Trader, by Charles M. Russell

THE McCABES

The Long Trail
One Man's Shadow
Return of the Gunhawk
Boom Town
Trail Drive
Preacher With A Gun
Johnny McCabe
Shoshone Valley
Thunder
Wandering Man
Going Home
Yesterday's Trail
Gunhawk Blood (Coming Soon)

OTHER BOOKS

Joe McCabe
Tennessee
McCabe County
Jericho
Early Trails

To Leon and Tula Shook

Good friends from Texas who, without even knowing it, helped inspire the direction for this novel

PROLOGUE

Wardtown, Texas
September, 1879

The man called Smith leaned on the bar with both elbows, and had one foot up on a brass railing. A glass of whiskey was resting on the bar in front of him, waiting for him. A brass spittoon was on the floor within spitting distance, but he left it alone. Chaw was one habit he had never picked up.

He had to make a decision. One he didn't quite know how to make.

His hair was long, touching his shoulders. His jaw was covered with a bushy beard that fell to the top of his shirt. His hair had stray strands of silver scattered throughout and his beard had a white streak that began just below his lower lip and extended all the way down through his chin and beyond. Like a long white stripe.

He wore a vest, and pinned to the left side by the lapel was a tin star. Holstered at his left side was a pistol. Not that he was a lefty, but the old horse doctor had been right. His gun hand was never again strong enough to squeeze a trigger. When he held a gun out, pointing at a target and pulling on the trigger, his hand would start shaking.

The back of his hand still had a jagged, round scar from the bullet that had torn through it.

When times of trouble were upon the town, he would grab a scattergun, because he wasn't much of a shot with his left hand. But this was a sleepy Tuesday morning in the second week of September. He didn't expect a whole lot of trouble so the scattergun was at the marshal's office.

He reached for the glass and took the whiskey down in one gulp, and said thanks to the barkeep and turned to amble out into the dusty street.

He didn't normally drink whiskey in the morning. But he had a decision to make and didn't quite know how to make it, and sometimes whiskey seemed to help him to think better. Sometimes not. This was one of those times that it did not.

A woman and child were walking past him on the boardwalk. She was the wife of the president of the local bank.

"Good morning, Mrs. Clayton," he said, reaching up to tip the floppy brim of his worn, dusty old sombrero.

She nodded politely at him. "Deputy Smith."

Most people in town knew him as Smith. Or Deputy Smith. Only a few knew him by his real name. Joe McCabe. Tremain did, and Josh, and Maddie. That was about it. But he was of no mind to tell anyone. Part of the long, complicated business that led to him not knowing how to make the decision he had to make.

He stepped off the boardwalk and crossed the open dirt street to the marshal's office. He turned the doorknob and stepped in.

Tremain was there, sitting at the desk. He had a cup of coffee in front of him, and was squinting his eyes at a ledger sheet. He looked up at the doorway.

"Joe," he said.

Joe nodded. "I wasn't expecting you back from the ranch yet. I've been wandering the town, doing my rounds. Over and over. Then I stopped at the saloon to see if a glass of whiskey might help me think."

Tremain said, "It's about what we heard at the saloon last Saturday. About your brother's ranch up in Montana."

Joe nodded. The summer before last, the ranch had been struck by raiders, and his brother shot and nearly killed. He had heard traces and whispers of the story over the past year, but so many tall stories about his brother circulated from among the saloons and cow camps that he didn't take it seriously. But then on Saturday night, a cowhand new to the area had details. He had been a freight wagon driver between Cheyenne and Bozeman until recently. Headed south to get away from the cold winters up Montana way, and landed a job at the Shannon Ranch. He had told the whole story.

Joe went to the small stove in one corner, and the coffee pot standing atop it. He grabbed it and a tin cup and began to pour. He said, "The thing is, I've been gone so long. I haven't seen any of 'em in over fifteen years."

Tremain nodded, thinking about what he was going to say. Finally he said, "Joe, I've never really asked what happened that set you on the run. You've mentioned bits and pieces, but maybe if I knew the whole story, I'd be able to give some advice worth hearing."

Joe walked toward the desk, tossing Tremain's words in his mind. He slid a chair out and sat down. He said, "Ain't never told another living soul any of this."

Tremain said, "None of it will go any further, either. You have my word."

This meant a lot, Tremain's word. Tremain was one of the finest men Joe had ever met.

Joe said, "You ever hear of a man by the name of Breaker Grant?"

Tremain nodded. "He owned a ranch a little bit north and east of here. The Broken Spur. I always thought that was a colorful name."

Joe nodded. "He was a former Texas Ranger. We worked for him for a short spell, my brothers and me. Back in the day. He's long gone, now. He was an old man when we knew him."

Joe took a sip of his coffee. Tremain waited.

Joe said, "I shot his son in cold blood. Coleman Grant. Put a bullet right between his eyes. Shot the life out of him."

Tremain stared. He hadn't been expecting this.

Joe said, "Ain't never did that before, and never done it since. It's not the way I was raised. Never shot a man in the back, my brothers or me. And never shot a man what didn't need killing. And the only one of us who just gunned a man down was me. Though, he really did need killing."

Tremain said, "You're a good man, Joe. I know that."

"Coming from you, that means a lot."

"There must have been a good reason."

He nodded. "There was a reason. Don't know how good it was."

Tremain took a sip of his own coffee while he waited.

Joe said, "He killed my brother's wife. Lura. Old man Grant's son, he shot and killed Lura. We always figured the bullet was meant for Johnny and caught her by mistake. But that was no excuse. We tracked the man for days. Johnny, our brother Matt, a cowhand by the name of Zack Johnson who had ridden with Johnny when they were with the Rangers, and me. We all tracked the sum'bitch for days. But then it rained and the tracks were gone.

"Matt, he always had a gift for words. Me, I never said much. Johnny usually did his talking with his fists or his guns. But Matt went into a speech about how Johnny should give up this search because they weren't gonna find the man, and the children needed him. We all agreed. We convinced Johnny, but it was mostly Matt's speech.

"But the whole time Matt was giving this talk, I had my foot on something I had seen on the ground. A big brass button with two little crossed swords on it. Grant's son wore a coat with buttons like that. He had hated Johnny from the start. It didn't help that Coleman's wife had almost thrown herself at Johnny."

"Did he hire it done?"

Joe shook his head. "Rode all the way out himself. I never did really understand what the hatred was all about, but as we were looking at the ground, with all of the tracks washed away, I saw the button. Sitting right there in plain sight. I put my foot over it, and then scooped it up when no one was looking.

"I stayed with Johnny for a while. Johnny packed up the children and moved them and the herd to Montana, to a little valley we wintered in with the Shoshone a few years before that. Zack Johnson came with us, and Johnny's late wife's aunt, to help with the children. The Shoshone were gone, so we built a cabin and survived the first winter there, and then we expanded on the cabin the following year, building a house. Then I told Johnny it was time I was moving on.

Told him I had the itch to see different territories. Either New Mexico Territory, or back to California to visit Matt. Matt had married a pretty little girl named Verna whose daddy owned a ranch. Wound up inheriting it. But the truth was, I rode back to Texas, to the Broken Spur.

"Breaker Grant had died by then, and his son now ran the ranch. I walked into Coleman's office one night, and he was still at his desk. I tossed the button down on the desk and told him he should be more careful what he leaves behind when he goes to try and shoot someone. Coleman, he turned white as a sheet.

"I told him to go fetch a pistol, because only one of us was leaving the room alive. He refused. He was always a little afraid of my brothers and me. I couldn't stand it any longer, and I just pulled my gun and shot him. Right there in his office. I done it so Johnny wouldn't have to. I was afraid Johnny would figure it out sooner or later. Johnny has a mind like that. Sort of like you. He can look at the facts and put things together, sort of like a puzzle. He would have made a good lawman."

Tremain said, "You shot the killer of Johnny McCabe's wife so he wouldn't have to."

Joe nodded.

"I've heard the stories about your brother's wife being shot. It's part of the legend. No one knows who did it. That's part of the intrigue about it, I suppose."

"Well, two people know who did it. Me, and now you."

Tremain shook his head. "Son-of-a-gun."

"Right then and there, I turned and walked out of the Broken Spur headquarters and got into the saddle and just rode out. And I've been riding ever since."

"Were there ever reward posters offered for you?"

"Not that I ever knew, strangely enough. It's not like I hid what I was doing. I just left my horse at the hitching rail in front of the house, and walked in without knocking. I knew my way around there because my brothers and I had worked for the Broken Spur for a time. I had seen a lighted window from outside, and I knew the place and knew it was old Breaker Grant's office. It was late, probably after ten. Late on a ranch, when the men are all up before dawn. I just left my horse outside and walked right in. I have no idea who else was in the house. The office was on the first floor. I walked in, had it out with Coleman and shot him dead. And then I just walked out the door, got on my horse and rode on. I can't believe no one saw me. But I guess no one did."

Joe took a sip of coffee. "It's not just the law I been runnin' from, though. I suppose I've been sort of running from myself all this time. The man needed killing. Of that, I'm convinced. But at the same time, to just point your gun at a man's head and pull the trigger and watch his life drain away. It does something to you. It leaves you feeling sort of sick and empty inside."

"You've never seen your brothers since?"

Joe shook his head. "How can I? How can I face them after doing what I did? I did it so Johnny wouldn't have to live with what I've been living with ever since. And so he wouldn't have to go to prison or get the noose. Those children needed their father alive and with them. But it doesn't change what I done."

Tremain's cup was empty. He rose to his feet, the springs of the wooden office chair creaking a bit as he lifted himself out of it. He strolled over to the stove, his boot heels clicking on the wooden floorboards. A couple boards groaned as he walked over them. He took the kettle and filled his cup.

"Joe," he said. "I returned from the War to find my family's old farmhouse gone. Burned to the ground. My parents had been killed and were buried out back."

Joe nodded. Tremain had told him this before.

Tremain said, "My brother Morgan had been told I died in the War. He rode out, and had been gone a long time by the time I got back home. I tried to find him, but his trail had long gone cold. It's been almost fifteen years. I finally stopped searching and made my home here. I guess what I'm trying to say," he was walking back to his desk as he spoke, "I wouldn't care what he had done. If I knew where he was, I would want to see him. If I found out he was in Utah, or Nebraska, or Oregon, I would hand the keys to this office to you and I would be off to find him. To see him. He's the only family I have left in this whole world."

"You sayin' I should go and see Johnny and Matt?"

Tremain nodded. "That's just what I'm saying. Johnny was almost killed in that attack on his ranch. Presuming it's not tall tales, and really happened. Go see him. And while you're at it, go to California and see your brother Matt. I can hold things together here until you're back. And I have Ken who helps out. And if I really need help, you know Josh Wilson would be here with a half dozen boys from the Shannon Ranch."

Joe nodded. Old Josh, he was one of the most reliable men Joe had ever met. Ken was a tall kid, barely twenty, skinny and all arms and legs. Worked as a swamper at the saloon and tended horses at the livery. He filled in as a deputy sometimes.

Tremain said, "Go. See your brothers. Your job will be waiting for you when you come back."

Joe leaned back in his chair. He was letting all of this sink in. "You really think I should?"

Tremain said, "Truth be told, between friends, I think you should have long ago. They're your brothers, Joe. If it was Morgan, I know what I'd be doing."

"You'd be heading on out."

Tremain nodded.

Joe put some thought to it. "Thing is, it's already half-way through September. It's already getting cold up Montana way. I've lived winters in the mountains, but I'm not outfitted for it. Maybe I should head to California and see Matt, first. He can tell me how Johnny's doing. Then in the spring, I'll ride on up to Montana."

Tremain looked a little surprised. "You're going to ride all that way on horseback? I figured you'd want to take a stage."

Joe shook his head. "I like to travel the land myself. Just me and my horse. Johnny was always that way, too. He and Matt and I rode all the way from Pennsylvania to Kansas once, and from there to Texas, and then from there to California."

"The stories around cattle camps is you left Pennsylvania in search of your father's killer. That really happen?"

Joe nodded. "I'll tell you the whole story, sometime. Now that you've got me talking."

In the morning, when the eastern sky was just starting to lighten, Joe got his horse from the livery and saddled up. He had no saddle bags, but he wrapped what little he had in the world into his bedroll, and tied it to the back of the saddle. He went out to a water trough and filled a canteen, and hung it from the saddle horn. Tremain had told him he could take a Winchester from the gun rack in the office, and it was now tucked into the saddle.

He pushed a foot into the stirrup and swung up and onto the back of the horse, and with his scattergun draped across the pommel, he turned his horse between two buildings and off to the long and low, arid hills beyond.

With the flat of his hand he patted the lower left vest pocket, and felt the tin star in there. He had taken the badge off but had it with him. He was deputy marshal of Wardtown, Texas. Something he took very seriously. Once this was all done, he would be coming back.

PART ONE

The Return

1

Johnny McCabe reined up at the top of a low, grassy hill. The top was fairly flat, and the grass tall. At the northern side, though, the hill fell off sharply, like someone had taken a giant shovel and dug away part of it. Down below was a small house. A barn. A corral with a horse pacing about restlessly.

Johnny swung out of the saddle and loosened the girth to let Thunder rest. It had been a long ride from Montana to these foothills in northeastern California. There had actually been little hard riding; for the most part, Johnny and Thunder had meandered their way through the mountains. Drinking from cold streams and sleeping out under the stars. Even still, Thunder seemed content to simply stand and chew on some grass.

Johnny took a few steps closer to the steeper side of the hill. It wasn't so steep that it was impossible to ride down. You would just have to take it slowly and let your horse find its footing. But if you were riding along and didn't know the hill dropped off like this, it could catch you by surprise.

Johnny gazed down at the ranch house. It stood only one level high, and its outer walls were made of upright planks nailed into place. It had a peaked roof. A chimney made of stones poked up through the center, and a thin trail of white smoke was drifting up from it.

This was the house that had once belonged to Johnny and Lura. Where they had made their home, and where their children had been born.

The earth smelled the same as it always had here. Rich and fertile. A light breeze picked up and touched his face. Made Thunder's mane ruffle a bit. A breeze like this was often kicking up in these low hills. Things had changed so little, it could have been seventeen years ago, he thought. He almost expected to see Lura, young and beautiful, stepping from the house to look up the hill at him and wave.

But this was not seventeen years ago. This was today, and his beloved Lura had been dead all this time. Shot by a bullet meant for him. Shot by a man planting himself on this very hill and aiming his rifle down to the house below. A Hall rifle, Johnny thought. Every type of gun had a unique sound to the trained ear, due to things like the caliber, the length of the barrel and the grains of gunpowder used. Johnny had heard a Hall rifle fired before, and thought the gunshot from this hill had about the same sound. And this shot had a throaty *boom* that often comes from a large bore. Johnny remembered some Halls had been issued in a .69 caliber. They had been out of production over forty years and you hardly saw them anymore, but seventeen years ago there had still been a few around.

Since the killer had never been found, Johnny didn't know for absolute fact that the bullet had been meant for him. He knew nothing at all about who the killer was or what he had been thinking. But he had always assumed he was the intended target, not Lura. She had no enemies in the world. No one who would have wanted her dead. She had been too full of love. She had a way of making the room seem lighter and warmer just by walking into it.

Johnny had been seventeen years younger. He had been riding home in the afternoon after a day of rounding up strays. His brother Josiah worked for them, along with Zack Johnson. Johnny couldn't pay them, but they stayed on for free room and board.

Joe and Zack were still with the herd, but would be riding in shortly. At the moment, Johnny and Lura had a moment alone. She was stepping from the house onto the porch, like she often did when she heard him ride up. She had always said she could tell it was him just by the sound of the horse. She had said a horse had a certain way of stepping when Johnny was in the saddle. It was like he and the horse were one, and the horse knew it and so stepped a little livelier. A little freer.

Johnny's face had lightened up when he saw her. It always did. He normally rode with a lot of heaviness in his heart because of men he had seen killed, and men he had been forced to kill himself. Even at the young age of twenty-five he had already lost count. Outlaws. Mexican border raiders. Renegade Comanches. Sometimes at night if he sat alone by the fire it started coming back to him. If he shut his eyes he could see their faces, hear the gunfire and their death screams. But when he saw Lura's face and her smile, all of that seemed to fall away, at least for the moment.

She had many smiles, depending on who the smile was aimed at, but there was one she reserved only for Johnny. One of love, filled with comfort and not a little joy, and a hint of daring. All of this wrapped up into one smile.

He swung out of the saddle and let the rein trail, and Lura stepped down from the low porch.

She said, "Where are Joe and Zack?"

"Back with the herd. They'll be along in a little while."

She raised a brow. "The children are down for a nap. That means we might actually have an entire moment alone."

"And what do you want to do with that moment?"

Her smile took on an extra pinch of daring, and then he took her in his arms and pressed his mouth to hers.

She pulled back after what felt like half an hour. "Why, Mister McCabe. You are such a flirt."

He chuckled. "I've been called many a thing before. But never a flirt."

She was grinning playfully. "And what are some of these things you've been called?"

This was the last thing she ever said. A gunshot roared to life from the hill behind Johnny, muffled a little with distance as the hill was easily a hundred yards away, and Lura was shaken as a bullet tore into her chest two inches below her collar bone.

Johnny stood in wide-eyed horror. He had seen many people shot. More than he could ever count. But not now. Not Lura.

She staggered back a step, and her eyes met his. She wasn't in pain or afraid. She was just looking at him with surprise.

Then her knees buckled and she fell backward.

Johnny caught her but she went limp and began sliding out of his arms. He went down with her, landing on his knees in the dust. He cradled her head. Blood was soaking the front of her blouse. She was going into shock from the rapid blood loss. Her eyes were open but she was no longer seeing.

"Lura, no," he said. "Hang on, Sweetie. Hang on."

She gave a shuddering breath, then another, and then breathed no more.

Tears streamed down, cutting rivulets in Johnny's dust covered face. He looked upward to the sky overhead, still blue in the late afternoon, and screamed out her name. Long and hard.

And his gaze landed on the rider sitting atop the hill. In the very spot Johnny had sat many times, looking down at his little ranch. Johnny couldn't make out the man's face from this distance, but he could see a dark, wide-brimmed hat. And in his hands was a rifle.

The man sat in the saddle a moment, then turned his horse and rode off. Johnny's horse still stood where it had been ground hitched. It had shifted a little to one side at the gunshot but had not bolted. Johnny considered leaping into the saddle and going after the shooter, but he considered this for only a moment. He couldn't leave Lura lying here in the dust.

And that was how Joe and Zack found him. They had heard the gunshot as they were riding in from the herd. They arrived only minutes after the shooter had ridden away. Johnny was on his knees, Lura's head in his lap. Tears were streaming and he found he couldn't even speak.

Zack was out of the saddle and at his side. They had fought in the Texas Rangers before. Saved each other's lives enough times that they had lost count.

"Who done this?" Zack said.

Johnny couldn't get the words out. He just looked off toward the low, grassy hill that was now deserted.

Joe McCabe, with a bushy beard and hair falling to his shoulders, and a Remington holstered at his belt and a Spencer in his saddle boot, was still on his horse.

He said, "I'll get the sum'bitch."

He turned his horse and charged toward the hill. But his horse was tired. It had logged a lot of miles chasing strays. By the time Joe got to the top of the hill, his horse was spent. To push it any further would probably kill it.

Lura was buried beneath an apple tree that stood out behind the house. Ginny had come out from San Francisco and stayed with the children while Johnny rode off to find the killer. Joe and Zack rode with him. After a day, Matt caught up with them and joined them.

The county sheriff, a man who was in his sixties but still strong and with a firm gaze, had said to him, "You let the law take care of this, son."

Johnny shook his head. "There's no law going to be involved in this. I'm going to find him. And I'm not bringing him back."

"Don't do this, son."

Johnny said, his voice low and almost hissing, "I'll say this once. Don't get in my way."

The sheriff didn't. Johnny never knew if it was because the sheriff really wanted Johnny to find the man himself, as only that would bring true justice. Or if the sheriff, as strong as he was, had been scared by Johnny. Zack had once said when Johnny was mad, when he was *really* mad, he was the scariest man Zack had ever seen.

was full and spread out like it was shading Lura's grave from the sun and rain.

Johnny remembered when he and Lura had stood on this very spot. It had been a spring day, and the scraggly little tree was covered with white apple blossoms.

Johnny's sombrero was hanging against his back by a chinstrap, and the twin Remingtons he carried then were slung low and tied down. She stood beside him, her hair the color of corn silk and tied back in a bun. His arm was around her shoulders and she was snuggled into him, the way a woman does when the man she loves puts his arm around her.

"Oh, Johnny. Look. An apple tree. I just love fresh apples."

He said, "I'm kind'a partial to apples, myself, I suppose."

"Let's build here."

"Right here?"

She looked up at him with an exuberant smile and nodded. "Right here. So when we come out the kitchen door, we'll be looking right at this little tree. And we'll have children and the tree will grow as they grow. And one day we'll be old, and this tree will stand tall and full and rain apples down on us in the fall. You'll bounce a grandchild on your knee, and you'll pluck a fresh apple and give it to him."

Johnny stood now, looking at the tree. It was big and full. And considering the age of the children, and the way Josh and Temperance looked at each other, it wouldn't be long before he would have a grandchild to bounce on his knee.

Madden said, "I'll leave you be."

Johnny nodded a *thank you*, and Madden stepped away. Back out front to tend to his horse, Johnny figured.

Johnny removed his hat. Not the same gray sombrero he had worn back then. He now had a brown hat that was flat brimmed and with a four-corner peaked crown, and had no chin strap. He still had his Remingtons, but they were in a drawer back at the ranch house in Montana. He now wore a single pistol, a Colt .44 Peacemaker. But like with the Remingtons, it was slung low and tied down.

He let his gaze fall on the tree. It was nearly four times the size it had been when he last laid eyes on it. The branches were curvy and a little twisted, which was the way with most apple trees. The branches fell almost to the ground.

He figured it was just the way she had imagined it would grow to be, all those years ago.

He allowed himself to imagine what she might have looked like today. She was nineteen when they married, and twenty-four when she was shot. Would make her forty-one today. Probably would have a few lines on her face. Maybe a strand or two of silver in that fine yellow hair of hers. But her smile would probably still be the same, or maybe made even more beautiful with a touch of wisdom added to it over the years.

He could imagine the two of them standing here. Him, the grizzled old gunhawk he now was, and her in a fine dress. The house would probably be twice the size it is now, because he would have added onto it as the years went by. A lady like Lura deserved a fine house. Josh would be out with the herd, and Dusty would be with him. Johnny figured Dusty would have found the family no matter where they were. Jack would be back east, studying to be a doctor, and Bree would be learning to be a lady at the hands of the finest lady Johnny had ever met.

He saw himself reaching up and pulling an apple from a branch and handing it to the love of his life, and her taking it from him with the smile that warmed his heart. He saw her taking a bite of the apple, relishing the taste. He would smell the gentle scent of peach blossom she often wore.

The apple tree was a McIntosh. He and Lura had never named the ranch, but he used an underlined letter M for the cattle brand, and he and Lura knew the M stood for McCabe, but also for McIntosh. For their tree. Locals had begun referring to the place as the M Bar, as many ranches were called by the brand. Hence the ranch in Montana was often called the Circle M.

Johnny had intended to one day build a front gate for people to ride through when they came a-visiting. The gate would be wrought iron painted black, and atop the gate would be the letter M. But the way things had happened, none of it came to be.

He could imagine himself looking into her eyes, saying, "Is it everything you wanted? This place? The children? The life we have?"

She would look up at him with that smile. "Everything and more."

But she wasn't here. The house no longer belonged to them. He had taken the children north, to the little valley he and Zack and Joe had wintered in a long time ago. The winter they had spent with the Shoshone. That village was now gone, but Johnny carried with him all he had learned from them. He and

Zack and Joe had built a cabin there. The next summer, they had expanded on the cabin, building a two-story ranch house of logs in the shape of a cape cod, like the family's old farmhouse had been back in Pennsylvania. The house Johnny, Joe and Matt had grown up in. The original cabin had become the kitchen.

Ginny had come with them, to help him care for the children. The old spinster who had lived a fine life among the high society in San Francisco now lived on a ranch in Montana. She had practically raised Lura, and now was doing the same for Lura's children.

Johnny had to wonder if things had been different, if Lura hadn't been shot and instead they raised the children here, a few hours' train ride north of San Francisco, would Johnny be a different man than he now was? Would he have become a fine gentleman rancher? A pillar of society here in the San Fernando valley? After all, life was much more civilized here than it was on their remote ranch in Montana.

He stood before Lura's grave with a deeply lined face and clothing that was dusty from the trail. His jaw was covered with a white beard, and he wore a gun that was ready for use. Ginny had said once that Johnny lived in a perpetual state of warfare. Zack had said once Johnny was this way because he had been shot at one time too many, and because Lura had been shot in front of his eyes. He wondered what he would be like, now. Would he have cut his Shoshone tail? Would his face be less lined? Would he attend cattle association meetings in a jacket and tie and smoke nice cigars?

He thought of the children. Josh wore his hair long, like his father. He wore his gun tied down. He was a tracker and knew how to survive in the mountains and how to find water in the desert. He was also a gunhawk, because he had to be to survive on the rugged frontier. How different might his life have been here in California? Would he have gone to a nice school in San Francisco? Would he have become a young businessman with short, neatly cut hair and finely tailored suits?

And what about Bree? A couple of winters ago she had ridden into the mountains with Johnny and she had shot a bear with a Winchester carbine. One of the best shots he had ever seen with a rifle. He had shown her how to gut the carcass, and they brought back the fur that was now a bear-skin blanket she used against the cold Montana nights in the winter.

He thought of the lady she would have become with Lura's tutelage. She would wear her hair all done up, and carry a parasol against the harsh California sun in the summer, and young gentlemen driving a carriage would come to call on her. She would attend soirees in San Francisco with her mother and her Aunt Ginny.

He had to wonder if maybe Bree was the one shortchanged the most by all of this.

He walked over to the headstone, ducking his head under one of the far-reaching apple branches. He stood with his hat in one hand, looking at the headstone. Ginny had paid for it. Engraved on it were the words:

LURA MCCABE
BELOVED MOTHER AND WIFE
1838 – 1862

The first time he had looked at this stone, the day it was placed in the ground, Zack had been standing beside him. The apple tree had been much smaller and the grave was touched by sunlight. Johnny had been filled then with a sense of disbelief, looking at those words. Seeing Lura's name on a headstone. He was struck with the same disbelief now, seventeen years later.

Madden had said his wife kept up the grave, and Johnny thought she was doing a good job. The stone was clean, almost polished looking. Like it had been the day it was shipped out from San Francisco and placed here. The grave was cast in perpetual shade because of the apple tree, but the ground about it was covered with little crushed rocks, and some wild flowers had been placed at the base of the headstone.

He knelt. He reached with one hand to the stone, letting his fingers trace her name. The stone felt smooth and cold to the touch. He let his hand fall away.

Touching the stone had been a way of trying to touch her, he supposed, but he had failed. The stone was simply a stone. The closest he had come to touching her had been in that vision he had while he lay in bed with his bullet wounds. It had felt so real. Maybe on some level it was. The Shoshone believed in spirits, that they can touch you while you sleep. And they believed in visions. Many tribes had rituals designed to bring on a sort of delirium so you could achieve a dream state while awake, and experience a vision. The Sioux and the Cheyenne with their Sun Dance, for one. Many people thought such rituals barbaric, but Johnny thought he understood.

The Shoshone believed the body died, but the spirit was eternal. Johnny felt in his gut that they were right. As such, he knew Lura was not really here. Only her earthly remains were in the ground.

Even still, he felt he should say some words. To come all this way, riding horseback from Montana through the Rockies, then across the deserts of Nevada and then through the Sierra Nevadas into this valley, and say nothing didn't seem right. So he said, "Hello, Lura."

The words seemed to ring a little artificial. She wasn't really here. And yet he felt that somehow maybe her spirit was. He even thought he caught the scent of peach blossoms on the breeze.

He said, "The kids are fine. Bree's fine. Ginny's fine. Josh is growing to be a strappin' young man. He'll be runnin' the ranch on his own, soon. And Jack's doing great at medical school."

He almost said, *he won't be the first doctor in the family*. After all, Lura's father was a doctor. But he wouldn't have said such a thing to her face, so he wouldn't say it now. Lura's parents had turned their backs on her when she married Johnny, and this had been a sore spot with her for the rest of her short life. It still angered Johnny a little. They wanted her to go to finishing school back east, and marry a lawyer or a doctor or a college professor. Instead she married a gunhawk.

Johnny was many things, he supposed, besides a gunhawk. A cattleman. Maybe even a business leader of sorts, in the remote little section of Montana where they lived. He was a tracker, a scout. Had even been an outlaw once—he chuckled at the memory of that.

When he had first met her parents he was in a range shirt and riding boots, and his twin Remingtons were tied down low. Didn't matter that he had his hat in hand, was freshly bathed and had brushed all the trail dust from his clothes. He was clean shaven and hadn't taken to wearing his hair long yet. He looked downright civilized compared to how he looked now, he supposed. And yet they were horrified and refused to give their approval. They didn't attend the wedding, and stayed away from the funeral, and to this day had never even seen their grandchildren. He wondered what they would think of Dusty, and again chuckled.

The preacher had stood here and read a passage from the good book. Johnny couldn't remember what it was, just the sound of the man's words droning on while Johnny stared down at the pine box lying in the grave. Zack was standing beside him. Somehow, one way or another, Zack always seemed to be standing beside him through the hard times. Joe was there, and Matt and Verna, and Ginny, and some of the neighbors. But Lura's parents were nowhere to be seen.

He drew a long breath and let it out slowly. In his vision, Lura had said to him he needed to live. He needed to stop grieving for her. She had said he needed to love again. When he woke up from that vision, much of the pain of her loss that he had been carrying all these years seemed to be gone. And it was still gone as he knelt on the crushed rocks and looked at her name on the stone.

He smiled. "We didn't have long together, but we had a whale of a ride."

He could imagine her smiling at that.

"I've gotta be going. Gonna be dark soon. I'm gonna ride out and visit Matt and his family. Might stop in Greenville on the way. According to Matt's letters it's changed a lot since the old days. Then I'll be heading back home."

He knelt silently for a few moments. Then he said, "I'll always love you. And I know you're waiting for me."

Even though most of the pain was now gone, he still felt a tear welling up in one eye and reached up to wipe it away. He didn't want his visit here to be a sad one. He wanted to remember the good times. He wanted her love to be alive in him, not the sorrow or the darkness he felt when she was taken away.

He rose to his feet. One knee was a little stiff and caught him in mid motion.

"Getting a little old, I guess," he said to Lura with a smile.

He had intended to head back around to the front of the house where Thunder was waiting, but he stopped and looked down at the grave one more time. "I wonder sometimes what you'd be like today. I suppose you would have stepped into middle-age as gracefully as you did everything else."

There was so much to say. He could have stood here for hours and not gotten it all out. But if it was true what the Shoshone say, that the spirit is eternal, then he was sure that wherever she was, she knew what was in his heart.

So he simply gave a silent nod of his head, turned away and pulled his hat down over his temples. He was much older now, and yet in so many ways the same man he had been when he married her. Still Johnny

McCabe. Still a cattleman, still a scout and a tracker. And still a gunhawk.

3

He gathered up Thunder's rein. He intended to find a spot somewhere off the main trail, maybe near some trees where he could find some dead falls to use for firewood. He had ridden near a thousand miles since leaving home back in July, and hadn't spent one night under a roof. He had camped with the stars overhead, sitting by a campfire. Much of his food he had shot himself. He had stopped in a small town along the way to replenish his supply of coffee and buy a few cans of beans, but then continued on.

He was about to push his foot into the stirrup when Madden stepped out of the house.

Johnny said, "I want to thank you again."

"Hey, listen, Mister McCabe," Madden said. "The wife wanted me to ask if you'd eaten yet. If not, you're more than welcome to join us for supper."

"I'd hate to impose," Johnny said.

"No imposition at all. Please. My son would really like to meet you. My wife makes some of the best roast beef you'll ever taste."

Johnny hadn't really noticed the smell of roast on the air until Madden mentioned it. He was hungry and now the smell was starting his mouth to watering. And so he stayed for supper.

The kitchen was much the way he remembered it. The table and chairs were new, and the curtains on the windows were different. Lura had used a white, lacey sort of curtain. These were off-white, and there was no sign of lace. But the cupboards were still the ones Johnny had built for Lura all those years ago. Beneath one window was a dry sink and an iron pump. Johnny had installed this so Lura wouldn't have to walk all the way out to the well for a bucket of water.

The wood stove was different. It was the same size, but not quite the same design. These things were made of cast iron and had a tendency to rust out if they weren't used. The house had been closed up for a few years before the Maddens moved in. Matt had used the range for some of his cows, but the house itself had been empty. Johnny was surprised the iron pump had held up.

Johnny washed a little of the trail dust off. He hung his hat on a peg on the wall, a peg that hadn't been there when this had been home to him and Lura. His gun stayed at his side.

Madden's wife was a small woman, and round in the matronly way a woman gets sometimes as she approaches forty. Especially if she's a mother. There were five children, a girl about Bree's age and a boy named Samuel, and three younger ones, one of them still in diapers.

They all sat down to the table, and Johnny found the roast was as good as it smelled.

Johnny said, "You run this place yourself?"

Madden nodded. "I run a small herd. I hire a couple hands once in a while, to help me move some head for a buyer. We're about twenty-five miles from the nearest railroad."

Johnny nodded. "The ranch I have in Montana now is a little further out. We have to ride all the way to Cheyenne to find the railroad."

While they talked, Samuel stared at Johnny. Made Johnny a little uncomfortable. He knew people talked about his exploits, expanding on them and adding to them. Jack had told him about a dime novel that featured him, written by some writer back east. The writer had wanted to meet with Jack to learn more about Johnny, and when Jack refused, the man just made up what he needed to.

As they all talked Johnny would let his gaze wander about the kitchen. He would glance toward the iron pump and see Lura standing there, cranking some water into a pitcher. Or at the stove, a coffee kettle bubbling away.

"Mister McCabe," Samuel said. "Is it true you rode into Mexico and shot it out with the Owen Carter gang? And rescued Petunia McBride?"

Johnny gave a polite smile. He had no idea what the boy was talking about. "I really don't know anyone by those names, son."

Mrs. Madden said with an apologetic tone, "You'll have to forgive him, Mister McCabe. He's read the novel. We keep telling him not everything in it might be true."

The boy said, "So you didn't rescue Petunia McBride?"

Johnny said, "Never met anyone by that name. When I was with the Texas Rangers, though, we did ride into Mexico a few times. Chasing Mexican border raiders. They would hit a small ranch and take some live stock. Sometimes burn the place."

"Would you shoot 'em all?"

"Samuel," Madden said.

Johnny thought it best to avoid the details. "Sometimes we'd get most of the livestock back, and sometimes we wouldn't. But you have to understand, the Texas Rangers are a law-enforcement outfit. That's what we were doing. Enforcing the law."

Johnny saw a little wind let out of the boy's sails. Apparently this novel depicted Johnny as some latter-day knight of the west. Johnny thought he might have to find a copy and see what was being said about him.

Johnny mentioned he was on his way to his brother Matt's ranch.

"Never actually met him," Madden said. "We bought this place from him, but like I mentioned earlier, it was actually his son Hiram did the paperwork with us."

Johnny shook his head. "The last time I saw them, Hiram was smaller than Samuel, here."

When they were finished, Johnny was invited to stay. Samuel volunteered to give up his bed and would eagerly sleep on the sofa. But Johnny wanted to be moving on. He wanted to sleep under the open sky. He was generally not happy sleeping under a roof, unless it was the home he had built in Montana. Somehow that place was different. But generally sleeping under a roof made him feel hemmed in.

He thanked Madden's wife for keeping up Lura's grave.

She said, "If there's anything you'd like done differently..."

"No, ma'am. It looks mighty fine just the way it is."

He stepped into the saddle, and gave a nod to Samuel. The boy was trying to hold his gleaming smile in, but you could see it in his eyes. Johnny doubted the boy's disappointment at finding Johnny had really not rescued some damsel-in-distress by the name of Petunia something-or-other would not last long. At the first opportunity he would be telling his friends he had met *the* Johnny McCabe. Larger than life and tougher'n a bear.

Johnny started away down the trail. Evening shadows now covered the land and the sky overhead had faded to a steel gray. The sun had long gone down. He doubted he would get more than a mile.

As he rode, he cast a look back at the house. Not his and Lura's house anymore. It was now home to another good family, one that seemed strong and filled with love. He thought Lura might give a little smile at that.

The trail followed a curve and ahead was a low ridge. Before he was taken beyond the view of the house, Johnny looked back for a final gaze at the old place, standing tall and sort of gray in the fading daylight. Madden and his wife and Samuel were still standing outside the house, watching him ride away. Johnny threw a final wave at them, which they returned, then he rode up and over the ridge, and the house was gone from sight. He wondered if he would ever see it again.

Madden's gaze was still on the darkening trail that was now empty.

His wife said, "Samuel, it's nigh time for bed."

"Yes'm," Samuel said with the same disappointment every boy of his age feels when it's time for the day to end, and he headed into the house.

Once the boy was inside, Madden said, "So, what'd you think? Not quite what we expected, was he?"

"Shorter'n I thought he would be," she said.

Madden nodded. "But much different from Hiram McCabe."

She said, "Hiram frightened me. I was glad when our business with him was done. There was something dark in his eye."

"They say Hiram McCabe shot a man in cold blood a few years ago. They say his father paid good money to cover it up."

"You believe that?"

He shrugged. "Never met Matt McCabe, but after meeting Hiram, after sitting with him while we signed the papers for this place, I wouldn't be surprised. It's just a gut feeling. The look in his eye. Something about his manner. I had the feeling there wasn't much he wouldn't be capable of."

4

  Johnny McCabe had spent most of his life on the frontier. He had ridden with the Texas Rangers, fought Mexican border raiders and renegade Comanches. He had run from the law for about a year, because of a misunderstanding in Kansas that led to a man being killed. He had punched cows and caught and broke wild mustangs. He had been shot at and shot back. He had poured down too much tequila in Mexican border towns and whiskey in cattle towns and bunkhouses, and he had endured hard winters. He had scouted and tracked. He had built a home for himself and his family in the harsh Montana wilderness. But never in all of his years in the west had he seen a cattle town transform into a mining town. Not until he rode into Greenville, California.

  Greenville was the little town where he had met Lura, all those years ago. It had been a sleepy cow town back then. Population maybe two hundred. He knew from the letters he got from Matt that gold had been found in the foothills near town, and mines had been built, and Matt and his wife had bought one of the mines, and Greenville was now a sort of combination cattle town and mining town. Yet, somehow, the way the human mind works, Johnny still visualized Greenville as looking the way it had. Wide streets with wooden buildings lining either side. An occasional rider working his way down the street toward the saloon in search of a glass of whiskey. An old-timer sitting on a bench chewing tobacco and enjoying the morning air. A shopkeeper sweeping off the boardwalk by his front door. Sleepy and quiet, except on the first Saturday after payday, when the local cowhands came in hooting and screaming and firing their guns into the air, intending to spend an entire month's salary on pharo, whiskey and women. He shouldn't have been shocked by the changes to Greenville. Yet he was.

There was nothing pretty about a mining town, and Greenville was now no exception.

The town had grown, and was now maybe four times its former size. The street he rode down was a river of mud. Thunder's hooves sank two or three inches with each step, then made a sucking sound as the hoof was pulled out to make another step. And the mud had a serious odor to it, because it wasn't just mud. It was the refuse from chamber pots and dishpans, simply tossed out the door. A light rain had fallen the night before, and that was enough to bring the contents of the street alive with a stench that was not much different from a poorly maintained outhouse.

Lined at either side of the street was row upon row of tents. Smoke drifted from stove pipes sticking out through holes cut in the canvas. A wagon was working its way along the street, the mules pulling in their harnesses as mud sucked at their hooves and rose almost halfway to the wheel hubs. Children, too young to realize how desperately poor they were, ran laughing through an alley.

An occasional wooden building was sprinkled in among the tents. One structure, with a crooked sign nailed overhead, had been hand-painted with the word SALLOON, spelled wrong. The building looked like it had been put up in a hurry. The roof was uneven and there were gaps in the boards in the walls.

Johnny had come to town for two reasons. One, because he wanted to see the old town again before he rode out to visit Matt. The other was because he found himself hankering for a taste of scotch. It was late afternoon, but he thought he had time for a drink before he continued on. He had been in the saddle all day, covering the distance between town and his and Lura's old home, and he figured Thunder could use a little rest. Then they would head out, find a place to camp, and arrive at Matt's in the morning. But after seeing the condition of this saloon, he found his hankering for a scotch fading.

The street emptied out onto the main street. Ahead of him was a bank, with brick walls and a peaked roof. This was new. The last time he had been here, the bank had been a structure of wooden upright planks. As he rode on, a series of houses he remembered from before had been replaced by a small train station. Sometime between then and now, the railroad had come through.

Ahead and on the left was another saloon. This one was called the *Cattleman's Lounge*. He remembered this from the early days. The roof was peaked, and the walls made of upright planks, but they fit firmly. Two windows faced the street, and a doorway that held two half-size swinging doors. Nice to see not everything had changed.

Johnny gave Thunder a light tug of the rein, and the horse stopped. He swung out of the saddle, his right foot burying itself ankle-deep in the mud. Johnny was in black riding boots that were dusty from the ride in from the mountains. He cringed at the thought of what he was stepping in.

He gave Thunder's rein a turn around the hitching rail. He said, "I won't be long, boy. We'll get out of here and find a camp with some firewood and some good grass."

You ride alone on the trail for three months, you wind up talking to your horse a lot. When your horse starts talking back to you is when you have to worry, Johnny thought with a grin.

A couple men milled about on the boardwalk. Dirty white shirts, woolen pants and suspenders. They wore laced-up boots and short-brimmed felt hats. Miners, Johnny figured.

They gave Johnny a stare. The tail of his hair was tied in fell a couple of inches longer than it had been when he left Montana, and his jaw was now covered with three inches of a beard that had been dark when he last saw this town, but now was a snowy white. His hat was flat brimmed and had a four-corner crease at the crown, and was dust covered. He wore a canvas jacket and jeans, and his Colt was tied down low on his right side. He figured he probably looked like a cross between a mountain man and a gunhawk. Which was probably an accurate description of him.

He nodded to them and they each gave a wary nod in return, and he pushed through the batwing doors and stepped into the saloon.

The barroom was a little bigger than he remembered. More tables. A couple of faro tables, and even a roulette wheel against one wall. A cloud of cigarette and cigar smoke clung to the ceiling and swirled about the rafters. When Johnny had last been here, the bar had been nothing more than two planks held up by upended beer kegs. But now there was an actual bar, like something you would see in St. Louis or San Francisco. Mahogany wood, and scrollwork.

Some miners stood about, and a few more were leaning an elbow against the bar. Some wore short-brimmed hats like the two outside, and others wore caps. Their faces all had the pallor of men who worked underground and saw little sunlight. Johnny heard accents he identified as Irish, French, the twang of New England, and an occasional Rebel drawl.

He counted three women moving through the room, trawling for business. Their dresses had necklines low enough that they would have drawn a scowl from Ginny. One looked thin and had a tired way of standing, like life had just worn her out. Which it probably had. There was no living Johnny knew of that was harder on a person than being a saloon woman. It was hard to guess this one's age, because saloon women often looked older than they were. The other two clearly looked to be in their late teens. Probably hadn't been at it all that long.

Johnny ambled up to the bar, shouldering past a couple of miners who didn't show the courtesy to move. They gave him a glare, but that's all they gave. He figured his rough look at the way he wore his guns made them want to be careful. Fine with him. He was looking for no trouble. He just wanted his glass of scotch and then to be on his way.

"What'll you have?" the barkeep said.

He was about Johnny's age, and had a tired look to his eyes. His jowls were fleshy and his stomach round. His hair was thinning at the top. And yet, something about the man struck Johnny as familiar.

Johnny had never been good about remembering names, but he was good with faces. Always had been. And this face connected itself in his mind to a name.

He said, "Crocker?"

The man gave a wary squint. "Yeah?"

"Artie Crocker."

The man nodded again.

Johnny said, "I guess it has been a lot of years, and I've been on the trail a few weeks and probably look like something the cat dragged in. Johnny McCabe. I used to work the McCarty ranch outside of town."

Crocker broke into a grin. "Sure enough. Johnny McCabe. Son-of-a-gun. How many years has it been?"

"Seventeen, if I'm counting right."

Crocker extended his hand. "How are you?"

Johnny shook the hand. "Mighty fine. And you?"

He held his hands out, indicating the room around him. "I own the place, now."

Back in the old days, Artie Crocker had been thin and with a wild mop of hair. He had made his living pushing a broom here and occasionally tending bar. A lot of the cowhands had liked to belittle young Artie. A man who chose to make his living pushing a broom rather than on the back of a horse couldn't be much of a man. But Johnny saw nothing wrong with earning an honest day's work, no matter how you earned it. He had shot the bull with Artie more than once, shared a cigarette with him, and an occasional drink. And now Artie owned the Cattleman's Lounge. Johnny wondered what those young cowhands from seventeen years ago would think, now.

"Drink's on the house," Artie said. "What'll you have?"

"You still carry scotch?'

"Do I still carry scotch?" Artie set a glass on the table. "For you, sir, a double."

Artie filled it half full.

"Mighty kind of you," Johnny said.

"Well, we don't see many from the old days, anymore. Most everyone's ridden on. The town's not the same anymore."

Johnny nodded. "I kind of noticed that when I was riding in."

As Artie talked, Johnny took a drink of the whiskey. The proper way to drink whiskey is not to just knock it back like a wild man, like so many did. The proper way was to draw a small breath, then take maybe half an ounce back on your tongue and swallow it, then exhale and let the flavor sort of drift its way up through you.

Artie was saying, "Old Doc Graham is still around. Sees a patient every now and then, but he's mostly retired now. You married his daughter, didn't you?"

Johnny nodded. "She and I settled down on a small ranch maybe a day's ride north of here."

As Johnny was speaking, the memories of those days were coming back to Artie. He looked like he regretted bringing it up. "I was really sorry to hear about her loss."

Johnny waved it off. "We're all doing fine, now. The kids are grown."

"I heard..," Artie was trying to recall just what he had heard. A bartender heard so many things. "You have a ranch up Montana way, now."

Johnny nodded. "Built ourselves a nice comfortable place."

"Good to hear."

"Anyone else still around?"

Artie shrugged and gave his head a slow shake. "Not that I can think of."

"You must see my brother Matt in town. He has the old McCarty spread, now."

Johnny saw an *oh, yeah* sort of form itself on Artie's face, but it wasn't a good one. "I don't see him in town very much, really. I don't think he comes to town much. One of his sons is the pastor at the Methodist church, off on Valley Street."

Matt had mentioned his oldest had become a minister. "His son Tom."

Artie nodded enthusiastically. "Tom McCabe's a good man."

"And Matt's son Hiram works alongside him running the family business, now. From what Matt has said in letters. Sort of like my son Josh is the ramrod at my ranch."

Artie nodded not so enthusiastically. "Hiram McCabe. Yep, that's what he does, I guess. He's the one we see in town. Him and his younger brother Dan. Checks up on the mine regularly."

Johnny got the impression there was something about Hiram that Artie didn't like. Not his words, but the way he said them. A wrinkle of the brows. A look of hesitancy when he spoke.

Artie said, "You riding out there to see your brother?"

"Eventually. I was riding right past Greenville, so I thought I'd ride in just to see the town and get a drink of scotch."

"What do you think of the old town?"

"Not what I remember, I'll say that."

Artie gave a bitter snicker. "That's a good way of putting it."

Johnny became aware of four men sitting at a corner table, who were staring toward him and Artie. These men weren't miners or cowhands. They had the dirty, longhaired look of gunhawks. Or at least wannabe gunhawks. There was a certain belligerence in their stare that you didn't usually find in men who worked for a living. And their faces bore the look of young men who indulged in whiskey a little too much. A little gaunt, a little pale. Reddened at the nose and around the eyes.

Johnny said to Artie, "Where could I find a halfway decent meal in this town, these days?"

Artie looked to a thin man with shaggy hair and an apron tied over the front his shirt. He was delivering a tray of whiskeys to a table where four men sat. A card game was underway at the table. At the center of the table was a pile of coins.

Artie called to him. "Little, go see what Mrs. Hanlon's cooking for our guests tonight."

With a nod, Little served the drinks then headed for the doorway.

Artie said, "Mrs. Hanlon runs a restaurant a couple doors down, and she fixes meals for my customers, too."

"Is the food any good?"

Artie nodded with a smile. "Home cookin'."

Johnny took another belt of whiskey, and turned to lean one arm on the bar and watch the card game. He glanced toward the men in the corner who had been watching him and Artie, and their gazes darted away from him. He hoped they weren't looking for trouble. He wanted none. He simply wanted to eat the home-cooking and finish his whiskey and be on his way.

Johnny noticed one of the men at the table was not a miner or a cowhand. He wore a black wide brimmed hat, neatly blocked and with a flat crown. His jacket and trousers were a charcoal gray with thin pin stripes, and he wore a checkered vest and a string tie. Johnny had a sideways view of him and could see a short barreled revolver was holstered at his belt.

Artie said, "That's Sam Middleton. Comes here almost every night. Professional card shark. I offered him a job running a faro game, but he said no. He said he just plays for pleasure, now. Though I've noticed he always seems to come away from the table with most of the money. I think he just doesn't wanna split any of his take with the house."

The other men at the table all looked to be miners, and the tired looking saloon woman stood behind one of them. The man wore a wool cap with a short visor, a blue shirt stained with dust and sweat, and suspenders over his shoulders. The woman was gripping those shoulders, kneading muscles that were swollen the way shoulders get from hard work.

"I'll meet your two bits and raise you two more," he said to the card shark, and tossed his coins to the growing pot at the center of the table.

The man to his right set his cards face down on the table. "I fold."

The card shark glanced to the saloon woman— was there some motion from her head? Did Johnny see her nod, almost imperceptibly? Or were his eyes just tired, becoming a little bleary from all of the smoke in the air?

The card shark had a very light blonde mustache and a matching crop of whiskers on his chin. He said to the miner, "I'll meet those two bits and raise you a full dollar."

The fourth man at the table tossed his cards down. "I'm out, too. This is gettin' too rich for me."

"Well, what's it going to be, Charlie?" the man in the black hat said. He spoke with a hint of the theater in his voice. Almost like he was reciting the words, and with a firm baritone that projected.

Johnny strolled over to the table, his glass in his left hand. Though he was right-handed, he usually held a glass or a cup in his left so his gun hand would be free.

The miner called Charlie looked at his cards hesitantly, then said, "I guess I'm out, too."

Johnny took another belt of whiskey. The gambler reached out to the table and scooped the coins toward him. Easily five dollars.

The gambler glanced toward him. "Greetings. Care to join us for a hand?"

Johnny shook his head. "Thanks anyway."

"Don't say we didn't offer." He was shuffling the cards as he spoke. He began dealing them, five to a man. Johnny noticed the man was older than he had first thought. The mustache and beard weren't blonde, they were white. And the man had fine lines trailing away from his eyes. But he sat straight like a younger man, and his shoulders were strong. "The game's five card draw, boys. Nothing wild."

This time, Charlie won, taking in a dollar. Then, on the next hand, Johnny noticed it again. The man Artie had called Sam Middleton glanced toward the saloon woman, and she moved her head ever so slightly up and down.

"I'll call," Middleton said, "and raise a dollar."

Charlie shook his head and laid his cards down. The other two did also.

"If I were you boys," Johnny said, "I'd take back the money I lost. Nothing fair about this game. The only thing sporting about it is how long it would have gone on before someone figured it out."

Middleton let out a long, exasperated sigh. "Now, was that really necessary?"

The three miners were looking at Johnny. Charlie said, "What's he doing? Dealing from the bottom of the deck?"

One of the others said, "I didn't see anything."

Johnny said, glancing with his eyes toward the woman, "She's working with him. She has full view of your cards. Nodding her head if you had a certain hand, doing nothing if you had nothing. From where she's standing she can also sneak a peek at your friends' cards."

Middleton rose to his feet, hooking his right thumb in his belt. He was smiling but his eyes showed no humor. "Friend, do you always go about accusing a man of cheating at cards?"

"Only when he is. Friend."

"Such a thing could get you very dead, very quickly."

"I'd leave that gun where it is," Johnny said calmly. "You're not dealing with a miner who's more used to a pick and shovel than the feel of a gun bucking in his hand."

"I suppose you're right," Middleton said. To Johnny's surprise, the smile became more genuine. "I suppose this town isn't big enough to survive the clash of two titans such as you and I."

Johnny couldn't help but grin. He had been called a lot of things before, but never a *titan*.

"Tell you what," Middleton said. "I shall let this go for now, simply because you have the advantage, due to your prowess with that pistol riding on your leg. But sometime when we're on more equal ground, we shall see which of us is the more worthy gladiator."

A man spoke from off to one side. "What seems to be the problem here?"

Johnny wasn't going to take his eyes from Middleton, but from the corner of his eye he saw two of the men from the corner table who had been staring at him were now on their feet and walking over.

Johnny said, "Nothing that hasn't been taken care of."

"Listen, drifter," one man said, one hand resting on his hip and the finger of the other hand pointing at Johnny. "You better watch yourself. We don't want no trouble in this town."

Middleton said, "Allow me to introduce what passes for law in this town. Marshal Gideon Wells, and his henchman."

Johnny then glanced at the man. "I don't see any badge."

The man called Wells said, "I don't have to wear it. Everyone here knows who I am. Now the question is, who are you?"

Middleton said, "Boys, go sit down. You're way out of your league dealing with just one of us, let alone the both of us."

"Look, city feller. I don't want to hear no sass from you."

A smile of amusement lit the gambler's face. But before he could say anything, Wells said to Johnny, "I think you'd better come down to the jail with us so's we can ask you some questions."

Johnny said, "I'm not going anywhere with you."

"Slow down, boys," Middleton said, "before someone gets hurt."

Wells said, "I've had enough of you, fancy pants. Shut your mouth or we'll haul you down to the jail, too. Cheatin' at cards is ag'in the law."

Middleton's smile was gone. "I think you boys had better go back to the hole from whence you crawled, before someone squashes you like the insects you are."

Wells and his deputy reached for their guns.

Johnny's right hand snapped to his holster, and his revolver was out and in his grip, hammer cocked. "Leave those guns where they are. This ain't worth dying over."

The eyes of Wells were wide as he stared into the maw of Johnny's .44. His own gun hadn't even cleared leather.

Wells turned away. "Come on, Bardeen let's get out of here."

They both headed for the door. Then Wells looked back to Johnny and said, "You'd best be gone by the time I'm back."

Johnny said, "You've got me real scared."

Wells turned and stormed out, pushing past Bardeen and almost knocking him over.

Johnny slid his gun back into its holster.

Middleton said, "I'd have given three to one odds that you would have at least spilled your drink."

Johnny's glass was still in his left hand, a few swallows of whiskey left.

Johnny said, "You're not surprised that I didn't have to kill him?"

Middleton shook his head. "Not in the slightest. I'd have given five to one against it. You wear that gun like you know how to use it. And I'm fairly sure who you are. And if you are who I think you are, I've heard that you never kill unless you have to."

The miners Middleton had been playing cards with were standing, but they had not left the room.

Charlie said, "We want our money."

"Oh, for crying out loud," Middleton said, "take your money."

The miners began scooping coins into their pocket, and then they filed out of the saloon. One of them threw an angry glance back at Middleton on his way. Middleton didn't seem to notice.

The man called Little then pushed in through the swinging doors, a tray of food in his hands. He brought it over to Johnny.

"Sit," the gambler said, "Share my table while you enjoy your repast."

"Mighty neighborly," Johnny said, "considering I was accusing you of cheating."

"Not neighborly at all." Middleton was smiling. "I just want you where I can keep an eye on you."

Johnny took the chair Charlie had been using. Little set a plate of fried chicken and potatoes in front of him.

Johnny said to Middleton, "Keep both hands on the table."

Middleton had returned to his chair. "I'm sure you'll do likewise."

Johnny cut into the chicken. Juicy and tender. Mighty tasty.

Middleton gathered up the cards and began shuffling. "By the way, if you're going to accuse a man of cheating, you should at least know his name. Sam Middleton."

Johnny nodded. "Mine's McCabe."

Middleton gave a grinning snicker. "Like I figured. Your age, the way you carry that gun, and considering this is Greenville. Part of the legend of Johnny McCabe is centered on this town."

"You know, Middleton, I can't quite figure you. You're no small-time card shark. And the way you were facing those two tells me you've been in a fight or two. What are you doing in a town like this?"

"Lying low for a while. This seems like as good a place as any. I wish you hadn't tipped off those local diggers as to what Peddie and I were doing, though. It gave us a tidy, little income. Small but steady."

"Is she your partner?"

Middleton smiled. "No. I usually work alone. She was just helping an old friend. She and I know each other from Saint Louis, where we were both enjoying better days."

As they talked, Johnny noticed one of the girls had gone to the bar. She was standing with her back to it and she was leaning against it with both elbows, and was watching him. Her hair was dark and fell in thick curls to bare shoulders. She was thin, maybe too much so. Her cheeks were a little hollow and even though she wasn't much older than his own daughter Bree, lines were already forming at either side of her mouth. The result of too many hardships and not enough smiles.

"That's Belle," Middleton said. "I think she likes you."

Johnny said nothing. He took another bite of chicken. He didn't usually truck with saloon women.

Middleton said, "Tell me something, McCabe. Why did you do that? Why did you step in and interfere with the card game? What did you care?"

"Because I have a respect for hard work, and those who do it. I've done more than enough of it in my life, and I'm sure there's a load of it waiting for me down the road. I hate to see someone like you trick hard-working people out of what little money they have."

Middleton shook his head. "How noble. Bravo."

He began dealing himself a hand of solitaire. "McCabe, hard-working people want to spend their money. There's a reason why poor people are poor. If they want to throw their money away, why not throw some of it my way? If they didn't do it at my table, they'd do it at the bar, or trying to buy five minutes with Peddie or Belle."

"At least then they'd be getting what they paid for. You were tricking them out of their money."

"In this life, you seldom get what you pay for, but you often get tricked. I would rather be the trickster than one of the thousands of victims waiting to part with their hard-earned cash."

Johnny decided to end this discussion. It was going nowhere. A man like Middleton could always find ways to rationalize his twisted beliefs. Johnny dropped a chicken bone to his plate and finished the potatoes, then he drained the remaining swallow from his whiskey glass.

He said, "Now tell me something, Middleton. Wells and the man with him. Were they really lawmen? And if they were, why were they spoiling for a fight?"

"Because you're new in town."

"I don't understand."

"I've had little dealings with the locals, other than what I see of them in here. But from what I understand, there is a group of thugs who work for the mine, sort of as enforcers. I don't know if any of them are actually official lawmen or not. They keep the peace in town, but I suspect they are actually protecting the mine's owner from anything the law might frown on."

"And what makes you think the mine owner has anything to hide?"

"Of course, since you're the brother of the mine owner, I probably shouldn't be saying anything."

Johnny shook his head. "My brother is a good man."

Middleton raised his brows. "You've been gone a long time."

Johnny had been intending to head back to the bar to pay Artie for the meal, then ride on out. He wanted to put some miles behind him before sunset. But instead he remained in his seat. Middleton now had his full interest.

"Say what you've got to say."

"Every stranger who comes to town, anyone who doesn't work for the mine or is a cowhand at a local ranch, is greeted as you were tonight. You drew their attention even faster, I suspect, because of the way you wear your gun. Of course, they have no idea you are their employer's brother."

"They seemed to be leaving you alone."

"They don't quite know what to make of me, so they watch from a distance. I dress like a dandy, but they can tell by the way I carry myself and the fact that I'm not afraid of them that I am much more than that."

This gave something for Johnny to think about. He knew Matt was a good man. And yet, he could see for himself that something was not right in this town.

He rose to his feet. "Nice chewin' the fat with you, but it's time I was riding on."

"Oh, and McCabe. Next time you bust up one of my card games, I may not be so forgiving."

Johnny looked at him curiously. "Threatening me, Middleton?"

He shook his head. "I don't threaten. I'm just stating a fact."

"Then don't let me catch you cheating."

Johnny went to the bar to pay Artie Crocker.

"Really good seeing you again," Artie said. "But watch your back around here. This town is really not the place it was back in the old days."

"Thanks, but I'm not planning on staying."

They shook hands and Johnny headed outside. The late afternoon sun was shining golden against the buildings across the street. Johnny figured he could get a couple of miles behind him before he would start looking for a place to make a camp. He generally preferred not to sleep with a roof overhead, unless it was his own house back in Montana.

He reached for Thunder's rein. "All right, boy. Let's get out of here."

He heard footsteps rushing up behind him. Light footsteps, too light to be made by a man. As he turned to see who it was, feminine hands grasped him by the arm. It was the saloon woman Middleton had called Belle.

"Walk me home, cowboy?"

"Look, ma'am. Belle. Thanks, but I'm not interested."

"Please. Just walk me home."

There was something in her eyes. A sense of urgency.

Johnny sighed. "All right."

She took his arm as they walked, though he hadn't offered it.

She said, "So, are you really Johnny McCabe? The gunhawk?"

He nodded. "So they say."

"Artie knows you. He had always said he knew Johnny McCabe, but none of us really believed him."

"Artie's a good man."

She nodded.

She asked about his family, and he told her he had a daughter almost her age. She said she came from a family of missionaries who were killed in an Indian raid when she was ten and she wound up in an orphanage, and then here.

He thought about Temperance, the girl living with him and his family in Montana. She and Josh were hopelessly in love. Johnny figured by the time he got back home they would be engaged. She was a solid young woman and would be a good mother to his grandchildren. But when Josh had met her she was in about the same situation Belle was.

"Well, here we are," she said, indicating a long building that was nothing more than canvas walls nailed to a framework of two-by-fours.

It was what passed for a brothel in this town. Johnny had seen this type of set-up before. The interior of the tent would be divided by blankets or sheets of canvas hanging from the ceiling. Each compartment would have a cot, where the women plied their trade.

"You sure you won't come in?" she said. "I'll make this one on the house."

Johnny supposed he should be flattered. But she was young enough to be his daughter, and that somehow left him with an unsettling feeling.

"Thanks, but no," he said. He decided to say what he was thinking. "You're young enough to be my daughter and that wouldn't be right."

"Not many men I've met would let that stand in their way."

Johnny touched the brim of his hat to her. "Take care of yourself."

She leaped at him, wrapping her arms around his neck.

"Get out of town," she said quickly, her voice no more than a whisper. "Get out quick. Ride on and don't look back, or they'll kill you."

"What are you talking about?" Johnny grabbed her by the hips to push her from him.

"No. put your arms around me. Pretend we're hugging. We're being watched."

She seemed really frightened. Johnny decided to play along.

She said, "Another man was here a few weeks ago. Like you. A stranger."

"But I'm not a stranger. I'm the brother of the mine's owner."

"Wells and the others don't know that. At least not yet. And maybe it wouldn't matter."

Johnny shook his head. "I know my brother."

"But you don't know his son Hiram. He's the one who does most of the running of the mine. We don't see his father in town. Hardly ever. Hiram has a cruel streak. Believe me, he's one of my customers."

That rankled Johnny a little. The idea of a woman being abused. His number of questions for Matt was increasing.

He said, "What happened to this man you speak of?"

"He rode into town and bedded down in the livery stable. They could have left him alone but he wore his gun like you wear yours. Like he knew how to use it. Made Wells and his men nervous. In the morning, the stranger just wasn't there anymore. All his gear is still at the livery, but he was gone. They came and got him in the night, is what happened. Everyone is saying Hiram McCabe had him killed."

"Has anyone found the body?"

"No, but that don't matter. Get out of town while you can. And don't bother with your brother. Just ride on. Don't look back."

He shook his head. None of this made any sense to him at all. Not Matt. If there was anyone he would have bet his life on being beyond corruption, it would be Matt.

He said, "I don't understand any of this. I know my brother Matt. He just isn't capable of anything like that."

She pulled back a bit until she was looking him in the eye, and she asked the question he didn't really want to hear. She said, "How long has it been since you've seen your brother?"

Seventeen years. He usually got a letter or two a year from Matt. But letters don't necessarily paint the whole picture.

She said, "People change, Mister McCabe."

"Not Matt." But he didn't say it with a whole lot of conviction.

She shrugged. "Maybe Matt."

He said nothing. He didn't know what to say.

She stepped back, and laid a hand gently at the side of his face. "You got a woman waiting for you?"

Again he said nothing. Too long a story to go into.

She said, "If you do, then she's one lucky woman."

And Belle turned and stepped into the brothel through the tent flap.

Johnny turned and started back down the boardwalk toward where Thunder waited for him. He glanced about casually and saw miners milling about here and there. Two cowhands riding down the street toward the Cattleman's Lounge. If anyone had been watching him and Belle, there was no sign of it.

He pulled Thunder's rein from the hitching rail and swung into the saddle. He intended to ride on out, and build a camp and sleep under the open sky.

Tomorrow he would be riding out to see his brother Matt, and he intended to find out just what was going on.

5

The fire danced in the hearth before her. She sat in a wooden rocker that creaked a little as she rocked a bit forward and then back. She sat with her back erect and her mouth was clamped shut. Her face was deeply lined, and her hair was now streaked with silver.

Her name was Verna McCabe, and the house about her had been in her family for a couple of generations now. It had been much smaller, of course, when her grandfather Ebenezer McCarty had first come to California. He had acquired the land from the old Spanish Don who had first settled here. The house had been little more than a kitchen, a small parlor and two bedrooms contained within adobe walls. It had been a single-floor place, then. Her grandfather had added onto it, expanding it. There was now a central building that was two floors high, with a wing shooting off in one direction and another in the other direction.

Her grandfather had worked hard to build this place. To start up a small ranch and then grow it into one of the larger ranches in the county. Her father then took it further. By the time of his death fifteen years ago, it had become one of the larger ranches in the state. In fact, the only one she knew of that was larger was one down Stockton way.

And now her husband had grown it from a ranch to a small empire. He had expanded the business beyond cattle, and they now owned two goldmines in California and one south of the border, and held significant stock in the railroad.

Actually, it wasn't her husband who had done this. It was merely part of the façade she created for the public. In reality, he was merely a puppet. He could speak eloquently, almost lyrically at times. He had a personal charm that made people want to listen to him. But it was Verna who had the intelligence. The business sense. And the backbone to make the hard decisions. To do what had to be done, even if what to be done wasn't pretty.

She had married wisely. She had had her choice between three brothers. It was obvious when they rode in twenty-two years ago that one of them was going to become her husband. None of the local young men had the breeding or the qualities she was looking for. Picking a husband was not unlike evaluating horse flesh, she thought. Her father had taught her horses and cattle, and all she had to do was apply that reasoning to men. With a few modifications, of course. When the three brothers rode in, obviously gunhawks by the way they carried themselves and wore their guns, she knew it would be one of them. After all, she had been twenty at the time. Well past marrying age, and she wasn't getting any younger.

The youngest brother, Josiah, she eliminated almost immediately. He said little, and he tended to hang back at the periphery of a crowd. Observing, but seldom taking part. He knew how to use his gun and he was an expert tracker—better than the other two—and he spoke a couple of Indian languages. He was wiley, of that she was sure, but she had learned men like Josiah McCabe were not quick to trust. And to do what she needed to do, to grow this ranch into an empire, she needed to have her man's absolute trust.

She gave the middle one serious consideration. He had a commanding way about him. A serious sense of leadership. When the ranch's ramrod had died, trampled by a stallion when they were out mustanging, her father had named the middle brother the new ramrod. He was also the fastest with a gun and the best fighter of the group. A true gunhawk. But he was strong willed. and while he was the best leader of the three, she doubted he could be led.

She then focused her attention on brother number three. The eldest of them. He had a way of speaking that made people want to listen. And he was the most civilized of the three. He looked natural in a tie and jacket. She had seen the other two dressed as such. The middle one kept pulling at his collar like he just felt uncomfortable, and the younger one had seemed comically awkward. No matter how they tried to fix his tie, it simply veered to one side or the other, and he wore his jacket like it was made of lead.

No, her husband was to be the eldest. Matthew, his name was. Winning his heart wasn't hard. After all, if you can break a horse, you can break a man. You just had to do it more subtly. You had to know which strings to pull, like with a puppet. You had to know how to approach a subject. How to get him to do what you wanted while letting him think it was his own idea. It helped that he was delightfully naïve.

The only ones who could have tripped her up were his brothers. The only two he would have listened to. The middle one set his eyes on the daughter of the local doctor, and she was killed only a few years after they were married. Fortuitous, Verna thought. The man took his family and moved them off to the wilds of Montana, far from the reach of her husband. If she had known that was what it would take to get him to leave the area she would have hired the killing done herself. And the younger one simply disappeared. Hadn't been heard from in years.

And so she controlled Matthew. Through him, she bought gold mines and got into the railroad. Through him she had built the empire her father had always dreamed of.

Her father had always wanted a son. Fate had denied him this, but Verna had proven he didn't need one.

And so she sat by the fire in her rocker. In her hand was glass of sherry. She sat, staring into the fire, sipping at the sherry and thinking. The next step, the most unfortunate in her years-long strategy, had finally arrived. She regretted what had to be done. Matthew had been a loving husband, but she simply no longer needed him. He had outlived her usefulness. Hiram was now old enough to take his father's place as the public face of the McCabe empire. He had his father's gift for speech and charm, and best of all, he didn't have to be manipulated. He shared Verna's vision and would work alongside her. This meant Matt had to disappear, and if she let sentiment get in the way, then she wouldn't deserve the success she was building.

She heard a rapping on the door. This was her time to be alone. She was never to be disturbed, except by one man.

"Come in," she said.

The door opened and he stepped in. A tall man with pale skin and high cheekbones, and short cropped white hair. He wore a dark jacket. Even though he was nearly fifty years old, he was solidly muscled and his shoulders were wide and filled the jacket out. His shirt was white and he wore a black tie and white gloves. At his waist was a red cummerbund.

He stood silently, waiting for her to speak. The firelight caught his white hair and gave it the color of sunset.

She waited, knowing he would not speak until so commanded. She relished the power that held him motionless.

She indulged in this for a moment or two, then said, "Yes, Timmons?"

"Does the lady require anything else?"

She nodded. "Yes, Timmons. Another log on the fire. The air carries a chill, this evening."

"Yes, indeed it does." He knelt by the hearth and selected a piece of oak from the wood box and set it atop the already blackened chunks of wood.

"Timmons," she said. "We've been together a long time."

Still kneeling, he nodded his head. "We grew up together, ma'am, under this very roof."

"You're one of the few people I can truly trust."

He rose to his feet. "You know I'll always be there for you."

She allowed a slight smile, and some of the commanding sense left her voice. "I know. I've always been able to count on that. Timmons, there are some hard decisions I've got to make. Hard things that are going to have to be done."

He nodded. She doubted he knew exactly what she was talking about, but she knew it didn't matter.

This man would take a bullet for her without even a question.

There was sudden noise in the hallway, beyond the door Timmons had left ajar. Footfalls from more than one man. And they were moving with a sense of urgency.

"Timmons," she said. "See to that."

He had been already turning toward the door. Part of having been with her family for so many years meant he could anticipate her needs.

He hurried into the hallway. Verna heard his voice, and the voice of another man. Then Timmons was back in the room again.

"Ma'am," he said, "It's Wells, from town. I know this is your time to be alone, but I think you might want to hear this."

One thing about Timmons, he had discretion and judgment. She had relied on both more than once. Whatever it was, she figured it must be pretty urgent.

She said, "Send him in."

Timmons went to the doorway and ushered Wells in. He was tall and needed a shave. His hat was in his hand, which she found made little difference because his hair was long and didn't look like it had seen water since the previous rain. A pistol was holstered at the left side of his belt and turned backward for a cross-draw. Verna's father had worn a gun the same way. At the right side of this man's belt was sheathed a knife.

The man was clearly intimidated to be in her presence, and shifted his weight from one foot to the other nervously.

"All right," she said, "Don't keep me waiting. What is so incredibly important that you had to ride all the way out here at this time of night?"

He said, "You told us to watch out for certain men. You give us a list."

She could tell by the way he spoke that he was nursing a wad of tobacco in one cheek. If he should spit any of that juice onto one of her floors, she was going to have Timmons take a bullwhip to him.

"Well," he said, "one of 'em has shown up in town. Tonight. Right out of the blue."

"Which one?"

"Johnny McCabe."

Timmons said, "How sure are you?"

"Well," he shifted his feet again. "We didn't know who it was at first, and I started pressing him with questions. Threatened to take him down to the jail. It was after he rode out I found out from the bartender Crocker who he was. Lucky I didn't wind up dead."

Verna nodded. "Indeed. Where is he now?"

"Rode out of town maybe three hours ago. I figured he might be on his way out here."

Timmons said, "We haven't seen him."

"Nor are we likely too," Verna said. "At least tonight. If he hasn't changed from the way I remember him, he always preferred to sleep under the stars. He's probably asleep by a campfire somewhere."

"So, tomorrow, then."

She nodded thoughtfully, letting her gaze drift back to the fire. Then she said, "Thank you, Wells. That'll be all."

"Yes, ma'am," he said, and turned and was out the door.

"Timmons," she said, "shut the door."

He did as instructed, then stood by the fireplace with his hands folded together in front of him, waiting.

She said, "This puts a whole new crimp in my plans. We'll have to make adjustments."

Timmons said, "We always knew he'd show up again."

"Yes. We always knew that, sooner or later, he would come to California to visit that grave, and then ride by here to say hello to his dear brother. Speaking of my husband, where is he?"

"In his room. Sleeping. I checked on him before I came here."

"And Hiram?"

"He's ridden into town. Presumably to visit some of the female companions he has there."

Which meant he was going to have a romp with one of the saloon whores. She so hated this side of him. But he was young, and young men seemed to have their needs. She was going to have to make finding a wife for him one of her top priorities. Once she dealt with Johnny McCabe.

She said, "Johnny will be here probably by morning."

Timmons said, "Maybe we'll be lucky and he won't be here for a long visit."

She glanced at him. She hated it when the people around her tried to think, but held back her reprimand. He had always been loyal, the one person she could trust. And in the upcoming days she would need his loyalty more than ever.

She said, "Think about the time of year it is. September. Unless he's changed entirely, he traveled all the way from Montana on horseback. Probably sleeping in the woods like a savage. He always seemed drawn to Indians and their ways. He will be heading back the same way, but the passes through the mountains are already probably buried in snow, or will be soon. No, Timmons, he won't be leaving until spring. And if I know my husband, he will insist his brother spend the winter right here, under this roof."

"That could present a problem."

"Indeed. Johnny McCabe always had an annoying sense of duty and honor, and self-righteousness. He must be swept out of the way." She hesitated while ideas swirled about in her head and took cohesion. "I want him arrested."

"On what charge?"

"Murder. That ought to keep him out of our hair."

"Murder? But he hasn't killed anyone."

She shrugged. She thought it was obvious. This was also an opportunity to kill the proverbial two birds with one stone.

She said, "What's the name of that saloon whore Hiram spends most of his time with?"

"Belle," Timmons said. "I don't know her last name."

"Belle. Yes. How quaint. I want her killed. And then have the good sheriff go after Johnny. It shouldn't be hard to find witnesses who can say they saw Johnny with her, going into her place of doing business."

Timmons looked a little confused. "Begging the lady's pardon, but how can we find witnesses who don't exist?"

She sighed wearily. Why was it no one could keep up with her? "You buy them, Timmons, like everyone else does. A small roll of cash, and you can get some people to testify to anything you want them to."

Timmons said nothing. He looked at her expressionlessly, which she knew meant he was appalled. She knew him well enough to read him like you would words on a page. But he would do as she said, regardless of how he felt.

"Ride into town. Once Hiram leaves the brothel, then find the girl and make it quick. I want you to do it yourself, that way we know it is done right. Nothing messy, just a broken neck. It has to be done quickly and without spectacle."

He nodded.

She said, "Once Johnny is here, I'll find some reason to get him back into town. Then the sheriff can make the arrest."

"What if he refuses? Is there anyone in town who could really stop this man, if he didn't want to be stopped? If everything I've heard about him is true?"

"Oh, it's true. He's the most dangerous man I've ever met. But one thing about the McCabe men, they're law-abiding. If the sheriff orders him to surrender, I think he will. But if he shoots Wells and runs, then all the better."

She said no more. There was nothing more to say. Timmons had his instructions. He gave a light bow, indicating he knew the meeting was over, and left the room and shut the door.

She was once again alone with a fire crackling away in the hearth. She took a sip of sherry and stared into the flames.

6

The following morning, Johnny rode out to his brother's ranch. The first time he and his brothers had been in this part of the world, it had been called the McCarty ranch. Johnny had actually been on McCarty range—or *McCabe* range as it was now called—for an hour before he came to the front gate.

The ranch house was twice as long as it had been the last time Johnny saw it, and it had been sizeable then. The central section was two floors high, with a single-floor wing that shot out from one side, and another that shot out from the other. The outer walls were made of adobe, and the roof was tiled. There were actually pillars standing by the front door, holding up a porch roof. Those hadn't been there the last time Johnny had seen this place.

This was the ranch Johnny and his brothers had been working on when Johnny had met Lura. The ranch had been run by the McCarty family back then. Matt had married old man McCarty's daughter, and it was now known as the McCabe Ranch. One good thing, Johnny thought. They didn't have to change the brand. The Bar M.

Matt had never bragged about his success in his letters to Johnny, but he alluded to a few things, and Ginny got some details in letters from friends in Frisco. Johnny knew Matt owned at least two gold mines, including the one in Greenville. He had bought into the railroad. He was clearly the most successful of Tom and Elizabeth McCabe's sons.

Johnny wasn't a bit surprised, either. Matt had always been the more eloquent one. Gifted with smooth, fluid speech. Johnny wasn't much for talking in front of a crowd but Matt could hold a group of people enthralled. He knew how to use words. Simply off the top of his head he could conjure up the right word and use it with just the right amount of flourish. He could give a eulogy and have you nearly in tears even if you had never met the dearly departed. There was talk in one letter of Matt considering a run for the California State Senate, but nothing more had been mentioned. Johnny wondered what had come of it.

Johnny rode along the small wagon road that led up to the ranch house itself, and two men came out to meet him. They were on foot, and it struck Johnny that they didn't look like cowhands. More like gunmen. They each wore their pistols low and tied down, and one had a scattergun in his hands. They were also a little older than you would expect for men working on a ranch. Most cowboys were somewhere between fifteen and twenty-five, hence the term cow*boys*. These men were a mite older. The one with the scattergun had a full beard and was chewing tobacco and Johnny would have put him somewhere in his thirties. The other one had serious lines cut into his face and a mustache that was streaked with silver.

He was the one who spoke. "Hold up there."

Johnny gave Thunder's reins a little tug, but the horse was already slowing its pace. Some folks considered a horse to be a stupid animal, but a horse that knows its rider learns to anticipate what's coming.

These two were sentries, Johnny realized. He had never seen a cattle ranch that needed to post sentries.

You didn't post sentries unless you were expecting trouble.

The older one said, "State your business."

"Are you folks expecting trouble of some sort?"

The older one was becoming visibly perturbed. "I said, state your business, mister."

"I'm here to see Matt McCabe. Tell him his brother's calling."

"It's okay, boys, let him through." A voice from the front porch. "I doubt you could really stop him if you wanted to."

Johnny glanced toward the porch. A man was standing there. His hair was white, and he stood tall but thin. It took Johnny a moment to realize it was Matt.

Matt had always had a build that was longer and rangier than Johnny's. And he was the tallest of the four McCabe brothers. But the man who stood on the porch was downright thin. His collar was buttoned and he wore a string tie, but there was some empty space between his collar and his neck, and his jacket sort of bagged on him. Matt had always stood ramrod straight, but this man's shoulders were stooped a little.

The two men were looking toward the porch, too. The older one said, "Yessir, Mister McCabe."

The younger one looked at Johnny with a hint of defiance in his eyes. Almost a look of challenge. He was young enough that it rankled him a little to be told he couldn't stop someone even if he tried. He was young enough that he took it as a challenge to his manhood. The older gunhawk had lived enough years to realize that bullets flying did nothing to prove anyone's manhood and there was no shame in picking your fights, so he gave a slap to the younger one's shoulder and said, "Let's go."

The younger one let his gaze linger on Johnny a moment longer, and then followed the older one back to one of the side wings of the house.

The wagon road had become a driveway by this point, and it curved its way around to the front of the house. Just like it had in the old days, except now there were pillars standing tall and announcing Matt's success to the world. Nothing wrong with it, Johnny supposed, but their father Thomas McCabe had been a simple man who took joys in the simple things in life, and he had raised his boys as such.

Johnny nudged Thunder forward. Thunder had already been inclined to do so, shifting his hooves a little. The horse knew as soon as the men with the guns turned away there would be no gunplay. The horse had been through more than one gunfight with Johnny and apparently knew what to expect. Johnny didn't have to give any instructions to the horse about direction—the horse just turned of its own volition and followed the driveway around to the porch, and stopped in front of Matt.

"Matt," Johnny said, grinning and squinting a little in the sun.

"Johnny." Matt was also grinning. "It's been too many years. Too many."

Matt stood with a cigar smoldering away in one hand. At some point over the years he had grown a mustache that was as white as his hair. He stepped down from the porch as Johnny swung out of the saddle, and they took each other in a hug.

"Still got that long Indian hair," Matt said. "You haven't changed much, really."

He glanced downward to Johnny's legs. "Carrying only one gun, now."

Johnny nodded. "These newfangled Peacemakers. So easy to reload a man doesn't need two guns."

"You haven't changed much at all," Matt said. He reached up and stroked his mustache. "It's like looking into the past. Like the way things were when we first rode in here, all those years ago."

Johnny wished he could say the same about Matt. Even the man's voice was different. Matt had always a strong baritone, and spoke like an actor projecting to the back of the theater. At the old farmhouse in Pennsylvania, he could be talking with someone in the kitchen and you'd hear him all the way upstairs. Now his voice was thin and reedy.

Johnny shrugged. "I've changed a little, Matt. A little white in my hair. More lines on my face."

Matt called out, "Diego!"

A young Mexican boy of maybe fifteen had already rounded the side of the house and was approaching. "Mister McCabe," he said. "They said you had a guest."

"Take care of his horse, please, Diego."

"Yes, sir."

Johnny said to Diego, "Don't try to ride him. Just lead him along. If he stops for any reason, don't try to pull him along."

Matt slapped Johnny's shoulder with a smile. "Diego knows how to handle a horse, Johnny. Come on. Let's go inside."

"I'm serious," Johnny said. "He could get hurt. He doesn't know this horse. It was born and raised in the mountains and is only half-broken."

Diego said, "I'll be careful."

"Come on inside," Matt said. "You in the mood for a scotch?"

The interior of the house showed some reflection of the way it had been in the McCarty days, but had been seriously refurbished. Johnny caught a glimpse of the dining room through a doorway as he followed Matt down a corridor. The dining room now had dark maple floorboards where before they had been pine. An elaborate crystal chandelier was hanging suspended over a deep mahogany table. Against one wall was a cabinet containing three shelves of china.

"You've done some work on the place," Johnny said.

Matt nodded. "We've been lucky. Had some success."

Johnny followed Matt to a doorway at the end of the hall. In the days of old Frank McCarty, the hallway had just ended at this point. But now there was a doorway that Matt opened, and Johnny followed him into a study. An oak desk filled one corner. A rifle rack was against a wall. A pool table stood in the center of the room, and against the far wall was a marble fireplace. A small sofa and a stuffed chair faced it, and a fire was already going in the hearth.

On a small table in one corner were two decanters. Matt tossed his hat on the desk and then took a decanter and filled two glasses and handed one to Johnny.

Matt raised his glass to his brother. "To old times."

Johnny nodded. "To old times."

They both took a drink. Matt then sat on the edge of the desk and shook his head. "Johnny. I can't believe you're actually here. It's been so long. What brings you out here?"

"Lura," Johnny said.

Matt nodded sadly. "I shouldn't have had to ask."

"The folks who live there take good care of the grave."

Matt grabbed the whiskey decanter and they went to the fireplace. Matt set another piece of wood on the fire, and took the stuffed chair. Johnny sat on the sofa.

They then heard some noise outside. A horse braying.

"What in tarnation?" Matt said.

Johnny grinned. "That's Thunder. He's letting Diego know he doesn't like to be led."

"A half-broke horse," Matt said. "Wild. Untamed. Kind of like my brother. I guess I admire that."

Their talk drifted to the old times, which was to be expected. Their adventures in Texas, when they were on the run from the law. Their travels had eventually brought them to California. Johnny met and married Lura. Matt married Frank McCarty's daughter Verna.

"How is Verna?" Johnny asked.

Matt shrugged a little uncertainly. "Oh, I don't know. Fine, I suppose. She's upstairs. She always rests, this time of day. She'll be glad to see you."

Johnny doubted that. There was always something about Verna McCarty that made Johnny a little uneasy. Something about the way she smiled with her mouth but not with her eyes. Something about the way she looked at a man as though she were sizing him up.

She's just shy, Matt used to say. *She's a great girl.*

Matt said, "Do you ever hear from Joe?"

Johnny shook his head. "He rode with us when we brought the herd to Montana, years ago. Zack Johnson was there, too. We built our home in that little valley I've spoken of. Where we wintered with the Shoshone. Then the next year, he just said it was time he moved on."

"Joe always was a loner."

"Never seen him again. I've never even heard anything about him. It's like he disappeared from the face of the earth."

Matt paused a little sadly. His gaze grew distant. "Maybe something happened. Remember those old bones we found that time in the mountains?"

Johnny nodded. He remembered. In the early days, Johnny and Matt and some of the other hands from the McCarty ranch had gone mustanging in the Sierra Nevadas. One ridge was covered with pines, and sticking out of the pine straw were the remains of an old Flintlock rifle. Looked to be a Hawken. The stock was all rotted and the barrel rusted.

Odd thing to be left lying around, Johnny said. They rode about, checking the side of the ridge and eventually finding what was left of a man. Mostly bones. The upper leg bone had been broken nearly in half. The skeleton had been tossed about. Probably feasted on by a pack of wolves.

There was a bowie knife, rusted beyond any hope of repair, lying with a couple rotted strips of material around it. What Johnny figured was left of an old buckskin sheath.

Matt had watched from the back of his horse while Johnny checked out the remains. Matt sat tall in those days. No bend to his shoulders. He said, *What do you suppose happened?*

Johnny said, *An old fur trapper, I'd bet. Got thrown from his horse and broke his leg. His rifle got tossed over yonder, or maybe it got dragged by wolves after he died.*

Matt looked at him with a little horror. *You mean he just laid here and died? Starved to death, or attacked by wolves?*

Their brother Joe had been with them. Long haired and with a full beard. He was the silent one among them. Seldom spoke, but when he did it was usually loaded with meaning. He was never one to waste words.

It happens, he said. *Man alone, out on a mountainside. Gets hurt. No one to hear his cries for help. Judgin' by that gun, it was probably more'n forty years ago.*

Matt sat in his stuffed chair and looked at Johnny with eyes that were sad and maybe a little afraid. "You think that's what happened to Joe? Got in trouble somewhere? On some mountainside, or off in a desert somewhere? Died alone?"

Johnny shrugged. "I hope not. But we have no way of knowing."

They were silent a moment, then Matt snorted a chuckle. "No. You wait and see. Some day, Joe will just ride in. He's all right."

Johnny nodded. He hoped so.

They talked of the farm back in Pennsylvania. How they still missed Ma and Pa. How their younger brother Luke was now running the farm. Living there with his wife and raising a passel of children. They wondered if the farm still looked like it did. Would they still recognize it if they were to just show up one day.

Johnny talked of the ranch in Montana, and how the children had all grown up.

Matt said, "It's mighty big of you, taking in Dusty like he was one of your own, the way you did."

This struck Johnny as a strange comment. "He *is* one of my own, Matt."

"Well, Verna and I were talking about it. She said a lot of people would be reluctant to just let a child like that into their family."

A child like that. The sound of it struck Johnny as wrong. As something the Matt of old wouldn't have said. Johnny wasn't the least bit surprised at Verna's comment. He could easily imagine her saying that. But somehow he just couldn't imagine the Matt he had grown up with, the Matt he had ridden with in the old days, saying something like a *child like that.* Johnny felt Dusty was as much his as any of the others. It was the way he had been raised. It was also the way Matt had been raised.

Matt went on to talk of building the ranch to what it is now. Buying some additional range. Investing in the railroad. Buying a couple of gold mines. Not that Matt knew anything about mining, but Hiram thought it was a good idea. Hiram had grown into quite a young man and was taking the initiative in many of the family's business ventures.

Johnny said, "There are some strange things going on in town, Matt."

"Where? In Greenville? I don't get in there much, nowadays. I've turned a lot of the operations over to Hiram. He handles the entire mining side of the operation. I still keep a hand in the cattle, though."

Johnny said, "People are scared, Matt. There are thugs running the town, calling themselves lawmen. They say your son Hiram hired them. Two of them almost drew down on me while I was there."

Matt laughed. "Would have been their funeral, eh?"

Johnny wasn't laughing. "Matt, I'm serious. I would have had to kill them."

"Johnny, I don't think it's all that bad. I'll talk to Hiram about it."

A man walked into the room. "Talk to me about what?"

He was maybe a little older than Josh and Dusty. He had dark wavy hair, like his mother. He wore a jacket and tie in the natural way of a man who seemed born to wear them.

Matt rose to his feet. "Hiram. Come here. I want you to meet your Uncle Johnny."

Johnny also rose to his feet. Hiram shook his hand. He had a firm handshake. "Pleased to meet you, Uncle Johnny."

Johnny looked for a sign of Matt in him and had to admit he saw little. Matt's face was kind of long and angular. Hiram's was squarely cut, and with a cleft in his chin. But there was a lot of Verna. Hiram was smiling, but in his eyes there was no smile. He looked like he was sizing Johnny up. Noting the way he stood and the way he wore his gun. What it would take to bring him down.

Johnny said, "There's some trouble in town."

Hiram raised his brows with surprise. "Oh?"

Johnny said, "A couple thugs passing for lawmen almost drew on me. I was told by two different people there that these lawmen have the town running scared."

Hiram shrugged, and looked helplessly to his father. "That sounds terrible. First I've heard of it, though. I ride out to the mine once a week, but I can't say I get involved with the goings on in town, much."

"Hiram," Matt said. "Tell Mabel we're having a guest for dinner. And have the guest room made ready."

Johnny said, "That's not necessary."

"Nonsense." Matt clapped a hand to Johnny's shoulder. "I insist you stay here."

Johnny was introduced to a hot bath, the first he had since he left Montana. He had washed in mountain streams, but it wasn't quite the same. He shaved the beard away, and in his bedroll was a folded broadcloth shirt, and some jeans he had last washed in cold mountain water a couple weeks ago. He put those on, and brushed the dust from his vest and boots.

The room he was given was elaborate by the standards he was accustomed to. The walls were plaster, the ceiling fairly high. In Montana, where the winters were icy and snow would sometimes drift up against the windows, ceilings were kept low to conserve heat. But here in California, the dead of winter was little more than late autumn by comparison, and the ceilings in this ranch rose to nearly ten feet. The head of the bed was made of dark wood and was scrolled into designs that reminded Johnny of ocean waves.

He fastened the top button of his collar and then reached for a string tie Matt had loaned him. He had slung his gunbelt over a chair, and he reached for it next, but then hesitated. He doubted Matt sat down to dinner loaded for bear. Matt had been wearing a tie and jacket, and this was probably his usual way of dressing. Johnny noticed Matt had not been armed. Johnny was about to leave his gun here. To go down to the dining room without it. But then thought better of it. Like Zack had said, Johnny had been shot at one time too many. His gut feeling said to bring the gun. When it came down to the brass tacks, his gut feeling said to *always* bring his gun. So he grabbed it and buckled it on and tied the holster down to his leg with the rawhide thong.

When he joined the family in the parlor, he found the simple hearth made of bricks that had been there years ago had been replaced by one of marble. Like the one in Matt's study but bigger. A crystal chandelier was suspended overhead. A sofa and three stuffed chairs were upholstered in a burgundy colored velvet that even Ginny would have thought elaborate.

Johnny was introduced to Matt's younger son, Dan. He was a couple of inches shorter than Hiram. If Johnny remembered right, Dan was two or three years younger. Johnny shook the boy's hand and found the grip firm. Nothing different than what he would have expected from a McCabe.

"Scotch?" Matt said.

Johnny nodded. Matt went to the wet bar and came back with two tumblers of scotch, and handed one to Johnny. Matt also had a cigar going, and offered one to Johnny. *Never say no to a good cigar*, Johnny thought.

"So," Johnny said. "Are Tom and his family joining us tonight?"

Matt glanced down at his feet. Dan looked away, and Hiram raised his brows in a sort of implied shrug, and turned to tend the fire. Johnny realized he had apparently struck a tender nerve.

Matt looked up to meet Johnny's gaze. "Tom doesn't come to the ranch much. There have been disagreements. I hope to work them out. Family means much to us and I hate to have a rift between me and any of my boys."

"Indeed," a woman said from the open doorway.

Johnny looked over to see Verna striding in. Again, he was struck by the changes over the years. She had been relatively pretty in her late teens. But now her face was hardened, and there were the type of stern lines you get around your mouth from not smiling. At seventeen she would stride into the room with arrogance, expecting all eyes to be on her. Johnny never understood what Matt saw in her, other than physically. But now she had a sort of commanding, regal way about her. And yet she seemed to be aging beyond her years. Deep lines were carved into her face, and her eyes had a bleary look to them.

She said, smiling with her mouth but not with her eyes—that much about her hadn't changed, "Johnny. So good to see you again, after all these years."

She extended her hand and grasped his gently.

Before he could say anything, she said, "Of course, it breaks my heart for there to be a rift between

Matthew and Thomas. But sometimes one has to simply wait these things out."

Johnny nodded. "Sometimes."

"Hiram," she said. "Would you get me a glass of sherry?"

Johnny noticed a man standing in the parlor doorway. He was about Johnny's age, with white hair cut short. He wore a black suit jacket and trousers, a checkered vest, and not a tie but a cravat. He simply stood and waited. Johnny made eye contact with him and the man nodded but said nothing.

It took Johnny a moment to realize he knew him. The man had been a skinny young kid when Johnny first met the McCartys. His father had been the blacksmith for the ranch, and his mother the maid. Johnny couldn't recall his name, but he remembered how the boy would stare at Verna from a distance. Probably thought he was being discrete, but it's hard to be discrete when you're staring at a girl.

Looked like the young skinny kid had grown up and was still following her around, but now as the family butler.

Johnny wasn't good with names, but after a few moments the name came to him. Timmons. Moses Timmons had been his father. Johnny didn't know if he had ever heard the younger one's name.

Hiram fetched his mother a sherry, and then she sat on the sofa and they all joined her. Matt milled about, idly puttering about the fireplace mantel or grabbing a wrought iron poker and prodding at the fire. The conversation was mostly Verna and Hiram, talking about the goings on at the ranch or their other business ventures. Dan listened in but offered little comment.

At one point, Verna said, "So, Johnny, how is Miss Brackston?"

"Fine," Johnny said. His gut feeling said to keep anything he offered to a minimum. Always follow your gut. "She runs the household, like she always has."

"Is there any chance of her coming home, and rejoining us in civilization?"

Johnny hadn't given this any real thought. The house without Ginny. They had never really discussed it, but with the children grown, he realized he wouldn't be all that surprised if she did return to San Francisco. What he did was give a shrug of his shoulders and said, "You never know, I suppose."

The light-hearted chat continued as they made their way to the dining room. Dinner was roasted duck served with some sort of sauce. Had a French name, but Johnny had never been into such niceties. He wanted nothing more than good old home cooking. Though Ginny could walk in this pompous world where Matt had seemed to make his home, she seemed perfectly happy to indulge in Johnny's simpler tastes.

In fact, Johnny really wanted nothing more than an open campfire and some deer meat roasting on a wooden spit he had whittled himself. A wolf or a coyote howling from somewhere off in the darkness. The gentle scent of balsam on the air.

Verna asked Timmons to fetch a bottle from their wine cellar. Again, some sort of French name.

He said, "The eighteen forty vintage, madam?"

She gave it a moment's thought. "Bring the eighteen twenty-two. We have a special guest tonight."

She was trying hard to show off for a guest who was not the slightest bit impressed. When the wine arrived, he held the bottle in front of her while she glanced at the label. He didn't actually allow his bare hands to touch it, but held it with a white cloth. She nodded and he pulled out a corkscrew and once the bottle was open he poured an splash into a glass which she then held to her nose and swirled the wine about and sniffed the ambiance. She then took a sip and nodded to Timmons, who began filling glasses. Johnny had seen this show before, but had never been really impressed.

Verna was at one end of the table, and Matt at the other. The two boys sat across from each other, and Johnny sat to Matt's right.

They ate and talked and somewhere along the line, Verna mentioned their cook was called *Pierre*, and was all the way from Paris, and my goodness he could do a thing or two with a duck. Johnny wanted to say one of the wives of the war chief of the Shoshone he had wintered with once was an artist with herbs and such things, and could make a venison stew that would leave you talking about it a week later. But he decided not to. The whole show Verna was putting on was about impressing people, and Johnny doubted the ways of the Shoshone would interest her much. Her people tended to think of the Indian as savage. The Indian tended to think people like Verna foolish. Johnny tended toward the opinion of the Indian.

Johnny noticed the dynamics around the table. Much of the conversation was actually between Verna and Hiram, just like in the parlor. They talked of conditions at the mine, and the problem they were having with some squatters in a canyon. Geologists believed a vein of gold ran through the cliffs of that canyon, and since no one had ever filed a proper claim on the land, Hiram had gone and done so. Hiram intended to expand the McCabe mining operation there. The squatters were trying to hang onto the canyon, but they had to be moved out before mining could begin. Matt would offer a word or two, which they would either politely respond to or ignore entirely. Dan sat and simply watched and listened, as though he was in awe of his mother and older brother.

Johnny wondered how Matt could have possibly fallen into this life. He had never been quite the man of the outdoors that Johnny was. Matt had always been more at home among civilization. But this whole situation, with all of the fineries, struck Johnny as artificial. Matt had never seemed artificial to him. And to sit by, eating his dinner and sipping his wine while his wife and son talked callously of moving people out of their home, seemed so unlike the Matt Johnny remembered.

"Johnny," Verna said from her end of the table. "You're not saying much."

She gave him a firm gaze which was anything but friendly, though her lips were spread in a polite smile. He gave the gaze back. *Don't mess with me, lady. You've met your match and then some.* But he figured she already knew that.

What he said was, "Not much to say, really."

Matt decided to chime in. "Johnny, there's talk of the railroad swinging up your way. To Montana. Have you heard anything of that?"

He shook his head. "Only idle speculation. Seems to be inevitable, though. There's gold and cattle in Montana. A fortune to be made."

"Really?" Verna said, feigning surprise. "Do you think it might be another California?"

Johnny shook his head. "The winters are too harsh. It takes a certain type to survive up there. But the gold is there, and cattle can be raised. Right now we sell beef to townfolk in places like Bozeman and Helena and Virginia City. Sell quite a lot to the Army, too. We pushed a herd down to Cheyenne to meet the railroad four summers ago. Josh was only seventeen. It was his first cattle drive. Zack Johnson was along, pooling his herd in with ours. That was before the war between the Army and the Lakota ended. That was an interesting cattle drive. A little tense at times."

Matt was grinning. Suddenly Johnny could see the old Matt in his eyes. "I bet it was."

Hiram spoke up. "What, pray tell, is a *Lakota*?"

Matt looked at him. "The Sioux. They've always called themselves the Lakota."

Johnny said, "They come from the Great Lakes country. Some bands of them moved west around seventy years ago to escape wars in that area, and others remained behind. It's said," he looked at Matt with a grin, "that the ones that stayed behind for some reason can't pronounce the letter *D*. So they call themselves Dakota."

Matt returned the grin. The other three were looking at them straight-faced. Matt said to them, "An old Indian joke."

Verna said, "I see."

Matt said to Johnny, "Remember where we first heard that?"

"That old Cheyenne scout we shared a campfire with. Utah Territory."

Matt shook his head. "That whiskey was raw, but it sure was good."

"He wouldn't have even taken us into his camp but Joe could speak Cheyenne."

Matt nodded with a grin and reached for his wine. "That's right. Joe had spent time among the Cheyenne."

Verna was giving Matt a silent stare that Johnny figured meant *shut up*. Matt caught the look and did just that. He tossed Johnny a barely perceptible apologetic shrug, and went back to eating.

Johnny shook his head, again wondering how Matt could have possible allowed himself to be caught up in something like this. How could a son of their parents have allowed this?

He could just imagine their father, with his gray eyes and square jaw and his graying hair swept back, pipe in hand, saying, *Son, we've gotta talk.*

After dinner, Johnny went out to the stable to tend to Thunder. Make sure the horse was all right. Diego probably knew how to tend horses well enough, but Johnny had ridden a long way on Thunder, and had a long ride home. One of the first lessons he had learned as a young man was a frontiersman takes good care of his horse.

This wasn't the same stable that had been here years ago. This one was bigger. Longer. Attached to one side was a series of carriage bays.

Johnny found Thunder in a stall.

"They treating you okay, boy?" he said.

Thunder raised his head to look at him. Thunder didn't look happy, penned in. Back at the ranch in Montana, Fred usually allowed Thunder to run freely in the open meadow behind the house that served as a pasture. The meadow was bordered by thickets and a convoluted mass of underbrush on three sides, which served as natural fencing. Thunder wasn't used to being kept in a stall.

"I know how you feel, boy," Johnny said.

He reached up to loosen his tie, then decided he had had enough of it and pulled the tie off and crammed it into a vest pocket, and loosened the top button of his shirt. He took Thunder by the hackamore and backed him out of the stall and then grabbed a brush from where it hung by a nail and began to work at the horse's back and shoulders.

"I don't know," Johnny said to him. "We're like fish out of water here. There's still some daylight left. Maybe we're better off just saddling up and riding on."

Verna spoke from the doorway to the stable. "He's not what you remember, is he?"

Johnny looked to the doorway. She was the last person he wanted to see. He decided to say nothing.

"Matt, I mean," she said. She came into the barn. She glanced toward the floor as she stepped along, as though there might be something on the floor that would get her shoes dirty. The stable was quite clean. Apparently Diego swept it regularly.

She said, "He's not the same as you remember him."

Johnny shrugged and went back to brushing his horse. "People change."

"Do they really?"

He looked back at her. "No, not really. A person might learn a thing or two over the years and change how they do things. But their nature doesn't change. Not really. There might be a certain aspect of their nature that becomes more pronounced as they get older, but it was usually already there. At least to some extent."

She had a shawl wrapped about her shoulders. It was a little cool. Hardly the weather they were probably getting back in Montana about now, Johnny figured, but cool by the standards of weather here in the great California valley.

Again Johnny was struck by how old she seemed. She was actually a little younger than Matt, but could easily have been ten years his senior. She stood with her shoulders a little bent, and she pulled the shawl tightly as though she was catching a chill.

But though she was looking more frail than a woman of her years should, her voice was strong and firm. She said, "I'm a hard woman, Johnny. I always was. I was taught early on to take care of myself. You have to take care of yourself because no one else will."

"Don't you believe in family taking care of each other?"

She shrugged. "Maybe to some degree. Maybe on the surface. It's a quaint notion. But in the long run, all you have is yourself. I play the game to win, Johnny. My father began building a small empire, here. I took what he built and I'm building it into a larger one. One of my sons will be a senator. Probably Hiram. He has the brains. I'm very disappointed in Tom. He could have had it all but walked away from it. And Hiram will have a son who could be president."

"Is there any limit?"

She shook her head. "The only limits are within ourselves."

"Maybe." He returned to brushing down Thunder.

"I could have had you, you know."

He hadn't expected her to say that. He turned to face her again, not even trying to hide his look of disbelief. "You really think so?"

"I know so. You can have anything you want, as long as you're willing to pay the price. I could have had any one of you three. Josiah...I dismissed him immediately. He didn't want anything but to ride his horse along a mountainside. He had no ambition. In you, I could see a potential king. You could have it all, if you wanted it. But you have this sense of nobility. This sense of trying to do the right thing. Trying to be everyone's hero. You never learned a basic lesson that I had already learned before you ever rode in."

"And what is that?"

"People don't want to be saved. When you step in and try to help, you're just ultimately wasting your time. And sometimes you incur their resentment. So, no, I knew I could never build an empire with you at my side."

"I take that as a compliment. Not that you had the choice you might think you did."

She ignored him. "Matt was the one. He spoke well, he had charm and charisma. And he was easily manipulated. Well, maybe not too easily. It would take time, but I was young and time was one thing I had."

"I take it you'll do whatever you have to, to protect your so-called empire."

She gave him a smirk. "Absolutely anything."

"And Matt doesn't know all that goes on around here." It was more of a statement than a question.

Her smirk grew larger. "He knows what he needs to."

Johnny gave her a long look, then returned to his horse.

She said, "You're trying to think of how to help your brother. How to right the incredible wrong you see being done here. Stay out of it, Johnny. Ride on. You have no place here. Your brother doesn't want to be saved. He wants to hide in his scotch and swim in oblivion."

Johnny kept silent.

She said, "Think about it. When you're in your old age, what'll you have? A drafty old log cabin in some remote section of the mountains? Your quaint Indian philosophies? A man of Matt's financial standing will be well cared for. He'll have the best, most comfortable housing money can buy. Silk sheets. A warm bedroom. The best doctors, if need be. Give it some thought, Johnny. Maybe he's not the one who needs saving. Maybe you are."

The brush Johnny was using on Thunder grew still, but he didn't turn to look at her.

"It's been nice having you here. Matt has liked it. But you don't belong here. You'll be trying to interfere in things that are none of your concern."

"What things? Like the things I heard in town?"

"Ride on, Johnny. Ride on right now. This evening. There's still maybe a half hour of daylight left. You prefer to sleep by a campfire, anyway."

She turned and headed for the door, still stepping gingerly along the stable floor.

She stopped in the doorway and looked back at him. "You have no place here. And you'll just make things harder for anyone who does. You'll make things harder for your brother. He's where he wants to be. He doesn't want to be saved. Ride on. Return to your mountains."

And she was gone.

Johnny stood by Thunder, leaning his elbow on the back of the horse.

Johnny said, "How about it, old boy? Do you think she's right? Should we just ride out of here?"

The horse swung his head around to look at him. *If horses could talk*, Johnny thought.

He looked at the stall he had backed Thunder out of. He didn't have the heart to return the horse to it.

His saddle was lying across a sawhorse in one corner. The bridle with it. His Sharps was in the saddle boot.

Johnny went and got the saddle and bridle, and brought them over to Thunder.

Johnny said, "The old lady's right about one thing. There's still some daylight left. I intend for this place to be miles behind us by nightfall."

7

Matt stood by the mantel in the room that served as his office. Verna was sitting in a chair behind him, her hands neatly folded.

He slapped the mantel with one hand. He said, "What'd you say to him?"

"I said nothing, Matt. He just knows the reality."

"And what reality is that?"

"That he's out of place here, Matt. As out of place as you would be in his world of mountains and Indians and sons who are half-Indian."

"Only one of his sons is."

"Matt, listen to yourself."

"I used to ride that trail. There was a time when I could have ridden right alongside him."

"But that was many years ago. You've left that kind of life behind you, and reached for so much greater."

"He's my brother, Verna. Dammit. I haven't seen him in seventeen years, and you just let him ride off like that."

"I didn't *let* him do anything, Matt. Since when does anyone *let* Johnny McCabe do anything? The man's a free spirit. As free as the wind. He wasn't comfortable here. I could see it, and so could you if you would open your eyes and see what's in front of you."

She rose to her feet and placed a hand gently on his shoulder. "Matt, you both come from the same roots, but you're not the same man you were when you both rode in here, all those years ago. You've grown and become so much more than you were, where he's stayed the same. He came, he visited a bit. You got to see him and he got to see you. But did you see how uncomfortable he looked at the table? Wearing a tie? Drinking fine wine? He's more at home scooping water out of a watering hole. Or drinking that awful, strong coffee you all used to drink in those days. With the grounds floating all through it."

He snickered and grinned, and looked at her. "That was pretty raw stuff, wasn't it?"

She returned the grin. "But you've left all of that behind you. Look at all you've built. It was good to see him again. And I'm sure he enjoyed seeing you. But he needed to be moving on."

Johnny had stepped in briefly to say goodbye to Matt. He had said he hadn't slept under a roof for so long he wouldn't know how to do it, really. And he had a lot of miles to be covering and winter was coming. There was probably already snow in the high passes.

"Can't you stay?" Matt said. "Just a little longer?"

Johnny shook his head. "I'll write once I'm home."

Matt gave him a couple of cigars to take with him. And then Johnny swung onto the back of his stallion and clicked the horse to a canter was gone, down the driveway and through the gate and off the way he had come.

A living legend, Verna thought. She was fully aware a dime novel had been written about him. People talked about his exploits. Whether they had really happened or not was none of her concern. She had used the connection to move more than one business deal. She had instructed Hiram to do so, too.

Matt shrugged his shoulders. "Maybe he did feel a little out of place here. It's so much grander than what it was when I first met you."

"And you built it, Matt. You've done so much."

He nodded. "It's just that sometimes I find myself missing the old days, you know?"

She smiled. "Well, of course you do. You've had a full life, Matt. A life most men could only dream of. You rode cross-country with your legendary brother. Lived off the land. Met wild Indians. You were even outlaws, for a while. Genuine desperados."

He smiled. "I don't know if we were really *desperados*."

"And then you married and had three wonderful sons, and built this place. Took a prosperous ranch and turned it into an empire that is still growing."

Matt looked at her. She could see doubt in his eyes. The whiskey was making him a little addled, but he was becoming more difficult to maneuver as he grew older.

He said, "You mean *you* took a prosperous ranch and made it grow."

She sighed. There was such a rift between them now, and it seemed to be growing. They had been in separate bedrooms for some years. Not that she minded, because theirs had been a marriage of convenience only, at least as far as she was concerned. But he was so much easier to maneuver when he was young and looked at her with love in his eyes.

This was why she had come to the decision she had, the night before. That this situation with Matt had to come to an end while she still had control of it.

That was when Hiram came in. "Mother. I think Dan has lost his mind."

She and Matt found Dan in his room. He was wearing a range shirt, and was buckling on a gunbelt.

"Dan," she said, "what on Earth are you doing?"

"I'm riding with the men, tonight."

She glanced to Hiram. He looked to her.

Hiram said, "I've been trying to talk some sense into him."

Dan pulled his gun and checked the loads, then slid it back into his holster. He wore it high on his hip. He knew how to shoot, but was no gunman.

Dan said, "These rustlers have been hitting the smaller ranches around here. Father, you said yourself they have to be stopped. Sooner or later they're going to start hitting our herd."

"But Dan, why does it have to be you?" Verna said.

"Because, Mother, we're business and societal leaders in this part of the valley. Being leaders means sometimes, well, you have to lead."

"Dan, you could get yourself killed."

"Mother, it's just something I have to do. I mean, the name McCabe carries a lot of weight."

Generally, when the name was spoken by people on this side of the valley it was in reference to Hiram or Matt. But she knew he was referring to another McCabe.

She said, "This is about your uncle, isn't it?"

"I sat at the table with him tonight. Not a legend, but a real man. Sitting right there at the table. And you know what? When he looked me in the eye, I felt small.

What would he do in a situation like this? He wouldn't hesitate to ride out there. He wouldn't let other men do it for him. He wouldn't even think about staying home while others rode out to defend his herd."

"Dan, you're not him."

"That's the point. The name McCabe carries weight. Maybe it's time I became a McCabe in more than name only." He looked at Matt. "You understand, don't you, Father?"

Matt walked up to his son and placed his hand on his shoulder. Verna could see something in his eyes. *It's pride. He's proud of his son.* That kind of pride could get Dan killed.

Matt said, "Yes I do, son. More than you know."

Dan grabbed a jacket and a stetson that was stiff with newness. He had hardly ever worn it. "I'll be okay, Mother."

He gave his mother a peck on the cheek. He said to Hiram, "You coming?"

Hiram said, "Maybe I'll catch up with you."

Matt said, "Be safe, son."

And Dan was gone from the room.

Verna followed Matt downstairs and back to his study. She shut the door behind herself. He was at the wet bar, pouring himself a scotch.

"Just what are you thinking?" she said. "He could get himself killed out there."

He filled the glass and turned to face her. "Sometimes a man has to do what he has to do, if he's going to call himself a man."

"He's not a man. He's a boy."

"He's a boy who's fast turning into a man. He's not much younger than I was when I first rode in here."

"That was a different time. People expected different things from a man, then."

He shook his head. "A man's a man. That much hasn't changed. In fact, I should be riding out with him."

She could see it in his eyes—he was actually considering it. "Matt, when was the last time you fired a gun? You'd just be in the way out there."

He said nothing. She knew she was still in control of the situation, even though her grip on him was becoming much less secure.

She said, "Matt, you have to talk with him. No one has to live up to the legend of your brother. He's a man of the past. Trying to hang onto a lifestyle that's fast fading. Dan will only get himself killed out there. You have to talk to him."

"Verna..."

"Your brother was here only a part of one day, and look at the havoc he's caused. Your son, thinking he's not good enough because he doesn't match up to some larger-than-life legend. And you, standing here thinking he might be right. Don't you love your son?"

He looked at her with a little exasperation. "Of course I do. What kind of question is that?"

"Then show it. Go out and talk to him. Explain that being a man doesn't mean having to live up to the reputation of your brother. Half of those exploits they attribute to him never really happened, anyway. Explain to him that being a man doesn't mean sitting on a horse in the night waiting to exchange gunfire with cattle rustlers. Explain to him that he's much more valuable to this family alive, than dying for an empty cause."

Matt looked at her long and hard. And she watched him soften, and he dropped her gaze. He was considering what she said, and reluctantly admitting she was right.

He finally nodded. "All right. I'll go catch him at the stable."

He set the glass of scotch on his desk, and headed out the door.

She was so glad Johnny McCabe had ridden on. If he had never been here today, then she doubted Daniel would be wanting to ride out and chase rustlers. And Matt was becoming hard enough to control, she didn't need Johnny showing up and reminding Matt of the man he once was.

Let Johnny ride into town, she thought with a smirk. Let him stop into Greenville for a glass of whiskey before riding on. Then she would be rid of the Johnny McCabe problem forever. Timmons had choked the life out of the little saloon whore Belle, and Wells had already secured a warrant for Johnny's arrest.

She went to the wet bar and poured herself a sherry. Either way, she thought, the problem of Johnny McCabe was over.

She meandered over to the hearth, the glass of sherry in her hand. The fire was dwindling down. She thought she might call for Timmons and have him fill the wood box.

Matt reappeared in the doorway. His eyes were wide with urgency.

"He's gone, Verna," Matt said. "Dan's gone. He had already ridden out before I could get out there."

She went to find Hiram. The parlor windows were all French doors that served as windows, with curtains that matched the burgundy upholstery of the parlor furniture, and opened to a long walkway that extended along the entire length of the back of the house. She found him out there, a glass of scotch in his hands. He was looking off toward the stable and the corrals. Beyond that were long grassy hills that stretched westward down into the valley. The sun had set and the valley was falling into shadows.

"Hiram," she said. "I talked your father into going to talk some sense into Dan, but it was too late. He's already gone."

He looked at her with disbelief. "Mother..."

"You've got to go find those men. Wells and Bardeen. You've got to tell them to call it off."

Wells and Bardeen were in Hiram's proverbial pocket. They worked in town as lawmen. Wells was the town marshal, but McCabe money had been spent to get him into that spot. By night, they were working a cattle rustling operation that was funded partly by McCabe money. It wouldn't do for the McCabe herd to be the only one in the area not hit, so tonight they were scheduled to ride in and shoot two or three McCabe cowhands. Mother had suggested they should take a few head, not a lot but enough to make it look good. Hiram was against this because each steer represented money. He decided Wells and his men weren't to take any cattle, but he would announce publicly that they had. Some of the McCabe cowhands were being positioned to watch for the rustlers, which had been Matt's idea. Hiram liked it, because it would make it easier for Wells and

Bardeen and their men to find them and shoot them down. Except now Dan was going to be with them.

Verna said, "Maybe if you ride out, you can intercept Wells and his men. Tell them to call it off for tonight."

He shook his head. "They're already out there somewhere. I wouldn't know where to find them. I don't know my way around out there. And it's getting dark."

"Your brother is riding into an ambush and there's nothing we can do to stop it."

He stared at her with dread. She stared at him likewise.

He said, "Maybe nothing will happen. Maybe he'll be okay."

"Maybe so." She said it, but didn't really believe it. She turned toward the darkening valley that stretched out before her. She had a very bad feeling about this.

She made a promise to herself. If Dan was killed tonight, then Johnny wouldn't have long to live. She had spent her life acquiring money and power, and power to the degree that she now had gave her a lot of reach. Even as far as Johnny's his little ranch off in his remote corner of the mountains.

8

Johnny rode across the valley floor. The land undulated in a series of low rising, grassy hills at this point in the valley, and was dotted with short, fat oak trees. Johnny followed no trail—he seldom did. He cut directly overland, heading due east.

The sun was hanging just above the horizon. Time to make camp, he knew. It would have been nice to make the foothills before dark, but he had lingered too long at Matt's ranch.

Ahead, he saw a line of trees stretching away to the north, and further along to the south. Looked to be alders and birches. Maybe a few maples. Trees have a way of lining the banks of a stream. He rode into the trees and saw he was right. A small brook ran over a rocky bed, and was making a chuckling sound.

He swung out of the saddle and knelt by the water and scooped some of it to his mouth. It was cold. He let Thunder drink a little, then said to the horse, "I think we'll make our camp right here."

He reckoned the Madden ranch was probably directly south of where he now was. Probably twenty miles or so. He thought briefly about maybe paying another visit to Lura's grave before riding on. But there would already be snow in the passes, and he had a long way to ride between here and home.

Maybe he could make it back in time for Christmas, he thought, though he doubted it. More than likely he could make it through the Sierra Nevadas, but by the time he reached the Rockies the snow would be too deep to get through, even with a horse like Thunder.

He would have to hole up in the mountains and wait out the winter. Build a lean-to and cut firewood and hunt his supper every day. He would have to make a pair of snowshoes. He had done all of this before. He had no coat warm enough for the winter, but didn't really need one. There was more than one trading post in Nevada where he could buy a couple of woolen blankets. With a hole cut in the middle, a woolen blanket could serve as a poncho and keep you respectably warm.

He doubted he would see his home in Montana before April. He knew the boys could handle things, but he was finding himself missing the family. Maybe seeing what Matt's life had become and what his son Hiram was like was giving Johnny extra appreciation for what he himself had, and he found himself yearning to be home again.

Well, he thought, at least he had left Matt's ranch behind him. The more miles between him and that place, the better. It occurred to him that he might never see his brother again, and that filled him with a little pang of sadness. He hadn't seen Matt in years and had found himself missing him, but even though he had seen him, Johnny found he was still missing him. The Matt he missed was the one from years before. The one who had been his older brother when they were growing up. The one who had gone west with him and Joe, searching for the killer of their father. The Matt Johnny remembered didn't seem to exist anymore, except for a quick flash Johnny had seen at dinner when they were talking about the old days. For the most part, Matt had become a stranger.

Johnny cleared away some dried leaves and twigs to make room for a camp. He then stripped the saddle and gear from Thunder, and began gathering up some firewood.

It got dark, and one hour blended into another. Matt paced in front of his desk. He poured a scotch and sat by the fire. He got up and paced some more, then looked at the ship's clock standing on the mantel.

He made his way to the kitchen and had the cook fix him a sandwich. He went upstairs and found Verna in her bedroom, sitting in her rocker by the fire. The ever dutiful Timmons was standing by her side. Matt talked with them for a few minutes and then wandered back downstairs.

He returned to his office and found Hiram there. Hiram had poured a scotch and was pacing, also. The clock on the mantel read 9:28.

Hiram said, "Father. I thought you had gone to bed."

On a ranch, you often went to bed early because the day began before sunrise.

Matt said, "I thought I'd wait up a bit."

"I can wait up for Dan. You should get your sleep."

Matt shook his head. "All I would do is lie there awake, staring at the ceiling. Might as well be down here."

He went to the wet bar and grabbed a glass.

Johnny sat by the fire. Thunder was picketed a little ways back, but well within the circle of firelight. Johnny had a tin cup filled with trail coffee in one hand. His left hand, so his right would be free should he need to grab his pistol. His gunbelt was still buckled on. His saddle was on the ground and his bedroll spread out, and his rifle was lying on the ground within reach.

Johnny had eaten a supper of canned beans. He now sat, thinking.

He didn't stare directly into the fire. When you stare into flames and then look away, it takes your eyes a few moments to adjust. In a life-or-death situation, it could make the difference. So he looked beyond the fire, to the darkness.

Something was pulling at him. Something about the day that had not seemed quite right. Something, he realized, about Hiram.

Johnny thought about their meeting. Shaking his hand. Sitting at the table with him and the others. And Timmons never far from Verna's side. Bringing out a bottle of wine. Always on hand should anyone need anything, but never positioning himself far from her.

Hiram, with his strong jaw and the cleft in his chin. A nose that was more like Verna's than Matt's. Eyes that were a dark brown, like Verna's. Eyes that never smiled, even when the rest of his face did.

Johnny thought about Timmons, who was a little taller than Matt. As a young boy, Timmons had been skinny and awkward, and had been so fixated on Verna. Puppy love, Matt had called it. And now he was a man, stepping through the door of middle age. His shoulders had filled out and the clumsiness of youth was gone. His hair was now white. But even though a lot of years had passed, he was still attached to Verna.

Funny thing, Johnny didn't think he had ever heard the man's first name. He was referred to as Timmons by Verna and the others. Years ago, when Johnny and his brothers had first ridden onto the

McCarty ranch, when someone used the name Timmons they meant his father, Moses. The boy was just referred to as Timmons' son, or Timmons' boy.

Timmons' father was about Matt's height, which had made him a little taller than Johnny, but was filled out with hard, bulky muscle. Johnny had seen him actually bend a horseshoe with his bare hands. But the man was not fierce. He was quick with a smile and loaded with humor. Johnny remembered the man's toothy smile and his cleft chin.

That was when it occurred to him. Matt had no cleft chin. Their father had been square-jawed, like Johnny, but there were no cleft chins in the family.

Hiram had a seriously square jaw, and a cleft.

Johnny was not one to think in terms of a family's dirty laundry. And yet, he found himself wondering. Was Timmons really the father of Hiram? If so, was Matt really this oblivious to the goings-on under his own roof? Johnny found he didn't want to know. In the morning, he intended to ride on and not look back.

Johnny finished his coffee and decided to climb into his bedroll. He wanted to get an early start in the morning.

It was nearly midnight and Matt was alone in his office. Hiram had gone upstairs to check on his mother. Matt paced about, a glass of scotch in his hand. His pacing brought him to the hearth, and he leaned one hand against the mantel.

When he had been young, riding through wild country with Johnny and Joe, he had felt strong. Like nothing could hurt him. But now with his youngest son out there somewhere in the night, a gun in his hand

and facing off against cattle rustlers, Matt felt weak. Tired. Old and helpless. There was one swallow of scotch remaining in his glass, so he downed it and then set the glass on the mantel.

How had he let himself become the man he now was? One step at a time, he supposed.

The doors to his office opened and Verna stepped in, followed by Hiram.

"You should be in bed," Matt said. "Hiram and I can wait up."

She said, "Nonsense. I'm not going to sleep until Dan is home and safe under this roof."

Hiram escorted her to a chair by the fire. She descended into the chair, and struck Matt as looking old and feeble.

Hiram said, "Would you like a sherry, mother?"

"No. But thank you. I think a cup of tea might be nice, though."

Timmons now stood in the office doorway.

Hiram said, "Timmons, could you get Mrs. McCabe a cup of tea?"

Timmons gave a silent nod and stepped out.

Matt was about to say something. To tell Verna she was wrong, that he should be out there with Dan. It was true, he might be a little out of practice with a gun, but he knew what it was like to be in a gunfight. He had been shot at, and had shot a man before. He was about to say all of this, but didn't because there was a sudden drumming of hoof beats from out behind the house. A number of horses, and they were moving fast.

The windows in his office were all the size of doors, and the ones on the back wall opened onto the long porch that ran the length of the house. Matt went to one of these windows and turned the latch and stepped out, Hiram and Verna behind him.

"Mister McCabe!" one of the men called out. Matt knew the voice. It was Ben Harris, the ramrod.

"Ben?"

The horses pulled up just short of the porch.

Ben said, "It's Dan. He's been shot!"

Verna stood on the porch, barely breathing. Hiram took her hand.

Ben had been riding with Dan on the horse in front of him. Two men jumped out of their saddles and hurried over to help Dan down.

"Hiram," Verna was saying. "Hiram, is he..?"

Matt found that while Dan didn't seem totally conscious, his legs were wobbly but trying to work.

Matt slipped an arm around his son's shoulders and said, "Let's get him inside."

They got him to the sofa in his office. Dan's hair at his right temple was soaking with blood, and his shirt was also soaked on the right side.

"What happened?" Hiram said.

Ben said, "We were ambushed, sir. It was like they knew we were coming."

Matt was on one knee in front of the sofa, checking the side of Dan's head.

Ben Harris said, "That one ain't a bullet wound. He got shot out of the saddle, and hit his head on a rock when he landed."

Matt found there was a lump on Dan's head, just above the temple. He had seen worse. Dan would have a serious headache for a couple of days, but the main problem was the bullet wound. Matt began to unbutton Dan's blood-soaked shirt.

Verna said, "How bad is it?"

"Hard to tell. There's a lot of blood. We need a doctor."

Verna said, "Hiram. Send Timmons into town to fetch the doctor. Hurry!"

Dan's wound seemed to be on the lower right side of his ribcage. Matt had seen gunshot wounds, and he knew what had to be done. Matt began pressing down on the wound with both hands, and told Verna to get some sheets to use as bandages. They had to slow down this bleeding. For years, Matt hadn't thought Verna could wipe her nose without Timmons there to do it for her, but she hurried to a linen closet and came back with two folded sheets.

Matt had Hiram press down on the wound while he tore a sheet into strips, and then placed a folded strip over the wound.

"Get a bucket of water," Matt said.

No one moved.

Matt looked to Hiram. For too long, he had taken a back seat to Verna and Hiram. For too long he had held back. He didn't know why and now was not the time to try to figure it out. He growled the words at Hiram, "Go and get a bucket of water!"

Hiram took off at a run, and was back within minutes with the bucket. Matt worked at cleaning some of the blood off of Dan.

Dan began to stir, and then opened his eyes. "Mother?"

Verna went to his side and took his hand. "I'm here, son."

"Mother. It's like they were waiting for us. They started shooting at us from two sides."

Verna glanced quickly at Hiram, who gravely returned the gaze. They had thought they were being discreet, but they weren't. Matt saw it.

Matt said, "Rest easy, son. You got a bullet in your ribs, and you hit your head when they shot you out of the saddle. Timmons has gone for the doctor."

Dan nodded, and closed his eyes. He fell back into a light sleep.

"Oh, Dan," Verna said.

Matt placed a hand on her shoulder. "He's made of strong stuff, Verna."

Greenville was only four miles from the ranch, and within less than an hour, Hiram was returning with Doc Benson. Young, for a doctor, maybe thirty-five, but Matt had found he seemed to be knowledgeable in all of the new medical theories.

He was tall and thin and with a thick mustache waxed into curls at both ends. He wore a dark colored bowler that he tossed into a chair, and went to work, poking about Dan's bullet wound. He then closed the wound with four stitches and bandaged it tightly, to close off the bleeding and to hold the broken rib in place.

When it was done, he met the family in the parlor.

"It looks worse than it is," he said. "Looks like the bullet cracked the rib but didn't go through. Must have ricocheted off."

Hiram looked a little confused. "Can a bullet do that? Actually bounce off a rib?"

Matt nodded. "Depends on how far away the shooter is. A bullet loses its force the further it travels."

The doctor said, "He's lost a lot of blood, and he's going to be sore. I wouldn't let him back in the saddle again for at least three weeks. But barring infection, he should be all right."

Verna said, "What *are* the chances of infection?"

The doctor looked at her, and shrugged. "It's a hard thing to predict. I don't want to give you false hope, but I don't want to scare you, either. But in the late War Between the States, the number one cause of death was from infection."

Matt nodded. He had seen men die of infection. He fully believed it. But he knew it could be prevented. He said as much.

Doc Benson shook his head. "No, Mister McCabe. I wish there were. But there's no way of preventing infection. Maybe someday, but I fear that day's a long ways away."

Matt was also shaking his head. "I've seen it work. Something an old Texas Ranger showed my brother."

"Johnny McCabe," Benson said, weariness in his voice, like he had heard the stories of Matt's legendary brother more often than he cared to.

Matt said, "I've seen it work."

"This is no time for old home remedies. What he needs now is rest. When he wakes up, try to get food and water into him. I'd recommend red meat to build his blood up. Beef stew, perhaps."

Verna nodded. "I'll have Timmons pay you, and escort you back to town."

He nodded with a smile. "I can get back to town myself, Mrs. McCabe. But thank you."

When the doctor was gone, Verna gave Matt a long look. She said, "You've actually seen this remedy work?"

He nodded. "I've seen gunshot wounds treated with it. And a boy working for the ranch here got gored with an antler once. Treated him with it, too. No infection at all. It was back when Johnny was ramrodding. Back when your father was still here."

She said, "Billy Hall. I remember that. I never knew anything was given to him to prevent infection."

Hiram said, "What remedy is it? How is it possible a fully trained doctor wouldn't know of it?"

Matt said to Verna, "Do you want me to try? I think we should."

He could see the wheels turning in her mind. Finally, she nodded.

Matt looked from Hiram to Timmons, to Ben Harris who was still there. "You boys are gonna have to hold him down."

Verna said, "What are you going to need to put this potion of Johnny's together?"

Matt looked over to the wet bar, and the whiskey decanter. "All we're going to need is right here."

Dan kicked and bucked like a wild man when the whiskey hit his wound, but once he settled down he fell into a comfortable sleep.

Matt returned to his office. The upholstery on the sofa was stained with blood. So was a braided rug under the sofa. Bloody strips of sheet were still on the floor where he had thrown them carelessly. He was in a gray satin smoking jacket which now also had random smears of blood on it.

He glanced at the clock on the mantel. Ten past three. He didn't realize how late it was. He had lost track of time when Dan was brought in.

He went to the bar and grabbed a glass and filled it with scotch. He then stood and looked at it. His son had almost died tonight. Matt should have been out there with him. Ben Harris was a good man but he was a cowboy, not a gunfighter. None of the men were gunfighters. Though Matt hardly considered himself one, both of his brothers qualified for the title and he had ridden with them for a long time. If Matt had been out there tonight, maybe he would have suspected the trap the rustlers had set for them.

He threw the glass against the wall. It shattered, and scotch splattered against the plaster.

I've had enough scotch, Matt thought. Too much scotch. If he had been out there on a horse instead of home with a glass in his hand, none of this might have happened. He should have grabbed his gun and saddled up and rode out after them. But Verna said for him to stay, so he stayed.

"What's happened to me?" he shouted.

With one hand, he grabbed the small table that served as a wet bar and sent it cartwheeling across the room. The decanter of scotch landed on the floor and didn't shatter, but the scotch emptied itself onto the floorboards. The decanter of Verna's sherry did shatter.

Papers and a quill pen and a bottle of ink were on the desk top. With a swipe of both hands, the desk top was cleared and the papers flew across the room, and the bottle of ink shattered and there was one more stain on the floor.

Matt went outside into the night. He needed to breathe. He wiped away tears, and he strode off the porch to the ground. He looked off into the darkness and wanted to raise his voice and scream to the heavens. But instead he stood, huffing for breath, his fists clenched.

From somewhere off in the distance, he heard a wolf howl. And he felt something come alive inside him. Something he had let die over the years. One step at a time. But now it was over, and he was back.

Come sunrise, he was in his office once again. Verna stepped in and said, "There you are. We were wondering where you had gone?"

Then her gaze traveled about the room. It looked like it had been ransacked. "Matt, what happened here?"

He didn't answer. She then realized how he was dressed. He was in a range shirt and a tattered old leather vest. The one he had worn when he first met her. He was in jeans and riding boots, and a pistol was at his side. A wide-brimmed brown sombrero was on his desk. The men on the ranch used the term *sombrero* loosely. Sort of a cowboy colloquialism. The hat was worn and tattered, with a brim that was wide and flat and a crown that was rounded. The hat he had worn when he and his brothers first rode into Verna's life.

Matt was standing by the gun rack, thumbing cartridges into a Winchester carbine.

"Matt," she said, "what on Earth are you doing?"

"I'm going after those men. The ones that shot Dan."

As he said this, Hiram stepped into the room behind his mother.

"Father," he said, "you can't be serious. You'll be killed."

"I should have been there with him in the first place."

Verna said nothing. She merely tossed a glance at Hiram. Her son stepped past her, and placed a hand on his father's shoulder.

"Father, put the gun away." He spoke gently, almost like a parent would to a child. "You'll just get yourself killed out there."

Matt shrugged off Hiram's hand. "It's time to take matters into my own hands. It's my own fault I let myself get talked out of riding with Dan. I've told Ben to saddle a horse for me."

"Well, I'll go and tell him to stop."

Matt had a strong voice, which Hiram had forgotten. Matt let it roar now. "This is *my* ranch! I gave *my* ramrod an order, and he's carrying it out. Either ride with me, or stay out of my way."

Hiram stepped back.

Matt said, "Before I go after those men, I'm going to go and bring back the one man we need for something like this. He shouldn't have too much of a lead on me. I should be able to follow his trail pretty easy."

Oh no, Verna thought. He's going to bring back his brother.

Matt said to Hiram, "Are you gonna ride with me?"

Hiram looked at him but said nothing.

"That's what I thought." Matt grabbed his sombrero from the desk. "I don't know when I'll be back."

He strode out onto the porch behind the house, and to the stable out back.

Verna looked to her son. "We have a problem."

9

Johnny knew he was being followed. When you've ridden enough trails, you know how to become aware of something like this. Little things, like a flock of birds a quarter mile back suddenly taking to the air. When he stopped Thunder and climbed out of the saddle and loosened the girth to let him blow for a while, the horse threw a glance toward their back trail. But mostly it was a gut feeling. Johnny tightened the girth and swung back into the saddle, cast one more backward glance, and continued on.

Johnny carried no time piece, but he guessed by the position of the sun overhead that it was late morning. Ahead was a small grouping of short, fat oaks, so he turned his horse into the grove and stepped out of the saddle.

He pulled his pistol and checked the loads. There were five. He usually rode with an empty chamber in front of the firing pin so if the gun got bumped it wouldn't shoot him in the leg. He thumbed in a sixth cartridge and then stood, gun in his hand, in the shade of an oak.

"We're going to have some company," he said to Thunder.

Thunder grazed contentedly. Didn't seem all that bothered.

Johnny was closer to the mountains now, and the land was rising into low, rounded hills, though they were still grassy with scattered oaks. From where he stood, he had a good view of a hill he had just descended, maybe a quarter mile behind him. Johnny waited what he guessed was over half an hour when a rider topped the hill and then began riding down.

Johnny recognized the rider, even though he hadn't seen him in a saddle in almost twenty years. Every rider has a distinct way of sitting on a horse, just like everyone has a distinct way of walking. This man rode erect, his head bowed a little as his eyes scanned the ground in front of him. He wore his gun high on his belt, and wasn't fast or flashy with it, but Johnny knew he could shoot straight. Johnny had expected he would probably never see him again, and couldn't help smiling as he watched him ride up.

The man could track, and he knew Johnny was waiting for him in the grove of oaks. He reined up by the grove and wasn't at all surprised when Johnny stepped out of the trees.

"Matt," Johnny said, dropping the sixth round from his gun and sliding the pistol back into its holster. "Not that I'm not glad to see you, but I am a little surprised."

Matt decided to get to the point. "Johnny, we need you. *I* need you. Dan's been shot. Ambushed by cattle rustlers last night. The fool boy went out with the men. I guess he thought he had something to prove."

Johnny said, "You're going after them."

Matt nodded.

"I'll get my horse."

As they rode back toward the ranch, Matt said, "You covered a lot of miles."

Johnny didn't know quite how to say this. In the past, he and Matt had never minced words with each other, but this was no longer the Matt he had known.

But he decided to follow the old policy and just say what had to be said.

"I really wanted to put as many miles as I could behind me."

Matt nodded. "It's not what you would have thought, is it? The kind of life I lead. Back in the day, when we were just three young men with a price on our heads, you never thought I'd wind up in a house like that, with servants."

"I have to admit, I'm not surprised by that part of it. If any of the four sons of our parents were to succeed, I'd put my money on you. But it's the way you seem to be going about it."

Matt nodded again. He knew what Johnny meant. "I don't know what's happened to me, Johnny. Somehow, I guess I just let myself slip away from myself. You know what I mean?"

Johnny's turn to nod.

Matt said, "I was so taken with Verna when I first saw her, standing on the front porch, all those years ago. She was so beautiful. I really did love her, at least in the beginning."

He sighed. "I know what she is. I began to realize, over the years. Love's blinders began to fall off, bit by bit, and I began to see what she is. But I couldn't just ride away. We had the boys, and they needed their father in the household. So I stayed, and just got used to turning a blind eye to the things she would do, and hiding in whiskey.

"And I know what my sons are. Hiram is just like her. Pains me to say that. Tom, he's a good man. There's no real rift between us. It's just that he had the good sense to get out. And Danny, he doesn't know what he wants. He looks up to Hiram almost like a hero. Wants to be just like him, but doesn't yet realize what Hiram is. Danny has heart. And gumption."

They rode in silence for a moment. Then Matt said, "I guess it got to be too easy to just lose myself in a bottle of scotch, and let Verna be Verna and Hiram be Hiram. And look where it got me. Danny was almost killed last night."

Matt told Johnny about the way Dan was brought home, and the extent of the wound.

Johnny said, "You might have been losing yourself in a bottle of scotch. I came close to that myself a time or two. But you're here now. Let's go find those men."

It was early afternoon when they arrived at the ranch. Hiram met them in the entryway. Timmons was with him. Hiram glanced at Johnny and said nothing, but his eyes said it all. Johnny knew he wasn't welcome here.

"How's your brother?" Matt said to Hiram.

"He's asleep. He's sleeping well. No sign of fever."

"And your mother?"

"She's resting, like she always does this time of day."

"She rests a lot," Matt said to Johnny. "I'm starting to wonder if she's ill. She hasn't looked well in a long time."

Johnny wanted to say, *all that rottenness is bound to wear a body out.* He wanted to say it, but didn't.

Timmons ignored Matt and said to Hiram, "Should I get her?"

But Matt answered, not giving Hiram a chance to. "No. Get Ben Harris and have him meet me in my office."

Without another word, Matt strode down the corridor that would lead to his office. Johnny noticed Matt hadn't asked, he had ordered. Johnny fell into place behind him.

Timmons gave a questioning look to Hiram, who shrugged and said, "I suppose you should go get Harris."

"What do you think is happening?"

"I have no idea, but it can't be good."

The door to Matt's office was closed, so he opened it and stepped in. To his surprise, the room had been cleaned. The blood stained strips of bed sheet were gone. The braided rug had been cleaned, and the entire sofa had been replaced. He wasn't surprised. The sofa had velvet upholstery, and blood wouldn't clean easily from it. What he was surprised about was how quickly it had been done. Even the small table that served as a wet bar was back in place, with two decanters and a small supply of tumblers and the tulip-shaped wine glasses Verna drank sherry from. The papers were back on his desk, with a new ink bottle.

He could just imagine Verna snapping orders to the poor crew who had the misfortune to work for her.

"I worked hard to build this place up," he said to Johnny.

"You built an empire. That's for sure."

"But somehow I let it get away from me. I'm starting to wonder if Verna had this planned all along. Manipulate me into making the business deals I needed to, and then gradually sweep me aside. Maybe I needed something like this, my son getting shot, as a rude awakening. Make me open my eyes and see just what's really going on. God help me."

"You need time to sort all of this out. But right now we have to focus on finding those riders."

"They probably have a big head start on us."

Johnny shook his head. "They've been hitting other ranches in the area. Safe bet is they're local."

"Then we'll find 'em." Matt went to the gun rack. "I saw that Sharps in your saddle. But you might want a Winchester, in case there's shooting."

"My Sharps will do me fine. You don't need a lot of shots if you shoot straight."

The old joke between them. When they had made their cross-country ride from Texas to California years ago, Matt had a Spencer repeater in his saddle, but Johnny carried an old Hawken muzzle-loader, and they had the same conversation a couple of times. Johnny grinned, and despite the distress Matt was under, Matt found a grin rising to the surface himself.

Then Johnny grew serious. "Matt, there's something to think about."

Before he could say anything further, Hiram came striding in, Timmons right behind him.

Hiram said, "Father, what you need is to slow down. Join me for a scotch."

Matt said, "I think I've had enough scotch over the years, don't you?"

He snapped the words maybe more than he had intended to, Johnny thought. Or maybe not.

Johnny said, continuing what he had started saying before Hiram interrupted, "Matt, from what you told me of it, those men who ambushed Dan and the others—they were waiting for them. They knew where they would be."

Matt said, "What are you saying?"

"I'm saying someone tipped 'em off."

Matt looked at him silently. With everything that had been going on for the past twelve hours, his mind had been overloaded and he hadn't considered this. Then he said, "Had to be someone here. Who else would have known?"

Hiram rolled his eyes. "Johnny, you can't be serious. Do you know what you're suggesting?"

Matt snapped his gaze to him. "*Uncle* Johnny to you."

Hiram gave a weary nod of acquiescence. "*Uncle* Johnny. Do you know what you're implying? And Father, you can't listen to this. Everyone here is loyal. I mean, what would anyone possibly have to gain by tipping off rustlers? It was our cattle they were stealing."

Johnny said, "I'm not implying anything. I'm outright saying those rustlers knew men from this ranch were coming out there. They laid there, waiting for them. I've been in a few gun battles, son. I know how these things work."

"I'm not your son." Hiram sneered the words.

There were boots scraping at the porch outside the full-length window, and then Ben Harris stepped in. He was wiping dust from his jeans, and a worn sombrero was perched on his head. He wore his gun high on the belt, like most cowhands did.

"Ben," Matt said, "I know you were up late last night, but do you feel up for a ride? I want you to take Johnny and me out to where it happened."

"Uh..," he glanced a little uncomfortably from Matt to Hiram, and then back to Matt. "Mrs. McCabe gave the order no riders are to leave the house without her permission."

Matt stepped up to Ben, stopping only a foot from him. Matt was thinner than he had been years ago, but he drew himself up straight. His tired posture now seemed gone.

He said, "Ben, you're a good man. But hear me. *I'm* in charge of this spread. From now on, you take your orders from me. Is that clear? Because if it's not, then collect your pay and get off this range."

Ben swallowed hard. "Yes, sir. Perfectly clear. I take my orders from you."

"Saddle up. And while you're at it, have Diego get me and Johnny fresh mounts."

"I'm all right," Johnny said. "I'll take my stallion. He's covered a lot of miles, but he can cover some more."

"All right, then. A mount for you, and one for me. Bring a rifle. I want to be riding out in ten minutes."

Ben nodded. "Yes sir, Mister McCabe."

And he was out the door.

Hiram was in a white shirt and a black string tie, and in a burgundy smoking jacket. His arms were folded and he took a few paces thoughtfully, then looked at Johnny. "Do you think you'll be able to track them?"

"In this dirt? It's dry, but not too dry. You haven't had rain for a little while, and judging by that sky out there, there's not any coming anytime soon. Should be as easy as reading words across a piece of paper."

"Maybe I should come with you."

Matt said, "Won't be necessary. Too many riders'll let 'em know we're coming. Stay here and watch after your brother and mother."

"When can we expect you home?"

Matt shook his head. "When the job is done."

Soon Ben was at the window. "We're ready, Mister McCabe. I had Johnny's stallion brought around back with the other horses."

Matt said to Hiram, "Tell your mother I'll be back when I can."

And he, Johnny and Ben were gone.

Hiram and Timmons stood in the office and listened to the hoof beats as the three rode away.

Hiram said, "Timmons, go wake Mother. Tell her we have some real problems developing."

Timmons nodded and left the room.

10

They rode for an hour, stopping every so often to let the horses blow. All about them were low grassy hills that rose to a small rounded summit. Occasionally they would pass a grove of trees. About them would be a couple hundred head of longhorns grazing away, and then they would be past them and riding through some open grassland, then would come to some more cattle scattered about. And all the time they were on Matt's land.

Impressive, Johnny thought. He knew Matt owned thousands of acres. The ranch was much larger now than it had been back in the days of Frank McCarty. But to read about it in a letter was not the same as actually seeing the land before him. He knew of few other spreads this size. The Walker ranch in Texas was one of the few. There was another a hundred miles or so south of here, near Stockton, and another in Nevada, in the Tahoe area.

They came to a long, deep ravine. It looked almost like God himself had taken a shovel and scooped away a section of the ground. The floor of the ravine was maybe twenty acres in size, Johnny estimated, and grass grew. It was almost a small box canyon.

Ben Harris reined up at the mouth of the ravine, and Johnny and Matt did the same.

"Here's where it was," Ben said. "The rustlers, they waited for us there," he pointed to one high spot at the ridge of the ravine, "and over there." He aimed his hand toward the other side. "They just shot at us, catching us in a cross-fire."

Johnny said, "How'd they know you'd be here?"

"This ravine, we found all sorts of tracks in there. Steers, and horses. We thought the rustlers had been using it as a sort of natural corral when they took stock from other ranches. I thought there was no reason they wouldn't be using it again last night. It was my idea to ride out here."

"But they knew you were coming," Matt said.

"Must have. It's the only way I can figure it. The moon was bright last night and the sky was clear, and maybe they saw us coming. But I doubt it. We were riding single file, and as quiet as we could."

Matt said to Johnny, "We're about a quarter mile from the edge of our land. Maybe less. This is sort of a four-corners country. Another spread abuts against ours, south of here. Another to the west. And one more to the north. All three of 'em have been hit by the rustlers. A few hundred head from each place. At the Colson place, to the north, one of their men was killed in the process."

Johnny turned Thunder up to the high spot Ben had pointed out, and stepped down out of the saddle. Matt and Ben followed him, and sat in their saddles while Johnny took a look around.

On the ground were crimped cigarette butts.

"They waited a while," Johnny said. "Had the time to roll a few smokes."

There were boot tracks, too. Some indicating where men stood, others that had the look of being made by a man in motion. As he was walking.

"Two men were here. Good, clear boot prints. A man about your size, Ben, and another maybe a little bigger."

Empty cartridges were scattered about, too. Johnny picked one up. "Forty-four. Probably from a Winchester. The rifle favored by most. It's too far from here for a pistol shot."

Matt backed his horse down from the low hill that formed the high spot. "They picketed their horses here. Tracks and droppings everywhere."

Ben said, "So they knew we were coming, but didn't know when."

Johnny swung back up into the saddle. "Who'd you tell about your idea to ride out here last night?"

Ben shrugged. "Mister McCabe, here. Hiram. Dan. Pretty much everyone at the bunkhouse. I suppose all of the men know about it."

Matt said, "We got us a snake back home. That much is clear. And I intend to find out who it was, and it's not going to go easy for him. That much I can assure you."

Ben said, "Who do you think it was?"

"It couldn't have been you or anyone who rode with you last night. No man in his right mind would knowingly ride into an ambush."

"Whoever it was," Johnny said, "we might find some answers when we find out who these tracks belong to. Looks like they regrouped here, and then headed south."

"All right." Matt looked at Johnny, squinting into the sun. "Let's ride."

The riders made no attempt to hide their tracks. One trick Johnny had learned was if you didn't want anyone to know how large your party was by the tracks you left, ride single file. But these men were riding along as though they expected no one to be able to follow them, and they seemed to be in no hurry. Like they were out for a casual ride.

"Appears to be four of 'em," Johnny said.

Matt nodded. "That's the way it looks to me, too."

Johnny glanced at Ben, riding along with them. Ben was no gunfighter, and there was no way to know what they would be riding into.

Johnny said, "Ben, it might be best if you rode back to the ranch."

Matt said, "You can tell Hiram and the others about our progress."

"If it's all the same," Ben said, "I'd like to ride along with you. I want a piece of 'em, too."

Matt looked at Johnny. "What do we do when we catch up to 'em?"

Johnny said, "That depends on how peaceable they are when we find 'em."

The trail took a leisurely bend to the southeast. They came to a small stream where the rustlers had stopped and let their horses drink. Probably took some water themselves. Maybe filled their canteens. A little later on, at a stand of alders, Johnny, Matt and Ben found where a small campfire had been made. A pile of old coffee grounds was by the fire, still damp.

"They stopped to make coffee," Johnny said. "They were in no hurry at all."

"Mighty curious," Matt said, scratching his chin. "You'd think they'd want to put as many miles between themselves and that ravine as possible."

They rode on.

The trail then curved its way directly east.

"They headed toward town," Matt said, clearly puzzled. "Greenvile's only a few miles ahead of us."

Ben said, "Wouldn't you think they'd want to hide out somewhere? And it would have to be a place where you can keep a lot of cattle."

"North of here, the land sort of becomes a bunch of ridges. Small ravines and such. It gets even more so beyond the Colson place. If I was stealing cattle, that's where I'd take 'em. Find some small canyon miles from anywhere. Some place where you could keep that many head without drawing attention to yourself."

"Maybe they are," Johnny said. "Doesn't look like they took any cattle at all last night. They were out for one thing only. To get your men in a cross-fire."

"But why?" Ben said. "It makes no sense a'tall."

"We won't find answers sitting here."

The trail continued eastward. The afternoon drifted its way toward early evening, and they found themselves on a small grassy knoll looking down at the buildings of Greenville.

"They rode right into town," Matt said.

Johnny nodded.

"So, what do we do, now?"

Johnny said, "We gotta find some way to smoke 'em out. I think I should start by asking some questions. I know Artie Crocker, runs the Cattleman's Lounge."

Matt nodded. "Artie's a good man."

"A bartender tends to hear things. I'll see what he's heard, and tell him to keep his ear close to the ground. There's also a gambler there. A man named Middleton."

"Think he might have something to do with it?"

"I doubt it. I wouldn't think cattle rustling or setting up an ambush would be his style. But he might know something. I have the feeling very little gets past him."

"All right. Let's ride on in."

Johnny shook his head. "Not you, Matt. You're too well known here. Half the men in town work for you. Men don't tend to be as forthcoming when the boss is the one doing the asking."

"You might have a point."

"Go back to the ranch. Check on Dan. I'll be along as soon as I find out something."

Matt nodded. "All right." He looked to Ben. "Come on. Let's ride."

Matt and Ben turned their horses away, and circled around till they came to the trail that would take them back to the mansion that passed for Matt's ranch house.

Johnny sat and watched them move along for a bit, then he turned his attention to the town below. The sun had set and it was getting dark. There were some lighted windows. He started Thunder forward and said, "Let's go, boy. Let's see if we can find out what's going on."

11

Johnny swung out of the saddle and left his tired stallion at the hitching rail in front of the Cattleman's Lounge. It was now fully dark, and the street was lighted from the windows of the saloon and others like it.

He had no intention of staying in this town any longer than he needed to. He would talk with Artie. See if he had overheard anything that might be helpful. Maybe talk with the card shark Middleton if he was still around. Then he would take Thunder out of town and they would make camp somewhere.

The town was busier than it had been when Johnny was here a couple of days ago. Riders were moving along the street, heading for the Cattleman's, or one of the other saloons in town. Or one of the brothels. Miners and cowhands walked along the boardwalk. One cowhand was walking with a saloon woman.

Johnny stepped in through the swinging doors. A man with a short brimmed derby and white sleeves pushed up by arm garters was rattling away a song on a piano that seemed to Johnny to be a little out of tune. Five saloon women were at work, getting men to buy drinks for them. One was the woman who had been working with Middleton. Peddie, Johnny remembered Middleton calling her. The one called Belle seemed to be nowhere in sight. Miners and cowhands and a few men who looked to be just plain drifters were at the bar or sitting at tables. Middleton was at a table with two miners and a cowhand, shuffling a deck. Peddie was at a different table, so maybe this game would be a little more honest.

Artie was not at the bar. An older man. Thin and with a tired looking face. He was filling mugs of beer and sliding them down the bar to the patrons.

Middleton glanced up toward Johnny. Probably caught motion at the doorway with the corner of his eye. He gave a nod of his head, as if to say *come over here a minute*. Since he was one of the men Johnny had planned to talk with, he made his way over to the table.

"Boys," Middleton said, a cigar clinched between his teeth, "I've got to bow out of this game."

He handed the deck to the man to his left. A miner.

"Hey," one of them said. "We want the chance to win some of our money back."

"You'll get it," Middleton said, pushing his chair back and standing up. "I have to talk to this man a minute."

He took the cigar from his teeth and flicked ash on the floor. He had exchanged his black jacket and hat for gray ones.

"Let's get straight to the point, McCabe. Belle's dead. She was strangled the night you were here. Only a few hours after you left, by my reckoning."

Johnny stared. He hadn't been expecting this.

Without waiting, Middleton continued. "The so-called marshall here, Wells, has decided you did it. You were seen talking with her outside."

Johnny said, "I walked her to her tent. She insisted. She warned me to get out of town. Said they had killed another man who had come to town."

"Quite right. A stranger who might be trouble is someone they don't like. They haven't got me quite figured out yet. I think I scare them just enough to leave me alone. But they've decided you did it, and they have announced their plans to arrest you if you ever came back."

"Why are you warning me about this? Why do you care?"

"Belle was a friend of Peddie's. And Peddie's an old friend of mine, which gives me an interest in finding out who did it. But I don't think you did it, and don't want to see the wrong man hang."

Johnny was about to say he was here to ask if Middleton had heard anything about the cattle rustling going on at ranches in the area, but Middleton said, looking toward the doorway, "Too late."

Wells was stepping in. He had a shotgun in his hands. Bardeen was with him, also with a scattergun. They were followed by a third man. All three walked toward Johnny, and then spread out maybe twenty feet from him.

There was a sudden scraping of chairs and drumming of boots on the floor as men cleared away from their tables. Some got to the other side of the room and others just got out of the building entirely. Middleton moved, too. Not to escape, but he caught up with Peddie and said something to her Johnny couldn't hear. She gave one nod of her head, and then pushed through the crowd and out through a back door.

Wells said, "Well, now, Mister McCabe. You came back to town. Not the smartest move on your part."

Johnny's right hand was by his pistol. "I want no trouble."

"Then you should have thought about that before you strangled the life out of poor Belle."

"I had nothing to do with whatever happened to her."

"You can tell that to the judge. Drop your gun."

Johnny shook his head. "I don't drop my gun for any man."

"Mister, you'd best do what your told. Or do you want a fight?"

"I don't start fights. But I finish 'em."

"There's three of us. Two of us have scatterguns. You know what a scattergun can do to a man at close range?"

"You'll have to actually fire that scattergun before I fire my gun at you."

Well's glance down to Johnny's holster. "Your gun is still in your holster."

The man who had stepped in with Wells and Bardeen was younger, maybe twenty. He was looking at Johnny wide-eyed, and he said to Wells, "That there's Johnny McCabe."

"I know who it is, Marty. Stand your ground."

"But..."

"He's just one man ag'in the three of us. Don't believe all the tall stories you hear."

Middleton had made his way to one side, and had drawn his pistol and it was cocked. He said, "No, gentlemen, but what you can believe is the reality of a cross-fire. I really doubt you can cock and fire those scatterguns before Mister McCabe can draw and get at least one of you. Probably two. And I'll be firing from here. Now, what would you say the odds are that the three of you will walk out of here?"

Wells glanced over to Middleton. "Stay out of this, you tinhorn. This ain't your affair."

"If it involves Belle, then it is. Now drop those weapons before the good mood I'm in fades. And believe me, you don't want to see me in a bad mood."

Wells looked at Johnny. Wells was thinking about it—Johnny could see it in his eyes. Could he really get a shot off at Johnny before Johnny could clear leather, and maybe one of his men get Middleton.

But then Marty's pistol hit the floor, and he backed up with his hands in the air.

"Marty" Wells said.

But then Bardeen took a step backward and said, "Look, Wells. I didn't sign on just to get myself riddled with holes."

Wells said through clenched teeth, "Stand your ground, dammit."

"I ain't bein' paid enough for this."

Middleton said, "All right, marshal. Make your decision. Do you go for your gun and get caught in a crossfire and torn to shreds, or do you want to live?"

Wells gave a long sigh. He was angry. Johnny knew the type. He was probably angry at someone getting the drop on him, and at his men for cowering down. He wasn't smart enough to realize that Middleton had just saved his life, because Wells had been facing Johnny without his scattergun cocked, and the one called Bardeen had been too. Johnny knew he could clear leather before either one of them could cock their gun, and Johnny's first bullet was going to be dead center into the forehead of Wells.

Bardeen had already placed his scattergun on the floor. Wells did the same.

"Now, gentlemen," Middleton said, "why don't you drop those sidearms, too? Nice and slow and gentle. I'd hate for you to make a sudden move and give Mister McCabe reason to draw down on you and end your pathetic lives."

Marty didn't even need to think about it. He unbuckled his entire gunbelt and dropped it to the floor. Bardeen gave a nervous glance at Wells and then did the same. Wells shook his head with disgust, and let his pistol drop to his feet.

"Now, kick them over to Mister McCabe."

They did as told. Marty had to give his gunbelt a solid kick to send it sliding all the way over to Johnny.

"Now, lie down on the floor. Face down."

Wells said, "Ain't gonna happen."

"Lie face down on the floor, or I'll put a bullet in your head and you'll fall down."

Marty didn't waste any time. He went straight down. Bardeen followed. Wells let out a sigh, his face almost a comical display of exasperation, and he did the same.

Johnny knelt down and grabbed each pistol and began unloading it. One was a Remington .45, and the other two were Colt .44s. Johnny tucked the .44 cartridges into a vest pocket. Ammunition was expensive.

While he did this, he said, "Don't think me ungrateful, Middleton, but I have to ask why. You have no stake in this fight, and you don't strike me as one to stick his neck out unless there's a potential profit in it."

"You might think me devoid of ethics, McCabe. But I do have a personal interest in this, which I'm not going to go into right now. But Peddie was a close friend of Belle's, and where Peddie's involved, *I'm* involved. I'm not going to let small-minded knuckle-draggers like these three railroad anyone into a murder conviction. I want to know who actually killed her."

"And what makes you so sure I didn't do it?"

"Because of who you are. Or maybe, more specifically, *what* you are."

Johnny rose to his feet, his vest pocket filled with cartridges. "And what am I?"

"A latter day knight. If this were a few hundred years earlier, you'd be riding around in shining armor, defending the weak and all of that. You have a nobility in you that I've seen in few others."

"And you can see all that in me even though you hardly know me?"

Middleton shook his head. "It was Peddie who saw it in you. Peddie and Belle. That's why Belle went to warn you to get out of town, because your very presence here would scare Wells and his men and the people they work for. And it was in doing this that Belle sealed her fate."

"How is that?"

Middleton still had his gun aimed toward the three men lying on the floor.

He said, "Because it gave her a connection to you, which is why I believe she was killed. I just need to prove it, and the one who strangled her will be dead, and so will the one who gave the order."

"You mean you think I was set up?"

"My, you're quick."

Johnny glanced to the three on the floor. Wells was looking up at him with as much hatred as Johnny had ever seen in a man.

Middleton said, "I would like to stand and discuss this all night, but you and I have to get out of here. I can contain these three for only so long before the people they work for realize what's going on and call in the cavalry. As in, more gunfighters."

Johnny received the message. Time to get moving. "I owe you one," he said to Middleton.

"Not at all."

Johnny threw one more glance at Wells, then was out the door. He half expected to find more men outside waiting for him with scatterguns, but the boardwalk was clear. Across the street a cowhand was standing, leaning against a wall. He had a large Texas hat and a big bandana draped across the front of his shirt, and huge spurs on his heels. He was talking to another cowhand who wasn't leaning against anything but was pacing about a little as they talked, scuffing one boot or the other against the boardwalk. Neither of them had any idea they had just missed a scene that was probably going to be talked about in saloons and mining camps and cow camps for years to come.

Thunder was waiting patiently. Johnny grabbed the rein and stepped up and into the saddle. He turned Thunder down the street, but then after a couple of buildings he turned the horse to the right and into an alley. A miner was there, trying to romance a saloon woman. Her back was to the wall, and he was standing in front of her, one hand against the wall, leaning in for a kiss. They both glanced at him briefly as he steered his horse through the alley, but it was at best a minor distraction. This was the west, after all. A man rode a horse into a saloon once, and hardly anyone thought twice about it.

Johnny emerged at the end of the alley, and out into the street behind the saloon. This was more residential. Tents serving as homes. Johnny could smell wood smoke in the air. It was October and the nights were turning off a little cool here in northern California.

Johnny followed the muddy street down to its end. Beyond the last tent was open grassland. The moon had risen and was giving off meager light, but it was enough to ride by. Thunder had covered a lot of miles today so Johnny kept him to nothing more than a fast walk as they headed off into the night.

12

As Matt rode through the front gate, every joint ached. He had been the saddle most of the day, something Johnny did often but Matt hadn't done this much riding in years. He also hadn't slept since the night before last.

Ben rode beside him and sat easily in the saddle. Ben was ramrod here and was in the saddle almost all day, almost every day. Matt had no intention of admitting to him how much he hurt. He hoped it didn't show.

The two sentries nodded to them as they rode up. "Mister McCabe," one of them said.

Matt realized he didn't even know their names. Hired by Hiram.

Hiram never called them sentries. He said they were "men stationed out front in case there's ever any trouble." But sentries was what they were. He had to wonder why Hiram and Verna felt the need for them. And he had to wonder why he was only asking himself this for the first time today.

He swung out of the saddle, hesitating a moment while his right foot hit the ground and his left boot was still in a stirrup, and something at the base of his spine snapped. He then pulled his left boot from the stirrup, and realized both knees hurt and felt a little wobbly.

You're an old man, he said to himself. Once he and Johnny and their brother Joe had ridden all the way cross-country. First from Pennsylvania to Missouri, then from there to Texas. And from Texas on to California. They were tired at the end of the day and slept on the hard ground by a campfire. But then in the morning they would be back in the saddle and moving on. He never hurt like he did now. But he had been young back then. Somehow, as he watched Verna build a successful cattle ranch into a financial empire, as he stood by and drank scotch and smoked cigars and tried not to see what he didn't want to see, he had grown old.

Ben said, "I'll take the horses to the stable."

"Thanks, Ben," Matt said, and took one painful step after another around the side of the huge house and onto the long back porch and then opened one of the floor-length windows and stepped into his office.

He unbuckled his gunbelt and dropped it onto the desk. It was the original gunbelt he had worn back in the day. Black finished leather that was now scratched and cracked in places. He tossed his hat on top of it, and ran his fingers through his sweaty hair and over his tired scalp. He then shuffled painfully over to the wet bar and grabbed a tumbler and pulled the glass cork from the decanter of scotch. But then he decided against it and returned the cork, and set the tumbler back on the table. He had had enough scotch over the years. He thought he might go out to the kitchen and see if there was any coffee.

His box of cigars was calling to him from the desk so he flipped it open and grabbed one, and struck a match on the side of his boot and brought the cigar to life.

Hiram stepped in from the hallway. He was in a gray jacket and matching trousers, and a string tie.

"Father," he said. "I thought I heard someone ride up. I was hoping it was you."

"How's Dan?"

"He's doing well. He was awake for a little while, and took down some beef stew. The doctor was out again and said he thought Dan was going to be all right."

Matt nodded. "I think I'll go up and see him." Then he chuckled. "As soon as I can climb the stairs. I've been in the saddle all day. I hurt in places I had totally forgotten about."

Hiram just stood and said nothing.

Matt said, "Is there any coffee on?"

"No, but I can get Juanita to put some on fast enough."

"No, that's all right. I might just finish this cigar and go upstairs. See Dan, and then get some sleep. Today has really reminded me that I'm not as young as I used to be."

Hiram went to the wet bar and picked up the tumbler his father had set down and looked at it curiously for a moment. Then he filled it with scotch for himself.

"So," he said. "What did you and Uncle Johnny find out?"

Matt told him what they had found at the ravine. Rustlers had waited to catch Dan and the men in a crossfire.

"They did more than what rustlers would normally do," he said. "Rustlers normally try to steal cattle but will run off at the first sign of gunfire. But these men were more like gunfighters, laying a trap like that. Their tracks were easy enough to follow, and we followed them all the way back to town. Johnny's there now, asking questions."

He realized Verna had appeared the doorway. How long she had been there, he didn't know.

Hiram said, "So, what do you plan to do if you find these men?"

"*When*," Matt said. "*When* we find them. And we will. And when we do, there won't be anything left of them to turn over to the law."

Verna said, "Do you really think that's the right approach?"

Hiram took a sip of whiskey. "We are societal leaders, father. What we do sets an example for the entire community. My recommendation is we go to Marshal Wells with this. It is his job, after all."

Matt said, "Your recommendation is duly noted. But I am the head of this ranch. I've sat by passively for far too long. Those rustlers almost killed my son. Your brother. If I had acted faster, maybe he wouldn't have been shot. I'm no longer sitting back. I'm taking an active role in this, from now on. There are to be no more business decisions made here without my approval."

Verna said, "Well, of course, dear."

Matt looked at her skeptically. He then said, "What I want to know is why you're not both more outraged than you are. Verna, Dan is your son, too, and he was almost killed last night."

"Well, of course I'm outraged. Of course I want those men brought to justice."

Hiram said, "It's like I said, that we're societal leaders, father. With great power comes great responsibility. We've built this from a ranch to a small empire. *You've*," he couldn't quite disguise his patronizing tone, "built this place into an empire. But with this comes responsibility. Society looks up to us for leadership. It looks up to you for leadership. We can't allow ourselves to revert to the concept of frontier justice. That might be the way things were done when you and Uncle Johnny were roaming the west like desperados, but those days are over."

Matt looked at him firmly. "I've met this Marshal Wells of yours. He's little more than a thug. I don't trust him to get things done. Johnny and I are going to find out who did this, and we're going to deal with it."

He turned and left the room, cigar in hand.

Hiram looked to his mother. "Things are going from bad to worse quickly, aren't they?"

"Everything will be all right," she said, "We're going to have to go ahead with my plan a little ahead of schedule, that's all."

He was a bit riled up now, enough that he was able to ignore the stiffness in his knees and back as he climbed the stairs. He intended to check on Dan and then have a hot bath and get some sleep.

The door to Dan's room was ajar, so he peeked in. Dan was awake and said, "Come on in, Father."

Dan's head was on a pillow, and the blankets pulled to his chest. He was in a nightshirt, and a lamp was burning low on a table.

"How are you feeling?" Matt said.

He shrugged and smiled. "Like I was shot. I'm okay, though. I'm filled with laudanum and feeling really fine right now. No pain at all. The doctor said as long as infection stays away, all I have to do is regain my strength and give the wound time to heal. He said it's amazing but there's no sign of infection at all."

Matt grinned. "Didn't think there would be."

Dan chuckled. "That was the most painful part of the whole thing. That really works?"

Matt nodded. "Your Uncle Johnny has used it on wounds again and again. It always prevents infection, as long as you bandage up the wound immediately afterward and keep it clean."

"I suppose he would know."

"Danny," Matt said. He was the only one who called him Danny. Matt pulled up a chair. "I really owe you an apology. You more than anyone else."

"Why?"

"If I had been taking an active hand around here, this wouldn't have happened. I would have taught you a lot more about how to handle yourself in a situation like that. And I should have been riding with you. I used to be a two-fisted sort of man. I don't know what happened to me."

"Father, there's no way you or anyone could have known they were waiting there for us. It was too dark."

Matt smiled. His son was young, and there was so much to learn. So much Matt wanted to teach him. Hiram was more Verna's son than his, and Matt had long given up on him. But not Dan.

Matt said, "I was out there today and saw where it happened. That ravine was the perfect place for an ambush. Almost too obvious. I know the land and have seen that ravine. If I had been with you, I would have had us split up and come up on that ravine quietly, from two different sides. Just in case there were men there waiting for us. At the very least, even if they didn't know you were coming, they might be using it to hold cattle and would have posted guards."

Dan nodded. He saw it. His father was right.

"Get some rest," Matt said. "Things are going to be different around here from now on. When you're feeling better, we'll talk."

"Yes, sir," Dan said.

Matt headed down the hall to his room. A lamp stood dark on a bed stand, and he lifted the globe and lighted the wick with his cigar. He was painfully tired and drawing a hot bath was starting to seem like too much work, and his bed looked too inviting. He set his cigar down in an ashtray, and then dropped face-down on the bed. *Aw, that feels good*, he thought. And that was the last thought he had as he fell into a sleep of exhaustion.

Mother had told Hiram to check on his father. See if he was asleep, and then report back to her. Hiram walked down the hallway carefully. He wore leather-soled shoes and the floors were hardwood, but oriental rugs with blazing reds and yellows were spread along the floor, and they served to muffle his footsteps.

The door to the bedroom was hanging ajar. Hiram decided to push the door open a little and step in. If his father was awake, then Hiram would have to invent a reason for being there, like he was just checking on him.

He tried the line in his head. "You looked so tired downstairs you had Mother and me worried."

No. Hiram was trying to be his own man. He didn't have to invoke Mother's name.

"You looked so tired downstairs you had me a little concerned. Thought I'd check on you."

Yes. That's what he would say, if his father should be awake.

He stepped in. The lamp by the bed was burning low and gave a sort of dim glow to the room. Father's cigar was smoldering away in an ash tray, and Father himself was lying face down on the bed, fully dressed.

"Father?" Hiram said quietly.

No response. Hiram could now see his father was breathing gently.

Hiram backed out of the room and headed downstairs. He found Mother in the study that Father liked to call his office. She was in a chair, facing the hearth, and a fire was crackling away. Both hands were resting in her lap, and in them was a glass of sherry. Though it wasn't cold, she had a shawl around her shoulders and was sitting as though she was chilled. Shoulders a little hunched. Arms drawn close to her side.

"Mother," Hiram said. "Are you well? You look like you have a chill."

Mother shook her head dismissively. "I'm fine. Got a little creak in my joints. Old age. It's to be expected."

Old age? Hiram was about to say she was not even fifty yet, but decided not to pursue it. Mother could grow angry when pushed, and he didn't want to deal with her temper. He was becoming his own man. He intended to one day rule this financial empire she was building, and he would do it on his own terms. But she was still here, still in power, and her temper was still something to be wary of.

Timmons stood off to one side. He was in a black suit and a checkered vest, and white gloves. His posture as erect as usual, and his hands were behind his back almost like he was in some sort of parade-rest pose.

Hiram was impressed with the air of power that seemed to radiate from Timmons. The man stood a few inches taller than Hiram, and even though he was as old as Father, he looked like he could lift Hiram with one arm. Timmons shoulders were broad, his neck thick, and his chest like a barrel. Hiram had seen miners built like this.

Hiram decided to get to the point. Mother didn't like needless small talk. He said, "Father's asleep."

"Good. Now is the time to act."

A small coffee table was in front of the sofa. Mother leaned over and set down her sherry, and rose to her feet. She stood slowly, placing each hand on an arm of the chair and pushing herself upright. Timmons began to reach out a hand to steady her, but she said, "I'm all right."

He withdrew the hand, as though she was a wild dog and might bite it.

"Hiram, we're going out to the secondary house tonight. I want you and Timmons to get Dan ready to travel. And be careful not to awaken your father. This is primary."

Hiram looked at her with surprise. The secondary house? Tonight? At this hour? But he allowed himself to do this for only a moment. To ask questions might mean to incur her wrath. You surely didn't want to do that. So he said, "Yes, Mother."

He started for the doorway and glanced to Timmons, who fell into place behind him.

The secondary house, as Mother called it, was a small house at the edge of the property that Mother had bought a few years ago. Considering the size of their property, the edge of it was a few miles away. Mother had kept the secondary house a secret from Father. Since the books were always kept by Hiram and Father never saw them, keeping the place a secret was fairly easy. The house wasn't even in her name. It was in the name of a dummy corporation Hiram had started for the both of them, for transactions they needed to make that they didn't want easily traced back to them.

Mother wanted this house because she said there might come a time when they would need to lie low for a while. It was actually a small two-level farmhouse. Timmons knew of it, and rode out once a week to see to its upkeep.

Hiram and Timmons climbed the stairs silently. The stairs were carpeted and their footsteps made no sound at all. They found Dan deeply asleep, which didn't surprise Hiram at all. Mother had told Timmons to double his laudanum dosage.

Hiram pulled the bed covers back and then gently tapped Dan's face. "Dan. Wake up."

Dan stirred, but nothing else.

"We can carry him. Just be careful not to open his wound."

With Timmons slipping his hands under Dan's shoulders and Hiram getting his feet, they got him downstairs. Mother had him deposited on the sofa in the parlor, and sent Timmons out to hitch a buggy.

After a time, Timmons returned, stepping in through one of French doors in the parlor. "The buggy is ready, ma'am."

He had pulled it out back so they wouldn't have to carry Dan as far. He and Hiram then lifted Dan and carried him outside. The buggy was a two-seater, so they deposited Dan in the back one and covered him with a blanket.

Mother said to Hiram, "Climb into the front seat and wait for me. You'll be driving. Timmons will be joining us once he finishes a task I have for him."

She stepped back into the house. Timmons followed her. She crossed the parlor and went through the doorway to the entryway, and stopped at the base of the stairs. Timmons followed her.

"Has the staff been sent away?"

He nodded. "There's no one else here."

"Good," she said, "Kill him."

Timmons nodded.

"Meet us out at the secondary house once you've finished. Don't let anyone see you leave."

"No, ma'am."

She laid a hand on his arm and met his gaze. A silent gesture of appreciation. He nodded.

She then stepped back into the parlor, and out to the buggy.

Timmons looked up to the railing at the top of the stairs. He reached into his jacket and pulled a five-inch long dagger that he always kept there. He then began to climb the stairs.

13

Sam Middleton said to the men lying on the saloon floor, "Now I want you boys to stay right where you are."

Wells was looking at him.

"Eyes on the floor. You look up at me, and I'll put a slug right in your head. I really am a good shot. Eyes straight down."

They did as they were told. They didn't know if Middleton would kill a man in cold blood, but he was a professional gambler and such men generally weren't known to be too strong in the ethics department. Wells decided he wasn't brave enough to find out, and neither were Bardeen or Marty.

Sam kept his pistol pointed toward Wells and his men while he backed up toward a door at the other side of the barroom. A door that opened into an alley. The patrons who had not fled the place formed a small crowd at the far end of the room. Sam threw a glance at them, and they were watching wide-eyed.

Sam stepped out the door and then ran down the alley and came out on the street behind the saloon. He saw a rider down the street, heading out of town. Looked like it was McCabe.

He ran down the boardwalk, revolver in hand. He needed to get to the livery, which was on the main street, but he didn't want anyone on the main street to see him. He knew Wells and Bardeen would be gunning for him, and Wells had other men who lurked about town, ready to be called into action. A call to them and there could be as many as seven or eight gunmen combing the town for him.

Middleton tried to estimate how far down he had to go to be parallel with the livery. He hoped he had guessed right, and turned into an alley. He could tell by the smell of horse droppings and hay that he had guessed right.

He holstered his gun and climbed up and over a fence, and then across the corral. Twice he stepped into piles that he knew wouldn't be pleasant, but he would worry about his boots later.

He could see light through gaps in the boards of the livery. He stepped in and found Peddie waiting for him, with two horses saddled.

An old man stood with her. Long white beard and bushy brows. A vest worn over an undershirt, and baggy trousers were tucked into riding boots. Old Harley Yates, who ran the livery.

Peddie ran to Middleton and threw her arms around him in a hug.

"I'm all right," he said. "We've got to ride."

The horses had saddle bags and a canteen each, but no bedrolls. Not even a rifle.

Old Harley said, "The young lady said the horses had to be saddled and in a hurry."

"Thanks, Harley," Middleton said. He reached into his vest and pulled out a silver dollar and handed it to him.

"A dollar? Thanks, Mister Middleton."

Old Harley was normally lucky to see a dime. A quarter was a large tip. Middleton always made a point to tip Old Harley excessively, because he never knew when he might need the old man's help. Middleton never stayed in a town unless he made preparations for a speedy exit. Such a thing had saved his life more than once.

He held Peddie's hand while she stepped up and into the saddle. Her dress and petticoats bunched out behind her. Sam then swung onto the back of the other horse.

Old Harley said, "Take good care of them horses."

Sam had bought the horses from Harley weeks ago, for just this type of occasion. He had bought one horse first, and then when he discovered Peddie was in town, he bought a second. He had left her behind before, but intended never to again.

"Harley," Sam said. "If they ask you, tell them what you need to, to keep them from getting rough with you. Tell them I took the horses at gunpoint if you have to."

They rode out back, into the corral. Old Harley walked along and opened a gate in the fence, and they rode out and through an alley, and to the street beyond. The one that ran behind the saloon.

Peddie had been raised on a small ranch. She could ride. Sam wouldn't have to worry about her.

"Okay," he said to her. "Let's ride."

Peddie said, "To Jessie's place."

"It might be better if we cleared the area entirely. Maybe we could get through the passes to Carson City before winter fully sets in."

She shook her head. "I have to make sure Jessie's okay, first. She was a friend of Belle's, too. In some ways, we were more family than friends. I have to make sure she's okay."

Sam smiled. Peddie was like a daughter to him and he could never say no to her, as much as he sometimes tried. "All right. Jessie's place it is."

Matt's dreams were filled with motion, like the sleep of exhaustion often is. He was back in the old days, riding across open grassland with Johnny at one side of him and Joe at the other. This was not the middle-aged Johnny with the long, graying pony tail. This was the young Johnny, before he had wintered with the Shoshone and began adopting some of their ways. His hair was a chestnut brown and short cropped, and his jaw covered with the fine whiskers of a young man. He wore a pair of Remingtons then, one at each side. This was long before there were pistols that took metallic cartridges, or railroad tracks beginning to crisscross the land. Before there were any towns between Missouri and California. No telegraph wires. Only an occasional Army fort or trading post.

They would laugh the carefree laugh of youth. They watched warily for any sign of Indians, because this was also before the Sioux or the Comanche had been rounded up and placed on reservations, and if they caught a lone traveler or even a small group, they would lift his hair and torture him to death. But Matt, Johnny and Joe were young. Despite the danger they found much to laugh about. They sat by the fire at night talking about dreams and looking off at the huge sky filled with stars or sometimes just sitting quietly listening to the coyotes howl in the distance.

And then his dreams took him today, covering miles with Johnny and Ben Harris. Following the tracks of rustlers who had shot his son.

Johnny now was graying, had the long Indian hair, and there were lines on his face. The Remingtons had been replaced with a Colt Peacemaker, a modern gun for the modern world. And Matt was no longer young and his joints creaked and he had fallen onto his bed like an old man on the verge of exhaustion.

He rolled over on the bed and stirred awake with a "Hmm?"

He didn't know what had awakened him. It was like he had heard something, but he didn't know what. He was alone in the room.

Then he realized he wasn't. Timmons was standing there. In his black suit and trousers, he had sort of been lost in the dim lighting of the room.

"Timmons?" Matt said.

Matt then realized Timmons was holding a knife in one hand.

"Timmons, what the hell?"

Timmons charged toward him, crossing the distance in two quick steps.

Matt was old. His joints creaked. He had been out of action for far too long. But the action he had seen in his days of riding with Johnny and Joe had left reflexes that were still there.

He raised one foot and caught Timmons in the chest. Matt's boots were still on and he kicked hard, enough that he figured he would leave a boot print on the man.

Timmons grunted and was pushed back a few feet. But he was tough and strong. Matt remembered old Moses Timmons. No one had filled the definition *bull of a man* better than him.

Timmons came at him again, this time raising the knife, but Matt doubled up and rolled off the bed in a backwards somersault, and the knife plunged into the mattress where Matt had been stretched out.

Too many years had passed since Matt had been involved in anything like this, however, and his backward roll was not as controlled as he would like it to have been. He landed on his feet but off-balance, and the roll continued without his say-so, and his back landed hard against the wall.

Matt didn't have time to catch his breath. Timmons leaped up and onto the bed with one running step, and then landed on the floor beside Matt and drove his knife toward him. Except Matt lunged to one side and the knife drove itself into the wall where Matt had been standing.

Timmons had driven the knife hard. It buried itself into a timber behind the plaster. He gave the knife a pull, but it didn't come out.

Matt drove a fist into Timmons' cheekbone. There was a smacking sound and Timmons' head was knocked a little to one side, but again it had been too long since Matt had done this sort of thing. His punch didn't have nearly what it would have back in the proverbial day, and on top of that he hurt his knuckles.

Timmons backhanded Matt across the face, knocking Matt against the wall and he fell to the floor.

Timmons gave up on the knife and decided to focus on Matt. Timmons had been expressionless until Matt punched him, but now his eyes were wide with fury.

He grabbed Matt by the back of his shirt and pulled him to his feet. He then wrapped both hands around Matt's neck, gripping hard. He apparently intended to choke the life out of him.

Matt drove a boot into Timmons' shin. No reaction. He did it again. Timmons grunted with the pain but held on. Matt knew he had only a few more seconds of Timmons' grip on this throat before he blacked out. He drove a knee up and into Timmons' groin. That hurt, and got the reaction Matt wanted. Timmons' grip relaxed, and Matt pulled away from him.

Matt stood a moment, rubbing his throat with his own hands, coughing and trying to catch his breath. Timmons stood bent over, enduring the aching pain that can come from a knee in the groin. Pain that reached up into his hips and down into his legs.

Matt then turned and tried to run for the door. Timmons dove across the bed and grabbed him. Matt was pulled to the floor and Timmons landed on top of him. Matt didn't wait for Timmons to try to reestablish his choke hold, and grabbed Timmons by the face and drove a thumb into his eye.

Timmons howled and Matt pushed him away. Matt struggled to his feet but Timmons grabbed him, wrapping his arms around him. Matt pushed him backward and they crashed into the night stand. Matt heard the lamp shatter on the floor.

"Hiram!" Matt called out. "Hiram!"

Matt couldn't wait for his son to get there. He snapped his head back and into Timmon's face. The cartilage in Timmons' nose cracked and he let go of Matt and again howled.

"Hiram!" Matt called out. There was no answer. Where was everyone?

Matt was in a fight for his life, he knew, and apparently there would be no one coming to help. He would have to deal with this himself. And this meant he was going to have to kill Timmons.

Matt ran, but not to the doorway. On the wall across from the bed was a hearth. There was one in every bedroom. It was to this that he ran.

Timmons was right behind him. Matt grabbed a poker and turned to face him. Timmons' eyes were crazed, and he grabbed for Matt.

Matt didn't swing the poker. He had been in enough fights in his younger years to know a swinging weapon like that can be parried. Instead, he thrust it straight out and into Timmons' face.

This was the third time for Timmons to howl, but this time it was serious. He staggered back, grabbing at his face with both hands. Matt thought he might have gotten the man's eye.

Matt then swung the poker hard at one knee, and Timmons was down. He then swung the poker hard once again, this time at Timmons' head. He made contact, and the sound reminded Matt of hitting a pumpkin with a stick.

Timmons didn't stop, though. In dime novels, a strike to the head induces instant unconsciousness. A writer's trick to render a character inactive for a little while. But in the real world, a strike to the head never has guaranteed results. A stream of blood immediately started through Timmons' hair and down his face, but he still managed to stagger to his feet and he lunged at Matt.

Matt jumped back to avoid the grabbing hands, and struck again with the poker. Caught him in the head again. Timmons was now on his hands and knees. Matt struck a third time, and a fourth. Timmons arms and legs went limp and he fell face forward to the floor.

Matt stood a moment catching his breath, iron poker in hand. It was only then that he realized flames were dancing at the other side of the room. He saw his bed was fully ablaze, fire rising almost to the ceiling.

His lamp, he realized. It had been knocked from the stand and shattered on the floor, but it had been burning.

He went to the doorway. "HIRAM!"

He looked back to the fire. A braided rug in front of his bed was already starting to burn, and the night stand was also in flames.

He needed something to attack the fire with. A blanket or something to beat at the flames. But the fire was spreading too fast. The lamp had been filled with oil that must have splattered when the lamp shattered.

He ran to Timmons and grabbed him by the hand, tossing aside the poker, and tried to pull him from the room. The man was heavy and Matt was not nearly as strong as he once was, but he pulled. The room was filling with smoke and he was starting to choke on it and it was burning his eyes, but he refused to give up and pulled the man from the room.

In the hallway, he rolled Timmons over onto his back and checked to see if he was breathing. He didn't seem to be. Matt forced open one eyelid—on the eye that hadn't taken the hit from the poker—and saw the pupil was fully dilated. The man was dead.

He let go of Timmons' and rose to his feet. He looked down the hallway and called out for Hiram again. Then for Verna. He got no answer.

He looked back to his room and it was alive with fire. The bed was now mostly gone, and the fire was dancing along one wall and the curtains on the bedroom window were burning. The entire braided rug was a small pool of fire. Black smoke was rolling out into the hallway and forming a cloud along the ceiling.

He knew what to do. He would run outside and get the men and they would put this thing out. Blankets to fight the fire with. Buckets of water. But first he had to get everyone out.

He ran to Dan's room, and found it empty. He blinked with puzzlement. Dan shouldn't be up and about. He then went to Verna's room, and then Hiram's. Both were deserted.

He ran downstairs, calling their names. He checked the parlor, the kitchen, his office. Every room was empty.

That was when it struck him. What had happened. Timmons trying to kill him. Everyone else gone, including Dan. At first Matt had thought Timmons had maybe gone out of his mind. But now he knew better. Verna and Hiram had ordered it. They were behind it.

He stood by the desk in his office feeling a chill run through him. Like icy fingers had reached out from the cold ground beneath the house and grabbed him.

His own wife and son had tried to have him killed. Timmons, the poor fool, had always been in love with Verna. Even when Matt was first meeting Verna. Back when she was seventeen. Timmons had been a young, love-struck fool then. He would have done anything for her, and apparently this hadn't changed.

Matt smelled smoke, and this brought him out of the reverie he realized he had fallen into. He stepped out to the entryway and saw it was filling with smoke. He glanced up to the railing at the top of the stairway, and saw the glow of flames. The fire had already spread out beyond his room.

What to do? Matt said to himself.

No. He was not going to allow himself to fall into indecision. He had allowed too much of this over the years. He had felt the man he once was waking up inside himself the moment Johnny arrived, and he was not going to allow himself to go back to what he had been becoming.

His wife had tried to kill him. If he was honest with himself, he supposed he had known she was cruel and cold, but he hadn't thought she was capable of murder. And he hadn't thought Hiram was, but if Verna said jump, the boy would ask how high. Anything she told him to do, he would. He had been that way his entire life.

Verna had ordered Timmons to kill Matt. Why, he could only speculate, but now was not the time for this. Now was the time for action. She had ordered Matt killed, and they had left, taking Dan with them.

He knew it would only be moments before someone outside saw flames from the window. He didn't want to be found here. Better to let Verna and Hiram think he had been killed, either by Timmons or the fire.

His gunbelt and hat were still on the desk where he had dropped them. He ran back to his office and grabbed his hat and planted it on his head, then buckled on his gunbelt. He checked the loads, old habit, then went to the rifle rack and grabbed a Winchester.

While he thought of it, he grabbed a second. In case Johnny wanted one. He intended to go find Johnny and they would tackle this situation together. He opened a drawer and grabbed a box of cartridges and stuffed it into one vest pocket, then on second thought grabbed a second box and stuffed into the other pocket.

He threw one last look at the room and said a mental good-bye. He expected to never see it again, even if this part of the house survived the fire.

His gaze fell on his desk, and he realized there was one more thing he was taking with him. He flipped open his box of cigars and grabbed a fistful. He had one more pocket in his vest, so he filled it with cigars.

He heard a knocking at the front door and someone calling. A man's voice. Probably the sentries from out front. He had to move now, before the men came running from the bunkhouse. He already heard a voice calling out, "Fire!"

He went to the French doors at the back of the room and opened one and stepped out back. He heard shouts from the bunkhouse. He had to move now. The roof of the house was roaring with fire and lighting up the yard, so with a rifle in each hand, he ran to the side of the stable that was hidden from the fire. It was late at night. Upstairs, after the fight with Timmons, he had noticed the grandfather clock gave the time as ten after ten. The last time he would ever hear that clock chime. He wouldn't miss it. The thing had been purchased by Verna, as had most of the furnishings.

As he hid in the shadows, men from the bunkhouse went running toward the main house. Ben Harris was among them, and so was Diego. Many of them were in undershirts and jeans with suspenders trailing. They had probably been in their bunks when the call went out. Had it been daylight, they would have seen him where he stood, but since it was night, they ran past the dark expanse of shadow and on to the house.

He waited until all of the men had run past, then he moved around to the front of the stable and the door. He lit a lantern and backed a horse out of its stall. The saddle he had used during the day was nowhere in sight so he grabbed another one that was draped over a saw horse. Once the saddle was in place, he tucked one rifle into the scabbard, then dropped both boxes of ammo into the saddle bags. He then led the horse to the door.

A canteen was hanging from a nail in the wall, so he grabbed it. He found it was empty, but he would fill it someplace else. He didn't want to be found on the property. Let Verna and Hiram think he was dead. It would give him time to figure out what to do.

Once he had the horse outside the stable, he led it away from the house, to the open grassy hills behind the bunkhouse.

He led the horse until he felt he was a safe distance, and then swung into the saddle. The moonlight was bright enough so he felt he could ride safely. Johnny was either still in Greenville, or camped outside town somewhere. Should be easy enough to find.

He sat in the saddle and allowed himself one last gaze back at the house. It was now fully ablaze, lighting up the night like a huge torch. He hoped none of the men got themselves hurt trying to put it out.

He then turned his horse and started away, toward town.

14

Matt had been too many years out of the game. When you live like he and his brothers had back in the day, you sort of develop a mentality of warfare. But he hadn't been shot at since he was twenty-five. Until the fight with Timmons tonight, he hadn't been in a life-or-death struggle of any kind since then. And he hadn't killed a man.

Now, as he sat in the saddle in the very early hours of the morning, looking down at the darkened town, he found himself having to force himself to think.

He had expected to ride through the grassy hills outside of town looking for a campfire. Such things are usually visible from a distance. There was a good chance any campfire out there would belong to Johnny. But there were no campfires. He hadn't expected Johnny to remain in town, but where else could he be? Matt surely didn't want to ride down into town, because if he intended Verna and Hiram to think he was dead, it would be better if no one saw him.

And yet, he didn't know what to do.

"All right," he said out loud. "Think. You gotta think."

He realized that even though he was the older brother, he had always allowed himself to take a sort of second seat to Johnny and Joe in their younger years. Both of his brothers had much more experience as frontiersmen and at warfare, and they seemed to even gravitate toward it. But this didn't mean Matt wasn't always observing them, and learning. Johnny, especially, seemed to have a natural way of thinking strategically in situations like this. Something that was never evident in their farm boy days back in Pennsylvania, but when they came west this ability seemed to manifest itself. Johnny also seemed to have natural leadership abilities. Matt was always the better speaker. To him it was almost showmanship. But when a leader was needed, men seemed to naturally be drawn to Johnny. It was Matt who married Frank McCarty's daughter and eventually inherited the ranch, but when Matt and his brothers first rode into the area, it was Johnny who Old Man McCarty had made his ramrod.

All right, he said to himself. What would Johnny or Joe do in this situation? After all, this really wasn't much different than chess, if you separated yourself from the life-and-death aspects of it all.

It occurred to him that finding Johnny should not be his first priority. Johnny would find him. His first priority was in town. After all, Matt had one more son. His oldest, Tom.

Tom had walked away from the family after an argument with Matt, but that argument had been about how Matt allowed Verna and Hiram to run the ranch, and the things they were doing. The things they were allowing to happen in town. The cruel way they treated the miners. The way they forced people off of their land in order to expand their empire. The things Matt had been turning a blind eye toward.

The main issue at the moment with Verna and Hiram was a canyon outside of town. Hiram's mining engineers believed a large vein of gold ore cut into the walls of that canyon, but that canyon had belonged to a man by the name of Bernard Swan. He was a gentleman rancher who ran a small herd in the canyon. The canyon floor was large and grassy, and Swan had moved in more than twenty years ago and took the land as his. He had never filed the proper claim, and he had died three years ago, but Matt believed a legal argument could be made that, due to squatter's rights, the land belonged to his heirs.

Matt remembered Swan well. A man of maybe sixty by the time he died, his hair had gone white prematurely and he had a barrel chest and bowed legs and sort of swayed from side to side as he walked, but when he sat a horse he moved like he and the horse were one. Never quite a gunhawk like Johnny or Joe, he was still a crack shot with a pistol or a rifle. There had always been something dignified about Swan. He pronounced his name *Ber*nard, not Ber*nard*.

Matt didn't know the whole story, as Swan had been a private man. Matt got to town seldom and took little stock in gossip. But the story went that Swan had taken some sort of liking to a saloon woman in town, and before anyone knew it, had married the woman and she gave him a child.

Hiram and Verna would never have tried to bully Bernard Swan from that canyon. But the woman and the child were still there, trying to hang onto the land. Hiram and Verna wanted that canyon, and they had no intention of paying for land they could simply take.

They had acquired a small farm at the edge of the McCabe Ranch a few years ago. They probably didn't know Matt was aware of this. He knew Timmons had been taking a buggy out there once a week to keep the place up. Matt had no idea why they would want the place, but he knew they had muscled the owner off of it, giving him the choice of taking their offer of less than half the going rate per acre, or being driven off. Like with the Swan canyon, the farmer had never formally filed a claim. An argument could have been made in favor of squatter's rights, but Verna and Hiram could afford a lot of legal help, and the farmer none.

Verna and Hiram were bullies. Something Matt had never wanted to see and had ignored for a long time. The scotch had helped him do that. And he now saw they were potential murderers, too. If Verna was willing to have Timmons try to kill her own husband, if Hiram could go along with having his own father killed, then what would stop them from doing the same to Bernard Swan's widow and daughter?

And what would stop them from hurting Tom and his family? There was nothing to gain financially from this, as Tom was a Methodist minister and lived in a little parsonage near the church in town. But Tom still legally owned a portion of the ranch and the other family businesses. Twenty percent. And that was a lot of money, considering the vast holdings that were now in the McCabe family. If Matt should continue to let Verna and Hiram believe he was dead—and the idea had its appeal, because it would allow Matt to just ride away from all of this—then the family fortune would be divided four ways instead of five. Tom would own twenty-five percent. As long as he was alive.

Money meant a lot to Verna and Hiram, but apparently life did not. At least, the lives of others. Matt had to get into town and warn Tom and get him and his family out of there.

The task seemed a little daunting to him, at first. To get into town without being seen. But he had ridden with Johnny and Joe and knew how to do this sort of thing, even though he might be a little rusty at it. He was a McCabe. Time to start acting like one.

With a rifle held across the front of the saddle and another one in the scabbard, he started his horse down the hill toward the darkened town below.

Tom McCabe drifted upward to consciousness. Someone was knocking on the front door downstairs.

What time was it? A lamp on a table at the bedside was burning low, and he could see the clock on the mantel across the room. Twenty after two?

He blinked the sleep from his eyes and sat up in bed. He was in his long-handled underwear, so he grabbed his trousers and pulled them on and stepped into slippers.

The knocking continued. A banging, actually. Like someone was taking their fist to the door, hammering at it with urgency.

Tom was a minister, pastor of the Methodist church in town. He was young, only twenty-four, but he seemed to be good at his job and the parishioners trusted him and often turned to him in times of need. It wasn't unusual for one of them to come calling in the night, needing help of one kind or another. But the rapping on the door sounded almost frantic.

Lettie was stirring, her head on the pillow beside the one he had been using. Her hair was dark and tied back in a long braid.

"Tom?" she said. "What is it?"

"Someone's at the door. I'll go see who it is. Go back to sleep."

"Well, if you need anything, come get me. If you need me to put coffee on, or anything."

She was used to callers at odd hours, too. She was a minister's wife.

Tom grabbed a lantern and struck a match to light it, and stepped out into the hallway and down the stairs. He hoped the pounding on the door wouldn't wake up the children.

"All right!" he called, as he stepped down to the small entryway. "I'm coming! Hold on!"

He was holding the lantern in his right hand. He shifted it to his left, then slid the bolt on the door back and opened it.

A man stood there, in the lantern light. About as tall as Tom, but thinner. Scraggly whiskers along a narrow jaw, and a face that reminded him of a shark. Not that he had ever seen a shark, but he had read about them and had a vivid imagination. Pinned to the man's vest was a tin star. Tom had met the man before.

"Marshal Wells," he said, a little surprised.

Wells grinned. Like a shark. "I been pounding on this door for five minutes."

"Well, I'm sorry. But it's late. I was sleeping."

"I'm looking for your father."

Tom blinked with surprise. "My father?"

"Yeah. You seen him?"

Tom shook his head. "My father very seldom comes here, I'm afraid. I never go out to the ranch anymore. I haven't seen him, I regret to say, in months."

Wells looked at him, nodding and smiling the smile that wasn't really a smile. He then raised a hand to the door and gave it a push, knocking Tom back a little.

"Hey," Tom said. "Now see here."

Wells stepped in. "Now you see here, Father. We're gonna search this place."

"I'm a man of the cloth."

"Be that as it may. I don't really trust men of the cloth. I put you in about the same class as gamblers and politicians."

Wells pushed past him, and was followed by another man, also wearing a badge. This man carried a scattergun.

Wells drew his pistol, and swung the door shut. "Bardeen, you search upstairs. I'm gonna search the downstairs."

Tom was furious. "You stay away from my family."

He started forward, fully intending to intercept the one called Bardeen but Wells placed the flat of his hand on Tom's chest and pushed him back.

Wells looked at him, the grin back in place. Tom realized Wells was laughing at him. Wells said, "The nephew of the great gunfighter, huh? You sure don't look like much."

Tom reached up and knocked the hand away and went to push past Wells, but Wells drove a fist into Tom's stomach. Tom doubled over and fell backward, landing on the floor.

Tom was as tall as Wells and was better muscled. But he did not advocate violence. When he was growing up, he had been taught how to shoot a gun by his father, but he had not fired one in years and had no guns in his house. He had never been in a fistfight.

Wells grabbed Tom by one arm and pulled him to his feet.

"Come on," Wells said. "Let's search this house."

Wells kept his grip on Tom's arm, and pulled him into the parlor.

Wells said, "Turn up a lamp."

Tom went to a lamp mounted on one wall. It was burning but low. Lamps were often left this way, so you could lighten a room just by turning one up and not have to go through the rigmarole of lighting one.

The room was simply furnished. A sofa, a couple of chairs. A small roll-top desk in one corner. A fireplace built into the inner wall. Tom and Wells were the only two in the room.

"All right. What's through that doorway? The kitchen?"

Tom nodded.

"Well, don't just stand there. Let's move."

They went into the kitchen and from there to the dining room, completing a circuit that brought them back to the entryway as Lettie was coming down the stairs with their young daughter. Lettie's eyes were wide with a combination of fright and outrage. She was in her nightgown and hadn't even been allowed to grab a robe. Mercy was five, and in a robe and clutching a stuffed bear. She looked serious and more alarmed than afraid.

"Leave them alone," Tom said.

Once Lettie touched down on the entryway, she hurried to Tom and he took her in his arms. Tom then scooped Mercy up and held her with one forearm under her butt and she clung to him.

Wells said, "Did you see anything upstairs?"

Bardeen shook his head. "He ain't here."

"Yet," Wells said. "Mister McCabe said to watch for him. Said he's likely to show up here."

"Mister McCabe?" Tom said. "Hiram sent you here?"

"Ain't none of your concern."

"What would you want with my father? What's happened?"

"Ain't none of your concern."

Bardeen said, "So, what're we gonna do?"

Wells looked at him with a little impatience. "We're gonna do like we was told. We're gonna stay right here and wait for him."

Tom said, "I want you men out of my house."

They ignored him. They didn't seem to feel that Tom presented any more threat than a fly buzzing around, and he was afraid they were right.

Wells said, "Let's move everyone into the parlor. Easier to keep track of 'em."

Tom reluctantly started for the parlor, followed by Lettie and Mercy.

At the doorway into the parlor, Bardeen said to Lettie, "You know, you're a good looking woman, for a preacher's wife. You'd actually stand up against them women down at the saloon."

Tom said, "Don't talk to my wife."

"What you need," Bardeen said, reaching a hand to her chin, "is a real man. Not some preacher."

Tom charged at him and drove a fist at him. Tom had been taught how to fight by his father, but he was too many years removed from it. His knuckles connected with Bardeen's cheekbone, but he didn't make his fist tight and didn't connect with the flat of his fist, but the side. Something cracked in the knuckle of his little finger. Bardeen's head was knocked back a little, but Tom stood grabbing his hand with pain.

Bardeen gripped his scattergun with both hands and swung the stock into Tom's face. Tom's legs were knocked out from under him and he landed hard on the floor.

"Tom!" Lettie screamed.

Mercy stood staring silently with wide eyes.

Tom was on the floor, propping himself up on one elbow. The gunstock had caught him in the side of the face, which had now gone numb. Blood was streaming from his mouth, and he couldn't move his jaw.

Lettie said to them, "Leave him alone."

Wells said, "We'll leave him alone. If you do what you're told."

From behind Wells came the unmistakable sound of metal clicking against metal. A gun being cocked. He turned enough so with his side vision he could see the bore of a pistol two feet from his head.

Matt McCabe was holding the pistol. "You've harassed my family enough. Drop your guns or I'll drop you both."

Wells let his pistol drop to the floor, then he turned suddenly and knocked Matt's pistol away.

Matt had been away from this sort of thing for a long time, but the man he used to be was coming back quickly to him tonight.

Matt stepped into Wells and drove his elbow into the man's nose. Matt then drove a fist into his stomach, and Wells doubled over.

Bardeen said, "Stop right there, McCabe. You wouldn't want a bullet to catch the little lady, wouldn't you?"

Matt saw Bardeen had grabbed Lettie and was holding her in front of him.

Matt hesitated. To drop the pistol would be to throw away any leverage he had and return control of the board to the two thugs. But if he tried to take a shot at the one holding Lettie, then Lettie could very well be shot.

"Drop that gun, McCabe," Bardeen said, aiming a pistol at Mercy, "or the little girl gets it right between the eyes."

Wells was straightening, catching his breath. He snatched the pistol from the floor and stepped around so he could have his gun on Matt.

That was when Johnny stepped in from the kitchen doorway, his pistol in his hand. Cocked and aimed at Bardeen.

"Johnny," Matt said. He hadn't known Johnny was here, and yet wasn't all that surprised.

Wells was down on one knee, still hurting from the punch to the gut.

Wells said, "Drop your guns, both of you, or I ain't gonna be able to stop my deputy from killing that little girl. Be a cryin' shame, wouldn't it?"

Johnny's arm was fully extended, his gun aimed toward Bardeen. "Don't drop your gun, Matt."

"Drop that gun," Wells said. "I ain't gonna say it again."

"Johnny," Matt said. "We can't take the chance."

Johnny said, "Matt, quit you're yammering. I'm trying to draw a bead."

Matt's mouth twitched into a sudden small grin. A conversation they had had before more than once, back in the day. This meant Johnny was about to attempt one of those impossible shots only he could make. Matt had never seen him miss.

"Lettie, Mercy," Matt said. "Close your eyes."

Both of them looked at him with puzzlement.

"Do like I say. Close your eyes."

They both did.

Bardeen was looking at Matt with a little confusion. Then at Johnny.

Matt said, "Drop your gun. Last chance."

Bardeen said, "I don't see what..."

Johnny's gun fired. Loud, almost deafening in the small room. Bardeen's head was snapped back, blood splattering against the wallpaper. His gun went off, but as he was being knocked back by Johnny's shot, and his own bullet went into a floorboard.

Lettie screamed and pulled free, and half leaped, half fell to Mercy, and scooped her up.

Tom was now on his knees, blood flowing from his mouth. One eye was swelling shut.

Matt's ears were ringing from the gunshot. Even still, he aimed his pistol back at Wells. "Now, I'm not the shot my brother is, but you know I can't miss from this distance."

Wells stared at him. But he said nothing. He let his pistol fall to the floor again.

Behind the house was an attached barn, and there Matt found a length of rope, and they left Wells tied up on the kitchen floor. Bound securely. Ankles and wrists. A bandana was tied around his mouth.

Johnny knelt down beside him, and drew his gun and poked the barrel into the marshal's cheek. "You picked the wrong family to try to bully. You're lucky you're alive. You know that?"

Wells was staring at him, truly afraid. He nodded.

"The good minister is above shooting a man. I'm not. Stay away from me and mine."

Wells nodded again.

Tom was in a chair in the parlor. The side of his face was bruising up and the eye had swollen shut, but the bleeding in his mouth had stopped.

He said to Matt, "Father. How did you know to come here?"

"There are things going on. I'll tell you all later."

Johnny appeared in the doorway from the kitchen.

Tom said to him, "I'm grateful to you. Please don't think I'm not. But that was an awful chance you took with my daughter's life."

Johnny said, "No chance at all. To surrender to those men would have probably gotten her killed anyway, along with you and your wife. After they were done with her."

Johnny looked to Lettie. "We've got to move. We all have to be out of here. How soon can you have some clothes packed?"

She shrugged. She hadn't been expecting this. "Half an hour?"

"Make it ten minutes."

Tom said, "I don't understand. You scared him right good. They shouldn't bother us again."

Johnny shook his head. "He's scared now. But give him some time, and that'll fade. And it'll be replaced by pure, all-out hate. And don't forget, he's the law in this town."

Matt said, "He, and your mother and brother."

Tom was truly confused now. "Mother and Hiram? What's going on?"

"We'll fill you in later. Right now, we have to move."

Johnny said, "What happened tonight, it's just the beginning. It's going to get ugly around here. A sort of ugly you can't even imagine. We have to get you and your family out of here."

"Ten minutes," Lettie said.

She ran up the stairs to the bedrooms.

Matt walked over to Johnny. "I'm glad we both think alike. I don't know what I would have done here if you hadn't shown up."

Johnny said, "I'm just glad you're alive. I had made camp outside of town but then I saw the glow of the fire off in the distance, so I rode to find out what was going on. I heard the men at your place talking. They're saying you might have died in the fire."

Tom said, "What fire?"

"But they found only one body and they couldn't identify it. I made sure they didn't see me, but the marshal was there and I heard him say he was heading here to wait for you, just in case that body they found wasn't yours."

Tom said again, "What fire?"

"Come on," Matt said. "Let's get you on your feet. We have some miles to cover."

"Where are we going?"

"Away from here."

Tom had three horses in the barn. Two were saddle horses. When he needed to visit a parishioner outside of town, he often went on horseback. He had a second saddle horse also, and sometimes took Lettie and Mercy for rides through the open hills outside of town. The third horse was a little larger, and used to pull a buggy.

Three horses and a buggy would be a little much on a preacher's salary, but as partial owner of the McCabe fortune, he had a hefty savings account. He very seldom accessed the money because for a preacher to be wealthy seemed somehow contradictory to the message he was trying to teach. But he had used a little of the money to buy the horses and the carriage.

"We can't take the buggy," Matt said. "It'll slow us down too much."

Johnny looked at his brother. "You speak like you have a destination in mind."

Matt nodded. "We can't outrun 'em. Not if they want to catch us. Not with Lettie and Mercy along. But there's a place that's easy to defend, and it's not far from here. Maybe an hour's ride. Ever hear of Swan's Canyon?"

Johnny shook his head.

But Matt nodded. "Yeah, you have. We herded some wild mustangs there, once. Back when you were ramrod of the ranch I was just a young, stupid cowhand chasing Verna. But it wasn't called Swan's Canyon, back then."

"I think I remember the place. A box canyon, if I remember right. Sheer, rock walls, but mostly grass at the floor. Maybe a couple hundred acres."

Matt nodded. "That's the place."

Mercy was with them. She said, "Mister, are you really the real Johnny McCabe?"

Johnny smiled at the question. "I guess I'm as real as I can be."

"Are you really my uncle?"

Johnny nodded. "I suppose I am. One time removed, or so, I suppose."

"Are you really a gunhawk?"

Tom said, "Mercy. Where did you hear a word like that?"

She said, "At Sunday School."

Tom shook his head with defeat.

Johnny said, "That's the label they put on me. So's your grandfather."

Mercy looked at her grandfather as though she was seeing him for the first time. "Really?"

But Matt shook his head. "No, honey. Maybe I used to be something of a gunhawk at one time, but that was long ago."

"I don't know," Johnny said. "From what I've seen the past couple of days, I think maybe we're witnessing the return of the that man. The return of the gunhawk."

Matt said, "May be. You never know, I suppose."

"Come on," Johnny said. "Let's get the horses ready."

Tom could ride a horse well, even as beaten up as he was. Lettie had been raised on a farm and never sat on a horse until she met Tom, but she was a fair rider. Mercy sat behind her, hanging onto her mother. Her eyes were wide and serious, and her stuffed bear was tucked under one arm. The third horse was now wearing the harness it normally did when it pulled the buggy. Pillow cases stuffed with clothing and some canned food were tied to the harness, forming a makeshift pack. Tom was going to lead the animal.

Matt said, "You remember the way to that canyon?"

Johnny nodded. "I haven't thought about it in many a year, but I think I do."

"You ride lead, then. There's a trail that takes you there in a roundabout sort of way, but I think we should ride overland. There's some rocky ground betwixt here and there. It might make it harder for them to follow us. And we should ride single file, so they won't know how many riders there are with us. Maybe make 'em a little less than certain."

Matt had been speaking with confidence. Not the sort of weak, uncertainty Johnny had heard in his voice a couple of days ago. And Matt's firm baritone seemed to be back.

Johnny nodded at his brother. "Welcome back, Matt."

PART TWO

The Canyon

15

They rode single-file. Johnny was in the lead, with one of Matt's Winchesters across the front of his saddle. Behind him were Lettie and Mercy, followed by Tom and the pack horse. Matt was bringing up the rear. He also rode with a rifle across the saddle.

They kept their horses to a walk, and the sun rose gently as they moved along. The grass was brown and stood to their stirrups. The sky overhead was blue and with only a light wisp of a cloud hanging motionless.

"It's such a beautiful morning," Lettie looked back to say to Tom. "Here we are, driven from our home, with only what we can carry on these horses, and the lawmen back in Greenville possibly coming after us. Last night we barely avoided being brutalized in our own home, and a man was shot and killed and his blood is still splattered all over the living room wall. And yet, the sun rises on a new day, like the old one never happened."

Tom said, with open bitterness, "Must be a lesson in there somewhere. Something I could make a sermon out of. But I can't seem to find it."

At the top of a low hill, Johnny stopped and looked back for any sign they were being followed.

Lettie's horse ambled past him, followed by Tom, then Matt reined up.

Matt said, "You think there's anyone back there?"

"Not that I can tell. Maybe we lost them in those rocks."

About a mile out of town, the country got rocky, a sort of spill-over from the rocky ledge the McCabe mine had been cut through. Johnny and the others had picked their way through it by moonlight. Matt had figured they would be less likely to leave readable tracks there.

Matt turned in the saddle and looked at their back trail. "We haven't lost them for good, though. They'll be coming."

They continued along.

By normal riding standards, the canyon was about two hours out of Greenville, but they had lost time finding their way through the rocky area, moving slowly so a horse wouldn't stumble. And they had been riding slowly since, keeping the horses mostly to no more than a fast walk, to make it easier on Lettie and Mercy.

Johnny figured they were three hours out of Greenville now, and if he remembered the lay of the land correctly, the canyon was still an hour away.

After a time, the hills began to grow higher and more distinct, with rocky outcroppings. The land was rising, and Johnny knew they would soon be in the foothills to the Sierras.

They stopped to rest the horses. Mercy stood with her mother, her stuffed bear held tightly in one arm. She was yawning. She had been awake most of the night.

Matt pulled two cigars from his pocket and handed one to Johnny. Matt said, "All that remains from my life that was. Brazilian cigars. You could buy a horse for the cost of three boxes of these."

Johnny bit off the end of the cigar and spit it into the grass, then struck a match and brought it to the front of the cigar and puffed it to life.

Johnny shook his head with supreme approval. "That's one mighty fine cigar."

"Came with too high a price, though. And I'm not talking about the money."

Johnny nodded his head. He caught Matt's meaning.

Johnny said, "From all the talk at the dinner table the other night, they all seem to believe a rich vein of ore stretches from the McCabe mine into one wall of the canyon."

Matt nodded. "That's what I've heard."

"Who'd you hear it from?"

Matt shrugged, "Verna and Hiram talked about it. I'm no miner. I know nothing about rocks and gold, and such."

They mounted up and continued on. As they rode, Johnny would draw a puff of smoke from his cigar, and with his eyes he would scan the land ahead of them and all around, and toss an occasional glance behind them. And he thought about that canyon. The layout of it. He was having to draw on memories more than twenty years old, but he had a good eye for the detail of the land around him, and a good memory for such things.

If he remembered right, it was a box canyon with sheer walls made of mostly rock. Walls that were impossible to climb from the inside or the outside. The pass into it was flat with no obstacles, but was narrow. No more than ten feet at the widest. The floor of the canyon was large and grassy. Two hundred acres Matt had said, and that went along with Johnny's memories of the place. Johnny remembered an occasional juniper attached to the walls, and in a few places, a stunted tree.

He remembered a ledge that was maybe halfway down the highest wall, putting it at maybe twenty feet above the canyon floor and at least as much from the rim. The ledge was sturdy, and ran flat for a while and then gradually sloped downward to meet the floor of the canyon. You could actually ride a horse up and onto it. Johnny and Matt had done this so they could look down at the herd of mustangs they had corralled below. Johnny remembered thinking if the canyon had been further from the ranch, they could have used that ledge to make a camp.

Johnny looked down at the Winchester he was holding. It was a carbine and held twelve shots. Forty-four caliber. A fine weapon, but it had a lot of moving parts and could jam. Johnny was old-school when it came to weapons. A single-shot rifle like the Sharps in his saddle couldn't really jam. His Sharps had been a cap-and-ball originally, but had been retooled to take metallic cartridges. A gunsmith in Helena had hacked off the cap lock and replaced it with the more modern mechanism. It could now be reloaded in five seconds, if you hurried, and had much more range than a Winchester.

The sun climbed higher in the sky and the chill of the night began to fade. Johnny pulled off his jacket and stuffed it into a saddle bag. He was in a flannel shirt and a buckskin vest, which would suffice.

The cliffs ahead were rocky, and Johnny knew they were getting into the ridge country where they would find the canyon. However, travelling overland it was sometimes kind of hard to come out specifically where you wanted.

Matt rode up beside him. "I think it's a little south of here. The trail from town goes right up to it, but travelling this way is sometimes requires a little more guesswork."

They followed the ridges south. Johnny heard Mercy saying, "When're we gonna get there?" And Lettie hushing her.

Johnny said, "It's been a long ride for a little girl."

Matt nodded and raised his brows. "It's been a long night for all of us, I think."

Then there was a gap in the rocks, which indicated they had arrived. Johnny saw a trail worn through the grass that wound its way from the gap, away toward the south and east.

Johnny reined up and the others did so too, and Matt again rode up to sit alongside him.

Johnny said, "I don't remember a trail being here before."

Matt said, "Not long after you moved north, a man named Swan set up in there and ran a small ranch. He's gone, but the ranch is still there, run by his widow. She comes to town. Folks from town ride out. I've been there a couple of times, before her husband died. Verna and Matt know all about it. Obviously."

"Which means someone could have guessed we might be bound this way, if they know the lay of the land and know we couldn't travel fast but needed a place that's well-fortified."

Matt nodded. His cigar was down to a stub. A long, flat outcropping of rock stretched out beside them, and Matt tossed the stub onto it. No need to risk starting a grass fire.

He said, "You think you and I should go in first?"

Johnny nodded.

Johnny nudged Thunder to take a few backsteps, to where Tom sat in the saddle. Johnny held the Winchester out to him and said, "You know how to use it?"

Matt said, "All my boys do. Even Hiram. I saw to it."

Tom took the rifle, and then held it out before him, looking at it as though he was looking at a gun for the first time.

He said, "I made a vow before God that I would never take a life."

Johnny was about to say a lot of good that did him when Wells and Bardeen pushed their way into his house. But he didn't. Instead he turned Thunder toward the gap that would lead into the canyon.

The gap was actually a winding pathway through abutments of rock. Johnny pulled his pistol and quickly checked the loads. Matt did the same. Johnny didn't like the idea of openly riding into someone's gunsights, but there was no other way to enter this canyon.

Matt said, "I should go first."

Johnny shook his head, at first thinking Matt was showing some sort of unnecessary bravado.

But Matt said, "You're the better shot. One of them gets me, you have a lot better chance of getting them than I would if one of them got you."

Johnny couldn't help but give a rueful smile. This was the kind of thing the Matt of old would have said. Johnny brought Thunder to a stop and let Matt ride on past him.

After they had ridden maybe five hundred feet, the narrow pass began to widen, and there were rounded rocks to either side. As they rode past one boulder the size of a wood shed, Johnny heard a gun cock from behind them. A man had been there, waiting for them, stepping around the rock to come out behind them.

The man said, "You make this too easy."

16

"You make this too easy," the man said. "I would have expected more from a titan such as yourself."

Johnny recognized the voice, and let out a small sigh of relief. He looked over his shoulder to see Sam Middleton standing by the rock, pistol in hand.

Matt said, "Huh? Did he just call you a titan?"

But Johnny said to the man, "You're about the last person I would have expected to see out here."

Middleton eased back the hammer and returned the gun to his holster. "I could say likewise."

Matt said, "I take it you know this man."

Johnny said, "Sam Middleton. Card shark."

Sam said, "Card shark, cad, and general ne'er do well, at your service." Sam gave a sweeping, theatrical bow.

Matt glanced at Johnny and gave a *what the hell?* look. But Johnny was grinning. As little as he actually trusted this man, he did owe him.

Johnny said, "We have some people with us. A man, a woman and a child. They're waiting outside the canyon for us."

"Then, by all means, go get them and we can ride up to the house."

When Johnny returned with Tom, Lettie and Mercy, Sam Middleton was now on a horse. It was an appaloosa with one white stocking. It was a little smallish, maybe a little more than fourteen hands. Johnny figured it had probably been a mustang caught and saddle broke.

A man stood by the rock. He was holding a Winchester in his hands, and Johnny figured him to be Apache by the look to his face. High cheekbones, darker skin tone. But his hair was cropped short and a sombrero was perched on his head, and he was wearing cowhand clothes. Except for the revolver at his side that was hanging low and tied down. Only a fool would wear a gun like that for show. This man was a gunhawk.

Sam said, "Allow me to introduce Wolf. He'll watch the pass. We always have someone watching it. Now, if you'll follow me..."

And with a theatrical wave of his hand that meant, *come along this way,* he started across the canyon toward the north wall.

This place was about how Johnny remembered it. There had been a little tree growth in spots, mostly near the walls, and a few scattered alders and oaks along a stream that ran through the center. Johnny had forgotten about the stream. Too many years away, he figured. It began at a crack in the wall at the eastern side of the canyon and trickled its way to a small pond toward the center. Now the trees were taller, and there were more of them.

Cattle were in random spots throughout the canyon, grazing contentedly like they had all the time in the world. Which, Johnny supposed, they did. He estimated possibly three hundred head in total. Not enough for a hugely prosperous ranch. At his own ranch in Montana, he and his boys ran close to two thousand head. He figured Matt ran more than triple that.

Against the northern wall of the canyon was the section of flat ledge Johnny remembered. Except now a house and barn were there. The house was a single-level, with white adobe walls and a roof that was tiled in the manner Johnny had seen Mexicans do. The barn wall was made of boards nailed into place upright, and had a peaked roof. The boards looked gray and weathered. A corral stood behind the barn, and a buckboard waited near the house.

In the corral, a black mare with three white stockings pranced about. Once as they were riding in, she reared up and pawed at the air with her front hooves, like she was feeling a little stir crazy and wanted to run. There were four others, all geldings. Three bays and another appaloosa.

A stone wall had been built along the edge of the ledge. It reminded Johnny of the old stone walls that criss-crossed their way through the woods and pastures of the northeast. In the colonial days, farmers had built their fences this way, so every scrap of wood could be used either for building or for burning. This wall stretched more than two hundred feet. Johnny figured every rock had been hauled in here by wagon and meticulously laid into place. This told Johnny two things. The man who had built this place was not afraid of hard work, and he knew how to fortify a position.

As they rode toward the house, Johnny fixed his eyes on the canyon rim.

"Is there any way up there?"

Middleton shook his head. "Not that I've found. Jessica, Mrs. Swan, says there's not. Not from outside the canyon, either."

The house had a small porch attached to the front of it, and a sloping overhang to serve as a roof. As they approached, a woman stepped out, a Winchester in her hands.

Middleton reined up, and the others followed suit. He said, "Everyone, allow me to introduce Jessica Swan."

Johnny reached up to touch the tip of his brim, and as he did so his eyes met hers and he found himself freezing in mid-motion. She stuck him as one of the most incredible-looking women he had ever seen. Something about the curve of her cheekbones made the breath want to catch in his chest. Her eyes were the color of the sky, and her hair was dark. Not quite the color of coffee. She was not in any way glamorous. She was dressed for ranch work, and her hair was pulled back into a bun, and her face was a little flushed. Probably had been working in front of a hot stove, Johnny figured. And yet he would have challenged any woman in a ball gown to keep up with her.

Her eyes were fixed on Johnny, and the two simply stared at each other for a moment. Johnny sitting in the saddle, and the woman standing on the porch with the rifle in her hands, the barrel aimed down and away.

Thunder didn't move. The horse had learned over the years if Johnny became stock still, the horse was to accommodate. He probably figured Johnny was about to begin shooting at something. But Johnny simply stared at the beauty standing on the porch before him.

Middleton caught the silent exchange, and grinned a bit. "Jessie, allow me to introduce the legendary Johnny McCabe."

Johnny tossed him a sidelong glance. He wished Middleton hadn't put it that way.

But she raised a brow and one corner of her mouth quirked into a little half smile. A smile that made something in his chest grow warm.

She said, "The legend himself. Here in the flesh."

Johnny said, "And my brother Matt."

She looked at Matt, and a less than friendly tone came into her voice, "I know who you are. What do you want here?"

Matt touched the brim of his hat, and said, "Refuge, ma'am."

Time for her brow to rise again, and she looked at Middleton.

He said, "I'll vouch for them all, Jessie."

She hesitated a moment. Johnny figured she was weighing the whole thing in her mind. After all, she probably saw Matt as evil. As the one trying to force her out of her home. But for some reason the word of this arrogant card shark Middleton weighed heavily with her.

While she was waiting, a second woman stepped out of the house to stand beside her. Johnny recognized her as the tired-looking saloon whore from town. The one who had been helping Middleton rig a card game.

"All right," Jessie said. "Come on in."

17

The front door opened to a small parlor, with a hearth made of stones. They looked a lot like the stones the wall at the edge of the small plateau was made of, in size and texture. A rack of long horns was mounted above a rough cut mantel, and a large bear skin served as a rug. One doorway to the parlor opened to a kitchen, and another to a small hallway where the bedrooms were. No dining room. Meals were taken on a large wooden table in one corner of the kitchen.

Jessica and Peddie took Lettie and Mercy down to one of the bedrooms. Lettie was hurting so bad from four hours on the back of a horse that she could hardly walk, and both needed sleep.

Middleton went to the kitchen and came back with a tray containing tin cups, the kind Johnny took on the trail with him, and a kettle of coffee, and he poured up.

Tom took a cup and sat at one end of a sofa. He was saying very little.

Johnny stood by the hearth, a cup in his hand. His left hand, which kept his gun hand free. A fire crackled low, and the heat felt good after riding through the cool air of the night and early morning.

Johnny said, "This place has a nice way about it. A good man built it. It's got his touch."

Matt sat in a chair made with a wooden framework and leather stretched over it. "Bernard Swan was that kind of man. Kept to himself, for the most part. But he just had a strength about him. The way he moved. The way he spoke. I've only been here a couple of times, and those were a years ago, but I've always liked this place."

Sam Middleton had hung his hat on a peg on a wall, and had a tin cup of coffee in one hand.

Johnny said, "Middleton, can you give me an answer?"

"Of course," he said. "Have I ever been anything but straight with you?"

Johnny shook his head. "No, but I haven't known you long enough for you to lie to me. Yet."

"Well, there you go. I've never lied to you. What's the question?"

"What brings you here?"

"To this house? Trying to avoid being shot by the good marshall and his band of thugs in town. Right before I came to your aid back in town, I gave Peddie a pre-arranged signal, which was for her to go and get two horses saddled. I always plan for a hasty exit, should one be needed. As it turns out, I seem to need such a thing wherever I go."

Johnny said with a little sarcasm, "I can't imagine that."

Middleton shot him a sidelong glance.

Matt said, "Johnny, how is it you two know each other?"

"I met him a few nights ago in town. He and the one called Peddie were running a crooked card game, trying to cheat some miners out of their hard-earned money."

Middleton gave a theatrical cringe. "Why, McCabe, you don't have to put it quite that way."

"How would you put it?"

Middleton gave a moment of thought. "Well, okay. You've got a point."

Matt said to Middleton, "You vouched for us. The good lady has every reason to hate me and suspect I am up to no good, considering the way she has been treated by Hiram and my wife. But you said you vouched for us. How did you know I wasn't here to try to harass her?"

Middleton said, without missing a beat, "Because you're with him." With a nod of his head he indicated Johnny. "I've heard the stories, many of them from Peddie. I know you want this canyon because you think there's gold in these cliffs, and Bernard Swan, God rest his ever eternal soul, never filed the proper paperwork for a legal claim."

Matt shook his head. "*I* don't want this canyon. As far as I'm concerned, this was Bernard Swan's, and now belongs to his widow. My wife and son, I'm ashamed to admit, are the ones trying to strong-arm Mrs. Swan out of here."

Johnny said to Middleton, "Why does Matt being with me hold any weight with you?"

"Because, my dear McCabe, you are the proverbial knight-in-shining-armor. The perennial do-gooder. Protector of the innocent, righter of wrongs, and all of that. You see a wrong being committed, and you cannot help but step in. Just like back in town, with the card game. I haven't met many like you, but just your very nature prevents you from doing anything under-handed. If your brother were here to cause trouble, then you wouldn't have allowed him to ride with you. In fact, if anything, I expect you to join in Mrs. Swan's struggle against the evil oppressors trying to take her land."

"It's not my fight."

"Of course, not. But can you really just ride away and leave a woman and her young daughter to face the likes of Verna and Hiram McCabe?"

Johnny took a sip of coffee, and didn't say anything. He wasn't sure if Middleton was complimenting him, or somehow laughing at him. Or in a complicated, bizarre way, both.

Matt said to Middleton, "Your word seems to carry a lot of weight with Mrs. Swan."

"She hardly knows me. My word holds a lot of weight with Peddie, and hers holds a lot of weight with Mrs. Swan."

"Why?" Johnny said.

Middleton gave him a curious look. "Your question could actually go two ways. Why do Peddie and I mean so much to each other, or why does Peddie mean so much to Jessica?"

"I think the first answer is obvious."

"Not as much as you might think. Peddie and I are not romantically involved. Never have been. I met her in St. Louis maybe..," he looked off into the air while he tried to figure the years, "maybe seven years ago. She's become like a daughter to me. She's another of those true and noble souls. Sort of like yourself. I pulled her out of a bad situation. Not my place to tell the story. But let me just say this about her. They say everyone has their price."

Johnny said, "So they say."

"I know I have mine. But there are people like Peddie in the world who simply would not betray someone. You can't buy them off, no matter what the price."

Johnny took another sip of coffee. A little weak for his tastes, but it was coffee.

Middleton continued, "McCabe, what would it take for you to put a bullet in your brother? Hide his body somewhere in the desert. What would it take?"

Johnny said, "What kind of a question is that?"

"A hypothetical one. Let's say you had a chance to gain total control of his holdings. It would make you a very rich man. Your brother might very possibly be the richest man in the state. And that says something, considering the level of prosperity down around the Frisco area. Let's say, hypothetically, you could have it all just by placing one bullet in the man's back. Sure, you'd feel bad about it. Probably for the rest of your days. But money can sure go a long way to compensate a conscience."

"I would never do it. Some things are more important than money."

"Let's say you could gain that kind of money by putting a bullet in my back. I'm not your brother. Just someone you met a few days ago."

"I've never shot a man in the back for any reason, and never would."

"Bravo. You just proved my point. Not for any reason, or any price. There are those who would. More than you might think. Betrayal is something many people are capable of, if the situation is right. If the price is right. I honestly don't believe you're capable of it. And neither is Peddie. At the risk of flattering you, I greatly admire that trait. I don't entirely understand it, but I greatly admire it."

He took a sip of coffee. "Whenever Peddie and I wind up in the same town, we take care of each other.

We watch each other's back. I've saved her life a couple of times, when customers got a little too rough. She put me up one time when I got cleaned out by a couple of highwaymen and was left with broken ribs and nothing but the clothes on my back."

Matt said, "And she knows Jessica Swan."

Middleton nodded. "That's a story for one of them to tell. Not me. It would be spreading gossip, and I don't do that."

Johnny said, "At least you have your standards."

Middleton shrugged. "Better than nothing."

"So, who's the Indian out by the pass?"

Matt answered. "That's Lone Wolf Martinez. They usually just call him Wolf. He was riding with Swan when they came to this area. I never heard the story from Swan himself, but they say Swan was in the Army, fighting the Apache, and Wolf was an Army scout. Apparently he stayed on after Swan died."

Middleton said, "According to Peddie, old man Swan saved his life at one time, and Wolf felt a loyalty to him. He made a crusade out of being Swan's right-hand-man, and now serves that function for his widow."

Johnny said, "Does anyone else work for her?"

Middleton nodded. "Ches Harding. He rode with Bernard Swan a lot of years. Helped him build this place. He's stayed on due to loyalty. Probably the oldest man I've ever met, but one of the most capable."

Jessica Swan spoke from the doorway to the bedrooms. "You seem to have a lot of questions."

Her eyes met Johnny's again, and again it struck him that she was one of the most breathtaking women he had ever seen.

He said, "I don't mean to pry. It's just that you seem to be in a bad situation, here. I'm thinking of lending my assistance, Mrs. Swan."

Middleton smiled and nodded at Johnny, as if to say, *you just made my point.* Johnny shot him a sidelong glance.

She stepped into the room. "We don't really need any assistance. We can take care of ourselves."

From behind her stepped a little girl. Maybe six or seven. Dark hair like her mother, and the same sky-blue eyes. She was in a nightgown and robe, and she held her mother's hand.

Jessica Swan said, "Lettie told me of your situation. You're all free to stay here for a few days. I don't have a lot of supplies but I would never turn away anyone in need. I'm going to make breakfast for Cora and me, and you're all welcome to join if you're of a mind."

Johnny's stomach was letting him know it was indeed of a mind. "That's mighty kind," he said.

18

Johnny was tired to the point that his joints were hurting. It seemed when he was younger he had to go a lot further to get to this point. But a lack of sleep combined with all of the hours in the saddle had a way of wearing on you. Not to mention the fact that he had added one more to the long trail of bodies that stretched back through the years. Killing a man still wore on him, even though he had to kill the man to protect Lettie and the others. Johnny had never killed a man who didn't need to be killed, and in his opinion, a man who would endanger women or children was a man who was on that list. Yet it was still killing and even though he didn't talk about it much, it weighed on him a little, and left him feeling weary and a little edgy.

There were two extra bedrooms in the house. Tom and his wife and daughter were given one, and Peddie already had the other. Middleton had said he was bedding down on the sofa. Johnny told her he would be perfectly happy to take the barn. Matt said that would be fine with him, too.

But before Johnny went to the barn to literally hit the hay, he thought he might pace about outside, and breathe the morning air. Try to take off a little of the edginess. In his younger days, patrolling the Mexican border with the Texas Rangers, he would have worked off the edginess with whiskey or tequila in a cantina in one of the border towns, but that had often led to more trouble than it was worth.

He stood at the edge of the stone wall, looking down at the canyon below. The Apache who apparently went by the name of Wolf was standing guard at the pass into the canyon. Johnny looked down at the pass, but couldn't see him. Johnny supposed if he could see him, then the man wouldn't be worthy of the label Apache.

Matt stepped out of the barn and walked over. He pulled out a couple of cigars and handed one to Johnny.

Matt said, "Beautiful morning."

Johnny nodded, and bit off the end of the cigar and spit it away. He then struck a match and soon the cigar was smoldering.

Matt said, "In some ways, this is a lot like the old days."

"You and me, side-by-side. And outside this canyon there's a whole passel of folks who would be happy to see us dead." Johnny grinned. "A lot like old times."

"Seems strange without Joe here with us, though."

Johnny nodded.

Matt said, "Wonder what ever happened to him?"

"No telling. I wonder if we'll ever know."

Matt took a draw on his cigar, and blew the smoke out slowly. The smoke formed a bluish gray cloud in front of him that spread out into the morning air and then was gone.

Matt said, "It still does this to you, doesn't it? Killing. Puts a sort of uneasiness on you. Just like in the old days."

Johnny nodded again. "Seems to. But there was no other choice."

"I couldn't count the number of men I've seen you kill. Maybe I could if I tried, if I could remember all of 'em. But I've never tried. But every single time, there was no choice. The first was when you saved that Mexican woman, back in Texas. Breaker Grant's young wife."

Johnny nodded.

"That Mexican bandito had her around the neck, not much different than that man Bardeen with Lettie. And you made an impossible shot and saved her life."

Johnny chuckled. "Coleman didn't seem all that appreciative. He hated me from the first time he saw me."

"Jealous, I think. He wanted his father's wife for himself. And remember how his old man took to us the moment he saw us. Old Breaker Grant was the kind of man who could chew nails. But he liked us, and I think it somehow didn't set right with Coleman."

"Coleman was spineless. Angry at the world. Hard to figure how a man like Breaker Grant could have a son like Coleman."

Matt nodded.

Johnny took another draw on his cigar. "I suppose I should write a letter to Ginny and the kids. Tell 'em it looks like I won't be home for a while. I had hopes of maybe getting home by Christmas, though I knew it was a long shot. I figured I'd visit Lura's grave, see you for a few days, and then start back. Traveling through the mountains in the early winter can be done, if you know how to do it. And Thunder's a good mountain horse. The best I've ever seen. But I just can't leave this woman and her daughter and the two men with her to face those men out there."

Matt grinned. "Are you saying that card shark is right about you?"

Johnny said, "Not that I'll ever admit it to him."

Matt chuckled.

Johnny said, "Don't know how I'd ever get a letter sent, though. Not like I can just ride into town without getting my back filled with lead."

"I can get it sent. There's a railroad water tower about thirty miles east of town. We can ride out there and meet the train. I'm an owner, remember? I'll have them take the letter to the train station in Cheyenne, and from there it'll go by stage coach to that little town you call McCabe Gap. Ginny should have the letter within a couple of weeks."

"That's faster than the postal service."

Matt nodded with a grin. "Pays to know an owner."

They stood a moment in silence, each enjoying the taste of a good cigar.

"You know," Johnny said, "the last time I think I had a cigar this good was from the desk of Breaker Grant, himself. All those years ago."

Matt held the cigar out in front of him. "I'm going to allow myself to savor every single puff off of these. I doubt I'll ever have cigars like this again, once they're gone."

This got a curious look from Johnny.

Matt said, "I've got to fight Verna and Hiram. In court, this kind of thing could take years to resolve. Assets will be frozen. Court order versus court order. Verna's lawyer against mine. And I don't even have a lawyer. I'll have to go to San Francisco and find one who has the expertise to go up against someone like Verna, and all of her financial clout. That is, if I can get there without someone hired by Verna putting a bullet in my back."

Time to ask, Johnny decided. "Exactly what happened at the house? I take it that fire was no accident."

"Well, it was. Sort of, I guess."

Johnny waited. Sometimes things that were hard to say took a little time in coming.

Matt took a draw on his cigar, and blew the smoke out and then stood looking at the cigar.

Finally, he said the words. Words Johnny wasn't really all that surprised to hear. "Verna tried to have me killed."

Johnny said nothing. There wasn't really anything to say.

Matt said, "She had her man, Timmons, try to do it. You remember his father? A bull of a man. Maybe the strongest man I've ever met. Timmons wasn't quite that strong, but he was somewhere in the same range."

Johnny caught the past-tense of the verb. "Was?"

Matt nodded. "He's dead. He came at me in my sleep. I was so exhausted from all the hours in the saddle. Somehow I came awake at just the last minute. Maybe somewhere deep inside me the old gunhawk still exists. I don't know. But he attacked, and we fought. And it was bad."

Matt stopped because he needed to. This was emotionally exhausting to talk about. Your own wife trying to have you killed. Her butler, essentially her henchman, attacking you in your own bedroom. Matt's voice had started to shake a little, and no man wants his voice to shake. Not even in front of his brother. Johnny gave him the time he needed.

Matt said, "I was never the fighter you are. And that Joe was. And I'm too many years removed from it. We struggled and I held my own, but just barely. He was clearly trying to kill me. I wound up killing him..." he had to draw a breath, as though he was trying to find the strength to say the words, "with a fireplace poker. That old mansion had a fireplace in every bedroom. But somewhere in the struggle we knocked over a lamp, and I didn't even realize it until the fight was over, and by then it was too late. My bed was entirely on fire, and the fire was reaching up the wall."

"What'd you do?"

"I got out of there. I had to think fast, something else I hadn't done in years. I knew Verna had put Timmons up to it. I don't think he would blow his own nose without her say-so. And if Verna put him up to it, it means Hiram was at least aware of it. He was always her son. He and I never were able to communicate. He always gravitated toward her."

Johnny was again struck with the thought that you could see a lot of Verna in Hiram, but nothing of Matt. But he could see Timmons. The square jaw, the cleft in his chin. Johnny had to wonder just where Timmons drew the line as to how far he would serve Verna. But he thought now was not the right time to bring such a thing up.

Matt said, "How do you face that? How do you find some sort of reconciliation within yourself about that? Your own son, trying to have you killed? Or at least being aware that his mother is trying to have you killed, and not doing a thing to stop it?"

Johnny tried to imagine that. Josh or Dusty or Jack, trying to have him killed. Or even Bree. Those four, along with Ginny, were more precious to him than life itself. They were family. And part of being family was a level of trust. Blind trust, actually. They had to trust each other without reservation. Just like the way you have to go into a marriage, if you want the marriage to work. It saddened him that Matt had married and produced three sons, but they didn't have that level of trust. When it came to Verna and Hiram, there seemed to be no trust at all, and Matt was only now realizing this.

Johnny said, "I don't know what to say. I really can't even imagine it."

Matt said, "In the heat of the moment, I had to think fast. I knew Verna had to be behind it. I figured it might be better if they all think I was dead. The house was blazing. Nothing I could do to stop it. I figured if I snuck out and the house just burned to the ground, then they would think I went with it and maybe that would buy me a little time to get my head in order. To figure out just what had happened. But that plan failed the moment Marshal Wells in town saw me.

"I had gone to Tom's to get him and his family out of there. I figured Wells and his henchmen would come after them. Verna might suspect I was still alive, and send them to Tom's just in case I showed up there. But I was too late. They were already there when I got there. If you hadn't showed up, then they probably would have shot me, and they would have done even worse to Lettie."

Johnny said, "I suppose the practical thing to do would have been to shoot Wells. Not leave him alive. But I just can't shoot down a man like that. In cold blood."

Matt shook his head. "Me neither. And I wouldn't ask you to."

"So, now what? We try to figure a way to get you to San Francisco, so you can find an attorney?"

Matt said, "I don't know if I even want to fight."

"That's just the fatigue talking. You're tired. Who could blame you for being tired?"

"It's more than that." He took a draw on his cigar, and looked off at the canyon floor below.

"What is it, then?"

"It's that I don't like the person I became. Rich. Lazy. Filling my day with scotch. Playing billiards with Hiram or Dan. Taking the train to San Francisco with Verna and having dinner in fine restaurants, or attending the theater. That's not the life I want."

He turned to face Johnny. "You know when I was happiest?"

Johnny shook his head.

"When you and I and Joe were riding across the country, with a price on our heads. Using assumed names. Remember what we called ourselves in Texas?"

Johnny nodded with a smile at the memory. "O'Brien."

"And when we first arrived in California we were calling ourselves Reynolds."

"I remember."

"Those were the happiest days of my life. At least as an adult. I was really happy in that old farmhouse in Pennsylvania, when we were growing up. Sometimes I wondered if maybe I should have done like Luke did. Stayed in Pennsylvania. Built a life there."

Johnny didn't know quite what to say about that. He knew he would never have been happy staying back home, working a farm. Not after he had gotten a taste of life in the west. And Joe even less so. But he wasn't so sure about Matt. Maybe Matt was right about himself.

Matt said, "Part of me thinks that maybe when this is over, I might want to just ride on. Just me, my horse, and what I can carry in my saddle bags. Leave everything else behind."

"If you want to come north, there's always room for you where I live. There are millions of acres surrounding the little valley where I live. Mountains heavily forested with pine to the west, grassy foothills to the east. A man can run cattle, or even farm."

"Thanks, Johnny. That means a lot. You never know, maybe I'll take you up on that offer."

Then they stood in silence by the stone wall, looking down at the canyon below and smoking their cigars.

Once their cigars were finished, Matt said, "I think I'm ready to get some sleep now."

"Yeah, maybe me too."

They went to the barn and Johnny rolled his bedroll on a layer of straw on the floor. His saddle was set for use as a pillow. Matt wrapped himself in his bedroll and was soon snoring away. But Johnny still wasn't feeling quite ready for sleep. He fished in his saddle bags and found a sheet of paper and a pen and a bottle of ink. He sat the paper on a small workbench attached to one wall, and scratched out a letter.

He didn't go into details. In fact, he didn't want them to think anything was wrong. No need to worry anyone. He just wrote that he was staying with Matt—not a lie—and some things were going on and Matt needed his help, so he would be staying the winter. He hoped to see them all sometime in the spring.

While he had never been the eloquent speaker Matt could be, he was even less so when it came to putting words on paper. But he figured it would be good enough. He had an envelope and addressed it to *The McCabe Family, McCabe Ranch, Montana.*

Now, he thought, he was ready for some sleep. He pulled his boots off, unbuckled his gunbelt and dropped it to the floor beside the bedroll, and climbed into the covers. He grabbed his pistol and pulled it free of the holster and quickly checked the loads, then set it on the floor by his saddle.

And as he drifted away to sleep, he found his thoughts drifting to Jessica Swan. Her smile. The way she moved. Her sky-blue eyes. The way she would raise a brow if she found something questionable or a little amusing. It had been a long time since a woman had occupied his mind this way.

He was awake again by mid-afternoon. Middleton was heading down to the pass to spell Wolf, but Johnny called him off and told him he would do it.

After a time, Jessica Swan stepped out of the house and to her surprise, Johnny was not down at the pass, but sitting on the stone wall overlooking the canyon. One foot was on the ground, and the other was crossed over his knee. He had one of Matt's cigars going. An old rifle was resting in his lap. She thought it might have been a Sharps. He heard the slight crunch of the gravel underfoot as she walked toward him, and he looked over his shoulder at her and reached a hand up to touch the brim of his hat.

"Ma'am."

She said, "I thought you were watching the pass."

"I am," he said. "Got a good view of it, right from here."

"What if someone were to ride in?"

"If it was an unfriendly rider, I could pick him off right from here. This rifle has a lot of range. It would be hard for more than two riders to get through that pass riding abreast of each other, and there's nowhere for cover once they get into the canyon. A bullet takes one of them out of the saddle, the other won't be sticking around long. He'll be turning his horse back into the pass as fast as he can. If there are riders in there coming up behind them, then there'll be all sorts of mayhem. All with one bullet."

"Can you really make a shot like that from here? I know the rifle has that kind of range, but can you really hit a target that far away with such precision?"

He nodded. It wasn't arrogance. It was simply fact, like the sky overhead was blue.

She said, "You really know this business of shooting, don't you?"

He nodded a little sadly. "It's what I do."

He turned his gaze back to the pass. The cigar was held in his left hand, and was smoldering away. He brought it up for a draw. His rifle was in his lap, held in place with his right hand.

She said, "Shouldn't you have your rifle ready?"

He said, "It is ready."

She looked at him like she was trying to decide if she thought he was boasting, or just plain out of his mind.

He said, "The longer you hold a bead on something, the more your aim starts to waiver. It's better to raise your gun, give yourself no more than a few seconds to sight in, and then make your shot."

She strolled up to the wall, to stand a few feet from him. She looked down at the canyon floor below her. "This place is all I have. I can't lose it."

"I'm not going anywhere. And neither is Matt."

"He's part of the reason I'm in this situation."

"Maybe he feels a little guilty. He let things get out of hand."

She looked at him with those incredible eyes. Again, he found himself stirred by her beauty. Only one other woman had ever struck him quite like this, and she was the mother of his children. Most of them.

She said, "But what about you? You owe me nothing."

"Being here isn't about owing you. It's about doing the right thing. Matt would be here too, even if he didn't feel guilty. Our father told us once that sometimes you just have to do the right thing because it's the right thing to do. Something his father told him, and so forth back down the line. I think it was the old man himself, the first John McCabe, who said it first. He was a frontiersman who was one of the first to explore the western Pennsylvania mountains, when that was still wild country. Back in the day."

"And you and your brother keep the legacy alive."

He nodded. "I suppose we do."

She looked off at the canyon floor again. A couple of longhorns were wandering about. Five more were grazing away. Johnny took a draw on the cigar and let his gaze travel the length of the Swan woman. A young man would have been focusing on the curves, which were striking and yet not overly so, like with the most beautiful of women. And Johnny had enough young man in him to fully notice. But once you've lived a few years, you begin to notice the little things, like how a woman carries herself. How she stands. Jessica had erect posture, but not too much so. She walked with confidence, and yet not arrogance. The way she turned her head or lifted a hand was with feminine grace, and yet she had a strength about her. It took strength, he thought, to live out here in a place like this. It said something about her that she could endure the hardships in order to appreciate the beauty of this canyon.

She said, "Is it true what they say about you?"

He shrugged. "What do they say about me?"

She gave him a sidelong glance. "You've heard the stories, I'm sure. That you rode into Mexico and killed an entire gang of outlaws who had captured a woman, and brought her back safely?"

He shook his head. "That one's the product of a writer from New York."

"And that you shot down twenty-five Comanches with twenty-five shots while they were charging at you?"

He shook his head. "*Ten* Comanches. It'd be might hard to shoot twenty-five, because you'd run out of bullets. Have to reload. You can't reload if you have that many men already within shooting distance, charging at you."

She was giving him a skeptical look. "You're laughing at me."

He shook his head. "Not at all."

"Okay," she allowed herself a little grin. She would play along. "You had to be using a Winchester."

"No, ma'am. That was back in '55. Winchesters hadn't come around yet. I was using twin Remington revolvers. You ever hear of a border shift?"

"I've heard of it. I've never seen it done."

"Well, it's not something done much anymore, I guess. You have to have two guns to do it, and with these new Peacemakers, you don't usually need more than one. And everyone has Winchesters. Some Winchesters hold eighteen rounds."

"You speak so casually of such things." She turned to let her gaze fall again to the canyon floor.

"Comes with the territory. But that doesn't mean such things should ever be taken lightly. I don't ever want to kill a man, and only consider it as a last resort."

"I suppose considering everything going on, the fact that there are men out there who want to turn my home into a war zone, I should just pack up and leave. But this is the only home my daughter has ever known. And Bernard worked so hard to build this place. He and Ches, and Wolf."

She turned to face him. "I know what they say about me, Mister McCabe. And yes, Bernard was a lot older than I am. But he was the finest man I ever met, and a great father to Cora."

"I'm not judging you, Mrs. Swan. I'm not from around here, and I've heard nothing about you at all. I just know you're a widow and have a daughter, and some people I have very little respect for are trying to force you off of your land."

"Bernard never filed a proper claim. It's open to legal interpretation."

"Matt said he knew Bernard Swan, and morally this land belongs to him. That's good enough for me."

She looked at Johnny long and hard. "Just like that? You're entering a situation that could very easily result in gunplay. Men could be killed. You could be risking your own life. And you do it without a second thought, just because Matt said Bernard was a good man?"

Johnny nodded. "Matt's word means a lot to me. There's no one I would trust more with my life. That, and now that I've met you, well . . ." he hoped he wasn't blushing. Gunhawks should never blush. "Begging your pardon, but I can see that you're a good woman and a good mother, and I won't let you be pushed off your land. Simple as that."

She glanced down at her shoes. "I appreciate the sentiment. Really, I do. But you and your brother, if he really is the man you say he is, are only two men. There is a small army of gunfighters in town, at the disposal of the marshal. And ultimately Hiram McCabe. How can you possibly hope to stand against them?"

Johnny shrugged. "Matt and I'll figure out something."

"Just like that? You and Matt will figure out something?"

He smiled. "We've been in worse situations."

She looked at him about as skeptically as he thought anyone ever had, and one brow rose a little. He realized she was at her most strikingly beautiful when one brow rose skeptically. He could easily see what the late Bernard Swan saw in her.

He said, "Once, I found myself in a situation with ten Comanches charging at me."

He grinned. She grinned.

She shook her head, "Mister McCabe..."

He said, "Call me Johnny. Please."

She looked him in the eye, with those incredible sky blue eyes, and he found her smile was even more captivating than one raised brow. She said, "Johnny."

He then noticed motion down on the canyon floor, motion that hadn't been there a moment earlier. He pulled his eyes from Jessica Swan, which wasn't easy, and saw a rider down there. He was already in through the pass, and heading their way.

Johnny could have kicked himself in the rump. As experienced as he was at warfare, he was allowing himself to be distracted from his duties by a pretty face. Well, not just a pretty face, a downright beautiful one. But still, such distractions in a situation like this could get you killed. Zack Johnson had said Johnny had been shot at one time too many. Apparently, Johnny thought, he hadn't been shot at enough.

The rider was coming toward the rise that would lead to the ledge the house was built on. His horse was moving at a light canter, and he would be there in about two minutes.

Her gaze had followed his, but before she could say anything, he said, "Get into the house. Now. And send Matt out here."

She didn't have to be told twice. When trouble arrived, she wasn't one to begin asking questions. She moved decisively. Johnny found one more thing about her to admire.

The door slammed shut, and Johnny then ran to the side of the barn. He leaned his rifle against the wall because it would do little good in a close-quarters gunfight, and drew his pistol.

The door opened and Matt came running out, and Johnny waved him back. Matt stepped back into the doorway, using the door jamb as a cover, and drew his pistol, and he and Johnny waited while the rider rode up.

The rider had a pistol holstered at his left side, and a scattergun held across the front of the saddle. He had long hair falling from under a worn, battered hat, and a bushy beard with a pronounced white stripe down the middle. Like someone had tied a skunk around his jaw.

Something about the way the man carried himself in the saddle struck Johnny as familiar. But Johnny didn't quite place him as the man reined up in front of the house.

Johnny stepped out from behind the barn, cocking his pistol. "Don't move a whisker."

Matt stepped out of the house, his pistol aimed at the man, but then Matt's tired face broke into first surprise, then a smile.

"Joe?" He paused, letting his eyes fix on the man, to make sure he was seeing what he thought he was seeing. "Joe!"

The man nodded, and said in a voice Johnny hadn't heard in nearly seventeen years, "Matt."

He turned to look at Johnny, and Johnny found he was looking into the eyes of his younger brother. "Johnny."

"Joe?" Johnny said.

Then he holstered his gun and Joe was swinging out of the saddle and Matt ran toward them and the three were hugging and laughing.

Jessica stood in the doorway, a little puzzled. Sam Middleton stepped up behind her. He was tall enough that he could see over the top of her head.

"Who is that?" she said.

Sam was grinning. "It looks like the legendary McCabe brothers are once again united. And our odds of coming out of this alive have just increased."

19

Johnny was going to take the first night watch, but Middleton said, "No, I'll take it. You go in and talk with your brother."

It was dark outside the windows. The only light in the parlor was from the hearth, a fire crackling gentle and low. Matt was sitting on the sofa with a cigar going. Joe was standing, leaning one hand on the mantel. In his free hand was a cigar. Johnny went into the house through the kitchen door and poured a cup of coffee and joined them.

"Joe," he said. "Where have you been all these years?"

Joe shrugged. "Here and there."

Just like Joe, Johnny thought. Never said much.

Johnny thought about taking the chair, but he thought about it for only maybe two seconds. He preferred to be on his feet because he thought better this way. He was more alert. One shout from Middleton outside that riders were coming, or one gunshot, and he would have to be ready for battle.

Matt said, "Were you in some kind of trouble?"

Joe shrugged. "It was complicated."

This struck Johnny as a little strange. Joe was one of the least complicated men he had ever known. "I like to keep things simple," he once said.

Johnny glanced at Matt, who glanced back at him. Johnny knew if you pried, then Joe would close up and say nothing. Such was his way.

Joe said, "I kept up with both of you, as much as I could."

He looked at Johnny. "I heard about you getting shot a couple summers ago. Are you okay?"

Johnny nodded. "I am now. For a couple days, they weren't sure if I was going to make it or not."

Johnny told him the story of how Vic Falcone and a group of guerilla raiders attacked the ranch, and how two of Johnny's sons pursued them. And he told Joe of the nephew Joe hadn't yet met.

While he was talking, Ches Harding drifted in and poured a cup of coffee and listened to the three brothers talking. Ches had a face that was deeply lined, and his hair was fine and white. His back was a little bent and he walked with a sort of bow-legged shuffle. He wore a hat that was wide-brimmed and with a tall crown and that had taken on a sort of neutral desert color over the years. It was floppy and worn in places, and there was a nick taken out of the brim in one place that looked to Johnny like the work of a bullet. Ches wore a gun at his belt, turned backward for a cross draw. Johnny had the idea he knew how to use it.

Ches sat on an ottoman, in front of the fire. He said, "Heard a lot about you boys when you were younger, and makin' a name for yourselves. They still talk about you around campfires. It's kind of a treat for an old man to be here in the same room with the three of you together like this."

He took a sip of coffee. "I actually come across an old wanted poster for the three of you, maybe seven or eight years ago. It was on a wall down San Diego way. Bernard Swan and me, we was down that way checking out a cattle auction."

Matt said, "You rode with Bernard a lot of years, didn't you?"

Ches nodded. "I practically raised him. I ran a small cattle outfit in Texas, and he grew up in the saddle, with a rope in his hand. Taught him everything I could."

"How old are you, if you don't mind my asking?"

"Eighty-seven."

Matt blinked with surprise.

Ches nodded with a grin. "Everyone always asks how an old cowhand like myself could live this long. I don't rightly know. Just never died, I guess."

Johnny said, "You must have seen a lot, over the years."

Ches nodded again. "I come west as a young man, back in eighteen and twenty. One of the first Texians. Had a young wife, and a baby. They was killed by Comanche raiders."

"Sorry to hear that."

"It was a long time ago. I just drifted for a while, then Bernard came into my life. Became like a son to me. We ran cattle for a while. Rode with the first Texas Rangers in the war with Mexico. We worked as drovers for a while, when the first railheads were comin' to life. Scouted Apaches for the cavalry in Arizona. That's where we met up with Wolf. Eventually, Bernard wanted to try California, so we rode this way and settled here in this canyon. Wolf come with us."

Joe said, "I've been living in Texas these past few years. A little town called Wardtown."

Ches nodded. "I know the place. Been there a couple of times."

Johnny said to Joe, "What've you been doing for work there?"

Joe said, "Mostly working as a deputy marshal. The lawman there is a gent by the name of Austin Tremain."

"I've heard that name a couple of times."

Joe said, "He's a good man."

Tom and Lettie had been getting Mercy to bed, and they drifted out to the parlor and sat at the sofa. Jessica appeared at the doorway to the hallway and since there was nowhere else to sit in the parlor, Matt got to his feet and motioned for her to take the chair, which she did.

The talk continued as coffee cups were emptied and then refilled. Talk of the old days, of the three brothers on the run from the law.

At one point, Ches wandered over to Jessica and said, "This is the stuff of legend, you know. These three, in the same room. Talking about the trails they rode. Someday Cora's going to tell about them being in their house, and people aren't gonna believe her."

Joe said to Johnny, "About the only thing missing here is Zack Johnson. How is the old hoss doing?"

"Fine," Johnny said. "He has his own spread now, on the other side of the valley from us."

Johnny added wood to the fire. Eventually Lettie and Tom headed back to the bedroom, and Ches thought that might be a good idea, and went out to the bunkhouse. Johnny would every so often glance at Jessica, finding the way the firelight danced across her face to be almost spellbinding. A couple of times her eyes met his, and one time she allowed him a small smile.

Eventually, it was just the three brothers in the room.

Johnny said, "I suppose I should get out there and spell Wolf."

Matt said, "No, I'll do it. You get some rest."

"I want you both to know," Joe said, "that I'm here now. You have one more gun in this fight. I heard in town what was going on from a bartender named Artie."

Johnny nodded with a chuckle. "He's a good man."

"Well, I had to be away. But now I'm here."

Johnny laid a hand on his shoulder. "Come on. We're bedding down in the barn. There's plenty of room."

Matt found Wolf by the stone wall at the edge of the small plateau, and told him he would take over. Wolf headed to the small bunkhouse behind the main house. He and Ches both had bunks there. Matt had thought about seeing if there was an extra bunk he might use, but Johnny had chosen the barn because he always seemed to want the most open-air sleeping conditions he could find. Matt joined him in the barn in case they had a chance to talk before going to sleep. After so many years apart, Matt wanted to spend as much time with his brother as possible. Matt had a practical reason, too. Johnny was hell-on-wheels in a fight, either with his fists or his guns. More so than any other man Matt had ever known. If Matt was to wake up to the sound of gunfire, which was a real possibility considering the situation they were in, he wanted Johnny close by.

Once Wolf was gone, Matt stood alone by the stone wall. Cigar smoke would taste good about now, he thought, but the drawing of cigar smoke tended to make the end of the cigar glow a bit. Nothing you'd notice by daylight, but in the dark such a thing could give away your position.

Matt had a Winchester in one hand, and he raised one foot to the stone wall and bent his knee and leaned on it, and looked down to the canyon floor. The sky was clear and the moon bright, and a sort of silvery light flooded the canyon. There were dark spots below, some of which were trees and others were cows. There seemed to be no motion, and he wondered how much motion he would be able to see from up here in the darkness.

He listened, too. If the cows suddenly seemed agitated, it might indicate something was down there that shouldn't be.

He then remembered something Johnny had said once. A horse in the night is as good as a watch dog. Better, maybe. It would let you know if something was out there that shouldn't be, but it would be quiet about it. He thought about maybe going to the corral and bringing out his horse and keeping it with him.

He then became aware of motion behind him. Something maybe heard like the soft sliding of a boot sole on the sand, or the rustle of trousers as a man stepped. Matt took no time to think about it, but whirled and pulled his gun as he moved. He had never managed a draw as smooth and quick as Johnny's, but he had his gun out and the hammer cocked.

"Easy, there." It was Joe. He had stepped out of the house and was coming up behind him with a cup of coffee in each hand. Cradled in the crook of one arm was his shotgun.

"Sorry," Matt said, and released the hammer of his gun and slid it back into his holster.

"Brung you a coffee. Just brewed a pot. None of that coffee Miss Swan was serving. Not that it's bad coffee, but I like mine a might stronger."

Matt took a sip. Black and strong and thick. Just like he used to drink on the trail with his brothers. "Haven't had coffee like this in a long time."

"In town, Artie said your house burned down and there was some folks thinkin' you were kilt in the fire. What happened?"

Matt told him the story, scanning the canyon below with his eyes as he did so, and taking an occasional sip of coffee. He told about how he had let himself become lulled into a state of complacency, living on scotch and memories of his younger days. And how Johnny's arrival had sort of jolted him back into rediscovering himself. He told of the ambush that got his son Dan shot, and then the attempt on his own life. And he told Joe that his wife had been behind it.

Joe said, "Maybe I should have stuck around. Maybe when I left Montana I should have ridden here, and worked for you on the ranch. Maybe we could've prevented some of that from happening."

Matt shook his head. "No, I don't think so. It was all my own fault. If a man's going to make a mess out of his life, he'll find a way to do it one way or another."

Joe was quiet a moment. Then he said, "The reason I stayed away..."

"If you don't want to talk about it, I understand. Johnny and I are just glad you're here now."

"No, I do want to talk about it. Just not to Johnny, because he's the reason. Sort of."

This caught Matt by surprise. "Johnny is?"

Joe toed the dirt a little with one boot, then said, "Matt, I found Lura's killer."

Matt blinked with even more surprise. "After all these years?"

Joe shook his head. "Nope. It was all them years ago. When we were riding with Johnny, following the killer's trail. I found out who done it, but I didn't say anything."

He then told the story he had told Tremain a few weeks earlier. Finding the brass button in the dirt, and then once Johnny and Aunt Ginny and the children were safely relocated to Montana, Joe headed to Texas to confront Coleman Grant.

Joe said, "I hated leaving them, but Zack was with them and there's no one more capable than Johnny, so I knew they'd be all right."

He told about his confrontation with Coleman Grant, and the shooting.

"I done it so Johnny wouldn't have to. I thought one day he'd figure it out and go shoot the man himself. I wanted to save him from prison or the noose, because his children needed him."

They didn't realize Johnny was standing by the barn door. He said, "Joe, I don't know what to say."

Joe muttered a curse word, and Matt said, "Johnny, how long have you been standing there?"

"Long enough." Johnny walked over to them. "Joe, I've thought about who could have killed Lura. I always figured it was some bounty hunter who hadn't got the word that our names were cleared. I gave up on ever being able to find his trail again after those tracks were washed away."

"I knew if you saw that button layin' there in the dirt you'd right off think of Coleman Grant, so I stepped on it so you wouldn't see it."

"Joe." Words escaped him. He just stood there and shook his head and then placed a hand on Joe's shoulder. "To take a burden like that onto yourself. I just don't have the words."

"Ain't no words needed. You'd have done it for me."

Matt said, "We all would have done it for each other."

Thunder was loose in the corral, and had been lounging idly. Dozing on his feet the way a horse will. But then his head snapped up and he gave a snort, and a couple of prancing steps backward.

Johnny heard the horse, looking over to the corral. "Something's down there that doesn't belong. That's the only thing that would rile Thunder like that."

Joe said, "Maybe we should go down and take a look-see."

20

Matt went to the bunkhouse and called to Wolf and Ches. Wolf appeared at the door, a rifle in his hands. Matt quickly told him they thought something was going on down at the canyon floor, and that Wolf and Ches were to go to the main house and be ready. Matt and his brothers were going to head down and see what was happening.

While they were waiting for Matt, Johnny went into the barn to his gear and pulled out a pair of buckskin boots. Joe stood watch while Johnny hauled his skin-tight riding boots off and slipped his feet into the others. These were a design he learned from the Shoshone. They pulled up almost to the knee and then tied together at the top with a strip of rawhide. Johnny then stood watch while Joe went to get his own pair.

Johnny was standing by the stone wall, scouring the canyon with his eyes when Matt returned.

Matt said, "Do you see anything down there?"

Johnny shook his head.

Matt said, "Could be nothing, you know."

"I hope it's nothing. And it could just be something like a coyote wandering in. But I want to make sure. Thunder has saved my life a couple of times like this."

Once Joe was in his buckskin boots, they began down the long sloping ledge that would lead them to the canyon floor. Matt stepped as quietly as he could, but his hard leather boot soles caught rocks a couple of times and sent them skittering along, and made scraping sounds as he stepped along.

Johnny stopped and looked at Matt in the moonlight.

"I'm making too much noise," Matt said. "I'll hang back. If there's trouble, I'll come running."

Johnny nodded, and he and Joe continued on.

The slope was dotted with junipers and a few short, fat pines. Matt crouched behind one of the pines and waited.

Johnny and Joe moved cautiously along. They were crouched, taking slow, careful steps. Even in their buckskin boots, a toe could accidentally catch a small stone and send it careening into another. Such a sound would carry in the night air.

Johnny had left his rifle back at the barn. There would be no call for long-distance shooting at night. Johnny was hoping it was just a wandering coyote that Thunder was reacting to, but he was prepared for the worst. And the worst would mean Wells and some of his men from town trying to make their way into the canyon and launch an attack. Johnny held his revolver in his right hand and Joe gripped his scattergun with both hands, ready for action.

After a couple hundred feet, Joe held up his hand to signal Johnny to stop. They could see each other clearly in the moonlight, and Joe cradled his shotgun in the crook of one arm and made a hand gesture using the sign language of the plains Indians. Johnny understood the language. Joe had made the sign for *horse*.

There were many tribes spread out from Texas to the Canadian border and each spoke their own language, but they also shared a universal hand-sign language. Johnny had no idea how it had developed, but it enabled a Lakota from Montana to communicate with a Kiowa from Colorado. Johnny had learned some of this language during their winter with the Shoshone, and Joe had learned it some years before that, when he had spent time with the Cheyenne.

Joe thought he had heard a horse, out there in the night. They stood still and listened, and after a few moments Johnny heard a sound. A steel shod hoof scraping on gravel. It wasn't loud, but Johnny had logged enough hours in the saddle over the years to recognize it as the sound of a horse walking. It was on the rising slope, not far from them.

Johnny pointed from himself to a short pine to the right, and then to Joe and an outcropping of bedrock that was maybe three feet high, to the left. Joe nodded and headed to the rock. Johnny got behind the tree. And they waited.

The horse came into view. One lone rider, keeping his horse to a walk. He wore a wide-brimmed hat and his face was lost in the darkness. He rode bent at the shoulders and hanging a little over the saddle horn, like he had ridden far and was bone weary.

Johnny cocked his pistol and said, "Don't make another move."

Joe said from the other side of the rider, "You're surrounded."

The rider's horse came to a stop, and the man raised his hands. "Don't shoot. I'm here to see my father."

Johnny stepped out from behind the tree. "What's your name?"

"Dan. Dan McCabe."

"You come alone?"

He nodded. "They're both gone. Mother and Hiram. He's gone to the mine and she's out of town. I was alone at the house, so I saddled up and rode out here."

Joe went to get Matt. He could have called out to him, but they were willing to err on the side of caution. They weren't sure which side of the fence Dan was on.

Matt came running, and said, "Danny. What're you doing? You shouldn't be in the saddle. You just got shot a few days ago."

"I had to see you, Father." Dan swung his leg around to swing out of the saddle, but he was weak and began to fall more than dismount, and Matt caught him.

Matt said, "Let's get him to the house."

They got Dan to one of the spare bunks in the bunkhouse. He had managed not to re-open his wound, but was exhausted. Ches said what the boy needed were fluids and food. While Dan sat in his bunk and ate some eggs and steak Jessica fixed in her kitchen, he brought his father and two uncles up to date on what his mother and Hiram were up to.

They were now living in the farmhouse Verna had purchased. The house was fully stocked and they had moved Dan there the night of the fire that took the main house. Dan told Matt his mother felt safe at the farmhouse because the purchase and upkeep of the house was done without Matt's knowledge.

Matt said, "Oh, I know about that house."

Dan blinked with surprise.

Matt said, "I knew more of what was going on around there than they realize. Maybe I tried to turn a blind eye to a lot of it, but I know about that house."

Dan told them Mother fully intended to rebuild the main house. Bigger and grander even than the first. Ben Harris and the men were working at hauling off the debris. Hiram had just come back from San Francisco, where he had met with an architect.

Matt said, "I'm surprised no one tried to stop you from riding out."

"Mother's asleep. And Hiram's in town."

Johnny nodded. He inferred from the way Dan said it that Hiram was visiting the brothel. He remembered what Belle had said about it. But he didn't know if Matt was aware, and so decided to remain silent.

Dan looked at Johnny, "They've posted a reward for you, for the murder of Belle, the saloon whore. You're wanted dead or alive. One thousand dollars."

"That's a lot of money," Johnny said. "More than the average cowhand makes in five years."

Matt said, "Been a long time since one of us was on a reward poster."

"You've got trouble too, Father," Dan said. "Everyone knows you didn't die in that fire. Wells saw you that night after the fire, and there was only one body found at the house. They've determined you murdered Timmons, and there's a poster for you now, too. Also a thousand dollars."

Johnny said, "I'm amazed at how they can just issue these posters. There have been no formal charges levied."

Dan nodded. "Yes, there have. They had two formal inquests yesterday, even though neither of you were there. Mother and Hiram have a judge in their pocket, and so the inquests were held without you because you are fugitives."

Matt said, "This goes from bad to worse, doesn't it?"

Johnny meandered into the kitchen in search of more coffee. Dawn wasn't far away and the eastern sky was starting to lighten up a little, and the shelf where the ranch house stood was now being bathed in a gray light.

Wolf and Ches had taken over guard duty while the brothers talked with Dan, both of them positioned at the stone wall. Now that daylight was coming, Wolf mounted up and rode down to the pass to stand guard duty there.

Johnny found Jessica at the stove scrambling eggs and frying up some more steak.

"Well," he said, "just so you know, you now have two official fugitives here. Reward posters have been issued for both Matt and me. They're trying to pin the murder of Belle on me."

"Belle was a friend of mine. As is Peddie. Peddie says you didn't kill Belle, and that's good enough for me."

Johnny refilled his cup, emptying the pot. "What makes Peddie so sure?"

"Because Sam Middleton told her you didn't do it. She trusts Sam with her life, and to me Peddie is family. As was Belle."

Johnny took a sip of the coffee. The last of the trail coffee. The next batch would be made by Jessica, and would probably be more civilized. Thinner. Brown, not jet black.

He said, "What makes Middleton so sure?"

"He says men like you and your brothers are like the knights of old. He says if you can't trust the three of you, you can't trust anyone."

"Yeah. He gave me a speech like that, too. With a man like him, you have to wonder what his angle is."

Jessica said to him, "She believes him, and she's no fool . She has trusted her life to him more than once, and he has never let her down. This is largely why I'm trusting my life to him. And to you and your brothers. Even though up until a couple of days ago I looked at Matt McCabe as my enemy."

Johnny said, "Matt's not a bad man. He made some bad choice, but now he's trying to make up for them."

Jessica scooped a pile of scrambled eggs from the skillet into a wooden bowl. "I'm glad his son is all right. But we're going to have a problem. Supplies are running mighty low around here. The store owners in town have been told not to do business with me. Part of Matt's wife's way of driving me out, I suppose. We have enough beef, and I have a small chicken house out back so we shouldn't run out of eggs, but that's about it. We're going to need flour and coffee. I don't have a butter churn."

"How are we fixed for water?"

"There's a natural spring out back that runs from a crack in the rocks. It feeds the stream that runs through the canyon. Cold, fresh water. Like a mountain spring. Better than any well water I've ever tasted."

"So, we just have to figure out an answer to the supply problem." Johnny took a sip of coffee. He was again, for more times than he could now count since riding into this canyon, taken with her beauty. Even though she had a bandana tied in a triangle over her hair and her face was a little flushed from the heat of the stove.

She said, "You haven't asked why I would consider two saloon whores from town to be almost family. Peddie and Belle."

"Not my place to ask," he said. "But one question I do have is why you stay here. How long can you hope to make a stand here?"

"Indefinitely, if I have to." She looked at Johnny. "According to Wolf and Ches, because of the nature of the pass leading into this canyon, two men could defend it against a small army. And have you seen the shape of the rim of the canyon? It's impossible to climb, from the inside or out. The only way in here is through the front pass."

"So, you plan to just stay here? Despite the overwhelming odds? Despite the store owners in town refusing to sell to you?"

Three steaks were sizzling away in a large skillet. She had been about to flip them, but then looked to Johnny. "This is my home, Mister McCabe."

"Johnny."

"Johnny. This is the only home I've known since I was a child. It's the only home Cora has ever known. Her father is buried out back, one of the finest men I have ever met. I can't just abandon this place. Where would I go?"

"Certainly, you must have family?"

She shook her head. "It's Cora and me. That's it. We have nowhere to go."

"Well, if it means anything, I have no plans to go anywhere. And I think I can speak the same for Matt and Joe. That's three extra guns alongside Wolf and Ches. We'll defend this place for as long as we can."

She allowed a small smile. It was weary and a little defeated, but at least it was a smile.

A call came from outside. "Riders comin'!"

The weariness was gone from her face like turning a page. In its place was alarm. Maybe a little fear.

Johnny placed a hand on her arm. "I'll check it out. You and Cora stay in the house. Tell the others, too. Tom and Lettie."

Outside, Johnny found Joe and Matt were at the stone wall. Matt had a Winchester in his hands.

Matt said, "Two riders just came in through the pass, and are heading this way."

"What happened to Wolf?" Johnny asked.

"They got past him somehow."

"I didn't hear any gunfire."

Joe said, "There's more than one way to take a man out."

Johnny nodded. There certainly were.

It was three riders. From this distance, all Johnny could see was that they wore wide hats and each one of them rode his horses like he was no stranger to it.

"Wolf's not with them," he said. Wolf had a buckskin jacket he was wearing this morning, and Johnny could see one rider seemed to have a red shirt, and the other two had darker shirts or jackets. The sun was up and Johnny could pick out the colors really well, and none of them were buckskin.

Johnny took a position at the barn, behind one corner. When the riders came into the ranch yard,

Johnny would step out from behind the corner. He would have no cover, but they wouldn't know he was there until he stepped out. Sometimes surprise was the best tool.

Joe went to a watering trough and crouched behind it. He would have cover, and he had his twin barrel scattergun in his hands. If he fired both barrels at once he could cause a world of hurt to three riders. Matt ran across the yard to a birch. Not much cover, but better than none.

The riders came into the yard, and Johnny stepped out and so did Matt.

The rider in the red shirt was actually wearing a red plaid wool shirt. He had a sombrero and wore his gun high on his hip. In the saddle was a Winchester.

Johnny recognized the man, but before he could say anything, Matt was calling out, "Hold your fire!"

It was Ben Harris, the ramrod of Matt's ranch.

The front porch had a rocker and a straight-back chair. Matt took the rocker and Ben the straight-back, and everyone else was standing. Jessica emerged with coffee cups and a fresh pot.

Ben said, "There's a lot of shady stuff going on back at the ranch. It don't take a genius to know something's wrong. How long have I ridden for you, Mister McCabe?"

Matt shrugged, doing the math quickly in his head. "You've been ramrodding for me for four years now, and worked for me for two or three before that."

"I know you didn't murder Mrs. McCabe's butler. There was always something creepy about that man, beggin' your pardon."

"Don't have to beg *my* pardon. I first met him years ago when he was more boy than man, and there was always something creepy about him. I wasn't all that surprised when he came at me with a knife that night."

Ben slapped his leg with one hand and looked at the other men. "I knew it. Didn't I say it? I knew something had to have happened."

The other two were nodding.

Matt said, "We fought and I had to kill him, but a lamp got turned over and caught the place on fire. It was out of control so fast I knew the house was going to be lost. I ran because I thought if maybe everyone thought I was dead for a while, it would give me some freedom of movement to go and figure out just what was going on.

"You see, boys, that butler, Timmons, wouldn't have tried to kill me on his own. He had to have orders. Who do you think they came from?"

Ben's mouth fell open. "Mrs. McCabe?"

Matt nodded. "Had to be."

"Gol dang." Ben looked at the other two, who were shaking their heads.

Ben said, "We took a vote in the bunkhouse last night. Whether to stay or ride on. Mrs. McCabe doubled everyone's pay the day after the fire, and everyone chose to stay, except us three."

One of them was a thin man with high, sharp cheek bones. He had a bushy beard that fell to the top button of his shirt, and was younger than Johnny had thought at first. Maybe early twenties. A beard has a way of making a man look older.

He said, "My name's Hatch. I ride for the brand. And I always thought you was the brand, Mister McCabe. I ride for you. My loyalty can't be bought off."

"Thank you, Hatch," Matt said. "That means more than you know."

The other man nodded and said, "Me too. We ride for you."

Jessica had returned the coffee pot to the stove to keep the coffee hot, and now stood in the doorway. Partly to get away from the heat of the stove, and partly because she was curious about what was going on.

Matt said, "We're mighty glad to have you men with us. But keep in mind, it could get ugly. It grieves me to admit my son Hiram is as corrupt as my wife, and they want this canyon. They believe there's a vein of gold ore running through these cliffs. And they've both shown they're willing to kill to get it."

Ben looked to Hatch, who stroked his beard thoughtfully. "Could be. I did some prospecting, at one time. Went to cowpunching because the money's better. The shape of the cliffs...a lot of it's just gut feeling, but I was thinking when we rode in here that back in my prospectin' days I would have wanted to work these cliffs a little."

Ben said, "We don't care if there's gonna be a fight, Mister McCabe. We're here with you." He glanced at Johnny and Joe. "All of you."

Jessica said, "I'm really much obliged, boys, but I can't pay you."

He hurried to his feet and snatched the hat from his head, as though he hadn't realized she was standing in the doorway. "Don't require no pay, ma'am. Just doin' what's right."

She looked at Johnny. "And, of course, this makes our supply problem even worse."

Matt glanced at Johnny.

Johnny said to him, "Mrs. Swan is running low on flour and many other things. The stores in town have been told not to sell to her."

"I'm not surprised." Matt shook his head. But then he looked at Johnny with the glint of a smile in his eyes. "But I think I might have a solution to that little problem."

21

Jessica fixed them a dinner of steak fried with wild onions.

"Steak is one thing we have a lot of," she said.

After the meal, the McCabe brothers stepped outside and stood by the stone wall looking down at the valley floor. It was now dark. Matt handed a cigar to Johnny and one to Joe, and then lit his own.

Joe said, "Are you sure you don't want me riding along with you? Three guns're better'n two."

Matt said. "We need as many guns as possible here at the canyon. What we're going to do, if two riders can't do it then three won't improve the odds much."

Johnny took a draw on the cigar. He was truly going to miss these once Matt's supply ran out. Johnny had a box of cigars on his desk back in Montana. They weren't bad, but they couldn't compare with these.

He said to Joe, "You're in charge while we're gone."

Joe nodded. "Just come back in one piece. Both of you."

Johnny saddled Thunder and picked a bay gelding from the Swan remuda for Matt. He saddled them both, but left his saddle bags and bedroll on the barn floor. He then checked the load in his rifle and tucked it into the scabbard, draped a canteen over the saddle horn and led both horses from the barn out into the ranch yard.

He found Jessica Swan waiting for him. She stood, her arms folded in front of her. The moonlight caught her hair and gave it a silvery edging.

"I don't want you doing this," she said.

"It's a sound plan."

"It's a foolhardy plan. There could be men lying in wait for you."

"We'll be careful. This is what we do. We've been through this kind of thing before. We know what to watch for."

She said nothing. He let both reins slip through his fingers and walked toward her.

He said, "We need supplies. You said so yourself. If we're going to keep this many men on, we need to feed 'em. And we need these men."

"They're not gunfighters. With the exception of you and your brothers, these men are cowpunchers. And Middleton's a professional gambler."

"I'm not sure what Middleton is. But I think he can hold his own in a fight. And these men, Ben Harris and the others. They're men to ride the river with. Like Wolf and Ches."

"I don't want you going out there. I don't want anything to happen to you."

"It'll be all right. Joe'll keep everyone here safe. And I don't think Wolf is any stranger to a gunfight. There's a certain look to his eye. You'll be all right here even if something happens to me."

"That's not what I meant." Then she glanced downward, suddenly embarrassed at what she had said.

And Johnny realized what she meant.

It had been a long time since a woman talked to him like that. It had been a long time since he wanted one to. He had spent so many years feeling guilty for the way Lura died, blaming himself. So many years alone.

"I'll be coming back," he said.

She met his gaze. "How can you be sure?"

He gave her a long look. A man could drown in her eyes. He finally said, "A gut feeling, I suppose."

"Let's just hope your gut feeling is right."

Matt came walking out. His cigar was now down to a short stub and he pulled it from his mouth and flipped it away.

He said, "Ready to ride?"

"Ready as ever," Johnny said.

Matt took the reins of the bay and pushed a foot into the stirrup and swung up and into the saddle.

Johnny took one last long look at Jessica. He said, "It'll be all right."

She nodded. She didn't look convinced.

Johnny turned and took Thunder's rein and swung into the saddle.

Matt said to him, "Do you have the letter?"

Johnny nodded and tapped the front of his vest. "Right here."

"All right. Let's ride." And Matt started down the slope toward the canyon floor.

Johnny turned in the saddle for one last look at Jessica. He hoped she would still be standing there watching, though he felt he had no reason to expect her to be. And yet she was. He nodded to her and she nodded back.

He turned and gave Thunder a light squeeze with both legs and a sort of *giddyup* motion with his hips and they started forward, down the slope. He rode with a feeling of lightness that he had not felt in a long time.

Wolf was standing guard down by the entrance to the canyon. He stepped out into view as Johnny and Matt rode up.

"I will stay here, at the opening," he said. "Until you come back."

Johnny and Matt rode through the entrance, rocks standing tall at either side, and then emerged from the canyon. Johnny reined up and Matt followed suit, and they sat in the saddle and looked at the landscape about them.

It was mostly flat, with a gentle rise or decline here or there. A lot of it was grass, which caught the moonlight like Jessica's hair had. Short fat oaks were scattered about.

Matt said, "I was bracing myself for gunfire. But there doesn't seem to be anyone out there."

"They're out there," Johnny said. "I think I know Verna well enough to know she's no fool, and she's not going to have any fools working for her. They have at least one man out there, watching this canyon. To see who's coming and going."

"Where would you place a man?"

"High ground, but not too far away." Johnny looked to his left. Maybe five hundred feet away the land rose a little and an oak stood. Short, with thick branches close to the ground. Easily climbable. "There. I'd have my horse back a ways, and I'd be in the tree. Maybe with a spyglass."

"Then maybe my plan will turn out to be a good one, because they won't be expecting us to ride in the direction we'll be riding in."

"Let's go overland. The moon's bright enough that if we take it somewhat slow we should be all right."

The trail that began at the mouth of the canyon wound its way south toward town. To the west was the McCabe Ranch. But Johnny and Matt turned southeast, away from either place, which they figured might puzzle anyone watching the canyon. Johnny figured they would expect the town or the ranch to be the two most likely places any riders from the canyon would head toward.

Johnny and Matt rode easily. At one point Thunder wanted to move into a light trot, and Johnny knew his horse had good judgment about such things so he let him have his head. Matt's bay fell into place behind him.

They rode for maybe three miles, then stopped and dismounted and loosened the cinch of each horse to let the horses breathe more easily and rest up.

Matt looked toward their back trail. "I would have expected pursuit."

Johnny shook his head. "They didn't expect us to come out at night and to ride off in this direction. There's probably only one or two men watching the canyon. They've probably been told to stay where they were and if they followed us they'd be abandoning their post. And they don't know if we'd be setting up an ambush for them."

Matt looked at his brother with appreciation and a little amazement. "It's like a chess game for you, isn't it? Warfare. It's a thing of tactics and strategy."

"I suppose that's what war is, when it comes right down to it."

"It's also about killing."

Johnny nodded. "That too. I guess maybe I've always been a little too good at both."

"Maybe you should have been a general."

Johnny shook his head. "All I ever wanted was a good horse beneath me, and miles of unbroken land all around me. A good gun at my side. A good knife. And I want my family safe."

Matt slapped Johnny in the shoulder. "Come on. Let's ride."

They rode another three miles. The land flattened out a little more and there were fewer trees. Maybe a half mile in the distance was a narrow structure standing as tall as a two-floor building.

"A water tower," Matt said. "The ten-eighteen will stop there for water. Pays to be part owner of the railroad. You keep up with the schedule."

Matt pulled a pocket watch from his vest and clicked it open, holding it so he could see the face in the moonlight. "We have about half an hour, if it's on time."

They covered the half mile in fifteen minutes. Johnny pulled his rifle free of the scabbard and stepped down to the ground.

"Stay with the horses," he said. "I'm going to climb up into the tower and have a look around. I want a look at our back trail and that tower will give the best view. I don't think we're being followed but it's best to be sure."

"What's the rifle for?"

"If we're being followed, then whoever's back there won't be reporting back."

Johnny climbed up and into the tower. The moon was not bright enough for him to have a clear view of much beyond a quarter mile, but he figured he would be able to see motion. The human eye is like that. Often it can spot motion before it can see details.

He let the minutes stretch by. Sometimes the most effective tool to survival is patience. And so he waited and watched for any motion that might indicate there was a rider behind them.

But he found none. After a time he heard a train whistle coming from the west. He looked in that direction and saw a light in the distance. He climbed back down to join Matt.

A locomotive came toward them in the night, its light growing larger. The whistle sounded again, and soon the train was close enough that Johnny could see the dark smoke rising from the stack in the moonlight.

The train came to a screeching, grinding stop, and then steam hissed from the engine. The engineer looked down at Johnny and Matt and said, "Evenin', boys. What can I do for you?"

Matt said, "We need to talk with the conductor."

The engineer nodded. He said something to his fireman, who stepped down to the ground and walked back past the wood car to the first passenger car and stepped up and in. Within a few minutes, a man in a dark suit and a cap stepped out into the doorway of the lead passenger car.

He said, "Something I can do for you gents?"

Matt stepped forward. "My name is Matthew McCabe."

The man stiffened with surprise. "Mister McCabe. Sir."

"You're heading east. We have a letter that needs to be dropped off in Cheyenne."

Johnny pulled the envelope from his vest and stepped forward and handed it to the conductor.

"I'll see it arrives, sir."

"Thank you."

"Mister McCabe," the conductor said. "Is everything all right? I mean, begging your pardon, but to be out here like, this so late at night."

Matt said. "Just see to it that letter arrives in Cheyenne."

"Yes, sir."

Johnny and Matt rode on, now heading west.

Matt said, "That house Dan talked about. The one Verna bought few years ago. It went to a small farm at the edge of the ranch property. She and Hiram tried to keep it secret, but I wasn't as oblivious as they thought."

Johnny said, "According to Dan, that's where they're staying until the new house is built. And that place must be stocked with supplies."

"That's what I'm thinking."

Verna sat in a rocker in front of the hearth. This was not the grand hearth she had enjoyed in her bed chambers at the mansion. This was a simple hearth made of bricks, by the farmer who had built this simple house years ago. The side of the hearth was a little uneven in places and the mantel nothing more than an old, rough-hewn timber. But it was functional. For now that would suffice.

In her lap was a saucer, and she brought a cup of tea to her lips. The cup shook a little. Her hand had always been steady when she was younger, but no longer. And she was tired. She was oh, so tired. When she climbed the stairs, she often felt winded. Back when she had met Matt, she had been able to run up the stairs at the old mansion easily. Matt had chased her up the stairs once, both of them laughing, and then she had hopped on the banister and slid all the way down. Now, such an effort would probably kill her.

She felt older, more worn out that she should be at this age, she thought. Maybe the pressure and strain of building this empire were catching up with her. She carried a lot of responsibility on her shoulders. She had been required to make some hard decisions over the years. Decisions that had impoverished some, and cost the lives of others. Most recently, Timmons. To make these decisions, you had to be strong. But after a time, no matter how strong you were, it was bound to wear you down.

A fire crackled low and Hiram paced behind her. He was in a string tie and jacket, and a glass of scotch was in his hand.

"Mother," he said. "Something has to be done. We are just sitting here."

"Actually, Hiram, you are standing." She said it with a little impatience.

Hiram had the proper values, she thought. He was free of the sentimentalism of Matt. She had seen to that. She had failed with Tom, and Dan simply didn't have the spine to do what had to be done. But Hiram had the right combination of strength and intelligence. What he didn't have, however, was patience.

He said, "But it feels like we're doing nothing."

"Patience is sometimes the most important attribute a person can have, Hiram. Unfortunately, it cannot be inherited. It has to be learned."

"But Dan is with them."

She sighed. "Regrettably, he has made his choice. I don't think he'll stay long, though. I don't think he has the stomach for it. Let him go hungry a while, let him live with the threat of a gun battle hanging over his head. In time, he'll return home."

"Is that what we're waiting for? For Dan to give up on them and come back?"

She shook her head. "We're waiting for the precise moment. I only hope that when it comes, Dan is not there."

"We're going to starve them out."

"A little hunger can work marvels on a person. They have beef, yes, and water. I remember that old canyon from when I was a young girl and Father would take me riding. Back then no one lived there. If I remember right, there's a natural spring there, so they'll have all the water they need. But there will be no flour. No coffee. No sugar. No one in town will sell to them—we've seen to that. And they have to live every moment on guard, ready for an attack. Such a thing can weigh on the nerves."

"I still say a rush attack is what we need. Catch them when they least expect it."

"What do you know of your uncle, Hiram?"

He shrugged. "I know I didn't find him very impressive. I would have expected more from a living legend. He's just an old man with ridiculous looking Indian hair, and living in the past. Quite frankly, I don't see what all the fuss is about."

"Don't make the mistake of underestimating him, Hiram. He is quite formidable. He has a natural head for warfare. I remember this from when he used to work for my father. Thinking strategically comes naturally to him. He was the only one I ever met who could beat Father at chess. Even I couldn't do that. And don't underestimate his physical prowess, either. The legends about him are based partially on truth. He has survived numerous gunfights, and you can't do that unless you are very good at what you do."

"You're saying he will make a worthy adversary."

She shook her head. "I'm saying he can make a truly dangerous one. The only one I've ever met who is truly on my level. Or, he could be if he chose to be."

"But he lives in a simple old cabin in the wilds of Montana. Probably not much more than this house here. Maybe not as much. Wouldn't a man on your level be building an empire of his own?"

She took another sip of tea. "He has two problems. One is the delusion that he is some sort of grand knight from the days of old. Riding in to save the poor peasants. Some sort of hero like in the days of King Arthur. The other is that he sees little value in wealth and the trappings that come with it. Give him his accursed mountains and a campfire, and he has all he wants in the world. He sees no value in power or wealth. If he had, considering who he married and the money in that family, he could have built a financial empire grander than ours. Virginia Brackston's father built a shipping business that was worth more than this ranch, back in those days, and your uncle's wife was her niece. Given your uncle's propensity for strategic thinking, he could have owned half the state by now. He could have been governor. Or a senator. He might have even been a candidate for the presidency."

Hiram made a dismissive, snorting sound. "Then why didn't you marry him, instead of Father?"

"Because I couldn't control him."

"Even still, he's an old man now."

"He's not that old. We still have to be very careful of him. Your father, by himself, is of no consequence to us. And the other people at the canyon—as I understand it, an old cowhand and some sort of an Apache scout. Small potatoes, really. And a former saloon whore and her ill-begotten child. No, the only one there of any consequence is your uncle."

"I understand the canyon's entrance is too easily guarded from the inside, and the canyon walls are too sheer to be climbed from the outside. But I still say if enough men rushed the entrance, those men with Father could be driven back."

She shook her head. "We would lose too many men in the process."

They heard Matt's voice from behind them. "Hello, everyone. I'm home."

Verna's breath caught in her chest and Hiram's whiskey glass fell to the floor, and they heard the sound of Matt's pistol cocking.

Verna rose from her chair and turned to face her husband. Hiram had turned, and he backed up until the hearth stopped him from backing any further.

"Matthew," she said, aghast. "What are you doing here?"

"Just being inconsequential."

"You heard us."

"Hard not to. The two of you talking away, leaving your backs unguarded. I really thought you'd be smarter than that, Verna. You're so good at strategic thinking."

"We have men outside."

"Not anymore."

The door opened and two men came in. Men Matt recognized as cowhands from the ranch's payroll. Jacobs and Snider. Cowhands now, but both had served in the Army fighting the Sioux and were no strangers to battle. Both in their mid-twenties. Longish hair, and with holsters at their sides. Though their holsters were now empty and their hands were held high in the air. Jacobs had a fresh, reddening bruise on his cheekbone. Johnny stepped in behind them, his Colt in his right hand.

"Evenin', Verna," he said.

Verna said nothing.

"Okay, boys, down on the floor. Face down."

They didn't hesitate.

Verna said, "What do you want?"

Matt said, walking around to Hiram, "First to apologize."

Hiram was looking at him with surprise because he apparently didn't expect his father to say that. And a little fear because for the first time in his life he was seeing his father as possibly a force to be reckoned with.

Matt said, "I failed you. I failed all three of you boys, really. Tom has done well regardless. And Dan's future is still his to shape. But you, unfortunately, are your mother's son. You are ruthless. You see people as pawns to move about or sacrifice for the sake of the greater good. And in your eyes, the greater good is your own good. I allowed myself to turn a blind eye to a lot that I shouldn't have. For that, I'm sorry."

Hiram only stared at him.

Matt then looked to Verna. "Now, for the reason we actually came. We need supplies."

She said, "You murdered Timmons and burned down the house, and now you intend to rob this one?"

"I didn't murder Timmons, and I think you know that. I killed him in self-defense. He was ordered to murder me. And who do you think gave the order?"

She said nothing.

He said, "I think Hiram knows. The sad thing is he doesn't seem to care. In the process of defending myself, a lamp was overturned and a fire was very quickly out of control.

"And taking supplies from here won't be robbery. Since the ranch and all of the property in the McCabe name belongs partially to me as long as I'm alive, you could easily say I'm just taking what's mine."

Johnny ordered Jacobs and Snider to their feet, and to begin carrying supplies from the kitchen to a buckboard out front. He then had them hitch a team to the wagon.

Matt kept Verna and Hiram in the house.

"Stealing horses now? And the wagon?" Verna said.

"Not stealing. They're partly mine, too."

Johnny tied Thunder to the back of the wagon and climbed into the wagon seat. He said to Jacobs and Snider, "Don't try to follow. I didn't kill you this time. I won't be so generous next time I see you."

Matt swung into the saddle. "Verna, as always, it's a pleasure doing business with you. Hiram, again, my apologies. If you have a change of heart, there will always be a place for you at my table."

He was about to ride away but then turned back to his son. "And be careful. Don't turn your back on your mother. You might think you can trust her, but she tried to have me killed. What makes you think she'd stop at doing the same to you?"

At that he turned his horse away and Johnny gave the reins a snap and the wagon began rolling away from the house.

Hiram and Verna stood on the front porch of the farm house watching them move away into the darkness.

"Don't listen to him," Verna said. "Of course I would never have anyone harm my own offspring."

"He has a point about one thing, though," Hiram said. "All of the family assets are partly in his name. All he has to do is get an attorney and he could make serious trouble for us. Freeze assets."

"He said the key phrase, himself. As long as he's alive."

"Mother. I was stunned that you tried to have Father killed once. You can't be thinking of doing it again. He might be pathetic, but he *is* my father."

"Oh, Hiram. Don't be ridiculous. Have you ever taken a good honest look in the mirror? Do you really think he's your father?"

She went back into the house and left Hiram standing alone on the porch.

22

It was nearly five in the morning as Johnny and Matt approached the canyon entrance. The going had been slow. Little rises and drops in the land, little outcroppings of rock, lumps of grass, things that a horse could step over or navigate around but which made traveling by wagon slow and tedious.

Wolf was standing guard and greeted them with a smile. Johnny turned the team up the grade that led to the house. He pushed on the brake with his foot and as he climbed down from the wagon, Jessica stepped from house. She was smiling widely.

He said to her, "I told you I'd come back."

"Did you have any trouble?"

He nodded. "Oh, yeah. But nothing we couldn't handle. And we didn't make any friends. Is everything all right here?"

Jessica gave a sort of I-don't-know shrug of her shoulders. "Sam's gone. Slipped out of the house without anyone noticing shortly after you left. Took one of his horses. He told Wolf he had something to take care of but said nothing more. But he left a note for Peddie saying he had an idea as to how to stop this whole thing, and to take care if he doesn't return."

"Sam's gone?" This made Johnny pause a bit.

Matt said, "Do you think he's the kind who would run out on a fight?"

Johnny shook his head. "I don't know him well, but somehow I have the feeling that's not his way."

Jessica said, "He's such a man of mystery. He always has been. Even Peddie knows very little about him. But if he were to cut and run, I couldn't blame him. It's not his fight. I just can't imagine he'd leave Peddie."

"Well, I'm not leaving. I promise you that."

Johnny was tired. Twenty years ago, the kind of night he and Matt had wouldn't have been physically taxing at all, but now he felt like every joint in his body was aching. Matt had already gone to the barn and climbed into his bedroll but Johnny felt too restless to sleep, despite how worn out he felt, so he poured a cup of coffee from a kettle Jessica had left on the stove and stepped outside.

He found Joe standing by the stone wall. His scattergun was cradled in the crook of one arm.

Joe was grinning. "You beat all, you know that? You probably added another page to the legend of Johnny McCabe."

Johnny took a sip of coffee. "This legend nonsense is starting to get tiresome."

"And yet you keep doing things that add to it. Just your nature, I guess."

"Something about this place," Johnny said, looking out over the darkened canyon floor. Soon it would be daylight, but the stars were still shining overhead. "I can see why Bernard Swan would want to build his home here. And I can see why Jessica doesn't want to be driven off."

"That's something I've been wanting to talk to you about."

Johnny took another sip of coffee. He didn't rush Joe. Many thought Joe to be a man of few words, but

Johnny had found if you didn't rush him, Joe had a lot to say. He just had to say it in his own time.

Joe said, "You're a good tactical thinker. As good as that man Tremain I work for back in Texas. Maybe even better."

Johnny waited. Joe looked off at the canyon floor. Johnny took another sip of coffee. It wasn't trail coffee, but it struck Johnny as surprisingly good. Or maybe it was just that Jessica had made it. Maybe he would like anything that had her touch.

Joe said, "I've had some thoughts about this situation we're in."

"I'm listening."

"How much money do you think they had in that house that went up flames? How much actual cash?"

Johnny shrugged. "I never thought to ask Matt."

"I figure probably not much. This land isn't really much of a frontier, anymore. The railroad's here, and banks. Most likely they have most of their assets invested in various places and have most of their cash in the bank."

Johnny nodded. "I 'spect so."

"And money is power."

Johnny nodded.

"Which means Verna has a whole lot of power. She can just hire as many gunmen as she wants to. A small army, if she wants to. And from what I understand, Bernard Swan never actually filed a claim to this place."

"He settled in here long enough ago that squatter's rights might have some precedence."

"That's something to be argued in court. If Jessica can afford an attorney. And Verna can hire the best.

And judges can be bought off. From what Dan was saying, it sounds like they've already done that."

Johnny took another sip of coffee, letting himself digest what Joe was saying. He then said, "I guess I'm not sure what you're getting at."

"What I mean is, this here is what you might call a hopeless situation. Not that Jessica isn't right morally. I think anyone with a good conscience would agree. But legal issues aren't decided on a good conscience. Verna has the power to buy her way in court, and to hire enough men to outgun us. How long can we really hold out here?"

Johnny looked off at the canyon floor.

Joe said, "I see how you look at her. Something like how you looked at Lura. And I understand, believe me. I know how a woman can grab hold of a man's heart and shape his thinking. But if you were in my place and looking at this more from the outside in, what would you say? From a military point of view, would you agree to make a stand here?"

"I'm not sure. But I do know Jessica's not leaving. I talked to her about that already. It's the only home her daughter has ever known."

"Understand that I'm with you no matter what. If you want to make a stand here, I'm with you."

Johnny said, "I know that."

"But I'm afraid that, if she doesn't leave she's gonna end up dying here. And so will the rest of us."

Joe turned and walked away and left Johnny standing alone with Joe's words fresh in his mind. Johnny took another sip of coffee and looked off at the canyon floor. In the east, the sky began to lighten to a dull gray with the first promise of morning.

PART THREE

The Stand

23

The weeks went by and November blended into December. The nights turned off cold, enough to warrant a fire in the parlor hearth. Another problem, Johnny knew, would eventually be finding access to firewood. Here in this part of California there was very little. Wood was usually brought in from the mountains and purchased, and this would present a problem because he was sure Verna wouldn't allow any firewood vendors to do business with them. And the mountains were too far away for Johnny and the others to feasibly cut the firewood themselves. He said nothing about this to Jessica, though he was sure she had thought about it as well.

He also thought about what Joe had said. About the futility of making a long-term stand here. But he said nothing about this to Jessica, either.

Johnny expected trouble from Verna. He doubled the guard at night. He had a man stationed at the canyon entrance and one at the stonewall. And yet, no riders came. He thought sometimes the waiting was harder on the nerves than an actual gun battle. Maybe this was part of Verna's plan.

Dan recovered from his wounds and began taking turns at guard duty.

"Look, Dan," Matt said to him. "I appreciate the fact that you're not standing with your mother and

Hiram. I really do. But you don't have to stay here. I don't want anything to happen to you."

"Father," he said. "I'm a man, now. And even more, I'm a McCabe. The name has to mean something. And standing for what's right is part of what it means."

Matt relayed this to Johnny one morning over coffee. Johnny said, "Looks like you raised him right, after all."

One morning Johnny asked Jessica to join him for a walk. He had a cup of coffee in one hand, and they talked of nothing and everything. The sunlight brought little freckles along her cheeks and nose to life. She would sometimes break into a smile as they talked. Her smile would seem to make any heaviness in his heart fall away. The heaviness he always walked with because of all the men he had killed and all of the killing he had seen.

The following day she suggested a walk, and soon morning walks with her had become routine.

He talked of Lura and how he had struggled with the loss over the years, and finally come to terms with it. He told her of his home in Montana and his sons and daughter. He told her of Dusty and how he had come to live with them.

"You love them all very much," she said.

He nodded. "They give me grounding. They fill my heart."

"And here I am, keeping you from them."

He looked her in the eye. "I'm where I'm meant to be. Where I want to be."

He touched the side of her face, and she closed her eyes the way a woman does when she likes a man's touch. And then their lips met. Lightly, gently. And then again.

He said, "I'm a fair bit older than you."

She merely smiled at him. "It makes no difference to me. What I care about is what's in the heart."

When he was taking his turn at the stonewall one afternoon, she joined him. She sat on the wall, placing both hands behind her and leaning back a little, and he stood with one knee on the wall and his rifle resting across it. The day was turning off cold. Nothing like the winters in Montana, but it was cold for California. Johnny was wearing his buckskin jacket, and Jessica had a thick, quilted shawl about her shoulders.

She talked of her life. Her parents had gone to California with the gold rush in '49 and she was born shortly afterward. Both parents died of fever when she was in her teens and she wound up in the saloons.

"Then Bernard Swan took a liking to me, for reasons I can't fathom."

Johnny said, "I can fathom it quite easily."

She gave him a smile that said she appreciated the nice words but still didn't understand it. She said, "When you look at what I was. The kind of work I was doing."

"Some of us look at the person, not the work. And some of us understand the way things are, that people have to do what they have to do to survive. It sounds like Bernard Swan was a good man."

She nodded. "He was. He was old enough to be my father, but he was so in love with me. He would do anything for me. He would buy an entire night with me just so I wouldn't have to be with anyone else, and we would just have coffee and talk. He would bring me out here to the ranch and I would have my own bedroom. But he never touched me, not until we were married. But he was so in love. It was impossible not to love him back. When he asked me to marry him I wanted to say no. I knew I wasn't good enough for him. I felt like I was taking advantage of him. But I wanted the life he offered me, and like I said, it was impossible not to love him back.

"Then he died. A couple of years after Cora was born. This is the only home she had ever known. Bernard was a good man, but one problem was that he was from the old way of doing things. When he was a young man in the west, there was very little of this business of filing claims. You just lived on a piece of land and said it was yours, and that was that."

"That's largely the way it still is in my part of Montana."

"But here, it's becoming more like it is back east. You have to file legal claims, and since Bernard didn't, the McCabes—apparently your brother's wife and their son—filed a claim on this canyon. It's now legally theirs."

"Matt thinks you would have a good argument in court because of squatter's rights."

"That would require a lawyer. I don't have much cash on hand."

Johnny nodded. He understood this. Most ranches operated with very little actual cash. They survived on credit most of the time, and repaid their debts when they sold some beef. There was usually not much extra cash left over.

"So," she said. "I suppose I know we're fighting a losing battle here. I guess I've known it all along. I know that's what's being said by the men here."

"Don't worry about what they say."

"I have to, John. They're all here for me and Cora. You are too. I know that."

He shrugged. "Well, I am a fugitive from the law, remember. I'm here, laying low."

"You could have just ridden out and gotten through the mountains before the snows. You stayed here because of Cora and me."

He smiled. "All right. Guilty as charged."

She returned the smile. "I stayed so long because this is the only home Cora has known, and the first one I've had since I was fifteen. But with so many of you here because of me, maybe it's given me an added sense of responsibility. I don't want to get anyone killed because of me."

"But if you leave, where would you go?"

She gave a long, slow shrug. "I have no idea. I really don't."

He touched the side of her face and she looked up to meet his eyes. He said, "I know where you could go. Have you ever seen Montana?"

"I can't accept charity. I never could."

"You could build a home there."

She shook her head. "It's one thing to be here, maintaining this ranch as best I can. But I know nothing of building a ranch from the ground up. And I know nothing at all about farming."

"Maybe you wouldn't have to start from the ground up."

She looked at him curiously.

Johnny knew where this was going, if he continued along this trail. But he found he didn't want to stop. It was soon. They had known each other only a couple of months. And yet he knew how he felt about her.

He wasn't watching the canyon floor as intensely as he should, but he didn't care at the moment. He said, "You and Cora would find my home warm and dry."

She looked at him as she realized his full meaning. "John, we hardly know each other."

"I've found it's not about how long two people have known each other, but how well they do. Look at Matt and Verna. They've known each other more than twenty years, but are only now starting to understand each other a little. And I think they're both a little surprised by what they're seeing."

She looked away, a little breathlessly. Then she looked back. "Are you really asking me to marry you?"

"It's not the proper place for a marriage proposal, I suppose. A nice restaurant would have been better. A bottle of fine wine on the table. Candles burning. But sometimes you have to alter your plans because of the times. You and Cora have no place to go, and I want you both with me. It's as simple as that."

"Is it really that simple? Is love really that simple?"

He nodded. "I've found love is one of the simplest things there is. We complicate it to pieces, but if you get right down to the brass tacks, love is simple. It's just there, or it isn't. And if it is, do you want it to grow? I know how I feel about you, and I want it to grow."

She said, "I'm not Lura."

"I know that. I don't want you to be. I'll always have a piece of my heart reserved for her. Just like I know you will for Bernard. And you know fully well I'm not him. But that doesn't mean we can't build a life together. Yes, I know, it's a little sudden, but I think the situation might require it."

She got to her feet.

He said, "You'll be living amongst gunhawks. But I think you know that."

"You're a man of the gun. I've known some over the years. Some are really bad men, but some are really good. You and your brothers fall into the second category, and I'm sure your sons do. But to me that's not a concern."

"It's rough country that I'll be taking you to. But it's good country. The valley we're in is three miles from a small community of maybe thirty people, and it's almost a day's ride to the nearest real town. But they're good people. Hard working, salt-of-the-earth types."

"So, when would we make this move? I'd like to hang on here at least through Christmas. It's only three weeks away. Do you think we could hang on that long? I'd like Cora to have one last Christmas in our home."

Johnny nodded and found himself smiling. "I think we can hold out that long. Maybe Joe and I'll take a ride into town tonight and survey things."

Her smile began to fade.

"It'll be okay. We know how to do this. We won't attract any attention."

She nodded. "Okay. Then," the smile was back, "maybe I should go tell Cora."

"One thing, though. You haven't actually said yes."

She grinned. Then she laughed. "Yes. Yes, absolutely. Yes, without a doubt."

And she leaped at him and he took her in a hug that lifted her feet completely off the ground, and they kissed and his rifle fell to the ground and he didn't notice, and he whirled her around and she laughed and they kissed again.

That evening in the barn, Johnny told his two brothers. He wanted them to know before he and Jessica made a general announcement to everyone.

Matt gave him a long look.

Johnny said, "I know it's kind of quick. It probably seems too soon. I've only known her for maybe two months."

Matt shook his head. "No. It's not too soon. I've seen the way you look at each other. When the two of you are at each other's side, you both look so complete. When you're apart, it looks like someone's missing. Even now, it's like there's an empty space at your side that's meant for Jessica to fill."

Johnny looked at his brother with wonder. Matt always did seem to know the right thing to say at the right time.

Matt said, "After all of the years you've been alone. All of the years you've grieved for Lura. I think she would want you to be happy. We all do. And there's no finer woman than Jessica Swan. This I've come to believe. I've been talking with Peddie, and she talks so very highly about Jessica."

"Thank you, Matt." Johnny extended his hand and Matt shook it.

Joe said nothing. Instead he simply held out his hand and Johnny shook it, and then Joe gave a little half grin. The closest he ever seemed to come to a full smile.

He then went to his saddle bags and pulled out a bottle of scotch. "I think it's time to celebrate."

Johnny said, "How long have you had that?"

"Got it in town, when I first rode in. Before I come out to the canyon. Got it from Artie. Figured if I was reunitin' with my brothers we should have a bottle of whiskey on hand. For old times' sake."

He pulled the cork out and handed the bottle to Johnny. Johnny took a pull from it.

He said, "We did go through a bottle or two back in the old days, didn't we?"

Joe was giving his half grin again.

Johnny handed the bottle to Matt. Matt said, "I really shouldn't, I suppose. I hid behind a bottle of scotch for so many years."

Johnny said, "An old friend of mine once said, it ain't how much you drink, it's why you drink. Apache Jim Layton."

Matt said, "You've mentioned him."

Johnny nodded. "An old scout and frontiersman. Sort of a mentor to me at one time."

Matt took a sip and handed the bottle to Joe.

Joe said, "Well, sometimes it *is* about how much you drink," and took a long pull from the bottle. Matt and Johnny laughed.

Joe handed it back to Johnny, and Johnny went to one corner to sit on the hay-strewn floor with his back to the wall. Matt joined him. Joe sat on the floor facing them, his legs crossed in what Johnny thought of as Indian-style.

Johnny said, "I really can't drink too much of this. I don't do a lot of that anymore."

Joe said, "You were known for some historic benders."

Johnny nodded with a smile. "That I was. But those days are behind me."

He took another swallow of whiskey and handed the bottle to Matt.

Johnny said, "We need to make some plans on how to get these folks out of here. Jessica wants Cora to have one more Christmas here."

Matt said, "Christmas is a couple weeks away."

"I think we can hold out that long. But I'm thinking you and I should maybe take a ride into town tonight and get a feel for things."

Matt had taken another swallow of whiskey and handed the bottle to Joe.

Matt said to Johnny, "I presume you're planning on taking Jessica and Cora to Montana."

Johnny nodded.

"You are a wanted man, you know. Even though the charges are false, the reward is very real. There's nothing to stop bounty hunters from coming after you."

"Then let them find me."

Joe handed the bottle to Johnny, who looked at the bottle silently for a moment, then decided two drinks was enough and handed it to Matt.

Matt held his hands up in a stopping motion and said, "No, I'm shutting myself off. I suppose a taste now and again won't do me any harm, but I don't want too much of it. Not anymore."

"Me neither," Johnny said.

Joe took the bottle back and returned the cork to it. He said, "We're gettin' old, you know that?"

Johnny looked at Matt. "I know what you're thinking. The bullet that took Lura was meant for me. And we didn't even have a price on our heads anymore. Those charges had been dropped."

Matt said, "Maybe I can talk to Verna. Make some sort of arrangement with her. I'm sure she's the one behind it all. Trying to find some way to eliminate you from the game."

Joe said to Matt, "What kind of a deal could you possibly make with her?"

"I can grant her a divorce and let her have everything, on the agreement she rescind the reward."

Johnny said, "I can't ask you to do that, Matt."

"I don't want it anymore. The wealth, the empire she's trying to build. I don't want any of it. Considering all of the under-handed things she's done to build it. She and Hiram, with me signing off on things I didn't even always know what I was signing off on. I can't believe the things she's doing now are anything new. How many people has she hurt along the way? How many has she killed? She and Hiram? No, I don't want any of it. Not anymore. That fortune is tainted. What I want, Johnny, is to ride to Montana with you. I want to maybe stake out a small claim. Run a few head. Build a small place."

Joe glanced at Matt with a little sparkle in his eye. Joe was always good at playfully needling his brother. "You thinking of Peddie? I've seen you talking with her quite a bit."

"Now, I'm not saying that." But Matt was suddenly blushing like a schoolboy who had been caught stealing glances at a pretty girl a few desks away.

Johnny said, "What's this? I guess I've been so focused on Jessica I didn't realize what was happening under my very nose."

Matt held his hands up again. "Now, nothing is happening. I just like her company, that's all."

Joe said, "Do you think she'd want to go to Montana?"

Matt nodded thoughtfully. "Maybe I might mention it to her. If it comes up. See what she says."

Johnny said to Joe, "So he has two reasons to make a deal with Verna."

Matt said, "Now, I didn't say anything."

Joe was grinning. "You didn't have to. You're turnin' red from your collar to your hat. Kind of says it all."

Johnny and Joe thought it might be best to wait until late to ride into town. Wait until people were asleep. So Johnny milled about. Smoked one of Matt's last cigars. Cleaned his rifle. All the while watching the clock.

Tom and Lettie and Mercy were asleep by the time Johnny drifted into the parlor. He tossed the stub of Matt's cigar into the fire. Jessica was sitting on the sofa with Cora.

Johnny said, "I'm going to miss those."

Ches was standing guard down by the canyon entrance with Ben Harris. The other men were in the bunkhouse. Johnny wasn't really sure where Joe was. Johnny had seen him rubbing down his horse a half hour earlier in the barn. He wasn't sure where Matt was, either, and noticed Peddie was missing. They were probably taking a little moonlight stroll. From what Johnny could see, he and Jessica and Cora were the only three awake in the house.

Jessica said, "I might go put on a pot of coffee. I don't plan on going to bed until I know you're back from town safe."

"I hate to make you lose sleep," Johnny said.

She grinned. "Get used to it. I never can sleep well unless all of mine are safe."

She gave Cora a hug. "I'll be out in the kitchen."

Cora nodded and yawned.

Jessica said, "You sit with Johnny and I'll tuck you in once I get the coffee going."

She nodded again.

Jessica stepped out into the kitchen, and Cora said to Johnny, "Is it true? Are you gonna be my new father?"

"C'mere," Johnny said.

She got to her feet and crossed the room and Johnny hoisted her up onto his knee.

He said, "You have one father, Cora. He's in heaven now, but he'll always be your father. I would never try to replace him. But that doesn't mean I can't be sort of your second father. I love your mother very much and I want you and her to come live with me and be my family."

He waited while she digested all of that. She was in some ways so similar to Bree at that age, and yet so different. Hair that was sort of a reddish blonde, and she had pronounced freckles along her nose and cheeks and forehead.

She said, "I guess that would be okay. But what should I call you?"

He shrugged. "What would you like to call me?"

"I called my father Daddy."

"Well, I don't think that would work. That name should be for him alone. Don't you think?"

She nodded thoughtfully. "Do you have any other kids?"

He said. "I have four of 'em. They're mostly all grown up now."

"What're their names?"

"Well, the oldest is Josh. He's twenty-one, now."

"Wow. He's gettin' *old.*"

Johnny nodded with a smile. "I'll make sure and tell him that. And then there's Dusty."

"Dusty?" she said with a giggle. "Is he all covered with dust?"

Johnny smiled. "Only when he comes back from working with the cattle all day. We call him Dusty because his name's actually Dustin. Then there's Jack. He's off in medical school, back east. Gonna be a doctor. And then there's the youngest, my daughter Bree. Her real name is Virginia Sabrina. We call her Bree for short."

"Do you think they'll like me?"

"Oh, honey, I think they'll love you. How could they not? You're a great little girl."

"Where's their mama?"

"Oh, she died a long time ago."

"Do you miss her?"

Johnny nodded. "Yes I do. I suppose I always will."

"I miss my daddy too."

"I think it's good to miss those you love, when they go to heaven. But that doesn't mean there's not a whole lot of people here to love, too."

"Sounds like you have a house-full."

That brought a chuckle from Johnny. He also heard a soft giggle from across the room and saw Jessica was standing in the kitchen doorway watching them.

"Well," Johnny said. "Looks like your mother is done with the coffee. I think it's probably time for you to go to bed."

Cora nodded. "Looks like."

She hopped down and said, "You smell like cigars and leather."

Johnny laughed again. "Is that all right?"

She nodded. "It'll do. Good night."

"Can I have a hug?"

She threw her little arms around him and he held her close. Then she scurried across the room to Jessica who took her hand and the two headed off down the hall.

Johnny drifted outdoors and went to the stone wall. No one was posted there at the moment because in the dark you couldn't see the canyon entrance at all. He stood a moment and breathed the air and listened. All sounded as it should.

The kitchen door opened and Jessica stepped out and walked over to him. "She's asleep."

Johnny nodded. "She's a great little girl."

"You seem to be really adept at winning the hearts of Swan women."

He pulled her to him. "Well, if you're gonna do something, do it well. That's what I always say."

Their lips met, then she stood beside him looking down at the canyon. His arm was around her and she let her head settle onto his shoulder.

"Be careful out there tonight," she said. "Come back to us."

"I plan on always coming back to you."

24

Matt said, "How do you plan on getting out of the canyon without being seen?"

Joe and Johnny were in the barn saddling their horses, and Matt was standing with them.

Johnny said, "No way we can ride out through that pass without being seen. If Wells is still having it watched."

"You think he still is? After all these weeks?"

Johnny nodded. "I do."

"Then, what're you going to do?"

Joe said, "We'll improvise."

Johnny pulled the cinch tight. "When you're riding into an unknown situation, it's best not to have too many plans."

They led their horses out of the barn. Jessica was waiting.

Johnny took Jessica into a hug.

He said, "I'll be back."

She said, "I'll be waiting."

Johnny swung into the saddle. Joe did the same. They started their horses down the long slope toward the canyon floor.

Jessica stood beside Matt and watched them go. She said, "I hate this. I wish he didn't have to do this."

"We have to find out what's going on outside of this canyon. See if we can figure out what Verna's planning. Johnny and Joe are the best two for the job."

She nodded. "Doesn't mean I have to like it."

"Come on. Let's go in. It's getting cold out here. I think I could go for some of that coffee you made."

Johnny and Joe stepped out of their saddles and let the reins trail. They made the rest of the way through the pass on foot, the rock walls of the pass standing dark to either side of them.

At the point where the entrance to the canyon widened out, they dropped to the earth and crawled out the rest of the way, stopping when they had a clear view of the terrain beyond the pass.

They could see a fire flickering away from the rise where the fat oak tree stood. The place where Johnny had told Matt that he would be positioned if he had been assigned to watch the canyon.

"Not too smart of 'em," Joe said. "Tellin' the world right where they are."

"Hard thing to stand guard at night in cold like this without a fire."

"It's chilly, but it ain't nothin' like what you get up at your home in Montana."

"Anything less than warm is cold."

"Maybe I should write that one down."

Johnny elbowed him.

Joe said, "It's dark. Quarter moon up there. Bright enough that riders leaving the canyon will be seen from that rise, but dark enough that a man on foot could make it. Especially if there was a distraction."

"Not a bad idea. And I know just the thing for the distraction. Come on, let's head back to the horses. I've gotta get my deerskin boots on."

Joe swung into the saddle and started for the open end of the pass, leading Thunder as he went. Thunder balked a bit at this.

"Be careful with him," Johnny had said. "The stallion's only half broke. Doesn't take too kindly to riders he doesn't know. There's only maybe five of us can ride him at all."

The stallion danced and pulled back on the rein. Joe had to grip it tightly.

"Hold on there, big fella," he said. "You take off on me too soon and this won't work."

The horse didn't listen. Joe didn't really expect him to. The horse gave a pull, letting go with a violent snort as it did so. If the rein had been in Joe's right hand, the one he had taken a bullet through a few years earlier in Texas, then Thunder would have pulled free. But Joe was holding it with his left, and he held on tight. To do this, he had to sling the scattergun over his back using a leather strap he had improvised. Thunder's rein was in his left hand, and he held his own horse's rein with his right.

With Thunder protesting, Joe rode from the canyon, keeping the horses to a quick walk. Once they were beyond the canyon entrance, Thunder gave a loud protest, a sort of shrieking whinney, and rose up on his hind hooves.

"Now hold on!" Joe shouted.

Thunder was not in a cooperative mood. He reared back again, with Joe barely holding on. His horse decided to join the festivities and pulled back, and Joe was almost pulled from the saddle by Thunder.

Thunder then stood and looked at him, then gave a lurching bolt backwards, and the rein was free, and the stallion turned and galloped away into the night. Joe let out a stream of curses and then charged after him.

Which was all according to what Johnny figured would happen if a man Thunder didn't know tried to lead him. Even Bree couldn't ride this horse. Thunder could be loud and put on a show, and he had not failed to disappoint this time.

And while the whole thing had been happening, Johnny made his way out of the canyon on foot.

He was in his buckskin boots. He left his rifle in the saddle because if any shooting had to be done, it would be with a pistol at close range. Though he hoped to get this done without any shooting. Partly because it would be bad strategically—the sound of a gunshot could carry, especially at night. But also because of the trail of bodies he had left over the years. He didn't want to add to it unless he had to, and he sometimes found it disturbing that he couldn't count the number of men he had killed. Though sometimes at night their faces would come back to him in his dreams.

He could hear the hoof beats of both horses fade into the distance as he crouched and made his way toward the rise. The breeze was brisk and coming from the rise toward him, which meant the horses the sentries had likely picketed wouldn't catch his scent.

He could hear voices.

A man, with a coarse voice. "What do you suppose that was about?"

Another man with a little higher vocal pitch, laughing. "I don't know. But I'd say the horse won that little battle."

"Where do you suppose he was goin?"

Another chuckle. "I have no idea."

Johnny was close enough now that he could see the men in the firelight. One man, the first who had spoken, lifted a bottle to his mouth. Then the man said, "You know, you gotta wonder why a man would need to bring along a second saddle horse."

The first man shrugged. He was kneeling by the fire, poking at it with a long stick. "Maybe he was goin' to pick someone up somewheres."

"I wonder if one of us should ride into town and tell Wells."

Johnny drew his gun and cocked it. The sound was loud in the night and the head of each man snapped in his direction.

Johnny said, "Neither of you are riding anywhere. And don't go for those guns or I'll plant a bullet in you."

He stepped into the firelight. "Mighty nice of you both to have this fire. Let us know you were here."

Both men raised their hands. The one with the whiskey bottle said, "We don't mean no trouble out there, Mister McCabe. We's just followin' orders."

"Then it's not worth dying over."

Both men shook their heads eagerly. The first one said, "No, sir."

"Then, draw those guns and drop the bullets on the ground."

They did as they were told. Both had Colt revolvers. They held their pistols upright, opened the loading gate on each, and spun the cylinders while the bullets fell out.

Johnny said, "Now toss those guns into the fire."

They did as they were told.

Johnny said, "I'm not going to steal your horses, but I'm going to borrow them. I have to ride after my brother and help him run down my stallion. Your horses will be in town waiting for you."

"But," the second man said, "how are we gonna get to town?"

"By walking. If you start now you should be there by morning."

Both horses were still saddled. The cinches had been loosened so Johnny tightened one and then swung into the saddle.

He said, "I would start walking now. It's going to get mighty cold standing out here."

The one with the bottle said, "If it's all the same to you, Mister McCabe, we'd like to wait by the fire tonight and start walking in the morning."

"Suit yourself," and Johnny turned the horse and, leading the other, started off in the direction in which Joe had disappeared.

25

Verna stood in front of the little brick hearth of the farmhouse. She would be in her new mansion within a month, but for the moment had to conduct business here. If she were a man, she thought, she would simply set up an office in San Francisco and work out of there. But women did not have their own offices. Maybe someday. There was a political movement starting to gain momentum back east. They called it Women's Suffrage in the papers.

In the center of the room stood Wells. Smelling of sweat and whiskey, like he usually did. And with him was a man who she found truly frightening. Long black hair fell to his shoulders. His face was deeply lined. In a couple of places she thought the lines might be scars, but for the most part his face looked like it did simply from rough living. He had a look of lifelessness in his eyes. Like he was so filled with sadism and the joy of killing that there was very little human being left within him.

Oh, Verna had killed. Sometimes it was necessary and she was not squeamish about it. But to do so simply for some sort of insane pleasure was a different thing entirely.

He wore a black stetson with a hatband that was decorated in what looked like Indian turquois and various shades of red. He wore a buckskin shirt. A knife so long it looked more like a small sword was sheathed at his right side and a pistol was at his left, turned backward for a cross-draw.

"Ma'am," Wells said, "this is Will Buck."

"Buck?" she said. "Is that short for something?"

The man shook his head. "Not that I know of."

Wells said, "Buck, this is Verna McCabe."

"The queen bee," he said.

She could not tell if he was grinning or sneering. Or both. Maybe a man like this didn't have enough humanity left within him to truly smile.

She decided to ignore his remark. Partly because she didn't want him to grow angry with her and decide to make her a target, and partly because she wanted to get down to business.

"I want to hire you," she said. "I need someone killed."

"Who?"

"Actually, very likely more than one."

She explained there was a canyon where some people were being holed up. She told him where it was and gave him a rough description of the features of the canyon. Namely that there was only one way in or out, and the walls were too sheer to be scaled.

"I need Johnny McCabe killed."

He raised a brow at this. "Johnny McCabe? The gunfighter?"

"The very one. And his brother Matt. And anyone else in that canyon who gets in your way. I'll pay you a full thousand for the death of each McCabe. Two hundred each for the others"

He shook his head. "Didn't know it was Johnny McCabe I was going up against. That could be suicide."

"Are you afraid?"

He didn't react. His eyes didn't even flicker. She wondered if he was even capable of human emotion.

He said, in a flat voice, "I ain't afraid of nothin', ma'am. But I know what I'm up against."

"Don't believe everything you hear about him."

"I actually met him once. Years ago, in a saloon. I could tell by the way he moved, the look in his eye. He's the most dangerous man I ever met. It's gonna cost you more."

She sighed. So this was it. Money. It always came down to money. She cast a glance at Hiram, who stood across the room from her. He gave a weary shake of the head.

"How much?" she said.

"Five thousand for him."

This made her eyes pop open. "Five thousand dollars? That's more than a miner will make in ten years."

"None of your miners are goin' up against Johnny McCabe."

Verna sighed. She didn't want to part with the cash. But she had hired a detective to look far and wide to find a man who was capable of holding his own with Matt's brother.

She said, "All right. I'll pay you half now and half when you're finished."

He shook his head. "I don't take money for a job till I done it."

"When will you do it?"

"Right now." He glanced at a grandfather clock standing against the far wall. It read twenty-two past nine. "I'll leave right now. If the canyon is where you say it is, I'll be a couple hours gettin' there in the dark. Another hour maybe, scoutin' the place out. Then I'll go in and do it."

"Just like that? Go in and do it? I'm sure they have the entrance well guarded."

"I don't want anyone to see me, they won't. I'll be back tomorrow to collect my money. Have it in twenties, fives and ones."

And without another word he turned and stepped out the door and closed it behind him.

Hiram had been standing back, watching the whole thing. "Mother! What are we doing now? Hiring thugs?"

"We hire the men we need to do the job, no matter which facet of the business we are dealing with." She looked at Wells. "Is he really as good as he says he is? Can he really just waltz into that canyon unseen and kill Johnny McCabe? Many have tried, and they're all in the ground."

Wells said, "I'd start getting the money together."

Johnny carried no watch, but estimated the time to be midnight or a little after, judging by the position of the moon. He expected the town to be pretty much closed up for the night. Stores with darkened windows and locked doors, houses in a similar situation, streets empty. And yet what he and Joe found were riders charging up and down the street firing their guns into the air. Shouting and cheering. Saloons were open.

Johnny and Joe slipped in through an alley. A bonfire in the center of the main street was burning wildly, but they held back in the shadows of the alley so they wouldn't be seen.

"Wonder what's going on here?" Joe asked.

"I can't imagine."

They heard a women laughing hysterically from above. They were in the alley beside the Cattleman's Lounge, and there was a second floor balcony overlooking the street. A man stopped in the street not far from the alley and took a deep pull from a bottle and then howled like a wolf.

A woman began screaming as she was dragged into the alley in front of Johnny and Joe. The man hadn't seen them. The woman's neckline was cut low, and from what Johnny could see in the firelight her makeup was a little heavy. Probably worked in the saloon.

She was screaming, "No! Let me go!"

The man shook her and slammed her backward into the wall. "Shut up," he hissed at her through closed teeth.

Johnny tapped him on the shoulder. The man turned around.

"Hi," Johnny said and drove his fist into the man's face.

The man's feet went out from under him and he landed on his back on the ground, and remained there unconscious. The smell of whiskey was radiating from him. Johnny didn't know if it was the punch that put him out, or the whiskey.

"Thank you so much," the woman said, then she looked Johnny squarely in the face. "Mister McCabe. I didn't realize it was you. My name's Rose."

Johnny was shaking his hand in the air. Punching a man in the face can bruise up your knuckles. "I'd like it if you didn't tell anyone I was here."

She shook her head. "I won't. I'll do anything to help you. I know for a fact you didn't kill Belle."

Joe stepped forward. "How?"

"Because I saw who done it."

Johnny said, "Who?"

"It was that boy. The son of the man who owns the mine. It was that man, the butler who died in that fire. They called him Timmons."

Matt stood by the stone wall, the Swan house behind him. The moon was only one quarter tonight and the canyon floor below was a void of blackness. He had a cup of coffee in one hand.

As he took a sip, Ches ambled up to him.

"Thought you'd have climbed into a bunk by now," Matt said.

Ches shook his head. "Tried. Couldn't sleep. Somethin's wrong."

"Wrong? Where?"

"I don't rightly know. Just a feelin' that somethin' ain't right. Call it a gut feelin', I guess."

Matt gave him a long look. One thing Matt had learned over the years was when you have an old scout or an old cattle hand available and he tells you something like this, you take it seriously.

Matt said, "You think something's happened to Johnny and Joe?"

Ches shook his head and shrugged his shoulders at the same time. "I don't rightly know. But you know that feelin' you get right before a battle? Right before the shootin' starts? You can feel the hairs on the back of yer neck just sort of start standin' up?"

Matt nodded. "I know the feeling."

"Well, I got it right now."

Matt looked back to the canyon floor. Then he glanced at the house. He turned his gaze up toward the rock wall that stood tall and sheer beyond the house. The wall was a sheet of blackness, but he knew it was there and he knew it was impossible to climb.

He said, "Who's standing guard down at the canyon entrance?"

"Wolf and Hatch."

"I think I might head down and check on things."

"I'll go with you."

Matt thought a moment. He wasn't the tactician his brother was, so he asked himself what his brother might do. "No, maybe you should stay here. Check the house. Are Ben and Price still at the bunkhouse?"

Price was the man who had ridden in with Ben and Hatch.

Ches nodded. "They're both sawin' 'em off in there."

"Wake them up and tell them to stand ready. Just in case."

Matt went to the corral and threw a loop on his horse and then saddled it. It was not even a quarter mile down to the canyon entrance, but no self-respecting cattleman would walk when he could ride. And Matt was getting back his self-respect. Discovering pieces of himself he didn't realize he had let slip away over the years.

In some ways, he was losing everything. The ranch, and his son Hiram. And he realized he wasn't actually losing Verna because he never really had her in the first place. The woman he thought she was had never existed. But in a way, with these realizations, he felt more alive than he had in a long time.

He led his horse out of the barn and then drew his revolver and checked the loads, then swung into the saddle and rode down to the rocks at the canyon entrance.

He found the horses Wolf and Price had ridden. They were both saddled, but the cinches had been loosened. The horses were where they should have been. Probably nothing was wrong at all, he thought. Ches was just being jumpy. Easy to get jumpy, though, standing around day after day and waiting for men hired by Verna to attack.

Matt swung out of the saddle and made his way along one side of the rocky canyon entrance. It was dark. It was almost like walking with his eyes shut. He knew when standing guard down here you took a position near the outside entrance, climbing up onto a rock so you had a look down at the pass itself, and had a little cover in case lead started flying.

He walked through the pass, listening as he moved. He could hear his hard boot soles making scuffing sounds on the gravel underfoot.

"Wolf?" he called out in a loud whisper. "Price?"

There was no answer. Matt walked a little further on. Now he found he was having a gut feeling that something was wrong, so he drew his gun. There was no rational reason for doing so, but he knew Johnny and Joe both survived by heeding their gut feelings. So Matt decided to do the same.

He was now near the opening. He called out again. "Wolf! Price!"

There was no answer, except the cool wintry wind whipping past and making a little howling sound as it made its way into the canyon. Matt wore no jacket, as it was not the chill-to-the-bone cold Johnny experienced in Montana, but he pulled his shirt collar close and hunched his shoulders a little.

He reached out with his left hand in the darkness and found the boulder Wolf liked to sit on when he was standing guard. Around to the side was an opening between the rocks and a little uphill grade that let you climb up and onto the boulder. Matt made his way slowly through this opening, his pistol with his right hand, and he held his left out in front of him so he wouldn't crash into anything should he be wrong about where he was. He walked by reaching forward with his left foot and then shuffling his right along to catch up with it.

He found the grade and then began climbing up, and his foot hit something. Could be a rock, he thought. He had never navigated this path in such pitch blackness. He reached down with his left, and found it was a man's boot.

He recoiled back, not expecting to find this. He needed light, he knew. He had a small box of matches in his vest pocket to light his cigars with. The light of a match might be visible from out beyond the canyon, but he had to risk it. He fumbled in the pocket with his left for the box and pulled it out and slid it open. Some matches tumbled to the ground but he paid them no mind. He managed to get a grip on one before it fell, then he let the box drop away and he struck the match on the side of his gunbelt.

Before him, lying on the ground, were Wolf and Price. Their throats had been cut.

Johnny said to Rose, "Are you sure? It was Timmons?"

She said, "I've seen him enough times. Everyone in town knows what he looks like. Every time that McCabe woman came to town, he was with her."

Joe said, "Well, what do you make of that?"

Johnny didn't know what to say. A lot was going through his mind at once. He hadn't expected to hear this. He had really thought Wells or one of his men might be the culprits. But he supposed he wasn't surprised. After all, Timmons had tried to kill Matt.

Johnny said to Joe, "From what Matt said about Timmons, this means Verna probably had it done."

Joe said, "So they could frame you for it."

Johnny said to Rose, "Would you be willing to testify against him if it came to that? If it came to a trial?"

"I sure would. I want Belle's killer to hang. But," she chuckled, "I don't see it going to court. That family owns the law. That woman and her son. And they own the local court. Money is power, and they have more than enough to rule this entire county."

The man Johnny had punched stirred a little.

Johnny said to Rose, "You'd best be getting along. You don't want to be seen talking to us."

"I owe you," she said. "For taking care of Frank, here. And any help you need regarding Belle, you let me know."

And she was out of the alley and on her way.

Joe said, "Come on. Let's try the saloon. That barkeep seemed like a good hombre. Maybe he can tell us a few things. There's probably a back door."

Most buildings had one, and so did the Cattleman's Lounge. Johnny and Joe slipped in through a kitchen that was empty and into a room they figured was behind the barroom.

When Artie Crocker left the bar and stepped out back for a moment, he found Johnny and Joe sitting at a table waiting for him.

"Johnny," he said. "How'd you get into town?"

"Carefully. Believe me."

"Wells and his men are looking for you. They're saying you murdered Belle."

"Yeah, I know what they're saying. What are all these men doing here in town?"

"Gunfighters, most of them. Some from south of the border. Matt McCabe and his son have hired them to drive out the folks holding up out at the canyon. That's where we all thought you were."

"That's where I was and where I'll be going back to when I'm done in town. But that's also where Matt is. He's standing with us. It's his wife and son who have hired the gunfighters."

Joe said, "That canyon would be really hard to attack. Just a handful of men could defend it for months. Verna and Hiram have to know that."

Artie said, "There's something I've gotta tell you. Word's out that they brought in Will Buck. He was in this very saloon just six hours ago, and he was seen riding out to the McCabe place. The farmhouse they're using while they rebuild the main house."

"Will Buck," Johnny said.

Joe said, "I've heard the name. They don't come any meaner."

"I met him once. I think he's everything they say he is. We gotta get back to the canyon."

Artie said, "What could one more man make? Yes, he's killed some men. But..."

Johnny was sliding the chair back and getting to his feet. "It's not just that he's killed some men. It's how he does it. When he was a child he spent eight or ten years with the Apache. He knows a thing or two about guerilla warfare."

Joe said, "A few men could hold off a small army in that canyon, but one man can sometimes accomplish what an army can't."

"Come on. Let's ride."

Matt took one step back from the bodies, then another, and his heel caught on a rock and he almost went over backwards. He flailed his arms out to catch his balance and the match went flying off into the darkness.

He had to get back to the house. Ches, Ben and Hatch. Tell them what happened. He hurried back through the darkened canyon entrance and found his horse where he had left it.

As he swung into the saddle, he saw flames glowing from up on the ledge where the house and barn stood. Something was on fire.

He kicked his horse into a full gallop and charged up the slope, pistol in hand.

Gunfire echoed against the canyon walls and as Matt drew closer he could see it was the barn roof that was ablaze.

Ches was face-down on the ground, in front of the house. Ben and Hatch were standing with guns in their hands, and there was a man Matt had never seen before. Long hair and a black hat, and he had an arm around Cora's neck pulling her toward him, and a long knife held at her throat.

Matt hauled on the reins hard and the horse came to a sliding stop in the gravel in front of the burning barn, and he leaped out of the saddle.

"Hold it right there, cowboy," the man said. "Another step further and I'll cut this little girl a new smile from one ear to the other."

Jessica was on the ground, propping herself up on one elbow. Blood was streaming from a gash over one eyebrow. Peddie was standing to one side, eyes wide in horror and her hands over her mouth. Matt's son Tom and his family were with her. Lettie was holding Mercy behind her, but Mercy was peeking around her mother and staring wide-eyed at Cora and the man with the black hat.

The man said, looking from Matt to Ben and Hatch, "I want you all to drop them guns. If'n you don't, then I'm gonna carve up this little girl right in front of you."

"You do," Matt said, "and you'll be dead."

The man was grinning. "You can fill me with bullets, but she'll be just as dead."

Tears were streaming down Cora's face and she called out, "Mama!"

Matt was trying to put together the situation as quickly as he could. He thought it looked like Jessica had been struck, not shot. This man had apparently made his way into the canyon and killed Wolf and Price, and then worked his way up to the house. Matt might have passed him on his ride down to the canyon entrance. Ches had been shot and was lying motionless, unconscious or dead.

Matt had to admit he didn't know what to do. His brother would probably pull off some historic stunt that would add to his growing legend, but Matt was not a legend. He was simply a man. And he knew he couldn't have this little girl's conscience on his hands.

"All right," Matt said. "We're dropping our guns. We don't want anyone else hurt."

Matt set his pistol on the ground, then looked to Ben and Hatch and they did the same.

"Good choice," the man said. He pushed the knife back into his sheath and then pulled his revolver. "Now, which one of you is Matt McCabe?"

"I am," Matt said.

"Good. I'm being paid a good price to shoot you."

"No," Ben said. "*I'm* Matt McCabe."

"Now ain't this cute. I know one of you is tryin' to be a hero. But this means I'm just gonna have to shoot the both of you to make sure. But before I do, where's the other one? Johnny McCabe?"

"Not here," Matt said.

"When will he be back?"

Matt didn't answer. The man leveled his gun at him again.

That was when they heard hoof beats coming. Two riders. Thank the good Lord, Matt thought. Johnny and Joe, coming back.

"Well now," the man said. "That could be him comin' right now."

But it was two riders Matt didn't recognize. But then he realized he did know one of them, though it had been a lot of years since he had seen him. Zack

Johnson, who had worked for Johnny at the little ranch he and Lura had owned. He had gone to Montana with Johnny and the others. Seventeen years older, and now with a mustache, but it was Zack. Matt didn't know the other rider, though. Young, about Dan's age. Long hair, a buckskin shirt, and he wore his gun like he knew how to use it.

They both swung out of the saddle and Zack said, "What's going on here?"

The man holding Cora said, "You two don't make another move or this little girl won't see another sunrise. One of you Johnny McCabe?"

Matt had to admit, the younger one did look a lot like Johnny. Or rather like Johnny had years ago, when they made their ride from Texas to California.

Zack took one look at the man.

"I know what you're thinkin'," the man said. "But a stray bullet could hit this little girl."

The man hiked her up until her feet were off the ground, and the top of her head was level with his chin.

Zack said to the younger one, "Can you make the shot?"

"In my sleep," he said, drawing his gun as he spoke.

He brought his arm out to full length, cocking the pistol as he did so, and squeezed the trigger. The man's head cocked back and Cora screamed and as he fell backward, she dropped to the ground.

Matt and the others ran to her. Matt scooped her up and she wrapped her arms around his neck and was sobbing. Matt looked to Jessica and saw she was now sitting up but just barely. Peddie was at her side, kneeling down in the dirt.

Zack walked over to Matt and said, "Are there any more?"

Matt said, "I don't know."

The young one was standing over the man he had shot, smoke still drifting from his pistol, and kicked his shoulder. The man didn't respond.

He said, "This is the one who won't be seeing another sunrise."

Zack extended his hand. "Matt. Good to see you again, after all these years."

Matt, still holding Cora, shook Zack's hand. "Good to see you too. You both came along at just the right time." He looked to the younger one. "That was one incredible shot."

Zack nodded. "Matt, let me introduce you to your nephew, Dusty."

26

FOUR WEEKS EARLIER

Ginny stood on the porch. The autumn winds were whipping past her with more fury than she thought was necessary. She was in a coat and had a scarf pulled about her neck. There was no snow on the ground, even though it was the second week of November. Kind of unusual for this part of the world. Ginny had seen winters where there was a foot of it on the ground before now. Not that it was in any way unseasonably warm. For the past couple of weeks the boys had found themselves having to break the ice on the watering troughs every morning. But the sky was clear. The sort of cold, wintry blue you got this time of year.

She looked off toward the other end of the valley. Not that she could see the other end from here. But she could see clearly down to the wooden bridge that crossed a stream a quarter mile away, and easily a mile of brown, grassy hills beyond that.

She could see a rider approaching from beyond the bridge. Even at this distance, she could see it looked like Zack Johnson. The way he sat in the saddle and moved with the horse. The set of his shoulders. Though she was no horse woman, and had somehow managed to live all these years in Montana without actually sitting on the back of one, she knew each rider moved with his horse in a way that was as individual as the way a person walked.

The house was striking her as feeling empty this morning. She supposed it was rather empty at the moment. John was off to California, Josh and Temperance had ridden into town to have lunch with Jack and Nina and Darby and Jessica. Bree was home but wouldn't be long, as she was in a mood to go on a ride through the hills. Something about riding through the pines and the bare, leafless trees in temperatures cold enough to freeze water made Bree feel alive. The very thought of it made Ginny want to wrap up in a quilt by a warm fire. But Bree was her father's daughter. Dusty was home, though. He had gone out back to fetch a horse and saddle it for Bree.

The rider drew closer. She could now tell it was indeed Zack. His horse was moving at what she had learned over the years was called a shambling trot. It was almost frolicking. Horses loved to run in the cold.

Dusty came walking from around the side of the house, leading the horse he had saddled for Bree. A black gelding with three white stockings and a patch of white on its nose. Bree's favorite. She had named him Midnight.

Dusty had his hat pulled down tightly against the wind and was wearing a wool coat buttoned tightly. The bottom edge of one side of the coat was pulled up and tucked behind his gun. Ever his father's son.

"Aunt Ginny," Dusty said, a little surprised to see her.

"I just thought I would get a breath of fresh air."

He nodded. "It sure is fresh on cold mornings like this."

Bree came out and skipped down the front steps. She was in a heavy wool coat, jeans and riding boots. A wide-brimmed hat was pulled down over her temples and her dark hair was pulled back in a tail. She held a Winchester in her hands, and tucked it into the saddle boot.

She swung up and into the saddle and said, "I'll be back before dinner."

Ginny said, "Please be careful out there."

Bree gave her a sidelong look. "When am I not?"

And she turned Midnight off toward the ridges and was gone.

Dusty said, "I'd feel better if she had a pistol with her."

Ginny gave him a weary glance. "You know how I feel about the thought of her with a sidearm."

Dusty shifted his feet a bit, and said, "Beggin' your pardon. I don't mean no disrespect, but it's always safer to have a pistol with you as well as a rifle when you're off in the mountains alone. And besides," he gave his aunt a little grin, "she is Pa's daughter. It's about time she learned to use a revolver."

Ginny shook her head. Bree had wanted her father to teach her to shoot a revolver for a long time. Ginny had held out against it for as long as she could, but she could see it was going to be a losing battle.

Her gaze drifted back toward the bridge, and he followed it and saw the rider.

"Looks like Zack," he said.

She nodded. "I should go in and put some coffee on. He'll be cold after the ride from all the way down the stretch."

"Wonder what brings him out this way?"

"Probably old habits."

That got a curious look from Dusty.

She said, "Normally when your father was gone, Zack would check in on us regularly. Now that you're here and Josh is grown, there probably isn't the need. But Zack has always been family, and old habits die hard."

They watched as Zack crossed the bridge, the iron shod hooves making a clattering sound they could hear clearly in the crisp morning air.

"Aunt Ginny," Dusty said. "Are you all right?"

"Why do you ask?"

"Well, it's just that for the past couple weeks or so, you seem kind of...I don't know. Not like yourself, I guess."

"I'm just thinking about your father," she said. "Probably worrying more than I need to."

"I'm sure he'll be all right. He's ridden through those mountains dozens of times."

"Even still, California is a far journey from here."

Dusty nodded. "That it is. My ride up from Nevada a couple summers ago was sure a long ride. But I'm sure he'll be all right."

She nodded, though not with much enthusiasm. "I'm sure he will be."

"There's no one more capable than he is."

Zack approached the house and reined up in front of the porch.

"Good morning," he said. "Just passing by. Thought I might pay you a little visit."

Ginny smiled. "You're coming by to check on us in Johnny's absence. Just like old times."

He shrugged. "I suppose it's not necessary."

She said, repeating what she had said to Dusty, "Old habits die hard."

"Yes'm, indeed they do."

He stepped down from the saddle, and Dusty took the rein and said, "I'll take care of your horse."

"Thanks, Dusty."

Ginny said, "We were just talking about California, and the long ride it is between here and there."

Zack glanced at Dusty, then said, to Ginny, "I'm sure he'll be all right."

She forced a smile. "I'm sure."

Ginny and Zack went inside and by the time the coffee was ready Dusty was coming in from the stable. He was rubbing his hands against the cold. "Boy that coffee smells good."

Ginny had just sat down to a cup of tea and Zack had a cup of coffee in front of him.

Ginny said, "Pour yourself a cup and join us, and shake off the cold."

Dusty shouldered out of his coat and dropped it and his hat on a chair, and pulled a mug from a cupboard.

Ginny took a sip of tea.

"All right," Zack said. "Beggin' your pardon, ma'am, but something's wrong."

She looked at him with puzzled innocence.

Dusty pulled out a chair and lowered himself into it. "You're worried about Pa, aren't you?"

"It's just..." she started to say and then cut herself off.

Zack said, "Did you have one of your premonitions?"

"I don't think I really have premonitions, Zack. Not in the traditional sense. Just a feeling that something's wrong."

He chuckled. "You always have that feeling whenever Johnny goes off on one of his long rides."

"This one's worse, though. It's almost a feeling of dread. I can't sleep without dreaming that he's in some sort of trouble." She shook her head and waved a hand dismissively. "Maybe it's just because of how badly he was shot the summer before last. Maybe I'm worrying unnecessarily. Maybe I'm just being foolish."

"I've known you a lot of years, ma'am. One thing I've never known you to be is foolish."

"It's just that he's alone out there. On horseback. If he would just take the train like anyone else. Take the stage down to Cheyenne and then board a train. But no, he has to ride a horse through the mountains like some sort of solitary mountain man, from the old days."

Zack took a sip of coffee. "I suppose, if you'd like, I could head out. We know he's going to arrive at Matt's place. I could take a ride down. Meet him there."

She shook her head again. "No, Zack. You have a ranch to take care of."

"Not much to take care of during the winter. Ramon can handle things till I'm back."

Dusty said, "We could cut west, through the mountains into Oregon. We could easily be through in two or three days. There's been a light dusting of snow up there, but nothing we can't get through."

"We?"

"I'm not letting you do this alone."

"We can do it in three weeks. Four, tops, if the weather's not agreeable. We won't meander like your father, riding down to Cheyenne and then going west and working his way to California. We'll do like you said, cut west through the mountains in as straight a line as possible, then directly south into California."

"Boys," Ginny said. "I appreciate this, but..."

"It won't hurt anything," Dusty said. "We'll just make sure he's all right. We can send you a letter once we get there, and then we'll ride back with him in the spring. Besides, I've never met my Uncle Matt. And it's like Zack said. Not much to do around here during the winter months. What little there is, Josh can take care of."

Zack nodded. "All right. When do you want to leave?"

"As soon as this coffee's finished. I'll throw some things in my saddle bags and Fred can get a couple horses for us."

Ginny said, "I hate to ask you to do this."

Zack said, "You aren't asking."

"How can I possibly thank you both?"

Dusty said, "No need. We're family. We take care of each other."

An hour later, Ginny stood on the back porch. She was once again in her heavy wool coat and had a shawl wrapped around her shoulders and neck. Dusty and Zack were riding across the bridge, their horses' hooves making the familiar clattering sound. Then they headed off toward McCabe Gap.

Ginny watched until they topped a low hill and were gone from her sight. She turned toward the front door, thinking about pouring another cup of hot tea, and realized the feeling of dread that had been nagging at her was now gone.

27

Johnny and Joe rode hard getting back to the canyon, and they found the barn reduced to an assortment of charred, smoking cinders. There were two extra horses in the corral but in the darkness Johnny couldn't tell if he recognized them or not. In the house they found Matt and Zack Johnson sharing a cigar, and Dusty was sitting in the parlor with Cora on his knee.

Dusty said, "Howdy, Pa."

Johnny was grinning and extended his hand, which Dusty shook.

Johnny said, "Not that I'm not glad to see you, but I have to admit I'm a little surprised."

"Aunt Ginny sent us. Said she had a real bad feeling about your trip to California. Looks like she was right."

Matt told Johnny what happened.

Johnny said to Zack, "I'm glad you came. It's always wise to take her gut feelings seriously. Not that I'll ever admit that to her, though."

Dusty said, "I'm just getting to know the girl who's apparently going to be my little sister. I see you've been busy."

Johnny found Jessica lying down in her room. Will Buck had struck her with the business end of his pistol, opening a wound over one brow. The blood was now cleaned off and a strip of bed sheet had been tied about her head.

"Peddie's a good nurse," Jessica said.

Johnny took her in a hug. "I'm so sorry I wasn't here."

"Your son is an incredible shot. He took that man Buck out with one bullet, and he made it look like it was as easy as swatting a fly."

"He keeps on the way he's going, they're gonna stop talking about me and start talking about him."

Come morning, Jessica was on her feet, though Peddie insisted on fixing breakfast and brewed the coffee.

Johnny checked in on Ches. He had taken a bullet that cut through some shoulder muscle. The bullet had passed through and not hit any major blood vessels. By the time Johnny and Joe had returned to the canyon, Peddie had already stitched up the wound using common sewing thread.

When Johnny stepped into the bunkhouse he found Ches sitting up on his bunk with one arm in a sling and with the other hand he was holding a cup of coffee.

"My head got the worst of it," Ches said, "It got hit on a small outcropping of ledge when I went down. I missed the whole thing. That shot your son made. I wish I'd seen it."

"I'm just glad you weren't hurt worse," Johnny said.

Ches shrugged it off. "I've lived this long. It'll take more'n just a poorly placed bullet to kill me off."

Then he said, "Actually the worst of it was Matt and your friend Zack, and their way of preventing infection. Never heard of such a thing."

Matt was standing there. "We lost the bottle of whiskey in the barn fire, but Mister Swan liked a drink of vodka every so often. Jessica still had half a bottle of it in the kitchen."

Ches said, "Gettin' that stuff dumped into my wound was a good incentive to get out of the way the next time some'n pulls a gun on me."

Dusty was down at the canyon entrance with Ben standing guard. Dusty said no one was going to slip past him, and Johnny had no doubt.

Johnny and Joe began sifting through the charred wreckage of the barn to see what they could salvage. Johnny found his bedroll partially burned.

"I won't be using this anymore," he said.

Joe found his saddle bags. They had been protected by a timber that fell over them and hadn't burned. He pushed a hand into the bag and pulled out the whiskey bottle.

He said with his half-grin, "At least the important stuff wasn't lost, after all."

Johnny said, "I asked Ben about the details of what happened. Apparently Will Buck got all the way up here without being seen. He started the barn on fire and then waited off in the darkness while everyone came running out of the house. Gunned down Ches and then grabbed little Cora to use her as a shield."

"I don't think we're gonna find much else here. I'm going to go grab some shut-eye. It was a long night."

Johnny nodded. He thought maybe Joe had a good idea, but then he caught sight of Jessica over by the stone wall. The white strip of bed sheet was tied around her head and she was standing with her arms folded in front of her, gazing off toward the canyon floor.

He climbed out of the barn's wreckage, his jeans and shirt blackened in places with soot, and walked over.

She heard the sound of his hard-soled riding boots on the earth and looked over to him as he walked up.

He said, "How're you feeling"

She said, ignoring his question, "We got lucky last night. We've been watching for riders all this time, expecting Wells and his men to try some sort of attack. We never figured they'd hire someone like Will Buck to come in at us the way he did."

"I was careless. I should have anticipated something like this."

"How could you have possibly known? You can't plan for every possibility."

"A good military tactician does. I should have looked at it from their point of view. I was so focused on the best way to defend this place I never gave any thought as to what might be the best way to attack it."

"Military tactician," she said wearily. "Don't you ever wish that you could be just a cattleman? Making your home out here, raising a family without having to have that gun at your side? Without all of the things you've had to do that have led to the legend?"

He nodded. "At least once a day."

He took her in his arms and she rested her head against his shoulder.

She said, "I've known you only two months, and yet I love you so incredibly much and I want to spend the rest of my life with you. I was so afraid last night that you wouldn't come back. That I would receive word that you had been shot down. And yet it was my dear, sweet Cora who was almost killed."

"I wish I had been here."

"I so wish we could begin our lives together right now. Right this very moment. Put this entire business behind us and start our new tomorrow right now."

"So do I."

"I wonder what they'll say. Your daughter Bree. Your other two sons. Aunt Ginny. I wonder what they'll say when you suddenly show up with a new wife and her daughter in tow."

"They'll love you."

"How can you be sure?"

"Because you are so incredibly worth loving."

If she could have melted any further into him, she would have.

She said, "I wanted to hang on here a little longer. Give Cora one last Christmas here. But it's too dangerous. Last night fully convinced me. Wolf was killed, along with Price, and we almost lost Cora. Matt's wife has won."

"No she hasn't. This isn't over yet."

She nodded her head. "Yes it is. You've all been staying here for me and Cora. But it's over. The time has come for us to pull out. If there's gold here, she can have it. I hope she enjoys it. The price of hanging onto this canyon is just too high."

Johnny held her tight. He wanted to find some way to fix everything. But he knew he couldn't. He knew she was right.

Matt filled a tin cup of coffee and walked off behind the house. The outhouse was off to his right, and beyond were the rock walls that climbed sheer and straight. At this point behind the house, the wall was nearly thirty feet high. Such an incredible geological formation, he thought, which made this place so easily defendable. And yet, despite this, the canyon had been invaded by one man last night, and Cora had almost been killed. And Ches. Wolf and Price were killed. In fact, if Zack Johnson and Johnny's son Dusty hadn't come along when they did, Matt would have gotten the next bullet. And perhaps Tom and Lettie and Mercy. Perhaps Peddie.

And it's all my fault, Matt thought.

He started walking. A grove of aspen stood behind the outhouse, and he stepped into the trees. You didn't see a lot of aspen in California normally. They tended to be found in cooler climates. But this canyon was at the edge of the foothills to the Sierra Nevada and the temperatures were much cooler than what was found further south toward the central part of the valley.

He stopped and leaned his back against one tree. He thought absently how aspens reminded him a little of birch trees. He realized the coffee cup was still in his hand and took a sip and found the coffee was growing cold.

He heard Peddie's voice before he saw her. "I thought I saw you head out here."

He nodded. He had wanted to be alone, but he couldn't ask Peddie to leave. He never wanted to be alone so badly that he didn't want Peddie with him.

Her light brown hair was tied back in a bun and a heavy shawl was pulled tightly about her shoulders.

"I wanted to be alone," he said.

"Would you like me to leave?"

He smiled. "Never."

She returned the smile. He wanted to put his arms around her but held this impulse back. It wouldn't be appropriate.

She said, "Are you all right?"

He shook his head, looking into her gray eyes. "You are so incredibly beautiful. Do you know that?"

She smiled and a touch of pink suddenly lit up her cheeks, and she looked down to her shoes.

"I'm sorry," he said. "That was so very inappropriate."

She looked up with surprising shyness in her eyes. "It's just that no one has ever said that before. Not and meant it."

A few strands of hair had come free and the brisk morning wind had brought them around and across her cheek and nose. He reached with his free hand to brush them back, and then allowed his fingers to remain where they were and touch her cheek and trail it along to the side of her face. She closed her eyes, liking his touch.

"Matt," she said. "You know what I am. What I've had to do for a living."

"I don't judge people by what they've had to do. I judge by what's in their heart."

She smiled. "That's what Jessica said your brother said to her."

Matt nodded. "We McCabes think alike."

"You know what my name stands for?"

He shook his head.

"Experience. Isn't that funny?" She snorted a bitter chuckle. "My parents named me Experience. If only they knew what they were condemning me to with that name. I've experienced more of the hard side of life than they would have ever imagined. My father ran off when I was too young to remember. My mother died of consumption when I was ten. I lived on the streets of St. Louis at one time. Then when I was old enough I took to the only way I could think of to stay alive."

"How did Sam Middleton play into all of this?"

She glanced away. Talking with him about the life she had led was a little uncomfortable. "One man who wanted things more rough than I allowed started hitting me and then he had his hands around my throat. We were in an alley. This was in Abilene. A railhead."

Matt nodded. He had heard of the place.

"Sam came along and stopped him. The man made the mistake of pulling a knife on him. Sam dispatched of him quickly and made it look easy. I was beaten-up bad. He took me back to his room and let me stay there until I recovered. Never laid a hand on me. He nursed me back to health. It took weeks. I had a broken collar bone, and that man hit me in the left eye so hard I still can't see right out of it. Sam paid for the doctor's bills. He said I was quickly becoming like the daughter he never had.

"He wanted me to stay with him and he would take care of me until I could find some work. But I knew the way things were. Once you're a whore, you can't find honest work. The label of whore just stays with you. But I couldn't accept charity, either. That's something I've just never been able to do.

"But wherever I go, whichever town I find myself in, he always seems to end up there. Like he's keeping an eye on me. I wound up in Greenville and met Jessica and Belle. And there was Sam. He goes away for a while, but he always comes back."

She was silent a moment, gathering her thoughts. "There's so much more to Sam than meets the eye. There's a lot about him I don't know. He's a gentleman, but he's also a killer if he needs to be. He's the most capable fighter I've ever seen, except for maybe your brother. If he had been here last night, that man never would have gotten as far as he did."

"But, Sam ran off. He abandoned you. All of us."

She shook her head. "I don't know where he went, but he didn't run off."

"How do you know that?"

"Because I know Sam. He left for a reason. Even if he hadn't left that note, I would know it because I know him. We haven't seen the last of him."

"Well..." Matt turned from her and looked off at the trees. He took a sip of the cold coffee and dumped the rest of it to the ground. "What happened last night shouldn't have happened at all. And it's all my fault."

"Now, how do you see that?"

"Because," he turned back to face her. "Because of what I allowed to happen for all those years."

Matt was silent a moment. He reached into his vest for a cigar, and found they were gone. "I'm all out of cigars. Kind of symbolic, wouldn't you say?"

Peddie walked up to him and placed her hands on his shoulders. "How did it happen? All those years with her?"

"Truth is, I don't really know. When I met her," he shook his head. "She struck me as so pretty back then. A rancher's daughter. Maybe the prettiest girl I had ever seen. Up till then, at least. I was young, not much older than Dusty is now. I rode into California with Johnny and Joe. Dusty looks a lot like Johnny did back then. We were all dusty and whiskers and shaggy hair that hadn't been cut in months. That was before Johnny grew his long, Shoshone hair. Three young gunfighters running from the law, covered with dust and with our guns hanging low. But I met Verna and it was almost love at first sight.

"I married her, not knowing what she possibly saw in me but grateful for it. Eventually we inherited the ranch and began expanding it. She had a great head for business and I deferred to her judgment."

He reached up to his shoulder to place a hand over hers. "I don't know what happened, really. I guess I was just an out-of-place country boy, grateful that this girl saw something in me. I could always speak well and I suppose I seemed so confident to others. But I wasn't. It's hard to be confident when one of your brothers was even at that young age on his way to becoming a legendary gunfighter, and the other was one of the best trackers and scouts you'll ever see anywhere. Even then, you could throw a quarter in the air and Johnny could shoot the center out of it before it hit the ground. And you could place Joe in the middle of a desert and somehow he would find water. I swear, he could track a jackrabbit over solid rock.

"So I let Verna run things. More and more I just sort of faded into the background. It didn't happen all at once, but a little at a time. At first I was too smitten to see what she really was. Then, as I slipped more and more into the background, the state of being smitten wore off and it was just too easy to stay out of her way. Indulge in whiskey."

"I'm glad you're free of all that. But I don't want you in the background. If I were to have a man like you to build a life with, I would want him at my side. And me at his. Working together as a team."

Matt turned to face her. "I'm a married man, Peddie. At least, legally."

She shook her head. "That's no marriage. It might be legal, on paper. But a real marriage is a thing of the heart."

"I'm a lot older than you."

"Don't bother me none, if it don't bother you."

He found himself smiling. "I guess it doesn't."

And then it happened. The first woman other than Verna he had kissed in more than twenty years. In fact, he didn't think he had kissed Verna in more than ten years. He touched the side of Peddie's face again with one hand, and she leaned in to him and their lips touched.

Then he said, "Wait."

"For what?"

"If we are to have a life together, if we and everyone else here is to be safe, then I have to end things with Verna. I have to get her to back off and leave us all alone. Only I can do that."

He turned and started for the house.

Peddie said, "Where are you going?"

"To set things right."

She scurried after him and grabbed him by the arm to stop him. "What are you going to do?"

"I'm going to make a deal with Verna. She can have everything if she gives me a divorce and leaves us alone." He looked into her eyes. Such a haunting shade of gray. "Will you be here when I'm back?"

She nodded. "Always."

He pulled her to him and kissed her again. Long. He wrapped his arms about her and her hands worked their way up his back. He found the back of her neck and then her hair came loose and fell in waves down over her shoulders.

He then stepped back, looking into what he realized were the most beautiful eyes he had ever seen, and then he turned and was once again striding toward the house.

He stepped around the house and off to the corral. Johnny and Jessica were standing by the stone wall and Matt moved past them, driving the heels of his boots into the gravel, not seeing them at all.

Peddie did see them, however, and ran to them.

"Peddie," Jessica said. "What's going on?"

"He's going to ride out and see Verna."

Johnny said, "He can't go alone. She's putting together a small army of gunfighters. They'll cut him down before he can even speak to her."

Jessica said, "That's probably what she wants. With him out of the way, she would have full title to all of their holdings."

Peddie said, "Oh, Jess."

Johnny turned and started toward Matt. "You two wait here. I'll see if I can talk some sense into him."

Matt was already saddling his horse. The saddle had been found in the ruins of the barn, one stirrup seriously charred but otherwise the saddle was usable.

"Matt," Johnny said. "What are you doing?"

"I'm going to offer Verna whatever she wants, if she'll leave us all alone."

"And what if she won't?"

He pulled the cinch tight. "Then I'll handle it."

Johnny grabbed him by the arm and spun him around. "What do you mean by that?"

"It means I'll do what I have to, to end this. What happened last night, it can't happen again."

"What happened last night wasn't your fault."

"Do you really believe that?"

Matt didn't wait for the answer. He pushed a foot into the stirrup and swung into the saddle.

Johnny didn't bother to argue anymore. McCabes were known for stubbornness and Matt was not lacking in that department. He quickly grabbed a rope and dropped a loop over Thunder's head. Matt would have a head start, but the way Thunder could go into a mile-eating gallop, Johnny would catch up to him quickly.

Matt rode down the ledge at nearly a full gallop. He saw Dusty on a horse riding back up the ledge.

"Hey, Uncle Matt," Dusty said, but Matt blew past him, Dusty's horse rearing up in protest.

"Easy, boy," Dusty said. "Easy."

The horse settled down and Dusty rode on up to the house. Pa had Thunder saddled and was mounting up.

"Where's Uncle Matt going?" Dusty said.

"He's heading off to confront his wife. End this all once and for all."

"He can't. There's a whole passel of riders approaching. I saw 'em from the pass. I was just riding up here to tell you."

Johnny turned Thunder hard and started down the ledge at a full gallop. But Matt was already on the canyon floor, turning into the rocky pass that served as the entrance. Johnny knew he wouldn't be able to catch Matt in time.

Ben Harris, standing guard where the entrance opened to the outside world, saw Matt coming and waved his arms at Matt, trying to get him to stop. But Matt charged past him and out of the canyon.

Ben heard more hoofbeats and saw Johnny and Dusty riding hard into the entrance, but it was too late. Gunfire began from outside the canyon. More than one gun. Ben knew the difference between the discharge of a pistol and that of a rifle, and he heard both. Matt had ridden face first into a hail of gunfire.

28

Matt charged from the canyon, kicking his horse into a full gallop, and didn't realize there were twenty-five riders waiting for him until they began unloading their rifles at him. Matt's horse came to a sudden stop, its hooves sliding on the grass, as Matt felt a bullet burn the side of one shoulder and another lifted the hat from his head.

The horse reared up in panic and Matt fell from the saddle to land hard on his back. First one bullet caught the horse and then another, and the horse went down and landed on Matt's leg.

Johnny and Dusty reined up, their horses turning and prancing frantically with the roar of gunfire. Johnny pulled the Sharps as he leaped from the saddle. Dusty joined him, a Winchester in his hands. He then stood with his feet far apart and the rifle held belt-high and began scattering shots. The Winchester was a long rifle and held eighteen shots. Johnny saw Wells sitting in the saddle in the middle of the line of riders, and decided he must be their leader and any good tactician knows you take out the leader first. So Johnny raised the Sharps and it fired with a roar and Wells was snapped to one side and fell from the saddle.

It was the riders' turn to deal with horses panicking from a sudden spray of gunfire. One man was knocked from the saddle. A horse reared and turned and threw its rider. One horse caught a bullet and went down. Wells' horse, now riderless, reared up and then collided with another horse, and the rider was knocked from the saddle.

Matt pulled his leg free and drew his pistol and tossed a couple of shots at the riders and began back toward the canyon entrance at a hobbling run.

Johnny held the Sharps now with his left hand only, and with his right drew his Colt and began firing. Ben ran toward Johnny and Dusty and took his place beside them, rifle in hand, helping lay down cover fire while Matt hobbled back toward the canyon.

"Fall back!" Johnny called out.

Some of the riders were now on foot, taking positions behind whatever cover they could find. A small bush, an outcropping of bedrock, a dead horse.

Johnny and the others ran back to the canyon entrance, throwing shots back at the riders as they did so. Dusty ducked behind a boulder and Matt ran behind the boulder where he had found Wolf and Price, and up onto the rock. Johnny and Ben were right behind him.

Johnny said, "Is everyone all right?"

Ben nodded. Matt said, "I twisted my leg when the horse fell."

Johnny risked peeking up and over the top of the boulder to see what was happening and was greeted with gunshots. He felt the breeze of a bullet whizzing past his ear, and another kicked up some rock chips in front of his face. He ducked back down.

Johnny called out, "Dusty! You all right?"

"I'm okay!" he called back.

Matt's shoulder was bleeding from where a bullet had grazed it. He pulled a bandana and pressed it against the wound.

"I guess I should have done a little thinking before I rode out there like a mad man," he said.

"We can talk about that later," Johnny said. "Presuming we get out of this alive."

Ben said, looking back toward the canyon, "More riders comin'."

It was Joe and Hatch, riding into the entrance but not too far, reining up and stepping out of the saddle. With rifles in hand they ran to the boulder where Johnny and the others were.

Joe said, "What's the situation?"

"Looks like Verna's changed tactics," Johnny said. "There's maybe fifteen men out there. Probably less now because we dropped a few. Matt ran head on into 'em. I don't think they were expecting that. They were probably going to try a charge into the canyon."

"Suicide," Joe said. "They can get ride in only two abreast. They'd be cut down."

"Maybe they figured if they caught us by surprise they could get some riders past the sentries."

Joe said, "Zack is back at the house with rifles. They're gonna be the last stand between us and the house if any men get past us."

Johnny nodded. He felt better about the safety of Jessica and Cora and the others with Zack there.

Joe said, "Tom's got a rifle, too."

Johnny wasn't surprised by this. "He's Matt's son."

Dusty called out, "Here they come!"

Gunfire began. Rifles going off from outside the canyon. Johnny and Joe climbed up onto the rock and saw eight men charging at the entrance, holding their rifles the way Dusty had, at the hip and jacking off shots. More men from further back were firing from behind cover.

Joe unloaded one barrel of his scattergun, followed by the other, and then ducked down to pop open his gun and pull out the cartridges and drop two more in. Johnny fired his pistol, not fanning it but holding it out at arm's length and cocking, firing and cocking and firing again. When he had fired five shots, his gun was empty and he ducked down to reload, and Joe stood again and fired more buckshot.

Dusty was holding his Winchester at his shoulder and firing. Bullets kicked up rock chips all around him and he ducked back down. Hatch and Ben went down the small slope from behind the rock to the entrance and began firing.

Five of the eight men charging at the canyon went down. Three of them got in. Dusty stood up to fire and was jumped by one man. The two others were cut down by Ben and Hatch. But one of them got off a shot while he was folding over from a bullet to the midsection and caught Hatch in the chest.

Dusty managed to kick off the man who had tackled him and the man swung a fist which Dusty ducked, and Dusty drove a right cross into the man's face. The man fell back and tripped over a small rock and fell backward. He had lost his rifle but reached for his pistol, but Dusty's was in his hand faster and he fanned a shot into the man.

Bullets began kicking up the dirt around Dusty and ricocheting off rocks behind him, so he ducked back behind the small boulder he had been using for cover.

Ben was dragging Hatch to the safety of the open space behind the larger boulder. Johnny said, "How is he?"

Matt knelt at Hatch's side. "Not good. Took one to the chest."

The front of the man's shirt looked like someone had torn at it with something sharp, and blood was starting to soak into the fabric. Matt took the bandana from his own shoulder and opened the man's shirt and pressed the bandana against the wound.

He said, "We gotta stop this bleeding."

Hatch tried to talk, but then coughed, and then got the words out in hoarse voice, "I'm hit bad, ain't I?"

Matt wasn't going to lie to him. Tell him he had seen worse. He hadn't. What he did say was, "You hang in there."

Ben climbed partway up the rock where Johnny and Joe were perched. He said, "We need a doctor."

Joe shook his head.

Johnny said, "Even if we could get past those men out there, it's a two-hour ride into town at best. Presuming we could find the doctor fast and get him on a horse, it'd be four hours."

Ben said, "He ain't got four hours."

Johnny glanced grimly at Joe, who shook his head again.

Dusty called out, "Here they come again!"

Johnny and Joe jumped up onto the top of the boulder. Five men were charging at the canyon, firing rifles as they did so. The rest of the men were back a bit, laying down cover fire. Johnny's pistol now had six shots and he began placing them. Taking down one man, then another. But bullets were zinging around him, and one bullet tore into his shirt and he felt it burn against his ribs, but he didn't flinch and kept shooting.

Joe was standing beside him, now holding a Winchester at his left hip and scattering shots. Dusty was firing from his position.

Two men were still on their feet and they pulled back.

Joe said, "How long do you think we can keep this up?"

"It depends on how many men Verna has hired. There might be more coming out from town. They have access to ammunition, but we have only what we have here at the canyon."

They looked back to Matt, who was now on his feet. He said, "Hatch is dead."

Johnny said, "Can you shoot?"

Matt glanced at the torn shirt at his shoulder. It was soaking with blood, but he wasn't going to let that stop him. "You bet I can."

"I'm gonna lay down some cover fire. You get across the pass and join Dusty." Johnny was pushing fresh cartridges into his revolver as he spoke.

Matt drew his pistol and quickly checked the loads. He had five in the cylinder so he pulled a sixth from his gunbelt and thumbed it in. "Give the word."

"Now!" Johnny jumped up into view and began squeezing off shots, the pistol bucking in his hand.

Joe joined him, holding his rifle at his hip. He wasn't much of a shot from the left side, but he was scattering shots and getting most of them somewhat close. His scattergun was behind the boulder, should he need it.

Matt ran. He threw a shot toward the men outside the canyon, covering the gravel expanse of ten feet from the larger boulder to the smaller one where Dusty was in three running steps, and dove behind the boulder. Dusty was kneeling behind the rock, squeezing off shots with his rifle.

"Nice of you to join me," Dusty said.

Matt scrambled to his knees. "Thought you looked kind'a lonely over here."

Matt began firing with his pistol.

"Cease fire!" Johnny called out. No need to waste any more ammunition.

Dusty said to Matt, "Ain't been to a shootin' match like this in a couple of years."

"Was the attack on the ranch two summers ago as bad as they say?"

"Depends on how bad they say. It wasn't much different from this. Except we were in the house and they were charging in on horseback."

"My fault," Matt said. "All my fault. Hatch is dead. He was a good man. I let this happen. How could I have done that?"

Dusty was thumbing fresh cartridges into his rifle. "Sometimes things just get away from us. Part of bein' human, I guess."

Johnny and Joe were again behind the rock. Johnny risked a peek up and beyond it, and a bullet ricocheted six inches from his head in response. He ducked back.

"They got us covered," Johnny said. "Looks like Dusty and Matt got a better view, but we show our heads and they take a shot."

"They can wait us out. Once night falls, they'll have the advantage. It was a quarter moon last night and will be even less tonight. Not gonna be much light."

Ben climbed up to join them. "What are we gonna do?"

"At this point," Johnny said, "we can't do much more than wait for their next move."

They didn't have to wait long. A man called out. "McCabe! This is Marshal Wells!"

Johnny said, "I guess I didn't place my bullet as well as I thought."

Ben shook his head. "That man has no right wearing a badge."

Joe snickered. "Ain't that the usual way with public office?"

Johnny called back, "What do you want?"

"We want you and Matt McCabe to surrender! And we want the rest of you out of this canyon by tomorrow mornin'!"

"We got women and children in here!"

"Ain't none of my concern!"

Ben said, "We could fall back to the house. Take position there. Shoot 'em as they come into the canyon."

Johnny shook his head. Ben was a cowhand, not a military man. "All they'd have to do is wait until night, and come in under the cover of darkness. Like Joe said, there's not going to be a lot of moonlight tonight."

Joe said, "And if reinforcements come from town, we could have as many as twenty or thirty men attacking the house in the darkness."

"I'm gonna have to turn myself in," Johnny said.

"Now, that's just plain crazy talk. There won't be any fair trial. They'll convict you in a kangaroo court and lynch you."

"Maybe they'll let Jessica and the others go."

"Do you really think they'll do that? Doesn't look to me like Verna or our nephew Hiram value human life all that much."

There was movement behind them and the three turned as once. Dan was there, holding a rifle.

"I come to fight," he said.

Johnny nodded. "We can use the extra firepower."

"Where's Father?"

"He's at the other side of the pass. A bullet grazed his shoulder but he seems to be all right."

They heard Dusty call out again. "Riders comin'!"

Johnny looked at Joe and cursed under his breath. "Here they come. The reinforcements you talked about."

They heard hoofbeats growing louder, but it sounded like there were only two horses. Seemed to Johnny there should be more. Two wouldn't make all that much difference.

A man called out, "Cease fire! All of you! This is Deputy U.S. Marshal Aikens!"

There was no gunfire from the other side. Johnny gave a questioning look to Joe who shrugged in response, and they climbed up onto the rock to see what was going on.

Two riders sat in the saddle between the canyon entrance and the men outside. One was a man Johnny had never seen before. He had a thick, long white mustache and a flat-brimmed hat pulled tightly onto his head.

The other rider was Sam Middleton.

29

Johnny, Joe and Matt walked out from the canyon. Johnny's Colt was in its holster, but he could grab it fast enough if he had to. Joe once again had his scattergun. Wells and one of his men had emerged from their cover and were walking toward the riders. Wells had some blood soaking his shirt at his left shoulder, and was holding his arm gingerly. He seemed to be in about the same shape Matt was.

The man with the big mustache held out what looked like a small billfold, and it fell open and Johnny could clearly see a marshal's shield.

"What's going on?" Johnny said.

Sam said, "I went to call in a favor. This man is Marshal Aikens."

The marshal said, "Which one of you is Johnny McCabe?"

Johnny said, "I am."

"And Matt McCabe?"

Matt said, "Right here."

"I have been out to see Hiram McCabe and his mother. I brought along a letter from State Supreme Court Justice McKinstry strongly urging them to have the charges against both of you dropped. They have been."

Johnny looked at Sam. "That must have been a whale of a favor you called in."

"It was. I helped them capture a fugitive. A murderer who has been wanted dead or alive for more than thirty years."

"Who?"

"Me."

That's when Johnny noticed there were handcuffs on Sam's wrists.

Allowing prisoners to indulge in social visits was not protocol, but Marshal Aikens thought the offer of a cup of coffee sounded good so he and Sam rode up to the house with Johnny and the others and Jessica put a pot of coffee on.

Sam stood in the parlor, his wrists in cuffs, a tin cup of coffee in one hand. The Marshal stood with him, a cup of coffee in his right hand, and his left was on the top of a wooden cane. He had surprised Johnny by producing it from his saddle where it had been tied on with a strip of rawhide. He walked as though his left knee had little strength and he used the cane with each stride.

Sam said, his voice lacking its usual theatrical flair, "I killed a man in Mexico when I was nineteen years old. The year was eighteen and forty-three. I had ridden down there with my brother and a few others. We had rustled some steers in Texas and gotten ourselves into trouble, so we rode south of the border to lay low for a while. That's when I got myself into real trouble.

"It was in a cantina. A young vacquero began harassing me. I was dancing with a lovely young senorita, but he took exception to this. Me being a *gringo*, and all. That's what they call us south of the border. Gringos. Except he preceded it with a few choice and very colorful adjectives. Needless to say, it led to a fight. He was good. I was better, but not by much. We battered each other almost senseless. But he died the following morning. The doctor said it was because of injuries he suffered in the fight. Possibly a fractured skull."

Sam paused to take a sip of his coffee. "Turns out it was the nephew of a very prominent Mexican general."

Johnny was standing across the room, a cup of coffee in his hand. Jessica was beside him, in a straight back chair Johnny had brought in from the kitchen.

Johnny said, "For a card shark, that was really bad luck."

Sam grinned, "You see now why I never trust luck. Why I had Peddie helping me out in that card game."

Johnny couldn't help but return the grin. There was something about this man that made it impossible to dislike him.

Sam said, "The Mexican government has had a price on my head for quite some time. A substantial price. I was almost caught about a year later. Put a bullet in a young lawman's leg when I was getting away. That young lawman, again unfortunately for me, was named Aikens."

Johnny shook his head and couldn't help but chuckle. Jessica looked up at him like she didn't quite get the joke. Peddie was sitting on the sofa with Matt, and she looked at Johnny with a little annoyance. She was protective of Sam because he had been so protective of her over the years. But Johnny couldn't hold the chuckle back.

Matt was smiling too. Joe was standing by the door with a coffee in one hand, and he was giving his crooked grin.

Sam couldn't help but nod and smile, and then he laughed. And Johnny laughed. And even Aikens found himself laughing.

Sam said, "I changed my name from time to time. A couple of times I tried to settle down and build a life for myself. After all, a man can run only so long. I even fell in love once. But my past always caught up with me and I had to run."

Aikens said, "I'll admit, I hated you for a long time. I've never been able to walk without a cane because of the bullet you put in me. But you were always a step ahead of us. More than a step, really. After the one time I almost caught you and you shot me, we were never even able to lay eyes on you. Not once. I eventually gave up the search. I had to, because it was eating me inside out. I doubt you ever would have been caught if you hadn't given yourself up."

Sam told them how he had walked into Aikens' house on a recent night. Aikens and his wife had been asleep. Sam poked Aikens in the side of the face with the working end of his pistol. Aikens opened his eyes and looked at Sam, who stood before him in moonlight drifting in through the window.

"As I live and breathe," Aikens said. "After all these years. You come to finish the job?"

Sam shook his head. "I'm here to turn myself in. Providing a couple of conditions are met."

Sam said to Johnny, "I knew he didn't rise to the position of Deputy U.S. Marshal without making some friends along the way. I didn't know he had made the acquaintance of Justice Elisha McKinstry."

Aikens said, "Justice McKinstry wrote a letter stating that if charges weren't dropped, there would be a federal investigation. All a bluff, of course. Just part of the deal we had to make for our man, here, to turn himself in."

Johnny said, "So, Sam Middleton is not your name."

Sam shook his head. "Allow me to introduce myself. Addison Jedidiah Travis. At your service."

Matt said, "That's quite a mouthful. What do your friends call you?"

"I have no friends."

Johnny said, "You do now."

After the coffee, the marshal and his prisoner went outside to their horses. Aikens tied the cane onto his saddle and then with his foot in the stirrup he had to bounce on his right toe three or four times to build up the momentum he needed because of his weakened left leg, and then swung up and over the saddle.

Matt and Peddie were standing with Sam by his horse. Johnny and Jessica were to one side. Everyone was sort of milling around.

Peddie said, "You've always been there for me."

He nodded. "I have to go away for a while. But," he looked at Matt, "take care of her."

Matt said, "I will."

She threw her arms around Sam. He couldn't return the hug because of his cuffed wrists.

She said, "I don't care what your name is. You'll always be Sam to me."

"I'd have it no other way."

She stepped back, wiping away a tear.

Johnny said, "What's the next step?"

Aikens said, "I'll take him to a cell in Sacramento. From there he'll be extradited to Mexico."

Johnny took a deep breath and let it out slowly. He didn't like the sound of that. He glanced at Joe and could see he felt the same.

Johnny said to Sam, "You're a man of many mysteries. I have a feeling we still don't have the full story as to who you really are."

Sam shrugged. "I don't think *I* have the full story yet."

"What you did here today won't be forgotten."

Jessica said, "We owe you."

Sam smiled at her. "No you don't. I'll be all right. Just live your lives. Treat each other well. Be happy. That's all I ask."

Aikens said, "Come on. Let's get riding. We have some miles ahead of us."

Sam swung up and into the saddle. Aikens started his horse along and Sam followed. He rode looking straight ahead in the saddle. He moved easily with the horse, a man who knew how to ride.

Johnny and Jessica stood and watched as Sam and the marshal walked their horses down the long slope toward the canyon floor. Matt and Peddie were beside them. Joe, standing alone. Ben Harris was there. Tom and Lettie. Matt reached down and placed a hand on the boy's shoulder. Dan was there, his gunshot wound now mostly healed. Zack Johnson stood silently, Dusty beside him.

They stood and watched until the riders had turned into the canyon entrance and were gone.

Hatch, Wolf and Price were buried out behind the house. A grassy patch near the grove of aspens. For headstones they used wooden planks with their names and birthdates and deathdates burned in them. Except for Wolf. Ches had heard his Apache name before but for the life of him couldn't begin to pronounce it, so they just used the name WOLF. Ches didn't know his birthdate, so they just burned on D. DECEMBER 18, 1879.

Tom read from the Bible. Not the usual piece about ashes to ashes, but instead the first section of the Gospel of John.

"In the beginning was the Word, and the Word was with God, and the Word was God. The same was in the beginning with God. All things were made by him; and without him was not anything made that was made. In him was life; and the life was the light of men. And the light shineth in darkness; and the darkness comprehended it not."

He had the Bible open, but Johnny noticed Tom wasn't looking at it, but down at the graves. He was reciting this from memory.

Tom said, "One of my favorite passages. I often turn to it when I'm in need of assurance. And in these days, I find myself in need of assurance a lot. These men, three good men, gave their lives for each of us present. As a minister, my job is to fill the air with words, to preach the holy gospel. But I find my words pale in comparison to their deeds. Their sacrifice for us is a greater sermon than I could ever deliver. So I ask instead that we offer a moment of silence."

Johnny stood in silence. Jessica was at his side, and her hand was in his. He could hear a crow calling from somewhere off in the distance. A winter bird. The leafless branches of the aspens creaked as they were touched by a light breeze.

After dark, Johnny stood alone looking down at the canyon floor. No more need for guards. He stood as easily as he ever did, which was never really very easy. Ginny had said once he was forever in a perpetual state of war. He supposed he was. As he had these thoughts, he reached down absently with his right hand to brush it against the butt of his pistol. Loosening in the holster, just in case he needed to draw it in a hurry.

Matt walked out. The moon overhead was a little less than a quarter moon, but provided enough light that Johnny could see Matt reach into his vest and pull out a cigar.

"Found this in my jacket," he said. "I thought I was all out, but I found this last one."

He broke it in two, and handed Johnny one half. Matt said, "Half of a good cigar is better than none at all."

Johnny struck a match and Matt leaned over and Johnny brought Matt's half to life, then went to work on his own.

Johnny said, "Mexican prison. That's what's waiting for him."

Matt said, "Yeah. I know."

"Prisons here in this country are no picnic. But what he'll go through there will be ten times worse."

Matt nodded.

"There's not much worse than a Mexican prison. You talked to Peddie about that?"

"Nope. Haven't said a word. I just told her he'll be all right."

"We owe him. You know that?"

Matt nodded again. "And a McCabe pays his debts. What've you got in mind?"

"Nothing legal, that's for sure."

Joe spoke from behind them. "First we gotta get them women and children to Montana. And the Swan herd. Then we can take care of business."

Matt said, "Joe. Didn't see you there. Sorry," he took the cigar from his mouth. "I would've broken it three ways if I had seen you there."

Joe said, "A cigar broken three ways ain't much of a cigar. Besides, I'm not really a cigar smoker. Them cigars of yours are mighty good, but too much of it can foul up the lungs."

"True."

Joe said, "So, first order of business is to get everyone to Montana."

Zack and Dusty were walking up. Zack said, "Then we'll deal with things, our way."

Dusty had a cup of coffee in his hand and his hat was flipped back, hanging from the chinstrap.

Dusty said, "You know, you won't be doing this alone."

His Pa said, "Dusty, I can't ask you to go along with what we have to do. We'll be breaking more laws than I'm even aware of."

"You're not asking. Your mission is mine. We're family, remember?"

Johnny grinned. "That's something I'll never forget."

Matt took a deep draw of cigar. Lord, but he would miss these. He let out a smoky exhale up toward the night sky.

"This isn't over yet," he said. "We have a reprieve, thanks to Sam Middleton, or whatever his name is. But there was nothing in the provisions he made that allow Jessica to keep this valley. If Verna believes there is gold to be had in those cliffs, she'll stop at nothing to get it. She'll find some way."

Johnny said, "What do you have in mind?"

"I still have to ride out and talk with her. Cut a deal. That much hasn't changed."

"Should be a might easier without folks shooting at you."

"Should be that."

"I'll be going along."

Matt shook his head. "No need to, really. It should be safe enough."

"I'd like to, though. I have a few things to say to her. She accused me of murder. I take that kind of thing personally."

"All right, then. First thing in the morning?"

Johnny nodded.

The men dispersed. Matt and Joe went out aways from the house and began building a campfire. With the barn gone there was no shelter for them and even though this was California, the nights still got cold. Not cold enough to freeze the water in the trough, but still downright cold. There was no room in the house, but Joe said, "We can sleep outdoors by the fire. We done it enough in the old times, and some of them nights were colder than this."

Johnny stepped into the kitchen for a last cup of coffee. Truth to tell, he was hoping to see Jessica once more before turning in. Maybe sneak a good-night kiss. In these times, discretion was the first order of business. Holding hands at the burial today was about as public as a respectable would get with their love.

What he found was Tom sitting in the kitchen with a half-finished cup of coffee. Tom was sitting with his shoulders bent, his elbows on the table like he was bracing himself for a strong wind, and he was staring at nothing in particular.

Johnny said, "That was a good sermon you gave today. Your father told me in a letter a couple of years ago that you had been ordained, but I've never heard you preach. If you'd like to come with us to Montana, and I hope you do, maybe you could build a church."

"They don't have one there?" Tom asked, but he continued staring. Not looking up from whatever point his eyes were fixed on.

Johnny touched the side of the kettle. Though the fire in the stove was burning low, the kettle was hot to touch. He grabbed a tin cup from the counter. There was some old coffee looking dark at the bottom. A cup someone had placed on the counter and it hadn't been washed yet. What the hey, he thought. It was trail coffee. Not much you can do to hurt that. He grabbed the kettle and filled the cup.

He said, "Yeah, we have a church up there. But it wouldn't hurt to have a Methodist church in the area, led by a good young preacher full of energy and spirit. You never know, you might even see *me* in the congregation once in a while."

"Are you a Christian, Uncle Johnny?"

Johnny raised his brows and tilted his head in a sort of shrug. "Well, my mother raised me Christian. I believe in Jesus. But life has made me Shoshone."

Tom nodded. "Legend has it you lived among the Shoshone for a while."

"I actually joined their tribe."

That got a pair of raised brows from Tom and now he looked at his uncle. "They would let a white man join their tribe?"

Johnny nodded, and took a sip of coffee. He could imagine Ginny scowling over the thought of drinking thick, muddy trail coffee and the image made him smile inside.

He said, "Most Indian tribes have prejudice. It's part of being human, I think. But their prejudice is not related to the color of a man's skin. It's focused entirely on which tribe you belong to."

Tom was looking at Johnny like he was speaking a foreign language.

Johnny continued, "To the Shoshone, anyone who is not Shoshone is potentially an enemy. The same with the Cheyenne, and the Lakota."

"The who?"

"White men call them the Sioux. Joe joined the Cheyenne years ago, and he used to wear a strip of fabric with Cheyenne colors on his gunbelt. He had to take it off when we went to stay with the Shoshone so they wouldn't see him as an enemy. We wintered with them in the little valley I now call home. We were with them nigh onto five months. I spent a lot of time with an old shaman. White men would call him a medicine man. He taught me their ways, and eventually invited me to join their tribe."

Tom said, "I had no idea."

Johnny nodded. "A lot of folks don't. For some reason, it never made the tall stories about me that circulate about."

"So, do you consider yourself Christian or Shoshone?"

"Both."

"How is that humanly possible?"

"Because I believe the Shoshone are just looking at the whole spiritual business from a different angle. Same truth, different angle."

Johnny expected to get a ministerial onslaught from him. Tom was, after all, a preacher. Lots of hellfire and damnation, and how he was going to hell and such. But instead Tom just looked away, back into whatever distance he was seeing.

Tom was in a white shirt and suspenders. His hair was a little unkempt and Johnny realized he hadn't shaved. Unusual for Tom. Despite living conditions more rustic than he was accustomed to, he usually found time to shave in the morning.

Johnny said, "What's eating at you, boy?"

"During the gunfight this morning, do you know what was going on back here at the house?"

Johnny shook his head. "Not really."

"We heard the noise. It was loud, when volleys of shots began firing. Something about the canyon and the acoustics. Like a giant cathedral, I suppose. We heard every shot, good and loud. And we were afraid those attacking would get past you and come up to the house. You see, I know my family, Uncle Johnny. My mother and my brother Hiram in particular. I know what they're capable of, which is why I washed my hands of them and stopped going to family functions. I don't want Mercy around them. I'm afraid some of the influence of whatever is so dark inside my mother and that has infected Hiram might fall onto Mercy, too. But even though I am out of contact with them, I keep my ear to the ground. After all, they exercise a lot of control in the town in which I live, and on the congregation I preach to. I know that my mother wants this canyon because geologists in her employ have estimated that there might be millions of dollars in gold ore buried away in those cliffs. And I know she would be able to lay claim to it a lot more easily if no one was left alive to challenge her claim.

"And so, we sat up here at the house, afraid. Listening to every shot. I held Lettie tightly, trying to make her feel safe, but realizing I could do absolutely nothing if those men came up the hill to attack this house. I grabbed a rifle, but knew I would be useless if they attacked, and Ches is in no position to fight, what with his bullet wound. It would all fall onto Zack's shoulders."

Tom looked at his uncle. "I'm the pastor of the Methodist church in Greenville. Some say I'm a good one. But I'm a failure as a man, Uncle Johnny."

Johnny drew a breath thoughtfully. "I don't know that I'd say that."

"Well, I do."

"How do you define manhood? By the guns that your father and I wear? Or your Uncle Joe or your cousin Dusty?"

"Or by the fact that as soon as you get Jessica and Cora settled in Montana you'll be riding down to

Mexico to free Sam Middleton? Even if you have to bust him out of prison?"

"And how would you possibly know that?" Johnny knew Tom couldn't have heard them talking outside.

"Because as I know my mother and Hiram, I also know my father. And through him and his stories, I know you and Uncle Joe. Yes, I know the legends about you, but through my father I know the *real* you, also."

Johnny pulled a chair and sat down. "There's more than one kind of man in this world, Tom. What you said out there at the graveside told me a lot about you. Many a preacher would have taken the opportunity to fill the air with lots of words. Trying to get everyone to repent. They would have quoted verses from the Good Book and raised their fist in the air. Sometimes I think these preachers are more about selling themselves than anything else. Enough of a fiery delivery can move a man emotionally and make him want to follow you. It seems to me a lot of people go to church to follow the minister, not God. But you didn't do that. You just said a piece, short and sweet. From the heart. One of the best pieces of preaching I ever did hear. People need this, Tom. They need real preaching that is not about theatrics and showmanship, that's more about God than the preacher."

Tom looked him in the eye. "Uncle Johnny, I want you to show me how to shoot."

"Didn't your father show you how to shoot a gun when you were younger? Dan seems to know."

Tom nodded. "Yes. He taught us all how to shoot. Even Hiram. He taught us how to hunt. How to track. He said it was important to know how to survive in the wild."

"He's absolutely right."

"But I want to learn how to really shoot. That shot Dusty made, killing that gunfighter, Will Buck. I want you to show me how to do that. Or that impossible shot you made when one of Wells' men was holding Lettie and threatening to soil her. I want to learn to shoot like that so I can defend my family. So I won't ever have to quake in fear if something like today should happen again."

"I can show you trick shooting. How good you become at it will be about your own personal self. But the shot Dusty made, or the one I made, no amount of trick shooting can show you that. It's about something inside us. Dusty's brother Josh, he's a good trick shooter. I've shown him everything I know. But he just can't do with a pistol what I do, or what Dusty can do. He's a crack shot with a rifle, though. Better'n me or Dusty. Even your father or Joe. As strange as it is to say about something so deadly, there's an art to it. And art can't really be taught."

"I still would like you to teach me what you can."

Johnny nodded thoughtfully. Weighing all of this. "All right. I'll show you what I can. But killing a man, that's something that can't be taught. And I hope it's something you never have to do."

"I suppose, in a way, it'll be a contradiction in terms. A preacher who can shoot."

"Not really. Not according to that Shoshone shaman. Their journey begins with learning to be a warrior starting in your late teens. By forty or so you're learning to heal. To be a physician. And by seventy you're a spiritual leader. As close to what might be called a pastor in our culture."

"But they're just heathens."

"That, I'll debate with you another time." Johnny got to his feet. "I have to get to sleep. Your father and I are riding out to pay a visit to your mother tomorrow, and we'll be wanting to get an early start."

Johnny stepped outside, his coffee still in hand, and he left Tom alone with his thoughts.

30

Matt said, "It seems kind'a strange to be able to just ride along without worrying about someone seeing you, or being shot at."

They rode side by side, and were keeping their horses to a shambling trot. Johnny held the reins in his left, his right hand near his gun. As always. Tucked into the saddle boot was the Sharps.

He said, "For the past two months, we've been living every day expecting a war. Now it feels like a pressure cooker with the steam being released."

They rode up toward the farmhouse. Four men on the front porch stepped down to meet them. Three held rifles in their hand. The fourth one, with long hair that didn't look like it had been touched by water since the last rain, stepped toward them. He wore his gun low on his side and tied down.

"Hold up right there," he said, squinting into the sun a little. "You two ain't welcome here."

Matt said, "We've come to talk to Mrs. McCabe."

"Like I said, you ain't welcome here."

The front door opened and Hiram stepped out. "What do you want here?"

"To talk to you and your mother."

Hiram said to the men, "Stand down. Let them in."

Johnny and Matt swung out of their saddles. A hitching rail stood in front of the porch so they tethered their horses there.

Long-hair stepped in front of Johnny. He said, "Cause any trouble in there, and you'll be leavin' feet first."

"You got me really scared."

Long-hair stood a moment, trying to stare him down. Long-hair must have been mid-twenties, Johnny guessed. The problem was, Johnny had done this with a lot of men over the years. The ones who backed down were still alive. At least they were the last time he had seen them. The ones who didn't were not.

Long-hair finally stepped aside, making it clear he was doing so reluctantly. Johnny shook his head with a little pity for him, and followed Matt up and into the house.

Verna was sitting in her rocker by the fire. It occurred to Matt that she sat in rockers a lot. She was often found in the parlor of their previous house sitting in a rocker by the fire. Or in her room at night, sitting by the fire.

"What do you want, Matthew?" she said without looking up.

"To talk."

"About what? You've won. At least for now."

"That's what I want to talk about." He stepped past Hiram and took a seat on the sofa so he would be facing her. He removed his hat because she was, well, not a lady maybe, but a woman.

He said, "This has to stop. I've come to cut a deal with you."

"What kind of a deal?"

"A full divorce."

"And you want half." She shook her head. "That's not going to happen. I've worked too hard building this financial empire to see half of it pulled away from me."

Matt said, "Not half. Leave me ten thousand dollars. The rest is all yours. All of the investments. Everything. I just want a divorce and ten thousand dollars. And I'll be out of your life. I'll leave the area and you'll never hear from me again."

She looked at him like a card player trying to read an opponent's hand. "What's in it for you, Matthew?"

"Freedom. A chance to start over."

"Do you really think you can build something like this on your own?"

He shook his head. "We'll never know, because I don't intend to try. All I want is to find myself a little plot of land and work it. Maybe run a few head."

"You haven't done a lick of real work in twenty years."

Matt was not going to be baited. "Think about it, Verna. The entire financial empire you've built, minus ten thousand dollars. That's a drop in the bucket considering all that you're worth. The entire thing minus ten thousand, all in your name alone. I will have no more legal claim to it. All I want is a divorce and a check."

She glanced at Hiram who visibly shrugged.

She said, "And what's your brother along for? Do you think you need a body guard?"

"Why would I feel safe here? You tried to have me killed once before."

She tried to give a look that said, *why, whatever do you mean?* But he said, "Will you please suspend with the theatrics? Everyone in this room knows you ordered Timmons to kill me. The poor fool was hopelessly in love with you and would have done anything for you. He proved it that night."

"I'll never admit to anything publicly, or in court."

"And I'm not asking you to. I just want the divorce and ten thousand, and I'm on my way."

"Where will you go?" Hiram said.

"Away from here."

Verna got to her feet. "How long do I have to consider this?"

"About forty-five minutes. That's how long it takes to ride into town from here. There's a lawyer in town. Gabe Simmons."

"The man's a fool."

"The man couldn't be bought. That doesn't make him a fool."

"Considering what I offered to keep him on retainer, only a fool would turn down money like that."

"Gabe's an honest man. For a lawyer. Johnny and I are going to ride into town to see him. If you and Hiram are with us, then I'll pursue divorce and you can have the entire estate except for ten thousand. If you're not with me, then I'm going for half."

Hiram said, "He's bluffing, Mother."

Matt said, "The reason I don't play cards is I'm terrible at bluffing."

Verna looked at him long and hard. Then she said, "Hiram, go hitch up the wagon."

Gabe Simmons was maybe sixty-ish and heavy set, with hair that was gone at top but white and bushy at the sides, and a walrus-like mustache that covered his mouth almost entirely. He did nothing but chuckle as he wrote up the papers. Gabe was friends with a judge from civil court, and Verna had the judge in her unofficial employ anyway, so the divorce was expected to go through without a snag. There was a small waiting period for the divorce to become official, but no one foresaw any problems. By the end of the day, Matt took a check to the bank and left with a large roll of cash in his vest pocket.

Matt said to Johnny, "I guess I'm glad I brought you along after all. This roll of bills would make me a target, but no one's going to tackle me with the legendary Johnny McCabe by my side."

Matt had said with a grin. One thing the McCabe brothers were good at was poking fun at one another.

"Oh, be quiet." Johnny couldn't help but return the grin.

They stood outside the judge's office on the boardwalk. One of their men had driven Verna and Hiram in a carriage. It was painted black with the words McCABE RANCH, GREENVILLE, CALIFORNIA on the side in red. He had left it at the livery and had now gone to fetch it.

Johnny had noticed Verna was standing with a cane, and when she climbed steps she did so as though each step was a bit of a struggle. But she said nothing and Matt didn't comment.

While Verna and Hiram stood waiting for their driver, and Matt and Johnny stood with them, Verna said, "Well, Matthew, it looks like you won this round. Cherish it while you can. When it comes to me, you are not able to play on the same level as I am. You don't have the brains, or the backbone."

Matt was smoking a cigar given him by the judge. Not the caliber of the cigars he had been sharing with his brothers, but good enough.

He said, "You fail to understand the situation, Verna. This is not a game. It's not about me beating you, or vice-versa."

"What is it then?"

"It's about you leaving me alone. Simple as that. Your vast fortune is yours. Just leave me and mine alone."

"It's never as simple as that."

"Sometimes it is."

Matt said to Hiram, "Son, you'll always be welcome at my fire. As long as you're not bringing trouble with you. Otherwise, I want to be left alone."

He then said to Verna, "I and the others with me plan to ride out of here. If all goes well, you'll never hear from me again. But understand this—the man I let myself become over the years is gone. I'm a gunhawk. I should never have let myself forget this. If you ever bring trouble to me or mine again, I'll deal with it like a gunhawk."

She rolled her eyes and sighed wearily. "And what, pray-tell, does that mean?"

"It means I'll put a bullet between your eyes."

With that he turned from her and walked toward the hitching rail where his horse and Johnny's waited for them.

Johnny gave Verna a long look. He had also come along to say some words to her. Let her know how little he appreciated having false charges levied against him. But nothing he could say could compare to Matt's parting words.

Johnny also had taken a cigar from the judge and smoked it down to a nub, so he tossed it to the boardwalk and followed his brothers to the horses.

Johnny was riding a roan gelding he had taken from Jessica's remuda. Thought he might give Thunder a little rest, considering they had a long ride ahead of them.

Johnny and Matt swung into the saddle. Matt gave Verna a long look, then reached a hand up to touch the brim of his hat to her, and he and Johnny rode away down the street.

"He's a dead man," Verna said to Hiram.

This caught Hiram by surprise. "Mother?"

Verna said nothing. She let her gaze drift down the street to where the carriage was approaching. A Mexican man in a flat-brimmed sombrero was on the seat. One of the men who had stayed when Ben Harris and the other two had ridden out. Pedro, Verna thought his name was. Or Mario. Or something. She didn't consider remembering the names of the men who worked for her important.

"Mother," Hiram said, "what are you talking about? We won. We have almost the entire fortune. Like he said, the ten thousand he got was barely a drop in the bucket. We won't even miss it."

"We won, yes, but on his terms. Not mine. It's not good enough."

The driver swung the team so the carriage would sidle up to the boardwalk, and then Hiram offered his mother a hand to help her up and into the carriage. There was a back seat, upholstered with soft leather, which she took. Hiram then landed beside her. The carriage had a roll-top which was lowered.

She said, "Take us home, Pedro."

It didn't matter what his name was. He was wise enough not to correct her if she was wrong.

"Yes, ma'am," he said and clicked the team forward.

"Mother," Hiram said, "sometimes a win is a win. We should consider ourselves lucky. A long, involved divorce proceeding could have tied up our assets in civil court for years."

"No," she said. "It's not enough to simply win. It's *how* you win. And my dear ex-husband is going to learn that. The hard way."

31

Johnny sat with Jessica at the kitchen table with coffee, and told her about his and Matt's meeting with Verna and Hiram. He left out Matt's parting words to Verna.

Jessica said, "That has to be the quickest divorce I've ever seen."

Johnny nodded in agreement and took a sip of coffee. "I suppose when you want something bad enough and have the money to make it happen, it can happen as quickly as you want it."

Matt and Peddie came into the room from the parlor. Matt said, "That coffee smells good."

"Help yourself," Jessica said.

Lettie was cooking dinner. Frying steak with some wild onions. Where Tom was, Johnny didn't know. He was concerned about his nephew. Not so much Tom's request to be taught how to shoot a man, which was essentially what he had asked, but the way he had asked it.

Jessica said, "Since the business with Verna is concluded, and since I've made the decision to give up this place, I'd like to get moving as soon as possible. Like you said, Johnny, the war isn't over. She lost the first battle, but this will never be over until we're out of this canyon."

Johnny said, "So, when do you want to leave?"

"Tomorrow, as far as I'm concerned."

"Well," Johnny glanced at Matt, "there are lot of logistics to be considered."

Peddie said, "Logistics?"

"A military term," Matt said. "Plans we have to make. We can't just start out without provisions. It's going to be a long journey all the way to Montana."

The door opened as Matt was speaking and Joe stepped in. He had been tending the horses. It was brisk outside and he was rubbing his hands together.

"Hey, Joe," Johnny said. "You want to join us? We're making plans for the journey."

Jessica said, "If we can't leave tomorrow, then I'd like it to be the day after tomorrow. We have three men buried out back, and the longer we stay here, the greater the likelihood that we'll have more."

Joe poured a cup of coffee and joined them at the table. "We're gonna need supplies. Lots of 'em. And a wagon. At least one."

Matt said, "We have money. I have a whole roll of it now. More than enough to bankroll this operation."

Jessica shook her head. "I don't want to be beholden to anyone."

"Well, it looks to me like we're all in this together, now. I'm the one with the money, Johnny and Joe and Zack have the expertise we'll need for a journey like this. I have the feeling Dusty knows a fair bit about such a thing, too. You have the cattle."

Peddie said, "I can cook. Jessie and Lettie can, too."

"Of course," Joe said, "we'll be needing to butcher a steer or two along the way for beef, and we'll lose a few head along the way because you always do in a long cattle drive. But most of 'em should make it to Montana."

Jessica said to Matt, "I wouldn't feel right if you didn't take partial ownership of the herd in exchange for the money you'll be putting up."

Matt shook his head. "I was thinking of maybe starting up a small ranch when we got to Montana."

And so, with a handshake deal, the Swan-McCabe Cattle Company was formed, with Jessica and Matt as the co-owners.

"We'll need two wagons," Joe said. "Big ones. And horses. We'll have to fill out the remuda a little. We'll have six drovers, from what I can see. Besides myself, and Johnny and Matt, we'll have Ben Harris. But we should only need four drovers with the herd at any one time. The other riders can be with the wagons, or scouting ahead."

Johnny said, "We'll need flour, lots of it. Sacks of coffee. Canned goods. A team of mules for both wagons. And ammunition."

Joe said, "We can go into town tomorrow. Presuming they'll sell to us."

"They'll sell to us," Matt said.

"Leavin' this time of year, we're gonna have to swing south. The mountain passes are gonna be filled with snow, so we'll have to swing south enough that it won't be a problem."

Johnny said, "Not as far south as the Mojave, but close enough. Then we'll have to cross New Mexico Territory, into northern Texas. Then, from there, start making our way north."

Joe nodded. "It'll be a lot longer than the first time we did this. It was late spring and the mountains were passable."

"We're adding three months easy to our travel time. Won't see Montana before May, I don't think."

Jessica said, "Maybe we should wait for spring."

Matt shook his head. "I don't think so. I know Verna better'n anyone here, and it's only gonna be a matter of time before she comes for us."

"But," Peddie said, "Marshal Aikens made them all back down."

"The marshal is on his way to Sacramento. She'll let things set for a while, but then she'll be hiring gunfighters and coming after us again. And I have the feeling she won't wait long. I'd rather have the extra months on the trail."

Joe said, "In a lot of ways, it won't be as hard as it was the first time. Back then, it was just open country between here and Montana. A couple forts. A few trading posts. Now there are towns. We can stop along the way, let some of the women folk grab a hotel room for a few nights to rest up from the trail."

"Women folk?" Matt said. "*I'll* be grabbing a hotel room to rest up from the trail."

They all laughed.

Joe said, "We'll need tents and cots. Lanterns. Cans of kerosene."

Jessica said, "We have an axe. Some pick-axes, too."

"Good. We'll have to bring 'em all. A few coils of rope. What was here got lost in the barn fire."

"There's one more thing." Jessica looked to Johnny. "I want us to be married before we start out. I know you wanted your children and their aunt to be present, but I want to do this journey as man and wife."

This caught him a little by surprise. Not that she wanted to marry him, but that she didn't want to wait.

She said, "When I make up my mind to do something, then I want to do it."

Johnny smiled. "I think that's reasonable."

"Sure is," Matt said.

The following morning, Joe, Zack and Matt started saddling up to get an early start into town.

Dusty said, "Want some company? I made this ride once myself, though I did it alone."

Matt said, "Any suggestions you might have would be welcomed."

Once in town, Matt strode into the general store. He had known the owner of the store for years. Phil Medwick. One of those men who was heavy-set but in a strong way. A thick stomach but a chest just as thick. Wide shoulders. Even his fingers were thick.

Matt dropped a roll of ten dollar bills on the counter top. "Phil, do you think you'll be able to lift the ban on doing business with us?"

Phil eyed that roll of bills. "I think I just might be persuaded."

Zack and Dusty picked out two wagons. They belonged to the livery, but the owner was willing to part with them for the right price.

Zack said, "Oxen or mules? Most settlers preferred one or the other. There's arguments for and against either."

"Mules," Dusty said, without hesitation. "In a pinch, you can ride a mule. I've never met a man who could ride an ox very far."

Joe and Zack would have both preferred contestoga wagons with bonnets, but buckboards were all that was available on short notice.

Dusty said, "We can cover the cargo with a canvas tarp. Better than nothing."

While Medwick was filling the wagons with the supplies Matt had, they all headed to the gunsmith shop.

Joe said to the man behind the counter, "We'll need all the forty-four-forty ammunition you have. Every single box of it."

"Let me see that rifle," Dusty said, indicating the rifle rack behind the counter, and the third rifle from the left.

The man handed it to Dusty. It was a lever action, but didn't have the customary magazine under the barrel as a Winchester did.

Matt said, "A Spencer."

Dusty jacked open the chamber to make sure it was empty—proper gun safety—then sighted in on an imaginary target across the room. "The best repeater ever made. Had me one, once. Been out of production now for maybe ten years."

Dusty looked to the man behind the counter. "How much for it?"

Matt said, "Throw it in with the lot."

"Uncle Matt, I can't ask you to pay for my personal rifle."

"You didn't ask." He looked to the man behind the counter. "Throw it in."

They returned to the canyon with two wagons each pulled by a team of mules. The wagons were loaded with sacks of coffee, flour and salt. They also had a few bolts of fabric to replace any clothing lost along the way. It might seem like a frill, but hole in the knees of your jeans could be mighty annoying when you're trying to stay warm and dry and still have a thousand miles of trail ahead of you.

They had bales of rope and lanterns and cans of kerosene. They had cans of beans and peaches. And they had cots, and four large Army tents.

"Can't have the women sleeping on the open ground," Matt said.

Joe even grabbed four bottles of scotch and one of Kentucky whiskey.

When they got back and Johnny saw the whiskey, Dusty said, "Jack's gonna wish he was with us. He has a passion for Kentucky whiskey."

Johnny looked at his son. "I didn't know that."

It occurred to Dusty that his pa thought Jack was back in medical school. He didn't know Jack had given that up and was now the town marshal back home.

Dusty said, "I got a lot of things to tell you about Jack. But it can wait. We have a long ride ahead of us. We'll have a lot of time for talking."

Johnny found Tom out back. Tom had an axe in his hands and his sleeves rolled up. They would need firewood for their journey, and the less they had to split on the road, the better off they would be. Matt had gotten a length of canvas to tie under the wagon for carrying firewood, and Tom wanted to fill it as much as he could.

Johnny noticed Tom's forearms were thick and strong, with veins standing out like most strong men had on their muscles.

Johnny said, "McCabes have always been strong men. It seems to come naturally. It's like there's a sort of power that carries on throughout the generations. Even my daughter Bree could beat most of the boys at arm-wrestling when she was in school."

Tom said, "I'm afraid I pale by comparison to you and Uncle Joe."

"You'd be wrong. I'm the weakest of my brothers. Always have been."

Tom looked at him with a little disbelief.

Johnny said, "Your father might be built narrower than I am, but he could always beat Joe and me at arm wrestling. Joe could beat me, but your father could beat both of us. And despite how diplomatic he can be, and a beautiful talker, I've never met anyone who could throw a punch like him."

Tom paused a moment, giving that some thought. Johnny thought Tom looked like a man who thought he had known his father, but was discovering little by little that he really did not.

Tom went back to the woodpile.

Johnny said, "I come looking for you. Jessica and I want to be married, and we want it to be today."

Tom was about to begin a swing at a chunk of wood that was about to become two or three smaller chunks, but stopped and looked at his uncle. "And I'm the only preacher available."

"Jess and I talked about it. You're the one we would want, regardless."

Tom held the end of the axe handle with one hand, and let the head drop to the ground. "I don't think I'm worthy. Up until a few months ago, I thought being a pastor was my life's work. Now I don't know what direction the Lord is leading me in. I thought I knew so much about faith."

Johnny said, "Some say faith brings you comfort. I've always found faith brings you questions, which lead to more answers and from there to more questions."

"I've thought long about what happened back at the house. That man who was holding Lettie. Threatening to do unspeakable things to her. And you ended the threat with one bullet to the man's head."

Johnny waited. He wanted to hear the man out.

"I've long followed the Good Book. I decided I wanted to be a minister when I was fifteen. And in the Good Book, it says *Thou shalt not kill.*"

"The Ten Commandments."

Tom nodded. "And Jesus said we are to turn the other cheek. And yet, there you were, faced with a situation that seems to me gave you two choices, both of them wrong. Kill the man, which violates the teachings of Jesus as well as the Ten Commandments, or let him assault Lettie. Which would also make you potentially guilty because if you have the ability to stop a crime but don't, it makes you guilty at least to a degree."

Johnny nodded. "I've had those thoughts myself, over the years."

"And yet you chose to kill the man, without even a second thought."

"I made a decision, long ago, that when I'm confronted with a situation like that, when I have two choices and both of them seem wrong, to pick the one that causes the least amount of harm."

"Just like that? You thought that through and came to that decision? Just like that?"

Johnny shook his head. "No. Not just like that. It was something I had to weigh long and hard."

"Do you have peace with it?"

"Not really. I still see their faces at night. I hear a creak in the house timbers at night, the house settling, and I'm instantly wide awake and reaching for my gun. It'll always be with me, I guess. But to have let that man brutalize Lettie would have weighed even harder on my soul."

Tom nodded, but said nothing.

Johnny said, "Many people try to live by the teachings of the Bible as though they are black-and-white. Turn one way or turn another. But I think what those teachings are meant to be is guidelines. You see, son, often in life we are met with things that happen that fall into a sort of foggy area between right and wrong. Sometimes we have only a few options, and all of them seem wrong. We have to look to the teachings of the Bible and decide, based on their intent, which is the least wrong."

"And how do we know what the intent was?"

Johnny shrugged. "I suppose by looking into our heart."

Tom nodded his head and looked at his uncle like he was seeing him for the first time. "Maybe you're the one who should have been a minister."

"No, I think the collar is on the right man."

Tom said, "So, you want to marry Miss Jessica."

Johnny nodded. "When I met Lura, I couldn't imagine ever loving a woman as strong as I loved her. When she was killed, I thought it would kill me. I hung on for the children. But you have to let yourself live. That's what Lura said to me, in a dream. You have to continue living, and you have to let yourself love again. And now I've met Jessica. We haven't known each other three months, but sometimes you just know in your heart when something's right."

"When you met Lura, how long did it take you to know you wanted to marry her?"

"The first time I looked into her eyes."

Tom nodded and grinned. "I would be happy to perform the ceremony."

At two in the afternoon, standing under some bare oak trees off to the side of the house, Johnny and Jessica were married. Johnny had no clothes worthy of such an occasion with him, but he put on a clean shirt and shaved. Jessica wore a dress she normally reserved for church. Tom fastened the top button of his shirt and borrowed a string tie that had belonged to Bernard Swan.

Dusty stood beside Johnny, who could think of no one better suited to serve as the best man. Peddie stood beside Jessica, but Cora was there also, holding her mother's hand.

Tom was about to read from the Bible, as he usually did when presiding over a wedding, but then he took a look at the people assembled here and decided to speak his own words instead.

"Every culture has one thing in common. The marriage ceremony. From the Hebrews of old Israel to the Shoshone, to this land of today. Some of the details might be different, but in the long run, the heart of the ceremony remains the same. One man and one woman wanting to build their lives together. And together they form a union that is, to paraphrase Aristotle, greater than the sum of its parts."

He then asked each in turn to repeat after him and they recited the wedding vows. Except when it was Jessica's turn to say *I do*, she said, "Absolutely." And Johnny said, "Without a doubt."

Then it was Johnny's turn to surprise Jessica. Something she didn't know about.

The morning before, Matt had asked Peddie if she knew Jessica's ring size. Women who are good friends tend to know this sort of thing about one another. After making purchases at the gunsmith shop, Matt and the others went to a jewelry store in town. Matt asked Zack and Dusty, who knew Johnny the best, which ring he would probably have picked out for Jessica. Both were in agreement. In the display was a simple gold band with a fine engraving of what looked like lace.

Dusty and Zack both pointed to it and said, in unison, "That one."

Matt had surprised Johnny with the ring, and now it was Johnny's turn to surprise Jessica. Tom knew what was going on, so he said nothing as Johnny reached into his vest pocket and produced the ring.

Johnny said, without prompting, "With this ring, I thee wed."

Jessica had tears in her eyes as Johnny slipped the ring onto her finger. It was a perfect fit.

Tom said, "You may now kiss the bride."

Standing in the sunlight on an unseasonably warm December day, with leafless oak branches reaching out above them overhead, Johnny kissed his bride.

Two of Joe's four bottles of whiskey didn't survive the festivities of the afternoon and evening. Lettie made a wedding cake, and beef was roasted over an open fire on a wooden spit.

That night, tents were set up outside. It was decided the house should be left for the newlyweds.

Peddie said, "They need their privacy."

Cora said, "But why can't I sleep in my own bed?"

Dusty knelt beside her. "Think of it as practice."

She knit her brows like he had just said the craziest thing in the world.

He said, "We have a long journey ahead of us, all the way to Montana. You're gonna be sleeping in a tent, on a cot, all the way. Best to try the cot tonight. Break it in a little. It'll be fun. It'll be like camping."

She grinned. "It'll be fun?"

"Oh, yeah."

"Will you sleep in there with me?"

He nodded.

"Are you really my big brother?"

He nodded and grinned. "That's something you can count on."

And she gave him a big hug.

Matt said to him afterward, "You know, you're going to be a great big brother."

"Never had the chance before. I don't really know what I'm doing. It's like I'm making it up as I go along."

Matt laid a hand on his shoulder. "That's often what being a part of a family is about."

Johnny and Jessica awoke early the following morning, and he fired up the stove for her and she put on a pot of coffee.

She said, "This will be the last pot of coffee I'll ever make in this house."

He stepped up behind her and wrapped his arms around her. "Do you have any regrets?"

She laid her head back and on his shoulder. "Wherever you and I are, it'll be home."

After breakfast, Johnny stepped out back. He walked past the graves of Hatch, Price and Wolf. Further back was a granite headstone. On it was the name BERNARD SWAN.

Johnny stood before the grave. He took off his hat and looked at the name.

"I never met you, but I feel like I have. The house you built, it says a lot about you. And the woman you took for your wife, and the daughter you both produced. I think you're a man I would have understood well."

Johnny paused a moment. The breeze was cool this morning and it touched his Shoshone tail. It had grown long over the months since he had left Montana, and fell between his shoulder blades.

He said, "I want you to know that I love Jessica. I'll treat her right. And I'll treat your daughter like my own. Even though I'm taking them far from this place, they'll be safe and warm in my home."

He stood a moment more, looking at the grave. He didn't know really why he was here, saying these things.

He supposed it was just that he had married this man's wife and was going raise his daughter as his own. He supposed something had to be said.

Dusty came walking over. He said, "I thought I saw you walking back here. We're about to start loading the wagons."

Johnny put the hat back on his head. "Let's go."

The beds were disassembled and loaded into wagons. Jessica thought it was especially important that in their new home, Cora have the bed that had always been hers. Most of the furniture wouldn't fit in the wagons, but they managed to make room for the parlor rocker. It had always been one of Jessica's favorites.

At nine in the morning, with the wagons fully loaded and the teams hitched, Johnny hefted Cora up onto a wagon seat, then took one of Jessica's hands while she climbed up. Then Johnny took his place beside them.

Thunder was fully saddled and tied to the back of the wagon. Joe was in his saddle, beside them. Peddie and Lettie and Mercy were in the other wagon. Peddie knew how to handle a team.

Matt, Ben Harris, Dan and Dusty had already rounded the herd up and got them moving, and the canyon floor was now empty. It had been a few years since Tom had worked as a cowhand, but he had grown up on his father's ranch and remembered what his father had taught him, so he joined in.

Ben had decided to stay with them and Matt asked him to become ramrod of the Swan-McCabe Cattle Company.

Jessica said, "I can think of no better choice."

He said, "It'd be truly a pleasure to work for you both."

"We can't pay you anything other than room and meals," Matt said.

"Ain't askin' for anything else. Sometimes you do something just because it's the right thing to do."

Jessica now cast a glance to the canyon floor, then back to the house. "The whole place looks so empty. So desolate. The house. The canyon. I've never seen the canyon without cattle milling about."

Johnny said to her, "You ready?"

She nodded.

"How about you, Cora? Are you ready to light out for our new home?"

Cora sat between them on the seat. Her hair was covered in a bonnet and she clung to a Raggety-Ann doll. She nodded. "Yes sir. Head 'em out."

Johnny laughed, and looked to Joe. "You heard the girl. Head 'em out."

And the wagons started down the long decline to the canyon floor, and then to the narrow pass that led them out of the canyon and to the grassy lands beyond.

PART FOUR

The Trail

32

It was December 21st when they left the canyon behind them. They made their way south, passing within a half hour's ride of the town of Greenville. Johnny wondered if he would ever see the town again.

Ahead of them would be the little ranch where Lura's grave rested. He had come to California to visit the grave, and now he was on his way back home with a wife in tow and a new daughter.

Johnny wasn't going to consider Cora a stepchild. He didn't believe in that sort of thing. A child who belonged to your spouse was your child also. He didn't know where he had gotten that belief. He supposed it had just developed over the years.

As they rode, Jessica said, "Do you want to stop and visit Lura's grave one more time?"

Johnny shook his head. "She's not there."

Jessica nodded with a smile. She understood.

They caught up with the herd by early afternoon. Two hundred eighty-one head, based on a count Dusty had taken a few days earlier. The Swan ranch had been a small one in comparison to Johnny's. And Johnny's ranch was small compared to the one Matt was leaving behind.

That night they slept in tents, with a minimal guard on the herd. Two riders were all that was necessary with a herd this size.

On the first morning, Jessica and Lettie and Peddie worked together to make a breakfast of steak and beans. A farmer had come out to the canyon the day before and bought the chickens from Jessica, as it would be almost impossible to bring chickens along on such a long journey. There would be no more eggs until they arrived in Montana. But on the trail you have a way of developing a hunger like no other, and the beans were welcomed by everyone.

On the second morning, Johnny stepped out of the tent and found Joe was gone.

Joe had decided to sleep outside rather than in a tent. "Sleeping under a roof makes me nervous," he had said. "Even in Texas, in the town where I'm deputy marshal, I often sleep outside."

But that morning he was gone.

Dusty stood scratching his head. "Is it like him to just haul out?"

Johnny said, "Not without saying goodbye. And not when there's a job to be done."

Johnny and Dusty walked a circumference around the camp, cutting for sign. They found one trail of hoof prints heading away.

Johnny said, "He led his horse out of camp sometime during the night. Then mounted up and rode on."

"I could follow him," Dusty said. "Find out what's going on."

Johnny gave that some quick thought. "No. I think we need you here. But make sure the men have rifles with them, and be alert. Just in case there's some sort of trouble developing. I'd like you to be with the herd, today."

Everyone else had set themselves to breaking camp while Johnny and Dusty scouted. When they got back to camp, Jessica was waiting for him by the wagon.

"Is anything wrong?" she said.

"I don't really know. It's not like Joe to do this."

"What are we going to do?"

Matt and Peddie had drifted over from their wagon.

Johnny said, "Let's get moving. We've lost a half hour already. But let's all be alert."

This day, Johnny handed the reins to Jessica and he rode Thunder. He rode with his Sharps held across the saddle.

The wagons moved a little ahead of the herd, so the dust the cattle kicked up wouldn't be in their faces. More than once, Johnny rode on ahead as much as a mile, scouting. Watching. Looking for tracks. Looking for anything that might be amiss. Every time, he saw nothing he didn't expect to see.

The sun was drawing low in the sky by five o'clock, so they made camp. They were now nearly fifty miles south of Greenville. There was a small stand of leafless alders and a stream, and the water was cold and fresh.

As it started getting dark and cookfires were started up, Ben called out, "Rider comin'!"

Johnny let his right hand fall to the pistol at his side. Jessica pulled Cora to her. Matt snatched a Winchester from where he had left it leaning against a wagon wheel and jacked in a round.

The rider came into camp. It was Joe. Tied to the back of his saddle crossways was a five foot long blue spruce.

He said, "It wouldn't do for Cora to have to go without Christmas."

Johnny couldn't help but smile. "You could have said something."

"But then it wouldn't be a surprise."

The following day, they celebrated Christmas. Johnny didn't have the heart to let Joe know it was only the twenty-fourth. Joe had always seemed to live by his own calendar, which was more about the alignment of the stars and the phase of the moon than anything else. Something he had picked up during his time with the Cheyenne, years go.

A dead alder had been chopped down the night before for firewood, and the stump was wide, moreso than the trunk of the Christmas tree Joe had cut. Johnny dug a hole into the stump with his bowie knife, and they stood the tree in it. Jessica had brought along a box of Christmas decorations, and soon the tree looked like a proper Christmas tree, complete with a wooden angel on the top.

Jessica said, "Bernard made that angel for Cora when she was an infant."

"Too bad there won't be any presents," Johnny said.

Matt shook his head and placed his hand on his brother's shoulder. "Wouldn't do for Santy Claus to forget about the kids, even out here on the trail. The boys and I did a lot of shopping when we were in town."

Both girls ended up with new dresses, and each got a little tea set. And they got new dolls and little wooden beds for their dolls.

They lost an entire day of travel, but everyone felt the delay was worth it.

The following morning, they packed up to be on their way as the eastern sky began to lighten. The decorations were back in their box.

Jessica said, "The next time they're used, it'll be on our tree in Montana."

As Cora took her place on the wagon seat, she looked at the little tree standing empty on the tree stump.

"It looks so sad and lonely."

Johnny said, "No, it's happy. It's where it needs to be. Out here amongst the other trees."

She nodded. That seemed to set comfortably with her.

Johnny took the reins and they rode on. Ben and Joe were with the herd that day, along with Zack and Tom. Dusty was scouting about, his newly acquired Spencer rifle in his saddle. Johnny had noticed Dusty seemed happiest when he was scouting the land.

About noon they stopped and were resting the mules. Johnny was taking a drink of water from the canteen he had slung over Thunder's saddle horn. Everyone was stretching their legs. The girls were running back and forth playing some sort of game, squealing with glee.

Johnny saw Dusty approaching from behind them. He had left a few hours before, riding away ahead of them. Apparently he had circled around.

Dusty said, "We could have a problem. There's a group of maybe ten riders, hanging back a ways. About a mile behind the herd. They been dogging our trail all day."

"You get close enough to see who they are?"

Dusty shook his head. "But they're staying even with us."

Jessica had drifted over. "What does this mean?"

Johnny said, "It means we haven't left trouble behind."

33

Hiram said, "You what?"

His mother sat in a rocker in her bedroom. All of the bedrooms in this farmhouse were small. Each bedroom in the new mansion would be even larger than the parlor downstairs, but for the next few weeks, this farmhouse would still have to suffice.

At least this bedroom had a small hearth. A fire was crackling, and his mother sat in front of it. She wasn't looking well, he thought. She had lost weight the last few days, and the lines in her face seemed deeper than ever. Her graying hair looked to have more salt and less pepper than he had noticed. She had started walking with a cane a week or so ago, and when she didn't have the cane she would have a hand on a table or against a wall. He had asked about her health and she told him she was fine, in the way she had that meant if he didn't drop the subject he would be sorry.

She sat with a quilt draped over her lap, and a cup of tea rested on a small end table within reach.

He had said he wanted to ride out to Swan Canyon in the morning. Everyone there had apparently left, and he wanted to scope the place out. Thought he might bring Wells and some of the men with him, just in case.

"Wells isn't available," his mother had said. "I sent him and some men off in pursuit of your father and the others. I told them I wanted no one left alive."

Which was why Hiram said, "You what?"

"It's not enough to win, Hiram. You need to understand this, if you are to be truly my son. If you are to inherit this financial empire I am building. And believe me, it will all be yours one day. Dan is with your father, and as such has sealed his fate. God help him. And Thomas and his ill-begotten family also. Thomas seems to have such faith in *God*," she said the word with contempt, "maybe it's time for Tom to meet him."

"Mother." He couldn't believe it. He found himself taking an involuntary step backward.

"This entire financial empire will be yours, Hiram. All yours. The mine in town. The mines in Mexico. Our shares in the railroad. The cattle ranch. I have invested money in the stock market in New York. You will very possibly become the most powerful man in California. One day, perhaps one of the most powerful in the world. To do this, you have to be smart. Which you are. But you also have to be strong. I won't always be there to do what has to be done. You will have to be able to make the hard decisions yourself. This is how I raised you. To continue what my father began and what I have taken and grown."

He found himself recoiling with disbelief. "But mother. There are women and children there. One of them is your own granddaughter."

She shook her head. "When Thomas left, saying he wanted nothing to do with the family business, I removed him from the will and as far as I'm concerned, he's no longer my son. His offspring is no longer any concern of mine."

Hiram was staring at her.

She looked at him with eyes that seemed old. Weary. "Being able to make the hard decisions is sometimes not easy. It sometimes takes a toll on you. But everyone has to know that when you speak, thunder rolls. It's through the power of intimidation that you get your way in this world, Hiram. You can't let up. Ever. You have to be powerful enough so if you speak, the governor will stop and listen. Someday perhaps even the president.

"I have groomed you for this, Hiram. You're old enough now that you have to start taking some initiative. You have to start being strong. These people opposed us. Matthew handed us the victory we wanted, but on his terms. Everyone must understand that we accept victory only on our own terms."

"You tried to kill my father once. It resulted in our entire house being burned to the ground."

She shook her head with exasperation. "Hiram. Is there no hope for you at all? Haven't you surmised by now that Matthew is not your father? Tillman served me in a variety of ways over the years. Loyal to a fault. And I had him serve me in one other way, too.

"You see, I have been grooming you to one day take over for me from the moment I decided it was time to conceive a second child. We already had Thomas, but he was too much his father's son. I realized my mistake. I didn't want my second child, the one I would groom to take over for me, to have McCabe blood. Those people have some sort of idiotic, misplaced sense of nobility. Look where it gets them. Something in their blood, I suppose. Matthew and his brothers are all like that. And I understand their father was, too. It all seems to have begun with the original John McCabe, a trailblazer who explored the mountains of Pennsylvania back when that area was a frontier. They make him out to be some sort of larger-than-life saint, like something out of a Fennimore Cooper novel, swooping into the forest to save everyone from villains. I wanted nothing of that delusional nonsense for you. So I made sure you weren't tainted with McCabe blood."

Hiram was speechless. He felt like he couldn't breathe.

"So, yes. Matthew and the others with him will die. And there will be no connection to us. No evidence that would stand up in court. But everyone will know. If you oppose us, you reap what you sow."

Hiram left the room and staggered down the small hallway to the stairs. He made his way down, hanging onto the railing. He felt dizzy. His legs seemed to move of their own accord, but they weren't moving well. He pulled at his cravat as it suddenly felt tight.

He staggered into the kitchen and opened the back door and lost his dinner.

He then stood by the open doorway and breathed. Sucked in the night air. It was December and the air was maybe fifty degrees. He took in another lungful and felt steadier. His legs were now strong and the dizziness was fading.

He went to the parlor. A man was there, a former slave, maybe fifty years old. Mother had hired him as a butler to replace Timmons. At least in some of the duties Timmons had. He wore a black jacket and white gloves.

"Would you like some more wood on the fire, sir?" he said.

Hiram shook his head. "Thank you, Luke, but what I really need is to be alone. You have the night off."

Luke bowed. "Thank you, sir."

Luke stopped at the door. "Oh, and sir? Merry Christmas."

Hiram nodded sadly. Wearily. "Yes. Merry Christmas."

Luke stepped out, leaving Hiram alone in the room. Hiram didn't know where he was stepping out to, and didn't care.

He said, "Merry Christmas, indeed."

He added a couple chunks of wood to the fire himself and then poured a scotch and dropped into a stuffed chair.

He finished the scotch while a clock on the mantel ticked away. He got up and grabbed the decanter of scotch and brought it back to the chair with him. He refilled his glass and then emptied it. And he let his mind reel with the things his mother had said.

He dozed. The clock bonged eleven times. He poured another scotch, drank it and dozed some more. The clock woke him up when it sounded again at the twelve o'clock hour.

He got to his feet. He had to talk to his mother. He had to have her call the men back. Being strong was one thing, but there had to be a place where you drew the line. Murder was where he would draw it. He didn't want any blood on his hands. Especially the blood of Dan or Tom, or Tom's daughter.

He climbed the stairs. His mother wanted strong, and so it was time for him to be strong. He would be ruthless. He would take what he thought should be his. Maybe even take some things that he shouldn't, like the gold people thought was waiting for him under the cliffs of Swan Canyon. He would use legal maneuvering to make sure the court never saw the canyon as belonging to the Swan woman. His mining engineers would take dynamite to those cliffs and blast them away and then his miners would dig and they would find the gold. But Hiram would not kill. That was where he drew the line. If old Bernard Swan's wife and daughter had to live on the street and beg, well it was their problem, not Hiram's. But he would not kill.

He knocked on the bedroom door. "Mother?"

There was no answer. She was probably asleep. Too bad. They needed to talk, and they needed to do it now. Part of being strong.

He rapped on the door again. "Mother? I want to talk to you."

Still no response. He turned the doorknob and stepped in. His mother was still in her chair, her eyes shut and her head listing a bit to one side. She had fallen asleep. The fire in the hearth was down to glowing embers, so Matt turned up a lamp that stood on a table by the bed.

"Mother?" he said.

She sat with the tea cup in a saucer in her lap. There was still some tea in the cup, now long grown cold.

"Mother," he said, and gave her shoulder a gentle shake.

The tea cup toppled and hit the floor, cracking into three pieces. But his mother didn't move.

"Mother?" He shook her shoulder again. Her head rocked a bit with the motion, but her eyes didn't open.

He didn't think she was breathing. He touched the back of his hand to her forehead and found it cold to the touch. He took the liberty of probing her wrist for a pulse—the old lady didn't like to be touched and would scream at him until his ears ached if she woke up to find him feeling for a pulse. But she didn't wake up and he found no pulse.

She was dead. He stood and stared. She had been sitting here in front of the fire after their last discussion, and sometime during the hours that had passed she simply died. Judging by how cold she was to the touch, she had died not long after he had left the room. She hadn't looked well for some time. Maybe she was gravely ill but he hadn't known.

You're supposed to cry when your mother dies. Hiram understood that as the normal way people responded to such an event. And yet he simply stood and stared.

Was it that he didn't love her? He asked himself did she actually really love him? Did she even know what the word meant? Hiram realized he wasn't sure that he himself knew what the word meant.

So, the old lady was dead. This meant the money, the assets, the properties were all his. He was the sole heir. Dan and Tom had talked themselves out of being included.

Hiram supposed he loved them enough not to want them dead, if not wanting someone dead was the definition of love. But he had no intention of sharing any of the wealth with them or with Father. They made their proverbial beds, and now would have to lie in them.

But he didn't want them dead. And mother had sent off Wells and the others to murder them. Hiram had decided where he would not cross the line, and he intended to stand by it.

He went outside to the two men who were standing guard. The two Johnny McCabe had gotten the jump on when he and Father had paid them a visit.

Hiram said, "I want one of you to saddle up and ride out and find Wells. Tell him and his men to come back."

The man looked at Hiram. "They left over a day ago. There's no way we could catch up to 'em."

Hiram let out a sigh. Like a sail having some of its wind knocked out of it. He shut the door.

So there was no way to stop the killing. He supposed it would make his life easier in the long run if he didn't have any of them coming to him one day and trying to lay claim to part of the fortune. He had no doubt he could defeat them in court, but family feuds could be bad for business.

He glanced at the stairs. Mother was upstairs dead. Soon Matt McCabe would be, too. Not his real father, he supposed. But his real father was dead, too. And Dan and Tom and Tom's daughter soon would be, too. Oh, well. Nothing he could do about it.

He thought about getting one of the men to ride into town and get the doctor. Have Mother declared legally dead. But then thought better of it. It could wait until morning.

The fire in the hearth was dying down so he set another chunk of wood in it and then poured himself another scotch from the decanter that was running low, and sat down to stare into the fire.

He would have to make plans. That was for certain. Mother always liked living on the ranch, but he thought maybe he would relocate their operations to San Francisco. The ranch would serve as a vacation home for when he wanted to get out of the city for a little while. There were debutantes in San Francisco and he was sure any number of them would jump at the chance to become his wife. A man needs a wife at his side if he is going to conquer the world. The new ranch house would be a small mansion, the way Mother had designed it. There were to be no pillars at the new house, but he liked pillars. The old house had had them. He would have some built to stand proudly out front, to overlook the drive leading up to the house and to welcome him when he returned from San Francisco.

He thought about the shipping business. The Brackston family had done well in it. He had thought for some time about getting into that business. Mother had shied away from it because she knew little about shipping goods back and forth between San Francisco and China, and she didn't want to get into a business she knew little about. Hiram didn't share that idea. He figured you can hire someone who knows the business. If you don't get the results you want, then fire the man and hire another.

He sat back in his chair and looked at the fire and took a sip of scotch. He couldn't help but smile.

34

Johnny stood by the fire, not looking into it but beyond it. His gun was tied down low at his right side and his Sharps rifle was within reach. He wore a waist-length jacket against the cold and his sombrero was pulled down tightly.

Dusty was with the herd, as were Ben Harris and Joe and Dan. Even though Ches had an arm in a sling, he was there, too. More riders than you normally need to ride herd at night, but with riders on their back trail Johnny wanted to take no chances. Each of the men was outfitted with a rifle, except for Ches who wouldn't be able to use a rifle until his shoulder had healed enough so he didn't need the sling.

The tent flap parted, making the almost silent whispery sound canvas makes when it is pushed aside, and Jessica walked up to him. She was wearing a shawl and her hair was hanging loose. He wrapped an arm about her waist and pulled her in for a standing-up snuggle. He used his left hand. His right was always free to grab for his gun. Especially on a night like this.

During the day, Johnny and Dusty had ridden out to scout their back trail, and the riders Dusty had seen. They hadn't been able to get close enough, but based on their tracks, Johnny estimated the number of riders to be anywhere from nine to twelve.

Johnny said to Jessica, "I thought you were asleep."

She shook her head. "I tried, but I kept lying there waiting for the sound of gunfire."

"Might be best for you to try a little more. Won't do us any good if we're all too tired to see straight come morning."

"I can be helpful, you know. I can shoot a rifle."

"Have you ever shot a man?"

"I was ready to once. Back when I worked in town. Back before Bernard."

He went to a wagon and pulled from the cargo box a Winchester carbine. One of the rifles that had been Bernard Swan's. "Why don't you sleep with this by your cot."

She took the rifle.

He said, "Show me you can chamber a round."

She jacked the lever-action down and back like she had done it all her life. He nodded.

"That got your approval, teacher?" she said.

He grinned. "You've got to be the most beautiful student a man could ever have."

She gave a wicked grin. "I could teach you a few things, too."

He pulled her in for a kiss.

Then she said, "I'll try to get some sleep. It'll be even more difficult, now."

She went back into the tent. He stood looking after her.

Zack walked over. A coffee pot stood by the fire, and he knelt and grabbed a tin cup. It was the one Johnny had been using, and it had a little cold coffee left in it, but Zack didn't care. On the trail, men often paid little attention to the importance of clean dishware. He tossed out the cold coffee and then filled the cup from the pot.

His pistol was belted on, and he carried a Winchester cradled in the crook of one arm. Because of the riders on their back trail, everyone was standing ready.

"What do you think of her?" Johnny said.

"She's a keeper," Zack said. "I never thought I'd see any woman other than Lura who could fit so naturally at your side. But it's like she was born to be there, and you at hers."

"It would be one thing if we were heading to Montana to build a home for ourselves. But I have four children pretty much grown."

"Dusty seems to like her well enough."

"But what will Josh, Jack and Bree think of her? And the house is Ginny's territory. Always has been. What kind of problems will there be?"

Zack shrugged. "Nothing your family can't work out. Look at the way Temperance fit into your family."

"She's become almost like a daughter to me."

"That's what I mean. I think your family will take to her and little Cora easily. I've already seen Dusty with Cora. He's falling into the role of big brother so naturally, it's like it was meant to be."

"I'm thinking maybe I should write Ginny another letter. Explain a few things before we get there."

Matt was walking up. He was holding a rifle in both hands and had been walking the perimeter. "We'll be nearing a town called Elkwood in a couple of days. There's a railroad line that goes through there on its way to Stockton. I can have the boys take your letter to Cheyenne, just like the last one."

"You're not a railroad owner anymore."

"Maybe they won't have heard the news yet."

Zack said, "So, what are we going to do about our unwanted guests back there?"

Johnny said, "I'm thinking we'll send the wagons and the herd on in the morning. If I remember the terrain right, we're near a small canyon. Not as big as the Swan canyon. Only a few acres in size. But it's not a box canyon. It's open at both ends. We can drive the cattle right through there to create some tracks that are real easy to read. And when the men back there approach the canyon, some of us'll be waiting for 'em. Hopefully we can get out of it without a shooting match. But if that's what they want, we'll be in a better position to deal with it."

"I want to be there with you," Matt said.

Johnny shook his head. "I'm going to need you with the wagons and the herd. You're a natural leader. And Joe can't do much more than shoot a scattergun, and that's only good at close range. He tried to use a Winchester back at Jessica's canyon, but didn't get very good results. So he should be with you. I'll take you, Zack. And Dusty."

Matt said, "Only three of you?"

Johnny nodded. "Three'll be enough. We can get the drop on them and catch them in a potential crossfire. Dusty's a good shot and my Sharps will make an excellent sniper rifle."

Zack smiled. "I do like the way you think."

"And if they don't fall for it and instead ride out and around the canyon, we'll just wait until they're gone then cut out and around them and catch up with the wagons before they do."

Tom stepped out of his tent. He had a Winchester carbine in one hand, and walked over. "Got any more coffee? I can't sleep. Too much on my mind."

There was an extra tin cup kicking about, so Matt turned it upside down to dump out any old coffee and dirt, and filled it with hot coffee for him.

Johnny told Tom their plan for the following day.

Tom said, "Will you be all right?"

"There are never any guarantees," Zack said. "But we've been through this kind of thing before."

Johnny said, "A few times."

Tom said to Johnny, "About that talk we had. About choices when there's no clear-cut right answer and you have to choose the one that's the least wrong."

Johnny nodded and waited for him.

Tom said, "I've made my choice. That's why I have this rifle. No one's going to hold a gun to Lettie's head again, or threaten my daughter."

Tom was dead serious. Johnny knew by the look in his eye that he could do it. Tom had asked Johnny to essentially teach him how to be a gunhawk. Johnny thought Tom might have just graduated.

Matt said, "You know how to use that rifle. Just remember everything I taught you when you were a kid."

Tom said, "Father. Things were so different then, between us."

Matt nodded. "I know. I have a lot of regrets about that."

"Well, it's just that, I wish I had known you like you are now."

Matt gave his son a long look. "That means a lot to me."

Tom took a sip of coffee. "Want me to go scout the perimeter?"

"No," Johnny said. "I think I'd like you right here, in case shooting starts. But it's been quiet so far tonight. Let's hope it stays that way."

There was a sudden bellow from the herd, followed by a chorus of bellows. Then a gunshot. And then more bellows and a sudden rumble.

"Looks like you spoke too soon," Zack said.

Matt said, "They're stampeding the herd!"

He went to run for a horse, but Johnny said, "No! Stay here!"

Matt looked at him like he was out of his mind.

Zack said, "The wagons are the target. The stampede is just a diversion. We can round the cows up in the morning. We've all got to stay here right now."

The rumble was growing louder. Johnny shouted so he could be heard. "Sounds like the stampede is coming right at us! Get the women and children out of those tents and under the wagons!"

"I'll do it!" Tom called out.

"Zack. Matt. At my side."

The ground was rumbling and the braying of the steers was loud, and everyone was already coming out of the tents. Tom ushered them under wagons and they didn't complain. Jessica gave Johnny one quick look. He didn't see fear in her eyes. What he saw was *be careful* and *don't take any prisoners*. Then she grabbed Cora and with the rifle in her hands was under a wagon.

Zack stood a moment, listening, then said, "They're driving the cattle right at us!"

There were gunshots. Some probably from the men trying to stampede the herd, but Johnny knew the men with the herd wouldn't let it happen without a fight. He heard a blast that he knew wasn't from a pistol or a rifle. More of a *boom* than a *pow*. It was from Joe's scattergun.

Johnny ran toward a wagon for cover, but the panicking steers were already on them. Charging through the camp. Panicking horses, kicking up dust and panicking the horses. Johnny ran for cover behind a wagon, but the wagon was hit by a cow and driven a couple of feet forward. Women and children under the wagon were screaming, and the wagon hit Johnny and knocked him forward. His rifle flew from his grip and his head struck something.

He rose to his hands and knees, choking on the dust. In the light of the campfire he saw a tent collapse and land on top of Matt, and then cows were charging over the tent. Then the firewood was scattered by hooves and fire was catching on the grass out beyond the small fire pit they had dug, and then the fire was extinguished by more crashing hooves.

Johnny wondered about Jessica and Cora. And Dusty and the others. His brothers. Matt was most likely dead. He had lost sight of Zack.

And then a steer charged between the wagons where Johnny was on the ground and slammed into him and sent him rolling over and over in the dust like he was falling downhill. And then he came to a stop. He tried to rise to his hands and knees but the world about him seemed to be falling into blackness, and he collapsed back to the ground.

35

A gunshot was the first thing Johnny heard when he gained consciousness. He didn't know how long he had been out. Dust was thick in the air, and he could taste it in his mouth. All was dark, but then he blinked a few times and could see shapes moving about in the moonlight. The light was muted, hazy, because of all the dust in the air.

Horses were picketed a little ways out beyond the wagons and men stood there. One was grabbing Jessica by an arm and pulling her out from under the wagon. One man was on the ground, and the one grabbing Jessica yanked the rifle from her hands.

"You killed him!" the man shouted, and gave Jessica a backhand slap that sent her sprawling.

Johnny pushed himself to his feet, reaching for his gun. That man was going to die. But Johnny found his gun was gone, and someone pushed him back to the ground. He realized his head was pounding and his neck hurt. His left shoulder hurt. One leg didn't feel right.

"Don't move, gunslinger," a man said from above him, "or I'll put a bullet in the back of your head."

Johnny quickly put what he saw together to make a picture. Jessica had shot the man on the ground before she was overpowered.

Johnny looked about quickly, for Zack and Matt. He couldn't see the tent that had collapsed on top of Matt because of the limited visibility, and Zack was nowhere in sight.

"All right," the man above him said. "Get to your feet."

Johnny did so, but found both legs were a little shaky. His head had taken a beating when the wagon smashed into him and his neck hurt. He turned his head to one side, the way he had seen his Shoshone teacher do to a warrior who had injured his neck in battle, and a joint in his neck snapped like a stick and then his neck pain was gone. But his shoulder still hurt and his head felt like he had just come off of a three-day bender. And one knee hurt and felt weak. He had to step gingerly to keep it from collapsing.

"Bring him out here," a man said. Johnny recognized the voice. It was Wells. Johnny had the brief thought that he should have shot the man back at Tom's house. Johnny showed him mercy and was now regretting it.

"Get moving," the man behind Johnny said, and Johnny stumbled his way out and away from the wagons.

Wells was indeed there. He was dusty and dirty and his left arm was in a sling, but he was smiling. He had a pistol in his hand.

He said to one of his men, "Line 'em up right here. The women and the children. I want to see who we got."

While this was being done, he looked at Johnny. "The big and bad Johnny McCabe."

Wells aimed his gun at Johnny's right eye. Wells said, "You don't feel so almighty big and important now, do you? Huh? Guess what? There's gonna be a new page added to the legend of Johnny McCabe. The name Gideon Wells, Marshal of Greenville, California, is gonna go down in history as the man who gunned you down."

Johnny said, "Shooting down an unarmed man won't put you in the history books, except maybe as a man facing the gallows."

"Oh, no," Wells was grinning. A wide grin showing jagged, broken teeth. Johnny figured he had been hit solidly in the mouth once. "According to my men here, you died with your gun in your hand. You just couldn't handle me. I killed you fair and square."

"All right, marshal," one of the men said. "We got 'em all lined up."

They were there. Jessica, now once again on her feet. Cora. Lettie and Mercy and Peddie. They all looked dusty and a little ragged, but they didn't seem hurt.

"Well, well," the marshal said. "Ain't you a ragged-looking crew?"

As Johnny stood there, he wondered where Tom was.

The eyes of Wells landed on Lettie. "It's sure good to see you again. You and me got some unfinished business."

Wells walked up to her. "Weren't we gonna have some fun back in town? And then we got interrupted by the livin' legend over there."

Wells reached up to her and moved some stray strands of hair from her face.

"Oh, you ain't gonna die," Wells said to her. "At least not yet. And if you play your cards right with me, you may not have to die at all."

Then Tom spoke from behind them. "Get away from my wife or I'll kill you where you stand."

Tom was standing at the edge of the camp with his Winchester to his shoulder and aimed at Wells. Tom was covered with dust and had a serious bruise on one cheekbone. His hair was flying wild and one sleeve had been torn clear to the elbow. But he was standing strong and was holding the rifle like he knew how to use it.

Wells laughed. "Preacher man. Here we are again. Me and your wife are gonna have some fun and there's nothin' you can do about it. And don't count on the gunfighter there to help you this time. He can't even help himself. Now put down that gun before you hurt somebody."

"Get away from her or I'll put a bullet in you."

"Now, preacher man, we both know you don't have what it takes to do that. You don't even have that gun jacked."

"I chambered a round already."

Wells began walking toward him. He holstered his pistol and drew a bowie knife from his belt. "You know what I'm gonna do to you? I'm gonna stick this knife in your belly and make you scream like a little girl. And then while you lay there dyin' I'm gonna take your wife. How's that set with you, preacher man? You like that?"

Tom squeezed the trigger. The gun went off and the bullet slammed into Wells' chest, stopping him in his tracks. He looked down at the bullet wound and then up and Tom, but Tom was already jacking the action to chamber another bullet.

One of the men fired at Tom, catching him somewhere in his left side. Johnny thought it might have been his shoulder but couldn't be sure. Tom spun around but retained his bearings and fired from his hip and took the man out.

Johnny, despite his injured leg, dove at a third man and pulled him to the ground. The man's gun went off and into the darkness and Johnny drove a fist into the man's face. The punch wasn't one of Johnny's best, but it was enough to stun the man and this gave Johnny the moment he needed to grab the pistol.

Johnny drove the handle of the pistol into the man's forehead, then rose to his knees and began to squeeze off shots, taking out one of Wells' men, and then another. Just like shooting at those Comanches that had been charging at him years earlier. Despite how much his head hurt, he felt a strange but familiar calm that the heat of battle often brought. The men were shooting at him, the bullets kicking up the cold, December dirt around him, and one bullet tore into the fabric of his shirt at his shoulder. But he didn't feel panic or fear. He felt centered and steady. He got a third man, then a fourth fired at him and missed, and Johnny put a bullet in him. The man was still on his feet but then a bullet from Tom got him and he went down.

Tom had dropped to one knee and was firing from his hip, jacking the gun and firing again. He missed with one shot, then with the other he caught a man in the chest.

Wells was still on his feet. He let the knife fall from his fingers and then drew his pistol. But then Tom put another bullet into him, and Wells was knocked backward to the ground and lay there, still.

Then it was quiet. Five men had been in camp with Wells. Five men, including Wells, were now down. The man Johnny had taken the gun from was stirring, so Johnny got to his feet and aimed the gun at him. Johnny thought the gun was probably empty, assuming there had been five bullets in it. The gun had gone off when Johnny jumped the man and then Johnny had fired four times. But there was no need for the man to know the gun was empty.

"Don't move a muscle," Johnny said.

The man said, "I ain't movin'."

Johnny looked at Tom, who was rising back to his feet. There was blood on his shirt, under his ribs. Where the bullet had struck him.

Johnny said, "You're hit."

Tom nodded. "It dug into me but went through. Just grazed my ribs. I'll be all right."

There was some shooting from out in the darkness. Johnny guessed the shots to be some distance off. Then there was more shooting, then all was silent.

Jessica was at his side, wanting to make sure he was all right. Cora was crying so Johnny took her in a hug.

"Everything's gonna be all right, Sweetie," he said.

They tied the one surviving man who had ridden with Wells to a wagon wheel. Officially, he was a lawman. He wore a badge pinned to his vest. He was maybe Dusty's age, and was long and thin with fine whiskers decorating his chin, and a black eye from where Johnny had punched him and a gash on his forehead where Johnny had hit him with the gun.

Johnny reached down and pulled the tin star from the man's vest. "You don't deserve to wear this."

Johnny's knuckles were roughed up from where he had punched the man, and one knuckle was bleeding. One finger had made a snapping noise when he delivered the punch, but it wasn't broken. The knuckle had snapped the way knuckles will. It felt a little sore, though.

Lettie was at Tom's side. Lettie was fussing about the blood on Tom's shirt, but this didn't stop Tom from lifting Mercy and giving her a hug.

Johnny looked at him and Tom's eyes met his, and Johnny nodded. Tom nodded back.

Peddie was standing in an open area of camp. The tent that had fallen on Matt was there, but Matt was not.

She said, "Has anyone seen Matt?"

There were more shots from the darkness, these ones closer to camp.

Jessica said, "We're not free of this yet, are we?"

"I don't know," Johnny said. "Get the women and children back under the wagons."

She did so.

The gun in Johnny's hand was a forty-four Colt, so he was able to reload from the bullets in his own gunbelt. Tom's Winchester was a .44-40, so Johnny handed him some cartridges and Tom pushed them into the rifle, then they stood side by side while they waited for whatever might be waiting for them out in the darkness.

"I'm not a drinking man," Tom said. "But I see why Father and the rest of you like whiskey so much. I could use a shot of it right now."

"You never want a drink before a fight like this. It might steady the nerves but it also takes away from your accuracy. And you don't seem to need anything to calm your nerves. You handle this like you were born to it."

"Should I take that as a compliment?"

"I don't rightly know."

They waited. Then someone started coming toward the camp. They could see him in the moonlight. He was on foot. Hobbling, Johnny thought. Favoring on leg. He came closer, and Johnny could see the white mustache and he knew it was Matt.

"Father," Tom said.

Matt came closer. Peddie went running toward him and threw her arms around him.

"Easy, woman," he said. "I've been trampled by a steer and shot."

"You want me to stop?"

"Never."

He looked over her shoulder at Johnny. "Got two of 'em. My gun's empty, though."

Johnny said, "How bad shot are you?"

"I'm on my feet. I gotta stop getting shot, though. It hurts."

"You better reload. This may not be over yet."

Matt did so, then went to stand beside Johnny and Tom.

Matt said, "Are you all right, son?"

"Strangely," Tom said, "yes. I don't know if it's a good thing or a bad thing."

"In a situation like this, it's a good thing."

They waited. And then riders came toward them from the darkness. Matt cocked his pistol. Tom jacked a cartridge into the chamber of his rifle. Johnny's pistol was already cocked.

One rider was Zack. The other was Dusty.

"We got three of 'em," Dusty said.

Dusty's hat was hanging from the chin strap and he was covered with dust. But he looked all right. Zack was holding right arm tight to his side, and held a pistol in his left. Zack had always been able to shoot with either hand, something Johnny had never been able to manage.

They quickly compared notes. Zack and Dusty had been caught by surprise when Wells' men stampeded the herd. Dusty had been thrown from his horse, but from the ground he shot one of the attackers out of the saddle and then took that horse. Zack's horse had reared and he found himself on the ground with a wrenched right shoulder, but he could shoot with his left and took two of them out of the saddle.

"I must be getting old," Johnny said. "I just didn't think they would try an attack like that. Not with so many gunhawks here, and the reputations we have."

Jessica said, "You can't be perfect. You can't always be on top of every situation."

Johnny nodded agreement just because he didn't want to talk about it any further at the moment. But these men looked to him for leadership and he felt he had failed them. He had made the mistake of underestimating his opponent. Must be getting soft, he thought. Too many years in the remoteness of Montana, he supposed. Too many years away from the line of fire. Aside from the attack on the ranch a couple of summers ago, he hadn't been shot at in years.

Dusty said, "I think we got 'em all."

Joe was still missing, as was Ben Harris. Ches rode into camp after a little while. Despite having one arm in a sling, he had ridden along with the herd, trying to head them off before they had a chance to scatter. His horse tripped on a rock in the darkness, though, and sent him sprawling, and he had just found it a short while ago.

"Afraid I missed all the action," he said.

Johnny said, "You're allowed. You've seen more than your share of it over the years."

Johnny rounded up Thunder and Dusty switched saddles with another horse and the two scouted about. They found one dead steer. Stampedes were dangerous for the animals doing the stampeding, also. And they found a couple more of Wells' men, dead.

They returned to camp and soon it was daylight. Jessica and Lettie made a breakfast for everyone, and the camp was cleaned up. The dead bodies of Wells and his men were hauled to a point outside of camp.

"We should probably bury them," Matt said. "If we leave them here they'll become coyote bait and we can't take them with us."

"What about the one that's alive?" Dusty said.

"I think we should make for Elkwood so we can regroup and nurse the wounded. We can turn over the one survivor to the marshal there."

Johnny was kneeling by the fire, chewing on a slice of bacon, and with a tin cup of coffee in one hand. He was not standing because he wanted to give his injured knee a rest. Nothing seemed broken but the kneecap was bruised and the joint didn't feel strong. A bullet had torn through his shirt and grazed his shoulder, but it was little more than a scrape.

Jessica and Lettie gone into a tent to tend to Tom. After a while, Jessica came out to the fire to pour some coffee, and Johnny asked how his nephew was.

"Hurt worse than he wants to admit," she said. "The bullet that grazed his ribs tore him up and we had to give him five stitches. He might have a cracked rib."

She took a sip of coffee. "I've learned to deal with wounds and injuries at the ranch. Broken bones. A cowhand got himself gored by a steer once. I had to treat gunshot wounds twice. But we could use a real doctor. I'd like that knee of yours checked out."

"It'll be all right."

She ignored him. "Matt's hurt, probably worse than he wants to admit. Like father, like son. Zack's shoulder is so bad he can barely move his arm."

"Matt's been talking about the town of Elkwood. Two days at the rate we've been traveling. Maybe we can push the mules a little harder and get there in a day and a half."

That was when he noticed two riders coming. He rose to his feet. Since the bacon had been in his left, he was holding the coffee with his right, so he tossed the cup away to free his gun hand. He was too hungry to toss the bacon away. One thing about a gun battle, it could make a man powerfully hungry.

He was about to call out that riders were coming, but he didn't. He recognized them. One was Joe, and the other was Dan.

"That coffee smells mighty good," Joe said, swinging out of the saddle.

"Where have you been?"

"Scoutin' the area. Makin' sure there weren't more of them out there. Found Dan out there."

Dan said, "I tried to stay with the herd. Tried to get ahead of 'em to turn 'em and slow 'em off."

Ches was sitting on an overturned barrel. "Sounds like we had the same idea."

"But then my horse went down and I got thrown. Lucky I wasn't trampled."

"Sounds like we had about the same results."

Johnny said to Joe, You could have told someone you were out there scouting."

Joe grabbed Johnny's discarded cup and filled it from the kettle.

He said, "Didn't want to take the time, and I didn't want anyone who might be watchin' this camp to know I was out there. But I could see you all were all right."

"We didn't see you," Johnny said, finishing off the bacon that had been in his hand.

He grinned. "Nobody sees me if'n I don't want 'em to.

He took a sip of coffee. "There's no one else out there. All of 'em are dead, except for the one you got tied to that wagon wheel. I scouted their back trail a few miles, and there's no one there. Ben's dead, though. Found his body. Or what's left of it."

Johnny shook his head. He didn't like that news. "Ben was a good man."

Jessica and Cora walked over to Johnny. He lifted Cora with one arm, despite the protests his knee gave him, and with his free hand he pulled Jessica in for a hug.

"I'm so scared," Cora said.

"Nothing to be scared of," Johnny said, "Not anymore."

36

Joe hadn't been injured so he stayed behind to round up some of the herd. After a stampede like that you couldn't expect to find them all, but he hoped to find most of them. Dusty was staying, too. Dan had been a little shaken up when his horse tripped and slammed him on the ground, but he wasn't seriously hurt so he was staying to help, too.

The wagons arrived in Elkwood the following afternoon. The doctor there determined Zack's shoulder was badly wrenched, but nothing seemed to be broken. He had been thrown by his horse and then struck by a steer, and the shoulder might have separated a bit, but was back in place now. Johnny's knee just needed rest. The doctor determined Johnny might have suffered a concussion when he was knocked unconscious, but the worst of it seemed to be behind him. His shoulder had been bruised but not badly. Matt had a twisted ankle and a cracked rib from where a bullet had grazed him, but he would be all right. Tom had a cracked rib also, and the bullet had cut into him more deeply, but the doctor thought the wound was clean and healing nicely.

"We'll wait here," Johnny said. "Rest up and give the boys time to round up those steers."

After seeing the doctor, Johnny and Matt headed to a small saloon that was attached to the hotel, and took a table. They each had a glass of scotch in front of them.

Matt said, "We're not staying in the tents. I still have a lot of money left, and we're going to use hotel rooms."

Johnny couldn't argue with that. Everyone was shaken up and he thought they would recover faster if they were in warm beds.

"In fact," Matt said, "I've been doing some thinking. Why don't we just wait out the winter right here? Not take that long, roundabout journey we had planned."

"It wouldn't be fair for you to burn what's left of your money on hotel rooms for all of us. Once your money is gone, it's gone."

"Don't think twice about that. I've talked to Peddie and Tom about it, and they're in agreement. We rest up here until the snow in the mountain passes has cleared away, and then we cut straight through and on up to Montana."

Johnny had to admit, he was tired. He had been through a lot since arriving in California and he was just plain tired. To the bone. His body was telling him he wasn't a young man anymore.

"All right," he said. "You've sold me on the idea."

They had been in Elkwood four days when Hiram McCabe arrived.

Johnny had enjoyed a long bath and was cleanly shaven and wearing freshly laundered clothes. He and Jessica were standing on the boardwalk in front of the hotel enjoying the morning air when they heard a train whistle.

"Won't be long before we're hearing those in Montana," Johnny said.

"Is that a bad thing? After all, it'll make delivering cattle to a buyer a lot easier. And shipping goods to and from."

"All of that's true. But in a way I hate to see it happen. I've always been drawn to remote areas. With the train will come more settlers, and the home I've built there will become less remote."

They stood in silence for a few moments, the way a man and woman do when they're comfortable with each other. Not every moment has to be filled with words.

Then Johnny said, "You know, I'm thinking maybe I should ride out and help the boys with the round up."

She shook her head. "Not with your knee the way it is. I think you should just stay right here in town and rest up."

"You do, do you?" He looked at her with a grin. "Been a long time since I had a woman care about me."

"I'm sure your daughter does. And Aunt Ginny."

"It's not the same thing"

"Well, get used to it." She returned the grin. "I don't plan on going anywhere."

They stood in comfortable silence for a few moments more. Then she said, "Is that who I think it is?"

Johnny saw she was looking down the street, so he followed her gaze and saw a familiar dandy walking along a boardwalk toward them. A bowler, a tie, a vest and a jacket. He had a couple of men with him who looked like two-bit wanna-be gunfighters.

"Hiram Mccabe," Johnny said.

Jessica shook her head wearily. "When will the trouble he's been bringing us end?"

Hiram stopped in front of them. "Uncle Johnny."

"Hiram. I'll honestly admit, I was hoping we had seen the last of you."

"That's not very friendly."

"Ain't feeling very friendly at the moment."

"I was looking for my father."

Johnny said, "He's in the hotel. In the dining room."

Hiram looked at Jessica and touched the brim of his bowler. She simply stared at him, not acknowledging his gesture with the usual nod of the head.

Hiram didn't say another word, but turned away from them and strode into the hotel lobby. One of the gunfighters stood a moment and glared at Johnny trying to make his presence felt. Johnny simply stared back. The man turned and he and the other one went into the hotel behind Hiram.

Johnny and Jessica followed them all into the dining room. Matt and Peddie were at a table having a late breakfast and looked up to see Hiram standing there.

"Father," He said. "We need to talk."

Matt rose to his feet. Not like a gentleman receiving a guest, but as a man expecting trouble.

Matt said, "I'm sure you heard what happened out there. The attack on our camp. The stampede."

Hiram nodded. "It was regrettable. I'm glad you survived."

"Are you really?"

Hiram looked a little wounded. "Of course I am. Murder is not a game I want to get into."

"Your mother seems to have no qualms about it. I have no doubt she sent those men."

"Mother's dead."

This gave Matt pause for a moment. "What happened?"

"She died in her sleep."

Matt supposed maybe he should say something. Offer a word of consolation. Maybe he should feel something. Sadness over a life lost, considering she was the mother of his children. But instead he felt nothing at all.

He sat back down, and Hiram joined them at the table even though neither he nor Peddie had invited him.

"Father, we need to talk."

"There's nothing more to say. You're my son and always will be. But you follow her ways. There's never been much of me in you, I'm afraid. I'm sure part of that's my fault. Maybe most of it. I don't know."

"I've got to tell you something. You're not my father."

This got Matt's full attention.

"Look at me, Father. Really look at me. There's no McCabe in me. Mother said Timmons was my father, and I believe her."

Matt let out a sigh. He wasn't shocked. He supposed on some level he knew it all along. He glanced to Johnny, who was still standing with Jessica by the table. He could see no surprise in his brother's eyes. Johnny must have figured it out, too.

Matt said, "Then why do you call me Father?"

"All right then," Hiram said. "Matt."

"What's next?" Johnny said. "Do you send more riders?"

Hiram shook his head. "I just want a promise from you," he was looking at Matt, "that you won't come back and make any legal trouble for me."

"I signed off my rights to your money."

"In this society, you can never really sign away your rights. You could always come back and fight for partial ownership. You might win, you might not, but you could tie up my assets for a long time."

"You have my word," Matt said, "that I don't want anything that's yours."

Hiram said, "I hope I can count on that."

Johnny said, "When Matt gives his word, it's as good as chiseled in stone."

Matt said, "Hiram, it's a little too crowded in here. There's not enough room for you and me. Why don't you do something about that? You know where the door is."

Hiram gave Matt a long look and then rose to his feet. He said to the two gunfighters standing behind him. "Come on. We're catching the next train back to Greenville."

They crossed the room and were gone.

Peddie reached over to Matt and placed her hand on his. "Are you all right?"

Matt looked at her and smiled. "Strangely, I am. For the first time in a long, long time."

Hiram reserved a private car on the train. He felt it would be unthinkable for a man of his stature in society to sit with the common people. He told his bodyguards to stay outside, then stepped into his car intending to have a glass of scotch and look at some ledgers. He was serious about acquiring a shipping business and would need to shuffle some funds so he could do so. He also wanted to write a letter to his lawyer in San Francisco instructing him to begin checking out residential properties for him.

He shut the door and took three steps toward his desk before he looked up and realized someone was sitting there.

It was his brother Tom.

To which, Hiram said the predictable thing. "Tom."

Tom was in a white shirt and a range jacket made of that new denim material some of the cowhands were wearing.

"Hiram," Tom said.

"How'd you get in here?"

"That's not the question," Tom said. "The question is, what *am* I doing here?"

Hiram didn't know if he should be afraid or not. But then realized there was no need for fear. This was Tom. His brother, who didn't have the spine to do what had to be done. Who had left the family to run a church.

"All right," Hiram said. "I'll play along. What are you doing here?"

Tom said, "I'm here to give you a warning."

Hiram chuckled. "A warning? You? Are you serious?"

Hiram then noticed there was something different about his brother. A look in his eyes. Steely hard. It reminded him a little of his uncle Johnny. What was going on here?

Tom rose to his feet and Hiram saw he was wearing a gun. A cartridge belt was buckled about his hips and a revolver was holstered at his right side. It was not slung low or tied down, but it was there.

"Tom, when did you start wearing a gun?"

"When men of yours attacked us. There were women and children there. My wife was there. And my daughter. I had to kill two of those men myself."

Hiram's brows rose a bit. "You? You killed a man?"

Tom walked toward him. "A line was crossed. And it wasn't just crossed by me. It was crossed by you, too."

"Tom, Mother's dead."

Tom didn't even flinch. "She's been dead a long time, Hiram."

Hiram didn't know quite how to react to that. But he knew that, for the first time in his life, his older brother was scaring him. He took a step backward.

Hiram said, "I didn't send those men. Mother did. Before she died. By the time I knew about it, it was too late to call them back."

"It doesn't matter."

Hiram took another step backward. "Look, Tom, I have two bodyguards outside."

"Go ahead and call them. See what happens."

Hiram didn't call them.

Tom stepped around the desk and stopped within reaching distance of his brother. He said, "Leave us alone, Hiram. If anything happens like what happened out on the trail, if you ever interfere in our lives again, I will find you. And I'll put a bullet in your head."

"I...I thought..," Hiram was stammering. He didn't usually face danger. He paid men to face it for him. "I thought you were a man of God."

"I am. But even a man of God has to make a stance sometimes. You forced me into it when those men attacked. Make no mistake, I'll put a bullet in you and not lose any sleep over it."

Hiram swallowed hard but said nothing.

Tom pushed past him and stepped out the door. He stepped past Hiram's guards without even looking at them, and climbed down to the street and walked away.

37

Spring brought with it warmer days, and a stand of oaks off to the west were full with green leaves. Wild flowers stood tall in the grass and bobbed their heads in a light breeze.

Johnny was in his saddle atop a low grassy hill, watching the wagons move along, and Dusty sat beside him. They had all left Elkwood that morning. Jessica had the team, and from the wagon seat she threw a wave at Johnny and he smiled and returned the wave.

Behind them, maybe a quarter mile maybe less, was the herd. Twenty-eight head had died in the stampede, and twelve more were unaccounted for. Not bad, Johnny thought. He had seen worse results after a stampede.

After a lot of thought, they had changed their plans. They were now headed north. They would ride into Oregon and then cut east and through the mountains into Montana. Reversing the path Zack and Dusty had taken.

Johnny had written Aunt Ginny a letter during their stay in Elkwood. Matt pulled strings with the railroad so it would be delivered to Cheyenne only a few days later, and from there taken to McCabe Gap. He wanted to tell her Dusty and Zack arrived safely and to prepare her a little for the changes in his life. Tell her about Jessica and Cora.

Johnny had felt so weary when they first arrived in Elkwood. Now he was rested and again felt alive. His love for Jessica was filling him, and he found himself enjoying the morning sun on his shoulders. His knee was much better. It was not entirely right. It creaked when he knelt down, and sometimes in the morning was a little stiff. Probably always would be.

A sweet scent drifted its way up from the flowers in the grass. He remembered Lura had loved mornings like this. At one time the very thought would have filled him with grief and the guilt he had carried with him for so many years. But now that was all gone.

It's a beautiful morning, Lura, he said to himself. On some level he thought maybe she could hear him. And he could imagine her smiling. He thought he caught a sudden touch of peach blossom on the morning air.

He would always love Lura. And he knew there would always be a piece of Jessica's heart reserved for Bernard Swan. But Johnny and Jessica were in love and would be building a life together, and he would be raising Cora like she was his own.

Of course, there was unfinished business. Sam Middleton, or whatever his name really was. Johnny owed him too much to let him rot in a Mexican jail. He knew Matt, Joe, Zack and Dusty would all be with him. But it would have to wait. As much as he owed Sam, his first priorities were getting Jessica and Cora safely to the ranch in Montana.

While they were waiting out the winter in Elkwood, Dusty had told him about Jack. Johnny thought about this now, as he and Dusty sat on the grassy hill looking down at the wagons.

Johnny said, "I still don't know what to think about Jack. I didn't realize he felt so intimidated by me."

"Not by you, exactly. But your presence. You don't realize how people look at you."

Johnny shook his head. He didn't see himself as a legend or in any way larger than life. He was just a man. Good at some things, not so good at others.

Dusty said. "It doesn't affect me much, but then I didn't grow up in your shadow. But for Jack and Josh, and even Bree, it's a little different."

"Well, now that I'm aware of it, maybe I can do something about it."

Matt rode along beside the wagons on horseback, and Peddie was sitting on his horse behind him.

"What do you think of them?" Dusty said.

"I think my brother allowed himself to become lost for a lot of years. And now he's rediscovered himself. And I think he and Peddie are going to build a life with each other."

Tom was on the seat of the second wagon, and Lettie and little Mercy were with him.

Johnny thought about Tom, and the journey he was on. Not just the journey to Montana, but the one he was on as a man. Tom was learning a lot about himself and maybe not entirely liking what he saw. But that was sometimes part of learning and growing. Of becoming more than you are.

"Come on," Johnny said. "Let's scout ahead a little."

Johnny and Dusty turned their horses and started riding.

Made in the USA
Las Vegas, NV
13 January 2024